FALLING

e.k. blair

For my husband

No fall could ever compare to the one I had with you.

"Your flaws are perfect
for the heart that is
meant to love you."

~Ash Sweeney

prologue

Two pills. Two fuckin' blue pills. I swore I'd stop this shit, but I can't stand the pain that still radiates in the back of my head where he shattered his beer bottle the other night. I hate that I'm just like him—dependent on this shit. *Fuck it.*

Tossing them into my mouth, I pour the cheap tequila down my throat and relish the burn that singes in my chest. My body falls lifelessly back onto the bed while the muffled music pounds through the walls.

"Give me some," Rene says. Or is it Rachel? Who the hell cares? She pulls the bottle out of my hand and takes a draw of the amber liquid.

Handing it back to me, all I see is a hazy shadow as I feel her crawl on top of me. This chick leeched herself to me when I walked into this party earlier. I knew she'd be an easy lay, and when she shoves her hand down my pants and grabs my dick, she proves me right.

I don't even try to focus as my body starts to weigh down from the effects of the pills. I love this feeling. Numb. Heavy. Warm. Hazy. It takes me over, and I don't even realize that this girl is now fucking me until I look up. Closing my eyes, I begin to drift. Drift from the hell that consumes me. It's Saturday night. The night he stays out late drinking just to come home and impale everything he hates about his life into me.

Waking up, head still heavy, vision clearer, I sit on the edge of the bed. I look over my shoulder and see some redhead, naked, sleeping. *Who is she?* I don't remember what happened, but I know we screwed because my pants are flung across the room, and I see the used condom on the floor.

My watch says it's after one in the morning, and I need to get home. Pulling on my pants, I stumble slightly as I make my way through the house filled with people I barely know, drinking, dancing, making out.

When I start my car, I know I shouldn't be driving, but I also know that I need to go because my dad normally drags his drunk-ass in around this time. I hate knowing that my mom will be there alone with him.

Pulling up to the dark grey, two-story house I have always lived in, I can't help but think about how the impeccably manicured structure is simply a mask for the madness that lives within. My stomach clenches when I see his truck in the driveway. I shut the car off and rush inside, but I know I'm too late when I hear my mother crying. Bolting through the house and into the kitchen, I get there just in time to see my dad swinging his arm around and smashing a coffee mug into the side of her head. Turning to face me, her face is void as she falls to the floor, blood everywhere.

"What are you looking at, you piece of shit?" he spits at me, and I fuckin' lose it.

My body roils with vengeance when I charge at him, and we tumble, crashing to the floor. Rage takes over as I begin to pound my fists into his face relentlessly. Over and over. Skin splitting. Blood gushing. The sounds of my mom screaming and the grunts I force out with every blow to his face are a distant echo in my head.

He thrashes beneath me, but I don't stop. I know I'm gonna kill him, and I hope I do. My teeth snap shut when he drives his palm into my jaw, causing me to bite my tongue. He continues to fight his way out from under me, flailing his arms, and dumping shit everywhere when he yanks one of the kitchen drawers out of its tracks.

My mouth fills with blood, and just when I spit it into his face, I fall over onto the floor.

"Fuck!" I scream through gritted teeth as I grab my side. I hear the clatter of metal falling to the ground and watch my father's black boots stumbling away from me.

Cold shivers prick at my body, and my vision fades as my breathing becomes more and more shallow. My mother's warm arms scoop my shoulders onto her lap as she cries, and I let my head fall to the side. When I see the bloody butcher's knife, I lift my shaking hand that's clutched to my side and raise it in front of my face. All I see is red.

I wake up the next morning, body sore and twenty-seven stitches in my side, along my ribs, where that son of a bitch stabbed me last night. Sitting up, I flinch against the stinging flesh. My mom is still asleep. I made her stay in my bed last night in case my father came back home, which he didn't.

I quietly make my way downstairs and feel the guilt from everything that happened last night flood through my veins.

If I'd never gone out, my mother probably wouldn't be sleeping in my bed with a concussion and stitches in her head.

I've been so selfish lately and getting too fucked up on ecstasy and alcohol to protect my mom. The drinking, the drugs, the rage that fired through me last night—I'm him. He's a part of me. He runs through my blood. I hate him. I don't want to be him, but I am.

Having him consume me like this makes me sick to my stomach, and I swear to God, I will do everything I can to avoid what I fear is destined to be my future. I've gotta stop the fuckin' pills. I've gotta . . .

A loud knocking on the door pulls me out of my thoughts, and when I make my way to the front of the house and open the door, two cops are standing there, staring at me with a look I can't quite make out.

Taking off his hat, one cop asks, "Is this the home of Richard Campbell?"

chapter one

"Hey, boss. That clown you call your friend is asking for you."

"I'm finishing up," I tell Max as I sign off on a few orders. "How long has he been here?"

Standing in the doorway to my office, he answers, "Not long. Half an hour or so."

I don't say anything as I finish up my paperwork and toss my pen on the desk, leaning back in my chair with a deep sigh.

"Everything okay?"

"Tired," I say as I look up at my friend. Max has worked for me for a few years now. He serves as security ever since business picked up at the bar after I bought it out from its previous owner. He's a good guy and extremely loyal, which makes him a commodity I can't afford to lose. Beneath his shaved head and insane build that intimidates most people that walk through the doors here, he's got a big heart.

"Call it a night, man. It's late, and you've been up here all day."

"Yeah." I push back from my desk and stand up, making my way out of the office. When I pass Max, I clap his back, saying, "I'm gonna go talk to Gav then head out."

Max follows as we walk down the stairs and into the bar that I've owned since I graduated from the University of Washington. This place has become a second home to me. It's where I spend most of my time.

Bumping shoulders through the crowd of people, I spot my old college buddy, Gavin, tossing back a bottle of beer.

"Ryan, dude? Where the hell have you been?"

"Working."

"Mel!" he shouts over to one of the bar girls. "Get this old man a beer."

"No, Mel. I'm good," I tell her, and she just shakes her head at Gavin, knowing what a partier he is.

"What's up with you tonight?"

"Tired, man."

"You not staying?"

Before I can answer, a tall blonde catches my eye as she starts making her way through the crowd and up to the bar. She steps next to me and leans over the bar top to get Mel's attention, and when I eye her, Gavin mumbles, "Yeah, you're staying," all too knowingly.

"Ryan, right?" the blonde asks as she turns to look at me, and when I nod my head, she introduces herself with a slow, "I'm Gina," trying to sound sexy, but it's lost on me 'cause I couldn't give a shit what her name is. Girls like her are an almost daily occurrence.

"Have we met before or something?" I ask since she already knows who I am.

"Not officially. I've seen you around though." She grins at me as she says this, but her fake tits are too distracting for me to focus on her face. It's when she giggles that I snap my attention up. "You own this place, right?"

I nod my head again. One thing about me, I'm not much

6

of a talker. I'm a pretty quiet guy for the most part, but with chicks especially, I don't talk. There's no need to. I don't care to delay the inevitable. I'm a straight shooter, and being as tired as I am, I cut the shit and say, "Wanna get to know me better in my office?"

Her smile grows, and I take her hand, leading her to the back stairs. I spot Gavin trying to nail his own bait, and he gives me a cocky grin when he sees me pass by.

We walk into my office, and I close the door, pinning her up against it, clasping her wrists in my hand above her head while I run my other hand up her skirt and between her legs. Letting go of her wrists, she works with my pants, anxious to get them off.

I fumble in my back pocket, and when I retrieve the condom, I quickly rip it open with my teeth, spitting out the shredded foil as she tugs my pants down. I waste no time. Closing my eyes, I shove her panties to the side and take her against the door.

I never care to look too much at the girls I bang. Honestly, I don't want to connect in any way.

This is me—disconnecting.

Screwing chicks as they come along. I don't talk. I don't watch. My escape lasts for as long as it takes for me to get off, then I move on. I've been this way my whole life, from a fifteen-year-old freshman in high school to a now twenty-eight-year-old man. I'm emotionally messed up, and I don't even try to hide it.

Clinging herself to me, legs wrapped around my waist, I bury my head in her neck, and the thick perfume she's wearing makes me screw her harder, wanting to finish up so I can go home and wash this shit off of me.

Pouring another cup of coffee, trying to wake up before heading out to the gym, my phone starts to ring. I know it's my mom before I even look. She always calls first thing Sunday morning—predictable.

"Hey, Mom."

"Hi, honey. How're you doing?"

Taking my coffee, I walk over and plop down on my couch as I say, "Good. Nothing new."

"What time do you think you'll be here tomorrow?" she asks.

"Around two," I tell her. My mom still lives in Oregon at the same beach house that I grew up in down on Cannon Beach. After high school, I moved here, to Seattle, to go to college, but I still go back home often to visit. "Tori's gonna come too. Sorry I didn't tell you earlier. Is that cool?"

"Of course. Is she bringing the kids?"

Taking a sip of my coffee, I laugh and say, "No. She's going crazy. That's why I invited her to hang with me for a few days. She's desperate to escape. She said that Connor has been a nightmare lately, throwing crazy temper tantrums. So she's going to leave the kids home with Trevor."

"Oh, dear. Four is such a rough age. I remember when you were four. You were always embarrassing me. You hated wearing pants, so it didn't matter where we were, you would just strip down bottomless in public for all to see." She starts laughing, and I can't help joining in with her when she continues through her chuckles, "I would be so embarrassed, but when I tried getting you to pull up your underwear, you just screamed and drew even more attention."

"I don't remember that," I laugh.

"Well, I do. Eventually, I had to tell you that it was against the law and the police were gonna come get you and throw you in jail if you did it again."

"Great parenting, Mom!" I say as I shake my head in pure humor. I love hearing these funny stories of my past since most of my memories are ones I wish I could forget.

"Well…" she squeaks out. "I didn't know what else to say, so I went with scare tactics."

"Did it work?"

"No," she says with a soft giggle. "Well, it'll be great to see the both of you."

"You too. I'm gonna go hit the gym, but I'll call you when I'm on my way tomorrow, okay?"

"Okay, dear. Drive safe, and I love you."

"Love you too, Mom"

I go upstairs to change before I head out to the gym to meet up with Max. We've always worked out at the same gym; that's how we first met. Making sure everything is locked up, I hop into my jeep and make the short drive to the Athletic Club. Max's car is already in the parking lot when I pull up.

"Hey, boss," Max shouts through the empty gym. Nobody is ever here on Sunday mornings, so we make it a point to get together at this time.

"What's up?" I say as I walk over to him. "You been here long?"

"Nah."

We head towards the indoor track to do a quick run before lifting.

"Oh, I forgot to tell you, but I'm going out of town for a few days, so Michael will be at the bar all week."

"Going to see your mom?"

"Yeah. Mostly plan on surfing with my cousin," I say as

we make our laps.

"Well, when you get back, I need your help."

"With what?"

"Traci is moving in, so I need you to help me with her furniture."

Looking over at him, I question, "She's moving in?"

Laughing at me, he says, "Ryan, don't act so surprised. We're almost thirty. Don't you think you should slow it down a bit yourself? Find a girl?"

"Nope. You know I don't do the whole girlfriend thing. Never have. I like being alone."

"No one likes being alone."

"I like being alone," I repeat, but it's a lie. Truth is, I've always been too scared to have a girlfriend. Too scared to allow myself to even have feelings towards someone else. Too scared of putting myself in a situation only to discover the person I believe lives inside of me. A person just like my father.

"Whatever you say," he teases as we continue our run. "My buddy, Chase, was wondering if we needed his help when classes start up in a few weeks."

"Working the door?"

"Yeah. He's a good kid. He's in school full-time but said he's free to work evenings."

Rounding another lap, I tell him, "Yeah. That'll work. Have him call Michael." Michael has been managing the bar for the most part lately. Knowing that the bar is in good hands and is running smoothly has allowed me more freedom with my schedule, and the income has been nothing but generous.

After a long workout with Max, I decide to stop by the office and take care of a few things before heading out of town.

"Hey, Mel," I say as I make my way past the bar to the stairs, and she gives me a flirty wink laced with mockery. Shaking my head at her, I go up to Michael's office.

"Hey, I thought you were out of town," he says from behind his desk. Michael started working here at the beginning of the summer. He's in his mid-thirties with a wife and kids. Dependent on the paycheck I write him, he's proven to be dependable.

"Tomorrow." Taking a seat in one of the chairs, I tell him, "Max has a friend that's gonna be calling you about a job. Check him out, and if he doesn't work, I need you to find someone who does. We need another guy to work the door. Summer has been a little slow, but shit always kicks up when classes at the university start."

"Got it," he says as he files through a stack of orders. "Anything else?"

"Yeah, I need you to start booking out the bands for at least six weeks. I'd really like to find a few we can book steady, so see what you can come up with. You can always call Gavin to see if he has any leads as well."

"Sure thing. When are you gonna be back?"

"Few days or so," I respond as I stand up to leave. "You got everything under control?"

"Yeah, man. Don't worry about things here. I'll catch you when you get back."

chapter two

"It's about time you got here."

"Sorry. Got tied up this morning," I say when I walk through the front door.

"Spare me the details," Tori teases as she shakes her head before giving me a hug.

Walking into the kitchen, I ask, "Where's Mom?"

"You just missed her. She ran to the store to get stuff for dinner."

"Wanna head out so when we get back you women have enough time to cook for me?" I joke while she gives me a jab to my ribs.

Tori is only three years older than me. Our moms are sisters, so we spent a lot of time together growing up. I have three cousins, all girls, but Tori is the closest in age to me and the only one that surfs, so we were pretty inseparable when our families would get together. We've always been good friends. She married Trevor in her early twenties and now has two kids. Seeing her as a wife and mother never deters me from giving her shit the same way I did when we were younger.

"You know Indian Beach is going to be insanely busy

today," she tells me.

"Yeah," I sigh and look out the windows onto Cannon Beach. The waves aren't hitting as hard here, but they're big enough. "Let's stay here then."

"You sure?"

"We can wake up early and hit Indian tomorrow before the crowds get there."

Nice weather is short-lived around here. Once the grey skies clear and the rain slows, everyone swarms to the Oregon coast, and Indian Beach is the spot that draws in the most people.

Hopping off the couch, she says, "Sounds good. I'll go grab my wetsuit."

We spend the next hour in the water until I hear my mother calling my name up on the beach. Paddling in, I walk out of the water, and my mother knows me too well when she starts taking a couple steps back, but I rush in and wrap my arms around her, soaking her clothes.

She laughs, and when I let go of her, she grumbles, "Now I have to go in and change. Thanks!"

"You're welcome," I tease.

Shaking off the mock irritation, she says, "It's good to see you, honey."

"You too."

She tucks a lock of her short blonde hair behind her ear and asks, "How much longer are you guys going to be out here?"

"Not too long."

She gives me a smile. "Okay. Well, I'll be inside whenever you two are done," and turns to go back in.

When I paddle back out, Tori is sitting on her board, and I join her as we bob up and down in the choppy water.

"What're you doing?" I ask.

"Taking a break," she responds as she looks out to the setting sun.

I can tell something is bothering her, so I come out and say, "Talk to me, Tor. What's up?"

She looks over at me, annoyed that I can read her like I do. Letting out a big sigh, she questions, "You ever wonder what it is we're doing?"

"Meaning?"

"Life," she says, taking a pause before continuing, "I guess I just thought I would feel more content than I do. Truth is . . . sometimes I feel like I'm too settled. Kids. Husband. Like I'm stuck."

When she looks over at me, I grab her board, steadying it next to me. "You're not happy?"

She doesn't respond.

"No," I answer for her.

"I didn't say that."

"You didn't have to. You're thinking too much."

"Are *you* happy?" she asks.

It's a loaded question. I'm numb most of the time. Friends are dropping off the scene, settling down with girls, and I'm still doing the same old shit. But the fear outweighs the jealousy, so I don't get too hung up on the fact that I'm emotionally incapable of having that. I never have had that. Never allowed myself the opportunity. All I know how to do is care for myself. I'm selfish just like he was. I'm not a provider the way a man should be; I'm a taker. I stay disconnected—and take.

"I'm as happy as I can be, I guess."

Tori never knew about my father, that he was a dick who used to pound his fists into his wife and son. Black eyes, broken ribs, bruises, and concussions. We kept it hidden well, my mother and I. They knew he drank, maybe not as heavily as he did, but that much they knew. Everything else, we never spoke about. Once he died, Mom was determined to start a new life. A life that had nothing to do with our past.

"Do you ever think about settling down?" she asks.

"No," I respond with forced ease.

"So you're happy? Having a different girl in your bed every night?"

I laugh. "Every night is an exaggeration, and those chicks aren't in my bed either. They stay downstairs."

"How is it that you haven't gotten the shit beat out of you yet?" she jokes in disgust.

My laughter grows as I say, "Lucky, I guess."

We sit for a minute or two when I finally ask the kicker, "Are you not happy with Trevor?"

It doesn't take but a second for her eyes to gloss over as she admits, "I don't know." When the tears fall, she reveals, "Maybe it's supposed to be this way. Maybe what I was expecting just isn't reality. My reality is . . . I've lost myself along the way somehow. Between two kids and not working, I'm just lost. I don't know of any other word to describe what I feel."

"What does Trevor say? Does he even know?"

"He doesn't want to hear me complain after he's been at work all day."

"Talk to him, Tor. Whatever is going on with you, he loves you and the kids. Maybe it's time for you to get out of the house. Go back to work."

She wipes her face and laughs softly. "The thought of not being with my kids kills me. I know you're right, but mommy guilt is a bitch."

"Yeah, I wouldn't know about that," I chuckle. Shifting, I lie down on my board and say, "Come on. Let's drink," before paddling back in.

After dinner, I walk into the kitchen to grab a beer and check my phone while Tori and my mom talk in the living room. Popping the cap off the bottle, I take a long sip before picking up my phone. I scan through some new emails that have come through and forward a couple to Michael.

Setting my phone back down, I lean against the counter and take another swig when my eye catches the cracked wood in the corner of the kitchen island.

"What the hell is your problem, kid?"

"I'm sorry. It was an accident."

Quickly grabbing a towel to clean up the juice I spilled that is now pooling under his briefcase, large hands grab my neck and shoulder. He abruptly throws me onto the floor, and the force of his strength sends me flying into the center island. The sharp corner pierces my back and sends a fire of pain up my spine as my head ricochets hard against the wood. I hear the crack and start crying. I'm scared he's gonna get more upset with me if he sees the damage.

I lie on the floor, avoiding eye contact, and grip the back of my head. I can already feel the bump growing.

"I'm sorry. It was an accident," he sneers, throwing my words back at me as he slings a dishtowel at me. "Clean this shit up."

That crack has been there since I was seven years old. It's such a faint line that I doubt my mother has ever noticed it.

"I'm calling it a night," Tori announces as she walks in and gives me a hug, pulling me out of my past.

"Early morning. Let's try and head out around seven."

"Sounds good," she says before she turns back to the living room to tell my mother goodnight and then heads upstairs.

My eyes shift back to the crack briefly as I turn to go into the other room. I walk over and sit down with my mom on the couch.

"How are you doing, darling?" she asks, patting my knee as I get comfortable.

Thinking back to my conversation with Tori in the water, I ask, "Are you happy, Mom?"

"Where is this coming from?" she questions, and I mindlessly find myself rubbing the back of my head where that bump from twenty-one years ago doesn't exist anymore, but the memory still does.

"You're all alone here in this house. I worry."

"I've always been alone in this house."

She never remarried after my dad died. I haven't even known her to date. We've never talked about it, but I just figured she was too scared.

"Can I ask you something?" I say as I turn to her.

"Anything."

"How come you never sold this house?" I wonder if the past still haunts her like it does me.

"What do you mean?"

"It's filled with so many bad memories."

"But it's filled with so many good ones too, dear." She smiles when she continues, "I remember holding you in my arms when I brought you home from the hospital. This is our home. It always has been. The one thing that bastardized this place is gone." She pats my knee as she says this. Nervous reflex. She isn't convinced of her own words. I'm good at reading people, especially her. "What about you?"

"Me?"

"Are you happy?"

I dig my thumbnail under the damp label on my beer bottle. Nervous reflex. I'm sure she sees it too. We are good at reading each other like that.

"I worry about you," she says softly.

"You don't need to worry about me. I'm good. Business is good," I assure her.

She leans back on the couch and lets out a sigh as she says, "I don't doubt that work is good, but I wonder how much longer you plan on keeping up like you are. I wonder when you'll decide to slow down and settle."

"You know why I don't settle, Mom." This is no secret between us. She has always known why I've never gotten involved with anyone. She knows my fears. I tell my mother nearly everything.

"You're nothing like him," she affirms sternly, and when I look at her, I deny her words.

"I'm a lot like him."

She doesn't respond, and I feel bad for cheapening her words. "Sorry."

"It hurts me to know this is how you think of yourself. I don't want you to be alone. I want you to find someone that you can be happy with."

"I want the same for you," I tell her.

"I know you do, but you're young. You have time on your side."

I can't help but laugh. "God, Mom, you act like you're a blue-haired lady at the bingo hall."

She laughs with me and says, "You know what I mean."

"I know." Letting out a deep yawn, I take the last swallow of my beer and lean in to kiss her on the cheek. "I'm gonna hit the sack. Tor and I are headed to Indian in the morning."

"What time will you guys be back?"

"Around ten or so."

"I'll cook you kids breakfast."

I smile at her referring to us as kids and say, "I love you, Mom," as I stand up and look down at her.

"Love you, too."

chapter three

Before the water gets too busy, Tori and I decide to call it and head back to shore. Tossing our boards aside, we sit and take a breather. The morning is cool, and the sun rising behind us casts a glow across the water. People filter in, trying to get as much of the sun as they can before the season changes and the rain and grey haze finds its home for the rest of the year. Personally, I love the darkness.

"I gotta head back tomorrow," Tori tells me as she unzips her wetsuit and tugs her arms out of it.

I start doing the same, saying, "I thought you were gonna stay for a few days."

"I was, but Trevor called late last night, and he just got a big case, so he has to go in this weekend." She digs her feet into the packed sand and shrugs, "Life of an attorney."

"You gonna talk to him?" I question.

She looks over at me and nods. "I'll talk to him."

"Good."

"So when are you coming back home?"

"I don't really know. Whenever. For sure Thanksgiving though."

"Connor was asking if you were going to take him trick-

or-treating this year."

I love her kids. Although they are my cousin's children, we've always just referred to them as my nieces and nephews. I have a lot; three nieces and four nephews. Being an uncle is great, and I take pride in spoiling them rotten despite their parents. "You know it's always a busy night at the bar, but I'll see what I can do. Don't say anything to him though because if I can't make it back here, I don't want him to be let down."

She smiles and says, "I won't."

"How is Bailey doing?" I ask about her one-year-old daughter.

"Crazy," she laughs. "She's a tiny diva. I look at her, and I know I'm in for trouble in about fourteen years."

"Well, if she's anything like you were . . ."

"God, don't even say it!" she whines.

We both laugh, knowing all too well how much of a partier she used to be when we were in high school.

Recalling a memory, I mention, "I will never forget seeing you hanging over the docks and puking into the water."

"Ugh! That was awful. I was trying to be cool in front of that guy, Shawn, so that he would notice me."

"Oh, he noticed you," I joke, laughing harder. We used to get together in Astoria, where she's from. We'd meet up with friends late at night and drink on the docks. Every now and then we'd get busted, but it never stopped us from going back.

"You ready?" she asks.

"Yeah, I'm starved," I respond as I stand up and grab my board. We head up the stairs, off the beach, and to my jeep. Loading everything up, we make the drive out of Ecola Park and back home.

The smell of coffee and bacon fills the house as we walk through the front door. We toss our gear into the laundry room then head into the kitchen where my mom is scrambling eggs.

"How was the beach?" she asks as I pour a mug of coffee.

"Good," Tori answers.

"Well, it's a good thing you guys went when you did. It's supposed to rain this afternoon."

"You know rain doesn't stop us," I say as I walk by and kiss her cheek.

She plates our food, and we all sit to eat.

"Tori has to bail tomorrow," I tell my mom.

"Oh, no. Everything okay with the kids?" she asks.

"Yeah, the kids are good. Trevor has to go into the office, that's all."

"When are you heading back?" she asks me before taking a sip of her coffee.

"I'll probably stay here for a couple of days. I'm in no rush to get back. Michael should have everything under control."

Finishing breakfast, I help my mom clean the kitchen before heading to my room to get cleaned up.

After my shower, I lie down on my bed and call Gavin.

"Hey, man. How's the beach?" he says when he answers.

"Good. Anything going on Tuesday?" Too many serious conversations yesterday and my head needs an escape when I get back home.

"Whatever you want to go on," he responds.

Gav and I have been friends for nearly ten years now. Through the years, I feel like our friendship, although it remains constant, has grown a bit superficial. He still parties the way we used to in college. We go out a lot, and he's into the chicks as much as I am. He's loud and obnoxious, where I'm more laidback, but he's my one friend that isn't tied down.

"Monkey Pub?" I suggest.

"Yeah, that works."

"I'll text you later then."

"All right, man. I'll catch you when you get back."

I spent the rest of my time with my mom, hanging out and taking it easy. It's always good to see her and catch up, although we talk on the phone often. She's always sad to see me leave. I know she was hoping I would move back to Oregon after I graduated college, but Seattle is my home. I love it.

When I get back in town, I head to Monkey Pub to meet Gavin. The lot is packed as I pull in to park. Walking in, the crowd is thick, and there are a few drunken college girls on stage, murdering a song in karaoke.

"Ryan," I hear Gavin holler, and when I spot him by the bar, I make my way over.

"Mel, what are you doing here?" I ask, but before she can answer, I catch her husband, Zane. "Shit, man. I haven't seen you in forever," I say to him as I clap his shoulder.

"Busy with the band. Things are finally starting to take off."

"God, don't get him started," Mel complains before she downs a shot.

"Fill me in," I encourage, and he proceeds to tell me that his band has been offered a contract for a recording deal.

"No shit? That's great," I tell him.

"Thanks. We're pretty stoked."

When I see the irritation in Mel's eyes, I question, "What's got you so pissy?"

"Zane forgot to mention that he would have to move to L.A."

"You'd think she'd be happy, but I can't get my woman on board to go to California," he tells me as he wraps his arm around her.

"I love Seattle. All my family is here," she responds.

"You guys will work it out. For better or worse, or some shit like that, right?" I laugh.

"Right," she sighs, not happy about the situation.

Turning around, I shout down the bar for a beer, and when the bartender gives me a nod, I take a seat next to Gavin.

"What did you do today?" I ask as he drinks his beer.

"Just work. Shit never ends."

"Dude, you love work. Don't give me that crap," I joke.

He laughs and says, "Not gonna lie, it's a good gig. I'm gonna go check out a new band the label is showing interest in on Thursday. Wanna tag along?"

"Yeah," I say as the bartender hands me my beer. Gavin has been working for Sub Pop Records for the past few years, so we hit up a lot of concerts.

He turns to a couple of girls that walk up and stand next to him as they wait to order drinks. Taking a quick look back at me, he shoots me a wink, and I laugh at him. When he turns back to them, he says, in tacky Gavin form, "Hey, ladies."

I sit back and drink my beer. Mel and Zane are off talking to friends, but when Gavin nudges me and says, "I got one for you," I turn around to see a tall, curvy redhead smiling at me.

Giving a slight nod, I say, "You go to college here?"

Small talk—it's almost annoying to me because if I do too much of it, it makes me feel like a dick for possibly giving girls the impression that I'm interested in more than just a fleeting hook-up.

"Uh huh. Education major," she tells me with a thick Southern accent, and I can't control the chuckle that slips out. "What about you?"

Is she kidding? "College was a few years back for me."

As she nods her head, she says, "Oh." Naïve. "So, what do you do . . .?" she trails off, not knowing my name.

"Ryan."

"Right."

God, this is painful. "I run a bar off campus," I tell her.

"Cool."

Looking over at Gavin, he's staring at the redhead and shaking his head. Yeah, I got the ditz outta the two, that's for sure.

"You need a drink?" I offer, and when she smiles and nods, I turn to get the bartender's attention. "What do you like?"

"Vodka."

"Shots?" I ask.

"Mmm hmm."

I shoot her a smile, and I know I'm in when she smiles back, biting her lower lip. I order four shots, and we waste little time knocking them back. We sit there as time passes, and she talks my ear off about school and moving up here from Oklahoma. I half pay attention but make sure I nod to give her the impression that I'm keeping up.

Her hand grips my knee when she leans in and begins talking closely into my ear as the bar grows louder the later it gets. Brushing her hair behind her shoulder, I let my fingers graze along her neck, and she shifts to look at me, no longer talking, just staring. When her hand tightens on my knee, I lean in and kiss her, tasting the alcohol and willingness as she moves her lips with mine.

She's not hesitant, but eager, so when I tug her hair, she moans into my mouth. Dragging her lips to my ear, she whispers, "Wanna get outta here?"

This one seems like she could be clingy. Not wanting to go to my place, and being tired after the drive back from Oregon, I lay it out there for her. "Car?"

She pulls back, looking at me with question in her eyes, and I explain, "I just got back in from being out of town. I'm tired."

When she doesn't respond, I ask, "That a problem?"

It takes a second, but eventually she shakes her head, and when I stand up, I see Gavin.

"You heading out?" he asks.

"Yeah, I'm gonna walk . . . umm . . ."

I look at the girl when she says, "Mary."

"Huh?" I question.

"My name. It's Mary."

I'm an ass. I turn back to Gavin and quickly tell him, "I'm gonna walk Mary out."

I take her hand and lead her out into the rainy night to my jeep. Not wanting to get my ass arrested, I go for the back seat, and she hops in behind me. She's on me quick, kissing me and running her hands up my shirt. I return the gesture and grab her large tits when she begins undoing my pants. Tugging them down, she leans over and takes me in her mouth.

"Shit," I exhale as I fist her hair and take control over her. Selfish? Yeah, I'm selfish. Escaping for my moment, not thinking. Enjoying. All thoughts vanishing from my mind. This is my vice. It used to be drugs. I rolled on X when I was in high school, but *this,* well this is just my version of a healthier release.

Zipping up my pants, she runs her fingers through my hair. This is the part I hate. I turn cold to make it clear that this wasn't anything more than what it just was.

"Thanks."

"Thanks?"

Opening the door, I step out and hold my hand out for her. "Like I said, I'm tired."

She hops down and hesitantly says, "You wanna call me sometime?"

"I don't do the whole girlfriend thing."

She nods her head, and my guilt appears as she turns to walk back into the bar without saying anything else. I take a moment and enjoy the rain that's falling, but when I hear my name being called, I turn around to see a familiar blonde walking my way from across the lot.

"Gina," she says, answering my unspoken question, and I suddenly remember the girl I had in my office a few days ago. "What are you doing out here in the rain?" she asks as she leans up against my car.

"Nothing. About to head home."

"Alone?"

"Alone."

She takes me by surprise when she shoves her hand in my back pocket and finds my cell, pulling it out.

"What're you doing?" I ask when she starts punching something into my phone.

"Storing my number," she explains. She hands it to me when she's done and says, "For when you don't want to be alone," before heading inside.

chapter four

"Dude! You said help with *some* furniture, not a whole house full," I complain to Max as we stand inside Traci's home.

"You have something else going on today?"

"If I said yes, would you let me off?"

He looks over at me with a straight face and admonishes, "You want me kicking your ass?"

Shaking my head, I laugh and say, "That's what I figured."

Walking over to her large sectional couch, he starts pulling off the cushions. "Come on."

We begin to load the furniture into the U-Haul when Max asks, "What are you doing later tonight?"

"No plans. I need to run up to the bar to see if Michael was able to get any bands booked," I say as I jump down from the truck to go inside for another load.

"You wanna stop by later? We're having a few friends over."

"*We're?*" I question.

Max just looks over at me and laughs. Although he and Traci have been together for a while, I know I'll be seeing much less of him now that they're living together. But hanging out with a house full of domesticated bliss isn't my idea of fun, so I tell him, "I'm probably gonna call it an early night."

"You sure?"

"Yeah."

We spend the next two hours loading everything up in the truck before driving it over to Max's house. Once everything is moved, I head into the office to get some work done and to talk with Michael. He was able to book a few bands and hire Chase, Max's buddy, to work the door. Since it looks like he has everything under control, I call it a night and go home.

Hopping out of the shower, I throw on a pair of pajama bottoms before going downstairs to watch some TV. I settle myself on the couch and flip on an old movie, one that I've seen countless times, but I watch it anyway.

An email notification lights up my phone, and I pick it up to see that it's work stuff that Michael sent. Not wanting to hack into it tonight, I start mindlessly going through my phone, opening apps, and wasting time. I begin scrolling through my contacts and stop when I see Gina's info scan by. I tap on her name and stare at her number.

"For when you don't want to be alone."

She's one chick that didn't make me feel bad after we hooked up. She got it. She accepted it for what it was, and clearly she's on the same page as me.

Before I know it, the phone is ringing, and when she answers, I say, "Hey. It's Ryan."

"Hi. What's going on?"

"Nothing. You busy?" I ask, keeping the chitchat to a minimum.

"Not anymore."

"Gotta pen?"

I give her my address, and when there's a knock on my door about thirty minutes later, I drag myself off the couch to see her standing on my doorstep.

Long blonde hair, tall, and wearing clothes that makes her look like she's trying a bit too hard for something that's a guaranteed giveaway.

Her heels click against my hardwood floors when she walks in, smile-clad face as she gives me the lookover. *At least I won't feel guilty with her.* I tell myself this a couple times before I take her hand and kiss her. She doesn't stop me or even slow me down as we stumble across the room.

It isn't long before she's bent over my couch, ditching her self-respect just to moan my name in what is nothing more than another throw of diversion. But I'm no better. I'm far from respectable. So the both of us use each other for the mere minutes that we're able to hold on before lust takes over, and we lose control of ourselves.

As I yank up my pants, she rights herself and turns to face me, sated.

"I'm glad you called."

I nod my head and start walking over to my kitchen to grab a drink. "You thirsty?" I offer.

"Yeah. Umm, where's your bathroom?" she asks, and I point down the hall.

"It's on the right."

"Thanks."

When she returns, she situates herself close to me on the couch, getting more comfortable than she should, but I don't say anything.

As she picks up her glass of water, she says, "So you have the night off?" before taking a sip.

"I don't keep a schedule," I tell her, and when she

doesn't respond, I clarify, "It's my bar. I own it."

"That's right. I remember hearing that from Gavin."

"How do you know Gavin?" I ask.

"He stops by my place every now and then."

Giving her a confused look, she assures, "Not to see me. My roommate, Ashley, and him have known each other for a while."

Nodding my head, she continues, "Bar must do pretty well."

"Why do you say that?"

"This is a big space you have. It's nice." She takes another sip of water and sets the glass down on the coffee table.

I bought this loft with the money my father left behind. When he died, everything stayed locked up in an account, untouched for years. My mother wanted nothing to do with it for the longest time. She lived off of the interest, which was more than enough to support us.

My father dealt in acquisitions, making a name for himself until he no longer had a name to make. I was still living with Gavin in an apartment after I graduated college when I fell into my business deal with the bar. I had been wanting a place of my own, but with the money I was sinking into the buyout, I couldn't afford anything. When I stumbled upon this place, it was perfect. The previous owner had done a full remodel, so it was turnkey ready. I couldn't turn it down, especially with the housing market in the shitter. I tapped into my father's money, bought it, and never looked back.

"It's getting late," I tell her.

"You don't talk much, do you?" Her inquiry is laced with curiosity to get to know me.

"No."

"Yeah," she sighs. "I'll see you later?"

Knowing that her offer is probably the one with the least repercussions, I say, "I'll call you." This chick is a no strings girl. Perfect.

She stands up, and I walk her to the door, giving her a chaste kiss before she leaves.

It wasn't but a few days after I had Gina over that she called me. We've been getting together for the past couple of weeks. It beats having to go out all the time only to wind up back at square one. But the last time she came over, she wasn't so quick to leave. I know my reputation; girls know it too. But if this one thinks that she's gonna be the one to tie me down, she's got it all wrong.

I know I'm only making it worse as I lie here, watching her pad out of the room to go grab me a bottle of water. But what she gives me is what I need. So I take.

When she walks back into the room, holding my camera, she says in a flirty voice, "What kind of pictures do you have stored on this?" She slips back into bed, still naked, and I take the camera from her that I left out earlier today when I was taking pictures of one of Mel's friends. "You photograph people?"

"Mainly."

"Really?" she responds with a hint of excitement.

"Really," I say.

I've always loved art, and photography is something I started tinkering with while I was in college. I don't do a whole lot of it, but what little I do, I enjoy. It's nice to have something to focus on every now and then.

Rolling onto her stomach, she peers up at me and

whispers, "Photograph me."

I step out of the bed and find my boxers slung across the room. Pulling them on, I walk back to where she's lying and focus on her back. She has a curvy figure, which enhances the sway of her spine. I zoom in and start shooting. She has no idea what I'm photographing when I stop snapping and look up to see her giving seductive looks into the camera. I don't want her face, just the line of her back.

After I get my shots, I instruct, "Sit up and face away from me."

She does, swinging her legs over the edge of the bed. I swipe the hair off of her shoulder and bring it around to her other shoulder. I then get a few shots of the contour of her neck. I'm close, and when I move to the side of her, she shifts to kiss me. There's something to it. Something I'm not feeling.

Quickly pulling back, I say, "You shouldn't do that."

"Why?"

"Because I'm not that guy."

"I don't believe that," she whispers, and it's now that I see the shift. I see the strings. "You've had me in your bed for weeks now," she says.

I don't want to make her feel like crap, but I don't want to lie either. "This isn't my bed."

When she shakes her head, confused, I clarify, "My bed is upstairs."

"Oh." Her brows dip slightly, and I can see the letdown.

Gavin warned me about Gina, but I blew it off. He found out from her friend, Ashley, that we were getting together regularly. He told me that Ashley said that she wasn't interested in anything casual with me. I blew it off 'cause Gina has never led me to believe otherwise. Until right now.

"I thought we were on the same page here," I say.

"No. We are."

"You sure? I'm not into hurting people, but I'm not into feeling either. So if that's what you're—"

"No," she says, cutting me off. "I just misread you for a second, that's all. No strings."

Her words aren't the least bit convincing. I see right through her, and wonder why she would put up with me for a hopeless shot at something more.

"I should probably go," she says as she starts putting her clothes back on.

When she's dressed, she makes her way out of the room, down the hall, and to the front door. Grabbing on to her arm, I turn her to face me. "Hey. I just need to be clear with you that this is all it will ever be."

"It's clear," she responds.

"Good."

After she leaves, I start to grow more uncomfortable with the situation. I shouldn't have kept calling her. I thought I was upfront but wonder if I was just leading her on. I stew around, thinking about how to remedy this situation, when my phone buzzes with a text.

Can I see you tomorrow?

Shit. She couldn't even wait an hour. Yeah, I've gotta cut this off. Looking at the time, I can't believe it's still so early. Not that our escapades last any longer than they have to. She likes it fast and rough, which works perfectly for me since that's all I like. But shit has to come to a stop. Sooner than later. The last thing I need is a clinger.

It's been a few days since Gina was here last, but tonight she stopped by unannounced, saying she had a stressful day at work and just wanted to vent. She spent the whole time bitching about some chick she works with that's friends with some other chick Gina used to be friends with. Shallow shit. Shit I couldn't care less about. But the fact that she thinks coming over here and talking to me about this crap is okay is all I need to know. She's getting attached, and it's time to cut it off. The calls, the texting—it has to stop.

I grab my keys and decide to head up to the bar to get some work done and to get my mind off of the situation I've created with Gina. When I walk in, it's packed. A good thing for a Monday night. Today was the first day of classes at UW, so business will pick up as it usually does after the summer. I look over to Mel, but she's too tied up with customers to notice me. I make my way through the crowd to the back stairs.

I stop in Michael's office to pick up some paperwork from him. When I go into my office, I look at the schedule he set up and start working on inventory orders. Time passes, and I'm deep into paperwork. We're closed, and I can hear the bar girls downstairs, laughing loudly as they clean up.

"Bad news, man," Max says as he walks into my office.

Looking up from my desk, I lean back in my chair, tired, and ask, "What is it?"

"The band that was scheduled for this Saturday night cancelled."

Throwing my pen across the desk, irritated, I gripe, "What do you mean they cancelled? They've been on the books for weeks."

"I don't know. I didn't take the call, but we've gotta fill that slot in the next couple of days. Classes at U-Dub started today, so this weekend is gonna be busy as hell."

"Shit!" I pause for a second, frustrated as fuck. "It's too

late to do anything about it tonight. I'll make some calls tomorrow and try to get another band booked. Oh, hey, if those fuckers call back, tell them to find another bar to play."

"Right, boss. You heading out soon? It's past midnight already."

"Yeah, in a little bit. I need to finish this paperwork and I'll be gone. Go ahead and go."

"See you tomorrow, man."

"See ya."

Time passes as I try working on the inventory supply sheet that I need to get in to our liquor distributor, but my mind is elsewhere. I really need to call Gina and tell her it's over.

A clatter outside snaps me out of my thoughts. I look down at my watch to see it's nearing one in the morning. *Shit.* When I start packing my things up to head home, I hear more commotion from outside. I shake my head, knowing it's probably just some drunk guys heading back home from a party. People are always cutting through the back alley.

I start locking everything up and make my way downstairs to the back door. "Crap," I mutter to myself, realizing I left my cell in my office. Walking back up the stairs to my office, I grab my phone off my desk.

I hear screaming.

A girl screaming.

chapter five

"Fuck!"

Bolting out of my office, I haul ass downstairs to the back door and out to the small employee parking lot in the alley.

"God, please! Stop!" a girl shrieks.

Before my mind can process what I'm seeing—naked girl, guy's hand between her legs, girl thrashing, screaming—the bastard smashes his fist into her face.

Adrenaline fires through my body, and I run. Yanking the guy off her, I start slamming my fist into his face over and over. I completely lose control of myself and relentlessly whale on him. I'm gone. My knuckles start to burn as the flesh begins to split open. He manages to get a few swift hits to my jaw and ribs, which allows him a quick moment to work out of my grip and flee.

Before I can charge after the guy, I catch a glimpse of the girl. It doesn't take but a second for me to refocus. She lies there, unconscious, bare, with her clothes ripped off of her. My stomach convulses at the image before me. I slowly approach her—scared—and kneel down next to her. Terrified to touch her, I take off my shirt and cover her naked, battered body. Her face is covered in blood and dirt, skin scraped off on one side and the other is already swelling from where the fucker's fist landed. Her knees are ripped open and covered in gravel. The blood between her thighs tells me exactly what that piece of shit did to her. My heart thuds hard in my chest, and my gut is in knots.

I pat my pockets for my cell, but it's not on me. I must have dropped it as I ran out here. Not wanting to leave her, I look around and spot her purse. I lean over and grab it in search of her phone. When I find it, I swipe the screen and dial 911.

My voice is shaky as I try to talk to the dispatcher. My thoughts are all over the place, and I stumble as I try to answer all of her questions. When she tells me that the police and EMTs are on their way, we disconnect. I slip the phone back into her gold purse and slowly zip it up as I stare at her. I don't want to look, but I can't stop.

As I sit next to her, she lies there, breathing peacefully. Whatever is running through her head right now has to be a million times better than the hell she's going to wake up to.

What the fuck just happened? I watch her. I don't know what else to do. She is so small, and when I look at her tiny hands, her nails are shredded. *Shit.* She fought. She had to have fought hard. The thought nearly makes me vomit, and when I shift my eyes away from her hands, I notice a little tattoo. An outline of a heart—simple black ink—on her lower hip that's still exposed. Sliding the shirt over a little to cover it, I finally hear the sirens in the distance.

"Thank God," I whisper.

The sound grows louder the closer they get, and when the red and blue lights strobe across the parking lot, I reluctantly stand to my feet, but don't move away from her until the EMTs approach.

"Sir, can you step over here?" an officer asks.

We walk over to the rear of his vehicle. He pulls out a clipboard from the car and opens the top of it, retrieving a few forms.

"I need to get your statement," he says while he organizes the papers under the clip. "You're the one that called 911, correct?"

"Yes, sir," I answer before turning my head to see them sliding the girl onto a backboard, strapping her down. She's now covered in a large blanket, and it's at this moment that I feel. Pain. Sadness. Anguish. It wells up and floods my eyes. I don't even know this girl, but I hurt for her.

"Where are they taking her?" I ask the officer.

"You know her?"

"No." I turn back and watch as they slide her into the back of the ambulance. Another EMT is collecting the scraps of her clothes that remain on the ground.

"Can you tell me what happened?" the officer asks.

"I don't know," I mumble. I can't seem to get my head straight. *What just happened?*

"Take your time. It's important that we get a detailed account of everything that occurred. Everything you saw."

"Is she gonna be okay?" I ask as the ambulance drives off.

"Do you need to sit down, sir?" I faintly hear the officer as he speaks. Pressure on my arm shifts my focus when I realize he has his hand on me, guiding me to sit in the front passenger seat of his vehicle. The door shuts, and I lean my head back against the seat. I watch him walk in slow motion around the front of the car. He sits in the driver's seat next to me.

"Start from the beginning."

"He raped her," I choke out.

"My God."

"He beat the shit out of her, Mom. I can't close my eyes without seeing it," I tell her. "I couldn't sleep at all last night. I just laid in my bed, replaying it over and over."

"Is she okay?"

"I don't know. They wouldn't tell me anything. It feels weird . . . to see that and not know."

"Are *you* okay?"

"How am I supposed to answer that? What do I say?"

"Say how you feel," she tells me with worry and concern.

"I feel sick. What he did to her . . . what I saw . . ."

"I hate that I'm not there."

"It's okay, Mom. I don't really wanna talk anymore; I just needed to tell you. I needed to tell someone."

"I'm so sorry that you had to see something like that," she says.

I've seen so much shit in my life. Too much to ever forget. You can't rid your mind of images that burn themselves into who you are. I've had to watch my mother getting the life knocked out of her at the hands of my father more times than I ever want to remember. But I also have her sounds etched in me. Her painful, pleading screams.

And now . . . now I have this girl. This unknown. A Jane Doe. Blanks that will never be filled.

"I'm so sorry I couldn't protect you better," I confess.

Guilt.

"Ryan, don't."

The knot in my throat makes my words painful to say, but I force them out. My confession. "I was right there. I heard the noise out back. If only I would have gone out there. Fuck, why didn't I go out there sooner?"

"How could you have known?"

"I could have stopped it. Prevented it. But instead, I ignored it." The whole time I knew there was someone back there, and I ignored it. I sat in my office while that girl fought so hard she had no nails left. "What have I done?" I breathe out, suddenly feeling the weight of the responsibility I now hold.

"You didn't do anything," she tries assuring me.

She's right. I didn't do anything. Nothing. I close my eyes, and I see it. The blood between her legs. The image I know will forever be with me. I toss the phone aside and rush to the bathroom, vomiting. Expelling the toxins, but not the images. Those remain.

Needing to move, needing to get out of the house, I drive up to work. I park out front and head straight to my office, shutting the door behind me. *Fuck. Why am I here?*

There's a knock on the door, and when I say, "Come in," Max walks in.

"Everything all right, boss?"

"Shut the door," I tell him, and he does.

"What's going on?"

I didn't get any sleep last night, and I feel like shit. I know I look it, and by the expression on his face, I know he sees it.

Folding my hands, I lean forward on my desk. "Something really fucked up happened here last night after you left."

He walks over and takes a seat in the chair.

"A girl was raped out back," I tell him.

"Christ," he breathes as he drops his head.

I don't say anything else. I'm not sure I can. We both sit there in silence as seconds pass by.

I finally speak the words that have me so fucked up. "I saw her."

"The girl?"

"I heard her screaming, and when I went out there, he was on her." I spin around in my chair and stare out the window that overlooks the street in front of the bar as it rains.

"I want cameras installed back there," I tell him.

"I'm on it," he responds. "You okay?"

Still facing the window, I admit, "I don't know, man. That shit was fucked up."

"Did the police come?"

When I turn back around to face him, I answer, "Yeah. I gave my statement, and they took her to the hospital."

"Was she okay?"

"I don't know. He beat her pretty badly. She was unconscious."

"And the guy?"

"Don't know. I had him for a moment, but I couldn't keep him in my grip. I couldn't leave the girl though, so he fled." I take a minute before telling him, "I don't want the girls walking to their cars alone. You and Chase need to be with them when they leave. Got it?"

"Of course." He takes a moment before asking, "You sure you want to be up here?"

Looking up at him, I let him know, "I can't be home. I need a distraction."

"I hear ya," he says then switches the topic, which I'm thankful for. "I talked with Chase earlier today, and he says he knows of a band that's gotten pretty popular lately. If you're tied up, I can get Michael to see about getting them booked for Saturday."

"Nah, I'll take care of it. Is he here?"

"Yeah, I'll send him up," he says as he stands and starts walking out. When he gets to the door, he turns back and says, "I'm here, man. If you ever . . ."

"Thanks." His friendship is genuine. It always has been. I might not be a man of many words, but I stop him before he walks out and tell him, "I really appreciate it," because I feel like he should know.

He gives a nod, accepting my words, and turns to head downstairs.

I spend the next few hours reviewing the financials and going over payroll. It's Michael's responsibility, but I absorb myself in it for the distraction. I speak with Chase, and I am able to contact one of the guys from the band he suggested and get them booked.

Filing some papers away, I notice the sky darkening. Somehow the day has passed, and I still feel like I'm on autopilot.

"God, please! Stop!"

I shake my head, trying to wash out the shrill of her voice. The panic.

There's a soft knock on the door, and before I can say anything, it slowly opens.

"What are you doing here?" I ask when I see Gina step in and close the door behind her.

This is the last thing I need to deal with right now.

"I never heard from you last night."

"I wasn't feeling well," I tell her. "Look, things are getting a little weird, and honestly, I'm just not feeling right about what we have going on." I should have told her this the other day, but I know that I can't keep having her come around, thinking that this has any value in it.

She sits down and questions, "What do you mean?"

Getting up from my chair, I walk around to the front of my desk and lean back against it in front of her. I need to lay it out there honestly for her so that there isn't any confusion.

"I'm starting to feel like what's going on between us is exactly what I try to avoid. It isn't working for me, and I'd feel like an ass if I led you to think otherwise."

She looks hurt. Proof that she's feeling too much. She plays it off well though when she says, "Well, it was fun while it lasted, right?"

I don't respond as I watch her stand up.

"Keep my number though," she says before turning her back to me and walking out.

I release a deep breath. A failed attempt to make me feel better. Truth is, I'm in a haze. A cloud. My mind is elsewhere—it's back in the alley. But that girl's cloud is no doubt thicker and darker than mine right now. *Why didn't I go out there sooner? What if I had?*

"Fuck!" I grit out, slamming the door shut, knowing I'm at fault, that I could have done a lot more if only . . .

chapter six

Walking through the back stockroom, I ask Mel, "Hey, have you seen Max or Michael?"

"Michael left a couple hours ago, and last I saw, Max was out back talking to Traci," she tells me as she loads her arms with a case of beer, almost dropping it.

"Here. Give that to me," I say, taking the heavy case from her. She follows me as I walk out and set the beer on the bar top. The place is starting to fill up. The band that Chase had recommended played here last week and really drew in a crowd. I went ahead and booked them again for tonight, and he wasn't kidding when he said they were well-known around here.

I help Mel behind the bar, stocking the beer while she serves customers. When I catch Max heading to the front door, I shout, "Hey, Max!"

"What's up?"

"You seen the guys yet?" I ask.

"Chasten is here, but I'm not sure about the others. Everything cool?"

"Yeah, if you see them before I do, tell them I need to talk with them before they go on tonight."

"Got it," he responds as he turns to head out to work the door.

I need to snag this band while I can. Getting them in a contract will alleviate the hassle of trying to book bands week after week. The guys seem pretty cool from what I got to know of them last week, which wasn't a whole lot aside from the guitarist, Mark. He stayed late that night, drinking and bullshitting with me and Gavin after he was done playing.

Gavin tried leeching some chick on him but got a good laugh when he found out that his hard work with the girl went down the shitter when Mark told him he was gay. The look of disappointment, that he wouldn't have another wingman, was something I selfishly took pleasure in.

He's been on my case lately since I ditched him a couple of times this week. I haven't been in the mood to go out just to find someone to use simply to make myself feel better. Ever since I saw that girl being attacked a couple weeks ago, it feels wrong.

"You got everything covered, Mel?"

"Yeah, Ry. I'm good," she says, and I start making my way to the back.

I spot Chasten and Mark talking and announce, "Hey, guys, can you get the others and meet me in my office real quick?"

"Yeah, no problem," Mark says and then introduces me, "Ryan, this is Jase, the guy I was telling you about."

"Jase, man, good to meet you," I say as I reach out to shake his hand.

"Yeah, same here," he responds with a note of hesitation, but I don't stick around 'cause I've gotta get up to my office to talk with everyone. "I'll catch up with you later, man."

"Sounds good," he says.

Once all the guys are in my office, I offer, "What do you guys think about making this gig a steady one?"

"You serious?" Aiden, the front vocalist, says.

"Yeah. I'm not gonna bullshit you guys. Finding bands is a bitch, so if you're in at a ten percent pay increase, all you have to do is sign this simple contract and we're good."

I take the contract and hand it over to Aiden, who reads through it first and confirms, "I'm in," before handing it over for the rest of the guys to read. When they are all on the same page with the agreement, they sign and call it a deal. Adding them to the payroll takes a load of stress off my back and simplifies my job even more.

When they leave to head down, I stay a little while to enter their info into our database. I write a note to Michael about the new payroll and employee additions and toss it on his desk before heading down. The band is just about to start playing when I make my way over to the bar and see Jase.

"Jase." I move to stand next to him, leaning my elbows on the bar top. "You ever been here before?"

"Yeah. This crowd is a bit insane though," he replies.

Watching Mel hand him his beer, I tell her, "Don't bother with a tab, Mel."

"Thanks, man," he says as he turns to me.

"No problem."

The music starts blasting through the bar when I say, "Your guy's band is fuckin' popular. They brought in a huge crowd last time they played here as well."

He keeps his focus on the stage, not responding, so I leave it and ask, "You go to school together?"

"Yeah," he hollers over the music. "We're in the same major."

"And what's that?"

"Architecture."

"That's cool," I say and then turn to yell for Mel to grab me a beer.

"Ryan! Fuck, man!" I hear Gavin shout with irritation from behind me.

I turn and question, "What?"

"That chick you flung on me last night was a fuckin' psycho."

Ignoring his complaint, I turn to Jase and say, "Jase, this is my dick of a friend, Gavin."

"What the fuck ever," Gavin says as he laughs. He looks to Jase and warns, "Watch out for this dipshit, and don't let him hook you up with anyone. His matchmaking skills suck balls."

"Find your own ass, Gav. I'm not your fuckin' hookup," I let him know because I'm not into his game tonight.

"Not anymore. What the hell has happened to you lately?"

"Nothing. Just sick of wasting my time."

I take a swig of my beer while Gavin tells Jase that I've been acting like a pussy, so I clip him and say, "Don't waste your time buddying up with Jase."

"Sad. I guess it's just me trying to get laid, huh?"

"Sorry. Looks like it," Jase tells him, laughing.

"Are these the same guys that played here last week?" Gavin questions.

"Yeah, they're gonna be playing here every Saturday now. They just signed a contract earlier."

"They looking for a label?"

"Ask this guy. I have no clue," I say as I tip the neck of my bottle towards Jase.

"You know them?" he asks Jase.

"Yeah, but I dunno," Jase responds. "I only know Mark and just met the drummer."

"This is Mark's guy," I tell Gavin.

He gives me a nod then says to Jase, "Yeah, I met Mark the other day. Cool guy."

I turn away from them and spot annoyance. Gina. She's here. I don't even say anything when I walk away and head toward her to see why she's here. She texted me the other day, but I ignored it. So seeing her here, when she knows this is my bar, winds me up a bit.

Weaving through all the people, I see her turn and spot me. Her smile grows along with my irritation.

"Hey, you," she says as she slides herself up next to me.

"What are you doing here, Gina?"

"Just wanted to see what you were up to," she flirts as she runs her hand down my stomach, straight towards my pants.

I grab her wrist and stop her, snapping, "If I were up to anything that had to do with you, you would know about it. You being here is just desperate." I suddenly feel like crap for my harsh words. But part of me, the big part of me that used to use people like I used her, pangs with regret.

She doesn't respond, and I know I just humiliated her, so I let go of her wrist and say, "Look, I'm sorry. I'm a dick, I know. But I need you to leave," before walking away and back to the bar.

"What the hell is up with you? That chick was all over your nuts," Gavin says when I approach, knowing damn well who Gina is.

Ignoring him, I lean over the bar and holler, "Mel, I'll be up in my office. I'll come down later, okay?"

"Yeah, no problem, Ry," she says as she's mixing a drink.

Gavin catches my arm and questions, "Dude, seriously? What the hell is going on with you?"

Jerking out of his grip, I tell him, "Not in the mood."

"You haven't been for a couple weeks."

"You wouldn't get it, man," I exhaust and then walk up to my office.

Shutting the door behind me, I flop down in the chair, and close my eyes.

"You're the one that called 911, correct?"

"Where are they taking her?"

"You know her?"

"Is she gonna be okay?"

"Take your time. It's important that we get a detailed account of everything that occurred. Everything you saw."

My eyes pop open, wanting to escape the scene that keeps creeping in. The rouse of my stomach weighs heavy when realization hits. My actions, though acted out on a totally different scope, are the same as that fucker who raped that girl. We both used someone to satisfy some twisted piece of our self with completely selfish intent. I've used so many people just to numb the ache I feel. *Fuck.*

I wonder how many girls I've hurt. I know of one for sure. She's downstairs, and I just made it worse after throwing my words at her. *What's wrong with me?*

I'm restless. It doesn't matter where I am, it follows me. But I need to move, so I head back down, not knowing what else to do with myself. Mel can see right through me, telling me to go home. I say a few quick words to Jase and then do as Mel says and go home.

chapter seven

It's been almost two months since I last saw Gina when she came by the bar. It's been longer than that since I've been with a girl. Ever since that night in the alley, my mind hasn't been in the same place. The images have started to fade, but I just can't continue to use people like I used to. When I think about going out to find a hook-up, all I think about is that fucker I let get away.

I never heard anything regarding my statement that the police collected, so I have to assume no charges were ever pressed or else I'm sure I would've been contacted by now. I've only ever mentioned that night to my mom and Max. I never told Gavin about what I saw. He's still running his game and has been hanging out with a couple of his buddies more often, now that I've been lying low. It doesn't bother me because I've been spending more time with Mark and Jase.

The two of them are pretty solid guys. Although they're a few years younger and still in college, I feel like we're on more of the same level than Gav and I are. We've been hanging out and hitting the gym on a pretty consistent basis. That, along with seeing them every Saturday night at the bar, we've gotten to know each other pretty well.

I ran into Gavin the other day, and he gave me some extra tickets to check out a band that Sub Pop is considering signing, so I invited Jase and Mark to meet me at The Crocodile where this band is going to be playing.

I throw on a black v-neck t-shirt, a pair of dark-wash jeans, and black boots. Running my fingers through my long hair that is due for a trim now that it's hit my ears, I grab my keys and head out to my jeep. When I drive past, there is a huge crowd gathered where the legendary club is located. I park down the street and walk. Once inside, I make my way backstage where Gavin told me to meet him.

"Ryan, you made it," he says when he spots me.

"I told you I would."

"Just didn't know if you were gonna bail." He gives me a friendly clap on the shoulder and then introduces me to the band before we head out to the bar to get a drink.

Mark is already there waiting on the bartender to take his order when we approach.

"Hey, man," I say to him. "When did you get here?"

"Just now. I ran into Mel's husband a second ago."

"Zane's here?" I ask.

"Yeah. He's around somewhere."

"Mel here?"

"I don't think so. Haven't see her," he responds.

"Mark, good to see ya," Gavin says after he's done putting in our drink order.

"You too. Thanks for the tickets."

"Have you ever played here?" he asks Mark.

"Shit, I wish," he laughs. "No, man. Before our gig at Ryan's bar, we were just taking anything we could get."

"I hear that a lot. Well, I gotta go meet a couple guys from work. I'll see you all in a bit," Gavin says as he grabs his beer and walks off.

I pick up the bottle that's on the bar for me and take a long pull when I notice Jase isn't around.

"Where's Jase?"

"Got tied up with a friend. He's not gonna make it," he tells me.

"Tied up all night?"

He nods his head and explains, "Yeah. She's going though some heavy stuff, so Jase is staying the night with her." He takes a sip of his beer, and then adds, "He'll be at the bar tomorrow though."

We sit and talk for a while as we continue to drink. The place is packed tight with people, and when the band takes the stage, the music blasts through the place, and there's no more talking.

When Zane finds us, he orders a round of Jack and Cokes, and it isn't long before Mark orders his second. He isn't paying attention when I hear a woman's voice in my ear.

"Did you need anything?" she asks as she sets Mark's drink down. She's hot. Deep tan, long brown hair, tall, and wearing a short black skirt that raises the question of what's underneath.

I shoot her a smile and nod my head for another Jack and Coke. She turns to make my drink, and maybe it's the alcohol that's already flowing through my veins, or maybe it's the fact that I haven't gotten laid in months, but lust takes over.

My indecent thoughts are interrupted when Mark stumbles into me, laughing uncontrollably. As soon as he opens his mouth to slur out his words, it's clear he's wasted.

"How many of these have you had?" I say as I point to his drink in hand.

"Check this shit out," he nearly shouts as he shoves his phone in my hand, and before I get a full view of what that chick is doing with a glow stick, I shove it back to him, saying, "Dude, that's fucked up."

Mark can hardly catch his breath, he's laughing so hard, and I'm getting a kick out of the show he's giving me, so I sit back on my barstool and laugh right along with him. Mark is a cool guy, much more outgoing and funny than Jase is. Jase tends to be more on the serious, calm side.

"I bet you'd like to be that glow stick, huh?"

"That's sick," I cringe. "Plus, you're the one that has that crap stored on your phone. Does Jase know that you get off on that?" I tease.

"You wanna see what I get off to?" he says as he starts scrolling through his phone.

"No. Love ya, man, but I don't wanna see what you're about to show me," I say as he starts pushing his phone towards me.

"Oh, come on," he taunts while I continue to laugh at him. "I know you think Jase is hot."

"What?"

"He's totally hot. Admit it! HOT!"

Holy shit this guy is far gone.

"I'm not saying a word," I tell him.

"That's a yes," he says in a singsong voice followed by an evil smirk. He's trying to get a rise out of me, and I find it pretty hilarious.

"It's not a yes."

"The dude is sexy as hell and you know it."

He's not gonna stop, so I just give him what he wants, and for the hell of it, I say, "Yeah, man. He's hot."

"I knew it!" he shouts through his laughter as I shake my head at all the attention he's drawing to himself. He takes a moment and then, with a straight face, sets his phone on the bar next to me and says, "Here, you enjoy glow stick girl. I gotta take a piss," before stumbling off.

I turn around in my seat and don't touch the phone. The girl behind the bar looks over at me and gives me a small grin. When she walks over, she looks at my glass and asks, "More?"

"I'm good."

"Your friend's pretty funny."

"My friend is pretty drunk," I tell her, and when she rests her forearms on the bar top and leans forward, she asks, "And what about you?"

"I'm in total control," I say in a low voice, and when I do, I get the look I was hoping for.

"We'll see about that," she says as she pulls back and walks away to continue helping customers.

I sit there for a while and nurse my drink. When I realize how much time has passed and Mark hasn't returned, I grab his phone to go look for him. I spot him towards the back of the club, talking with Gavin. When I step up to them, I hand Mark his phone and tell Gavin, "Call this guy a cab, will ya?"

"Yeah, man," he responds. "You heading out?"

"Not yet," I say, heading back towards the bar, but before I can get there, I run into the bartender as she's about to turn down a hall that looks like it leads to an office.

"You leaving?" she asks.

Wanting to know if this is worth wasting my time, I cut to the chase. "Not if you don't want me to."

An all-too-transparent grin spreads across her face before she says, "Come here."

She takes my hand and starts leading me down the hall. Opening a door to a small closet, she pulls me in and shuts the door. I can't see shit; it's so dark, and the smells of bleach and booze fill the room.

Her body presses up against mine, and I begin running my hands up underneath her top, grabbing her tits. She starts kissing my neck while fumbling with my pants, and the heat takes over. We begin moving at a frantic pace. I yank her top up and pull her bra down as she shoves her hand down my pants, fisting me tightly.

I throw my head back and hear the *thunk* as it hits the wall.

"Are you okay?"

"Is she gonna be okay?"

Suddenly, I'm back in the alley as my words play back in my head. This chick is all over me, but in an instant, my mind is somewhere else completely. Somewhere it hasn't been in a long time. I try to shake it off, but it's so dark in here that my eyes have nothing to focus on.

"God, please! Stop!"

"Stop."

"What's wrong?" she pants.

"Stop," I repeat and move her away from me. Buttoning up my pants, I know I can't do this. I know that she isn't, but all that floods my head is that this girl could be *that* girl. And what the hell am I doing with her anyway? Using her for a quick fuck to satisfy some sick need I have that I can't seem to get rid of? *Fuck.*

"Did I do something?" she questions, and the last thing I wanna do is make her feel like shit.

"Pull your shirt down," I tell her before opening the door. When I do, I look at her and say, "You didn't do anything. I'm just . . . I just can't do this. Sorry." I turn to walk out and back into the club. I don't even look for the guys; I just head straight out the door and continue to my jeep, to head home and jerk off.

I sit in my office at the bar, drinking beer and not getting much work done at all. Last night was messed up, and I know I can't be doing that shit again. I need something else to focus on, so I spent the morning clearing the images off of my camera and loading them onto my computer to start editing and enhancing. I figure I can work on those to suck up all the free time I seem to have on my hands at night now.

When the door to my office opens, Jase walks in.

"Hey, man," he says as he walks straight to the little fridge that's behind my desk that I keep stocked with beer.

"Can you toss me another one of those?" I ask as I throw my empty bottle into the trash.

Handing me the beer, he asks, "So, you been up here all day?"

"Pretty much. You know how Saturdays are—crazy as hell all day." I take a drink and then add, "Missed you last night. Mark said you got hung-up with a friend."

"Yeah, sorry about that. She's been going through a rough time, so I decided to stay with her last night."

"You missed a pretty good show," I tell him, referring more to his boyfriend than the band.

"That's what Mark said."

I can't help but laugh at the thought of him last night. "Your guy's a little crazy when he drinks."

"I'm not even gonna ask, but he was in a piss-ass mood when I saw him earlier."

"Ha! I bet. He drank a shitload, probably hungover as fuck."

We both laugh when the door opens and Mark walks

through. "What's so funny?" he asks as he stands there.

"You, man," I chuckle.

"If this is about last night, I don't even wanna know what the hell I did. My head has been pounding all damn day, and now I have to play for the next two hours."

"Go find Max. He always has earplugs," I tell him.

"Not a bad idea." Turning to Jase he asks, "Can I stay with you tonight? My new roommate just decided to tell me that he's throwing a party tonight."

"Yeah, no problem."

"Well, I gotta run. I just wanted to catch you," he says before he heads back down to the bar.

I start to shut down my computer when I ask, "So, is she okay?"

"Who?"

"Your friend. The one you were with last night," I say.

Standing up, I grab my beer and start to head out when Jase stands to follow me, saying, "She's getting there."

chapter eight

Since that night at The Crocodile a few weeks ago, I've been out of touch with Gavin and spending more time with Jase and Mark. I hit the coast the other week to get a break and do some surfing. I've finished working on several of the photos that were stored on my camera and picked up the mattings from the framer yesterday. I don't know what I plan on doing with them, but I spent so much time working on them, that I felt like I needed to finish them off by getting them matted.

I had to call Tori to let her know I wouldn't be making it back home for Halloween. I know she was disappointed, but Michael has had some things come up at home and hasn't been at the bar very much. Not sure what's going on with him, but I've had to be at work more than usual, covering for him.

Pulling out my phone, I open up my video chat and connect to Tori. I promised her I would call to say hi to Connor and Bailey before they leave to go trick-or-treating.

The call connects, and I see Tori when she answers.

"Hey, Ryan," she says, and I can tell she's flustered. The background is filled with the kids laughing and being loud as usual.

"You look rough," I tease.

"Connor had a Halloween party at a play date we went to earlier, so the kid is hopped up on sugar," she explains.

"Put him on. I wanna see him."

"Connor, Uncle Ry is on the phone," she hollers over her shoulder, and I see a miniature Superman with not-so-miniature padded muscles.

"Buddy! When have you been hitting the gym?" I ask.

"I have muscles," he says and then crooks his arm up with an intense face and growls, "Arrrr."

I laugh at his mock intensity and say, "Dude, you're getting bigger than me."

"Show me yours, Uncle Ryan," he requests.

Crooking my arm in the same way he did, and giving him the intensity right back, I flex and growl, "Arrrr."

His eyes grow big, in the way only an innocent four-year-old's can, and he says, excitedly, "Wow!"

"Yeah, man. Keep lifting those weights, and you'll get big guns like me."

"You're ridiculous," Tori teases as she pops her head back on to the screen.

"Hey, Connor. Don't let your mommy make fun of me, okay?"

"Mommy, be nice," he scolds her, and I let out a laugh.

"Where's your sister, little man?"

I watch as he runs off, red cape flying behind him. These kids have a way, in a matter of only seconds, of putting me on top of the world. I doubt I'll ever have any of my own, so I try to get the most out of my cousins' children.

"Here she is," I hear Tori say as she hoists Bailey onto her lap.

She's the sweetest little poodle I have ever seen. "My

little angel's a poodle," I say, not able to wipe the smile off my face. The cuteness is too much.

"Say hi," Tori encourages, as Bailey raises her chubby arm and waves at me before pointing, pressing her finger against the screen and saying, "Wy-Wy."

"That's right. It's Ry-Ry," she says to Bailey.

"Give Ry-Ry kisses," I tell her.

Perking her lips, she gives me an exaggerated, "Muah."

"Muah," I give her back in return.

"Are you coming for Thanksgiving?" Connor asks when he walks up, standing next to Tori and Bailey.

"Yeah, buddy, I am. Promise! I miss you guys so much, you know that?"

"I miss you too," he says.

"Well, I'm gonna let you guys go. Make sure you get a ton of candy. Be good for your mommy and daddy, okay?"

"Yay! Can we go trick-or-treating now, Mommy?" Connor asks with way too much energy, and I have no clue how Tori and Trevor are gonna get through Halloween without the aid of alcohol.

"Yes, we can go. Say bye to your uncle."

"Bye, Uncle Ryan," he shouts before running off.

"Say bye-bye," Tori tells Bailey.

Waving her hand again, she says, "Bye-bye."

"Bye, sweetie," I tell her.

"We gotta go before Connor drives me crazy," I hear Trevor, Tori's husband, say as he walks up.

"Okay," she responds.

"Hey, Ryan. What's up?" Trevor says into the phone.

"Not much. Looks like you have your hands full."

"You have no idea. Get your ass here and help us out," he jokes.

"Soon, man. You guys have fun tonight."

"Same to you. Bye."

"Bye," Tori adds.

"Take it easy, guys," I say before disconnecting the call.

I take the next half hour to call my other two cousins and check in with their kids. Envy starts to move slowly inside of me, and before I let the feeling take over, I go upstairs to my room, blast some music, and hop in the shower. It's gonna be a busy night at work, and I don't need to be in a funk. I love my family, but the idea of having my own worries me. What I grew up with was far from perfect. I've never had to take care of anyone other than myself, aside from my mom. But she's a strong woman, always has been. I don't really know what it means to provide for someone else emotionally. Even if I did, I doubt I would be capable of it. I live a selfish life. I only take care of myself, and at times, I feel like I do a shitty job of it.

After my shower, I grab a bite to eat and watch a little TV. I find myself focusing on the rain outside rather than the show that's playing. It's pouring as I stare out the solid wall of windows. I've always loved the weather here, never getting tired of the constant rain.

My phone rings, and when I look at the screen, I see Max's name.

"What's up?" I say when I answer.

"When are you getting here?"

"What time is it?"

"Almost ten. We're already at capacity, and I feel like shit," he complains.

"I'm leaving now," I tell him as I drag myself off the couch and start heading out.

I walk out to my black Rubicon and decide to grab a coffee before I go to the bar. It's gonna be a late night, and Mel sucks at making coffee. I drive around the corner and spot a coffee shop right off campus. Not that hard to do since there are coffee shops on every street corner.

Throwing the car in park, I step out into the heavy rain. I keep my head down as I walk to the door, getting soaked. When I go inside, my phone buzzes with a text from Jase. He's asking when I'm heading in, and I'm distracted when I walk up to the counter.

I briefly notice a girl sitting on a stool behind the register, reading a textbook, studying. She sees me and hops up as I turn my attention to the drink menu on the wall.

"Hey, what can I get for you?" she asks softly.

Still looking at the drinks, I settle on my usual. "Uh, just a twenty coffee. Black," I tell her when I start typing my text back to Jase.

"Easy enough."

On my way now. Give me 15min. Busy?

Insane.

"That's one ninety-three," she says as I shove my cell into my pocket.

Pulling out my wallet, I hand over a five. Finally, not distracted, I look at her. I think I know this girl 'cause something about her seems familiar. I stare, trying to pinpoint who she is, but she's so different from any girl I would ever go for, so I'm just confused. She has a small frame, can't be much taller than five feet. Her hair is a deep brown like mine, and it's pulled up, messy, on top of her head.

"Everything okay?" she asks, catching me staring, as she hands me my change. This girl has me so caught off guard that I don't even realize I haven't responded when she questions, "Anything else?"

The small features of her face, aside from her large hazel eyes, seem more delicate with her fair, almost porcelain-like skin. Not my usual type, but God she's pretty.

"Um, no. No, that's all," I say like an idiot, and I can tell I'm freaking her out when she nervously takes a step back and stumbles into her stool.

I turn to leave before I say anything else that makes me look any more like a moron, but dammit if I can't help turning to look at her a couple more times before I leave. As soon as I step out in the rain, it hits me.

"God, please! Stop!"

Snapping my head back to get another look at her through the rain-covered window, I feel my heart begin to pound. Her back is to me, so I can't see her face. *No. It can't possibly be her. What are the chances? There's no way.* Fuck, my head is really playing with me tonight. I get into my jeep and start driving. My mind is consumed with crazy thoughts that I need to dispel because none of them make sense to me.

She's tiny . . . just like the girl from that night. But her face . . . there's no way I could even make a comparison because that girl's face was so badly beaten and covered in blood. There's no way to know what she really looked like.

All I can think about is that night in the very alley I just pulled into and parked. I get out of my car and walk over to the dumpster, to the spot I found her. I rack my brain, but there are no real details I have to link these two girls.

The images flood through me. My stomach knots up, and I feel sick. That was a fucked up night that I wish I never had to witness. I wish I could forget. I wish my head would stop messing with me. *Give it up, man. Let it go. Just forget about it.*

When I head inside, I go straight to my office. Sitting down at my desk, I pick up my desk phone and call downstairs to the bar.

"Blur," I hear Mel answer.

"Mel, it's Ryan. I just got here. Can you send Max up to my office?"

"Sure thing."

Hanging up, I sit there, anxious for some reason, but need to talk, and Max is the only one who knows about that night.

"Hey, boss."

I look up at Max as he walks in, and when he sees me sitting there, soaking wet, he questions, "You okay?"

"Do you think it's possible . . . to connect two strangers . . . I mean . . ." I trail off, not able to get my thoughts together to form a coherent sentence.

He takes a seat and says, "What are you talking about?"

I breathe in a deep breath and let it out slowly when I tell him, "I went to grab a coffee before coming here, and the girl working there . . . well, when I saw her, my mind went straight to the girl from the alley. The girl who was attacked here a few months ago."

"You think it's the same person?"

Raking my hand through my wet hair, I fist a lock of it in frustration before saying, "I don't know. I mean, I guess for a second I did, but really, the chances would be next to nothing, right?"

He doesn't respond. I know I must sound crazy, but I continue anyway, "It's probably not. That girl was unrecognizable. I don't even know why my mind even took me there."

"I think it makes sense."

"You do?"

"Yeah. After it happened, it really bothered you that you didn't ever know what happened to her. If she was even okay. So it makes sense that your mind would still need closure and that it would come out at random times trying to make that connection." He takes a moment in thought, and then adds, "I dunno. Just my thought."

"No, you're right. I'm probably subconsciously trying to put an end to that situation. But that's not gonna happen. I just need to let it go."

"Yeah, 'cause you're gonna do nothing but drive yourself crazy," he says.

"That chick probably thought I *was* crazy. I couldn't stop staring at her, like some sick perv or something," I joke, trying to lighten the mood.

"She wouldn't be too off base," he throws back at me, and I laugh with him. "I gotta get back to the door. You gonna come down soon? Jase is here with Zane."

"Yeah, I'm gonna try and dry off, and I'll be down."

He turns back before walking out of my office and says, "That girl, whoever she is, I'm sure she's okay. It's been almost three months since it happened."

"Yeah. You're probably right," I reluctantly agree.

"Like you said, just let it go."

chapter nine

I couldn't let it go like Max told me, like I told myself even. I went back to Common Grounds a few days later. Back to the coffee shop and she was there. I just had to see her again. Had to get the confirmation that there wasn't a connection. The only similarity I could see was that the two girls are petite. That's all. No other connection. So now . . . now I let it go.

Before I hit the gym today, I need to stop by the bar to pick up a few files that I have to drop off to my accountant. It's early in the morning, so when I get there, I'm surprised to see Mel's car in the back lot. Walking in, it's dark. None of the lights are on, and the sun hasn't started to rise under the cloud-covered sky.

When I walk out from the back, I see Mel sitting on top of the bar with her legs crossed, nursing a cup of coffee.

"Hey," I say softly as I approach her.

She looks up and that's when I see the tears streaming down her cheeks.

"He's gone," is her only response, and I know she means her husband.

Zane, back when he was her boyfriend, played gigs here

every now and then. They would hang out here a lot, and when Mel needed a job, I brought her on.

I sit on one of the stools in front of her, and when she looks down at me, she explains, "They signed the deal, and he left."

"Why aren't you with him?"

As she lets her head fall, she says, "Because he didn't want me to be."

I clasp my hands together, not knowing what the hell is wrong with Zane. "I don't understand."

She wipes the tears from her eyes and sits up a little straighter. "He said he was tired of hearing me bitch about something he'd been working towards for years. He knew I didn't want to move to L.A. My life is here. My whole family is here. I didn't want to leave all that, but it was pissing him off. He feels like I'm not supporting him."

"Do you support him?"

"I don't know, Ry. Honestly, between you and me, even though I don't want to be alone, I'm kinda glad for the break. We haven't been on the same page for a while." After she says this, she hops down behind the bar and walks over to refill her cup of coffee. "Want some?" she asks.

"Yeah."

She pours it black, like I always take it, and sets it in front of me as she stands on the opposite side of the bar top.

Taking a slow sip, I then ask, "So, why are you here?"

"I just had to get out of the house, and I knew nobody would be here. That is, until you decided to crash my pity party," she jokes, laughing at herself. "What are *you* doing here at six a.m.?"

"I'm on my way to the Athletic Club. I needed to pick up some paperwork to drop off to my accountant later today."

"You coming back?"

"Nah. I'm gonna take the day off."

"That sucks," she complains.

"Why?"

"'Cause Michael is boring as hell, and he's been in a shit-ass mood the past few days," she tells me.

"You know why?"

"Not for sure, but I overheard him on his cell the other day."

"Eavesdropping?"

She starts laughing, and says, "You know it! But anyway, from what I heard, I think . . . and don't say shit about this, Ryan. Got it?" she warns.

"Yeah, whatever. Just say it."

"I think his wife is having an affair."

"That fuckin' sucks."

"I know. But you didn't hear that from me, and I'm not saying it's true. It's just what I pieced together from what I heard," she defends.

"Well, for his sake, let's hope you're full of shit and your eavesdropping skills suck."

The ringing of my phone interrupts us. I look to see that it's Gavin before I answer.

"Hey, what's up?" I say.

"You at home?"

"No. I'm at the bar."

"Even better. I wanted to drop off some tickets that I can't use for a concert this Saturday."

"Dude, I'm not in the mood to hit up another club."

"No club, man. It's a private concert over at Spines."

"The book store?" I ask.

"Yeah. My boss gave me a few tickets, but I had another work thing come up, and I have to bail. You want 'em? It's for The xx. They're in town for a couple days before their overseas tour," he explains.

"Yeah, definitely, man," I respond. That's one band I've been dying to see, but never had the chance before now.

"Great. Don't go anywhere. I'm about five minutes away."

"Later," I say before hanging up.

After Gavin dropped off the tickets the other day, I wound up running into Jase when I made it to the gym. We spent a couple hours lifting, and he took a few of the tickets off my hands, saying that he would go with Mark and bring along one of his friends, who I assume is the same person that Mark was telling me about a while back. We also made plans for the three of us to head down to Mount Rainier to go hiking next weekend.

After talking to my mom, I'm now running a bit late. I take a quick shower, fix my hair, and throw on my typical dark jeans, grey shirt, and black boots. I make my way downstairs and grab my jacket before I head out. The night is misty as I drive across town to Spines, a local book and music shop that has managed to stay open and alive while most of the others have closed.

I swing by one of the many espresso stands in this town and grab a cup of coffee. I don't plan on drinking tonight, so I need the buzz of caffeine to keep me going since I was up so early this morning.

I pull into Spines and park my jeep. When I walk in, the place is dimly lit, with people everywhere. The store is small, so even though there aren't too many people here, it feels like there are. The band is already playing, and I leave my jacket on one of the coat racks before spotting Mark.

He's by himself, hanging out next to a low bookcase, and I make my way over.

"Hey, Mark."

He turns around and claps my arm. "Hey. You just get here?"

"Yeah. Where's Jase?" I ask.

"He's grabbing a few beers," he responds. "There he is," he says as he looks over my shoulder.

When I turn around, I'm taken by surprise when I see that Jase's friend is *her*. Her eyes catch mine, and she coughs against the sip of beer she just took, looking shocked to see me just as I am her.

She's dressed casually in a long-sleeved, white v-neck shirt, jeans, and worn, brown leather boots that run up to just below her knees. She stands small next to Jase when she speaks, "You again."

"You two know each other?" Mark asks.

"Not really," I answer, finally breaking my eyes away from her.

"He's come into Common Grounds a couple times to get coffee. How do you guys know each other?" she asks Mark.

"He owns Blur, where the band has been playing lately."

"And the guy who gave me the tickets," Jase says and then turns to me and adds, "Thanks, man."

"No problem at all," I tell him and flick my eyes over to the girl, only to see she now has her back to me as she listens to the band play.

Mark and I go find a table to sit down while Jase stays back for a moment with his friend. *I still don't know her name.* I sit down and look over at them. She looks upset when Jase reaches down and holds her hand. I immediately wonder if her mood has something to do with me being here. *God, why am I feeling so self-conscious?*

They start heading over, and she sits down across from me, slipping her leopard scarf off her neck and laying it on the table. The two times I've seen her, her hair has been pulled up, messy, but for some reason, it looked good on her. Tonight it's down, thick and layered. She pulls my focus when she says, "I'm sorry, but I never caught your name."

I smile. I don't know why, but something about her is intriguing, so I let it linger on my lips when I tell her, "Ryan. Ryan Campbell."

"I'm Candace." She looks at my cup of coffee, and teases, "Ever drink anything besides coffee?"

"I work a lot of late nights."

"So, Ryan," Jase starts, "Candace will be graduating this year as well. She's a dance major."

I notice Candace looking annoyed at Jase for saying that, but I shrug it off and ask her, "Dance. What kind?"

"Ballet," she tells me and then takes a sip of her beer.

"Can't say I know anything about that," I say with light laughter.

"It's okay. Nobody ever does."

This chick seems way out of the realm of the girls I normally talk to. *A ballerina?* I find myself wanting to keep her talking because I like the sound of her soft voice. "So, I take it you're the best friend who loves this band?" I question, nodding my head toward the stage.

She shifts, almost nervously, in her seat. "Yeah."

She looks over at Jase, who is sitting next to her, and I watch their silent exchange, unsure of what's going on. I think back to what I've heard Mark say about this girl.

"She's going through some heavy stuff . . . Jase is staying the night with her."

Watching her peel off the label on her beer bottle, I try to push whatever is bothering her away, and ask, "So, Candace, what do you plan on doing when you finish school?"

When she looks up at me, I notice the coloring of her eyes. They're a light gold that almost flake into a deep emerald green.

"I hope to dance professionally while time allows. Not sure where that will happen. New York was always the plan, but I'm not so sure now." She looks over to Jase again, but he's engrossed in a conversation with Mark. I notice one of her brows twitch up. Nervous tick. I wonder if she's even aware that she has one.

Man, this girl is easily distracted. I bring her back in when I say, "I love New York. You ever been?"

"Yeah, several times. It's a great city. I actually lived there the summer before my senior year of high school. I had a scholarship to one of the conservatories in the city."

"So, your parents just let you live there alone for the summer?" I ask, surprised that a parent would let their teenage daughter run off to New York City all by herself.

"Umm, yeah. My parents are . . . well, not your typical involved parents," she tries to explain.

Moving past it, I continue, "So, that's where you'd like to wind up then?"

"That's the plan," she says with a hint of a smile, which also reveals a hint of a dimple in her right cheek.

Damn, I feel like a deprived puppy, infatuated over details of a chick I don't even know.

"What are you two talking about?" Mark asks, and I take the distraction, answering, "New York City."

The band starts in on another song, and I know it well—'Infinity.' I watch Candace stand and walk back to the bookcase Mark was at earlier. The three of us get up and follow her over, and I step next to her, resting my elbows on the bookcase as I lean forward.

I listen to the music, all the while feeling her eyes on me. I know I shouldn't look, but I do anyway, catching her. She gives me a soft grin and turns her attention back to the band.

Mark and Jase head to the bar, and I notice Candace taking a step back. I don't look at her. I don't want her to know that I want to. I'm not even sure I know why I want to—but I do. I keep my eyes forward, and when I can't help myself, I turn my head back to see her eyes locked on me. She's flustered as she stumbles around and runs smack into Mark, whispering something in his ear. Mark turns to Jase, and when he does, Jase steps over and asks her, "You ready to go?"

Mark looks to me and says, "Hey, man. It was good seeing ya. We'll catch up later this week."

"Yeah, catch you later," I tell him and then hold my hand out to Candace. "I'm glad I ran into you again."

Hesitantly, she slips her hand into mine, and I like the way it feels.

"Yeah, it was nice," she says, quickly pulling her hand back and turning to leave.

Interactions with this girl are weird. Jase told me, when I gave him the tickets, that the friend he wanted to bring didn't do well with crowds. Maybe the small space was making her uncomfortable.

Looking over, I spot her leopard scarf still lying on the table. I go over and pick it up. The greedy man in me is happy that she left this behind, giving me an excuse to see her again. The pull of this girl has me confounded, and I know I should make the smart move and stay away.

chapter ten

Coming back from the gym, I finally make the decision to just go and see her. I could just as easily give the scarf she left behind the other day to Mark, but I keep holding on to it. I've never chased a girl. It's always been the opposite. But I'm curious to get to know her and that curiosity surprises me, but I decide to go with it.

I take my time getting cleaned up. I'm not even sure if she's gonna be at work, but I'll take the chance and stop by before I head into the bar for a few hours. When I walk downstairs, I look out the large windows to see that it's another rainy day. Grey and cold.

Shrugging on my jacket, I walk over to the coffee table to grab her scarf. Her scent is encased in the fabric. Light and floral. I laugh at myself for being so shot with this girl that I actually smelled it the other night.

When I pull up to the coffee shop, I park my jeep and pick up the scarf. *Why am I nervous?* Walking through the door, I immediately spot her and happiness swarms, thankful that she's here and I didn't miss an opportunity to see her again.

She's talking to a chick with crazy hair and wiping down

the counter. She doesn't see me, but her friend does and gives me a smirk as she continues to talk to Candace. Finally, looking over her shoulder, she spots me as I make my way to the counter.

"You're gonna get an ulcer," she teases, and it's cute as hell.

I laugh and say, "I didn't come for coffee," as I hold out the scarf.

"Oh, I thought I had lost this," she says as she takes it from my hand. "Thank you."

"No, you left it on the table, but you rushed out so fast, I didn't have a chance to catch you."

Her head lowers, embarrassed I'm guessing, before quietly saying, "Sorry."

"No need to apologize."

She takes her apron and sets it on the counter when I ask, "Are you taking a break?"

"Um, no. My shift is over."

"Perfect timing." I smile and take this opportunity to spend a little time with her. "Want to have a quick drink?"

"She'd love to," her friend says over Candace's shoulder, and when Candace shoots her an irritated look, she starts to stumble over her words.

"Actually, I . . ." she starts, but never catches her sentence when she finally gives up. "Sure," she resolves. "Let me go grab my bag."

I watch as she walks away, and her friend steps up with her tattoo-covered arms and asks, "What can I get you?"

"Coffee. Black."

She gives me a wink as she turns to get my drink, and when she returns to me, she sets down two cups. "Candace likes hot tea," she says with a smirk, and I wonder why she's so eager.

When I pull out my wallet, she tells me it's on the house, and I go to find an empty table by the front window. Sitting down, I look up to see Candace walking towards me. She eyes the drink that's on the table, and I tell her, "Your co-worker said you like hot tea."

"Oh, thanks," she says as she takes a seat. "She's actually my boss. Roxy." She seems nervous, just like the other night. She takes a sip of her tea and focuses her attention out the window.

"Did Mark tell you we are heading down to Mount Rainier on Saturday?" I ask to try and draw her attention back to me.

"Yeah, Jase mentioned something like that to me."

"You should come with us."

"I don't know . . . I have a lot of studying I need to get done."

I can tell she's avoiding me. I'm not used to girls not being interested in me, but this one . . . she hardly seems to notice me.

"Well, if you change your mind, we are heading out in the morning around eight."

"How did you know I would be here today?" she asks, changing the subject on me.

"I didn't," I say, trying not to be too transparent. "I just thought I would stop by, and if you weren't here, I was just going to leave your scarf with whoever was working," I tell her, not needing her to know that I'd been hanging on to that scarf for days, hoping when I did stop by that she would be here.

"I didn't mean for that to come out rude."

"It didn't."

Watching her small hands clutch her cup of tea, I shift my eyes up and ask, "So, what are your plans for the rest of the day?"

"I have class in a couple hours, then I go to studio until five o'clock."

"Studio?"

"It's dance class."

Nodding, I question, "You do that every day?"

"Yep. Two hours a day except for Tuesdays and Thursdays, which are three hours. But I tend to go in on the weekends as well for extra practice."

"That's a lot. When do you have time for anything else?"

"I don't," she says with a shake of her head.

"That bother you?" I ask, wondering if she does anything besides school.

"No . . . Why?"

"I don't know. When do you ever get down time?"

"I don't. But I love dance, so I consider that my down time. It relaxes me."

"So school and work, huh?"

She grins and responds, "Pretty much."

"That doesn't sound like very much fun," I joke.

Shifting her eyes down to her hands, she doesn't respond. She's difficult to read, so I back pedal, and say, "I didn't mean for that to come out like it did."

Her eyes catch mine when she looks up. "I just like to stay busy."

I back off the questions and offer her another tea, but she says she has to get going.

"I'll walk you out," I tell her. We slip on our coats, and she gathers her things before we head out into the rain. She nods her head to a sporty, white Acura, and we start walking that way.

"Thanks for the tea," she tells me as she opens her door and slides into her seat.

Gripping the frame of her car, I lean in slightly and say, "Think about Rainier."

"I will," she tells me with fake intent, but I laugh it off and shut her door before she pulls away.

I hop into my car and head to the bar. When I get there, I go upstairs to my office and run into Max in the hall.

"Hey, boss. I didn't know you were coming in today."

"Yeah, I need to get a few things done. I'm not staying tonight though." I had made plans with Mark and Jase to go shoot pool, so when I leave here I'm gonna hang out with Jase at his place before we head out.

"You seem upbeat," he remarks as he follows me into my office.

Shutting the door, I walk over to my desk and take a seat. "So you know that girl from the coffee shop I told you about the other week?"

"Yeah."

"I had coffee with her this morning," I tell him.

"What? Why?"

"Turns out, she's friends with Jase and Mark. I ran into them a few nights ago, and she was with them."

He looks at me with a curious tilt of his head, and I admit, "It's weird."

"What's weird?"

"Her. I mean . . ." I can't seem to find the words to explain what I'm trying to say, but he jumps in and asks, "You like her?"

"I don't know her," I immediately defend, knowing that the first word that came to my mind was yes.

"You don't have to know her."

Sitting back in my chair, I tell him, "There's this pull she has that no one has ever had on me before. But she's not like any of the girls I've ever been with."

He laughs at me and says, "That's probably a good thing."

I laugh with him for a second. "She's a ballerina."

"No shit? So why is she hanging out with you?" he teases.

"That's the thing . . . I don't know. She's really standoffish, and I can't figure out why."

"Maybe she's just not into you. That is possible, you know?" he jokes with a knowing grin on his face.

"Yeah, man. I know," I give him right back. "But it isn't that obvious. More like she's got thick boundaries. I dunno."

"You gonna see her again?"

"I have no idea. She's very evasive."

"I think I like this one," he says with a cocky smile.

"Oh yeah. Why's that?"

"She doesn't stroke your ego like most chicks do. She's gotten under your skin."

"She's not under my skin," I refute. But is she? Maybe he's right.

"Whatever you say," he sighs as he stands up and starts walking to the door.

Taking a swig of beer, I mindlessly watch Mark and Jase finish up their round of pool. My head is back at Jase's apartment where she is. She stopped by unexpectedly while Jase and I were hanging out. Flustered. Something had upset her from the time I saw her earlier today at the coffee shop. She didn't say anything, but I overheard her asking Mark if she could stay the night with Jase, which I find a little odd.

"So when did you see Candace?" Jase asks me, knocking me out of my thoughts.

"What?" I say as I grab my cue and chalk it.

"When you mentioned our hike."

"This morning. She left her scarf at the concert. I stopped by her work to drop it off," I explain right before I break.

Jase is protective over her. I see how he acts with her; I saw it the night of the concert. Holding her hand, touching her back—almost assuring her. Of what? I don't know. But I see it with Mark too. These guys care deeply for her, there's no question about that.

When I look up at Jase, he's staring at me, almost zoned out. "You're up," I say.

He moves to make his shot, sinking his ball into the side pocket.

"You guys want another bucket of beers?" Mark asks.

"Yeah," Jase tells him before Mark heads over to the bar.

I take this time to try and get a little more info on this girl, so when he lines up his next shot, I ask, "So, what's her story?"

"No story," is all he says and then misses his shot.

I walk around the table, looking for my play, when I try to casually ask, "You've known her a long time?"

"She's not like that, man. Not even close," he quickly responds, and I suddenly feel like I'm way out of my league. Jase doesn't know me like that, but knowing Gavin, I'm sure he's told Jase stories. By the time I met Jase, and even Mark, I had pretty much stopped fucking around.

I lean over the table, ready to take my shot, when I peek up at Jase, who's staring. "She's like a sister to me," he adds, and I know he knows I'm interested in her. And I also know that he doesn't think I'm good enough. *Maybe he's right.*

chapter eleven

Call me when you get a chance.

I read the text from Jase while I'm working from home today. Our conversation a couple nights ago was a little awkward, so I'm curious as to why he wants me to call him. I don't waste any time thinking too much about it when I tap his name and it begins to ring.

"Hey, what's up?" he says when he answers.

"Not much. Just getting some work done. You?"

"Heading home from class," he says before adding, "Look, I'm sorry if I came across short with you the other night. I wasn't trying to make you feel like you couldn't hang out with Candace. I just get a little protective of her at times."

"No worries. I know the two of you are close, so I wouldn't ever . . ." I trail off, not even sure of where I'm going with this statement, but he cuts the silence and says, "Yeah, I know. But, hey, if you wanna come over tonight, Candace and Mark will be here. We're just gonna lay low and hang out."

"Yeah, man. I've got some things to take care of, but I'll stop by later."

"See ya."

"Later," I say and then hang up.

I spend the day taking care of a few work things. I'm trying to lessen the time that I have to spend up at the bar, so I've been getting most of my work done from home. Michael has been putting in the hours, and I feel I'm at a point where the bar is running smoothly without me having to be around all too often.

It's a little after eight when I head over to Jase's apartment building. When I get there, Mark lets me in, and I look over to see Candace wrapped up in Jase's arms on the couch. My head takes me to wishing it was my arms wrapped around her. I shut that thought down fast, but it lingers in the back of my mind. Truth is, I've never been that way with a girl in my whole life, so to see Jase have that with someone who's only a friend makes me a little envious.

He looks up at me when I walk by and says, "Hey, there's beer in the fridge. Help yourself."

Giving him a nod, I head straight into the kitchen to grab one. When I turn around to get the bottle opener, Candace walks in, holding an empty wine glass.

"Could you hand me a bottle of water?" she asks, and I open the fridge to grab one.

Handing it to her, I take the wine glass out of her hand, and with a smirk, I say lightly, "I thought you never did anything fun."

When I walk over to the sink to set her glass down, I hear her respond, "I never said that. I said I like to keep busy."

I turn around to face her and lean back against the counter. She stands there in what looks to be a pair of Jase's boxers and a UW t-shirt. Her hair is piled on top of her head again, and I don't think she could look any more attractive than she does right now—relaxed.

"Did you have a better day today?" I ask, knowing that the last time I saw her something had clearly upset her.

"It was okay. How about you?"

"Hung around my place for the most part."

"Candace," Jase calls from the other room, "It's back on."

She doesn't say anything else to me, she just turns to go sit next to Jase on the couch, pulling her legs up as he wraps his arm back around her. I sit on the other end of the couch while Mark is comfortable in a chair.

I turn to the TV to see some drunk jackass climbing his kitchen cabinet just to have the whole structure rip off the wall and fall of top of him, dishes and all. When I hear Candace laughing, I turn to her and ask, "What the hell are we watching?"

"'Ridiculousness,'" she answers, keeping her eyes fixed on the TV.

Jase looks over her to me, and says, "For such a refined girl, she loves this show."

"You're the one who first told me about it," she accuses him.

"Just ignore their banter," Mark says to me. "They both love trash TV."

I listen to the three of them go back and forth and their connection seems strong with one another. I know that Mark just recently started dating Jase, so to see them interact like this, like they've known each other for years, makes me realize just how alone I am. The deepest friendship I feel like I have, outside of my mom and Tori, is Max. But it's nothing like these people have. So I sit here, drink my beer, and enjoy the company.

Before I call it a night, I catch Candace quietly sneaking off to go to bed in Jase's room. My curiosity grows as to why she's staying here, but I don't ask. Mark tells me to meet him at his place in the morning to pack up for our hike as I head out.

After about three hours of hiking, we start making our way down Tolmie Peak. It's been raining for the better part of the hike and the four of us are cold and drenched, and when I hear, "Crap!" I look back to see that Candace has fallen in the mud.

Jase and Mark are further down the trail, so I go back and hold out my hands for her to grab on to, pulling her out of the mud.

"You're a complete mess," I tease.

"Yeah, I know," she says, almost unfazed that she's covered in mud.

She keeps her hold on my hand, and I like it, as we make our way down to the bottom. Once there, she lets go as we continue our trek back to the car. Jase and Mark are several steps in front of us, lost in their own conversation, and it's not long before Candace starts talking. She seems more comfortable around me, but we did just spend most of the last three hours hiking without the company of Jase and Mark. They've been keeping their distance from us.

"So, how did you come about owning a bar?" she asks me.

"Just kind of fell into it. When I graduated college, the economy was starting to decline, and I couldn't find a job. So, when I found out that the previous owner of that bar was about to shut the place down, I worked out a deal with him and was able to do a slow buyout."

"You went to U-Dub?"

"Yeah, I graduated back in 2007."

"So, that makes you . . .?" she pries.

Laughing at her, I answer, "Twenty-eight."

"What did you study?" she continues, and I like that. For once, I'm not having to struggle to get her to talk.

"Business Finance. So, it wasn't too far out of reach that I would come to own my own business."

"You enjoy it?"

"I do. When I did the buyout, I changed the whole place out and created a new vibe for it. It wasn't before long that the business was taking off quicker than I expected. At this point, the staff pretty much runs the place, and I have a trustworthy manager, so my schedule is very flexible."

"Sounds like the perfect job."

"You ever been there?" I question.

"No. I don't really ever go out." She smiles and adds, "I'm sort of a workaholic. Jase is always nagging me about that."

"Well, you should stop by sometime."

"Yeah. Maybe," she says, but I know she doesn't mean it.

Laughing, I joke, "You're full of shit, aren't you?"

"Yeah. Maybe," she repeats as she laughs with me. Her smile is perfect and that shallow dimple makes it hard to not lean over and kiss her, but this girl has walls—unbreakable ones—that I'm determined to start chipping away at.

Getting back to Mark's house, we each take our time showering and cleaning up.

Mark and I tune in to the Washington vs. Colorado football game. Mark throws a couple of logs onto the fire, and when I pull out my cell to order some pizzas, I see

Candace walking through the room and straight into the kitchen. I'm distracted when the line is answered and I'm putting in the order.

"What kind of pizza do you want, Candace?" I holler into the kitchen.

"I don't care. I'll eat anything at this point," she tells me as I order the pizza.

She walks back into the room carrying a bottle of wine to share with Mark. Those two have proven to be the wine drinkers of the group while Jase and I watch the game and toss back a couple beers, but apparently I haven't kept that good a count 'cause Jase has definitely had more than a couple when he starts screaming at the penalty that was just called.

We all laugh at him when he runs into the kitchen to answer Candace's phone that starts to go off.

He walks back in, total mood shift, mouthing 'I'm sorry' as he hands Candace the phone.

"Who is it?" she asks quietly.

"Your mother."

She looks irritated when she heads outside to the patio to take the call.

"What's that all about?" I ask Jase.

"Her parents are assholes to her," he blurts out and Mark butts in, almost scolding when he calls his name, "Jase."

He looks to Mark and says, "What? They are. They treat her like shit and she doesn't deserve it."

Getting up from the couch, I head into the other room where I watch her through the glass French doors. I can hear her yelling, "Of course this is my fault, right? You are unbelievable, Mother!"

"It's not my fault. I swear."

I watch my father's glare as he spits out, "It's never your

*fault, you piece of shit," before grabbing the broom and
whacking the wooden handle into my back. I hear the wood
splinter and crack when it slaps across my skin, sending
shards of heated pain up my spine.*

*"Get your ass up and walk to school. Don't ask me to
drive you again. You miss the bus, you walk."*

Coming out of my thoughts, I fight the urge to storm out
there and take the phone from her so she doesn't have to
listen to whatever her mother is saying to her that's making
her so upset. Instead, I stand here and watch her. When she
hangs up and shoves the phone in her pocket, she sits back in
one of the chairs and stares up into the sky. She's sad. And
it's not just tonight. Underneath the few conversations that
we've had, I can see it buried in her. On the drive to Mount
Rainier this morning, she must have had a nightmare or
something when she fell asleep in the back seat of the car
while Mark and I were up front. I didn't want to give it too
much attention because I didn't want to embarrass her, but
she was scared. She was in Jase's arms in a matter of
seconds, and now, watching her staring into the blackness, I
feel there's more to her than she lets on.

When she stands and turns, she catches me watching her,
but I don't even care. I open the door and ask, "You okay?"
because I really need to know.

But when she blows it off and says with mock humor,
"My mother's lost her mind, that's all," I see her walls.

"Wanna talk about it?" I keep on, trying to chip as she
walks past me.

Turning to face me, she casually says, "Nothing to really
talk about."

I want to touch her, just brush her cheek, something, but I
don't. Being with her today, talking with her, laughing with
her—she's different. Sweet, funny, athletic, and soft. God,

she's soft. But it's more than that; she has depth to her. A depth I've never seen with the girls I've been with. Not that I've been with them in a way to even notice if they did, but they all seemed so shallow. Even though she doesn't mean to let on, I can tell there's a lot going on under her exterior, and I feel this eagerness to explore.

When she walks back to Jase and lies down with her head in his lap, he asks, "What did she want?"

"She wanted to know when I would be home for Thanksgiving."

"When are you going to leave?" Mark asks.

"I told her I would be there Wednesday night. I'll probably leave Saturday morning," she answers as I walk across the room and take a seat on the stoop of the fireplace.

"When are you and Mark heading out?" she questions Jase.

"Our flight leaves around noon on Tuesday," he tells her.

"When do you guys get back?"

"Late Sunday afternoon."

"What about you?" she asks me as she rolls onto her side to look at me.

"I'm going to go spend a few days with my family down in Cannon Beach in Oregon. My aunts and uncles always come to my mother's house with my cousins for a big dinner."

"Will you be there for the weekend?"

"Nah," I tell her. "I'll come back home that night. My mom and her sisters spend the day plotting for Black Friday, so I always come back home and just lay low."

"Sounds like you have a big family," Jase says.

"Yeah, man, three cousins and between them they have seven little kids. I love them, but shit they're loud," I say as I laugh.

"Must be nice though. I'm an only child with no cousins. Small family," she tells me.

"So, it's just you and your parents?"

"Mmm hmm."

"They live very far?" I ask her.

"No. They still live in Shoreline where I grew up."

Knowing that Jase is going home with Mark to Ohio for the holiday, I offer, "Well, I'll be around."

When I see a hint of a smile, I feel like maybe I've finally made a nick in her exterior.

chapter twelve

When I pull into my mom's driveway, I see my family's cars littering the street. I'm the last one to get here, and when I walk in, the noise confirms it. I make my way through the foyer to the back of the house, and the scene looks the same as always. The guys are drinking beer and watching football while the kids run around and play. The girls are all in the kitchen with the babies, laughing and gossiping.

"Sweetheart!" my mom squeals when she notices me walking into the kitchen. She gives me a big hug, and I wrap my arms around her. I feel like a lot has changed since I last saw her, so I take the embrace I feel like I've been missing for these past few months.

We exchange our 'I love you's' and 'I've missed you's' before I say hi to everyone else. The kids are running wild, excited to see me, as I hand Tori the keys to my jeep so she can go bring in the bags of gifts that I always have every time I see the kids. I love spoiling them, but it's also my method of distracting them, and giving them new shit to play with keeps them occupied and out of their parents' hair for a while.

When Tori walks back in, arms full of gifts, she mouths

'thank you,' desperate for the reprieve. I laugh and follow her into the living room where all the kids are. I sit on the floor with them as they rip through the paper, finding puzzles, toy cars, dolls, and a small bubble machine that is sure to keep these kids entertained by the hour.

"And where did you plan on the kids playing with that?" my mother gently nags, in only the way a mom can do.

"In the playroom upstairs."

"Can I send you the bill for the carpet cleaning?"

Rolling my eyes at her, I say, "It's bubble solution, Mom, not a turd."

"What's a turd, Uncle Ryan?" Madison, my three-year-old niece, asks.

Smiling at her, I say, "It's poo poo."

"Ewwww!" she squeals through her fit of laughter, and her mom, Katie, scolds me with a simple, "Ryan!"

I love getting a rise out of my cousins when it comes to their kids. I swear they can take the most harmless thing and make a big issue about it.

"Katie, they know what poop is. Relax."

"Connor, you're a turd head," we overhear Madison say, and then I get *the look* from Katie as I start laughing.

"Hey, Tor. Can you grab me a beer?" I holler over to her while I sit next to her husband, Trevor.

"All these men are helpless," I hear her tell my aunts.

My mother gathers the older kids and takes them up to the playroom, and when Tori hands me my beer, she sits on the floor between her husband's legs.

After taking a long swig, Trevor asks, "So, man, how's life in Seattle?"

"Good. Can't really complain."

"I need to get some free time to get up there and run around with you for a few days," he tells me.

"You should. I haven't been going out as much as I used to though."

"Oh yeah?" he questions before Tori butts in and adds, "Why's that? You seeing someone?"

Shit. This girl sees right through me, so I quickly defend, not wanting to reveal my personal shit to anyone, "What? No. Just been busy and haven't had much time."

Narrowing her eyes at me, she says, "You lie. You told me last week that the new manager is freeing up your time and you haven't been going into the office as much."

"Dude, who is she?" Trevor pipes in with a nudge to my arm.

"Who's who?" my mother says as she walks down the stairs.

God, my family is nosey as hell.

"Nothing, Mom. They're just giving me crap."

My mom walks into the kitchen to join her sisters.

"Seriously, Ryan," Tori pries.

Looking down at her, I say, "Seriously," in an attempt to clip her curiosity.

"Don't listen to her," Ethan, Katie's husband, tells me. "Enjoy the freedom."

I give him a nod and take another sip of my beer, while Tori teases him, "That's nice, Ethan. Does my sister know that you miss your freedom?"

"Every. Single. Day," he jokes right back with her, and the three of them start laughing.

"I can't lie, I miss it too," Tori admits through her chuckles.

I listen to them while they complain, wishing I knew what it felt like to have what they do. Someone to share their bed with, kids, a family to make a home with. I've been alone my whole life. I feel like I don't have a choice. I see what my cousins have, and it seems happy. But what I had, what I *know*, is a stark difference. It was pure chaos and dysfunction. Misery. I fear I'll wind up just like my dad. I don't know what it takes to be functional with anyone. I was never exposed to what a healthy relationship looks like. But when I think about where I'd like to wind up in life, it isn't alone.

I head upstairs to my room to grab a coat and then make my way out to the back patio that overlooks Cannon Beach. It's cold and windy with a faint mist under the grey sky. I love it out here, so I sit and kick my feet up onto the wooden railing in front of me.

I hear the door open, and when I look back, I watch my mom join me as she sits in the chair next to me.

"What are you doing out here in the cold?" she asks as she ties her leopard scarf around her neck, and my mind goes to Candace for a second before I answer, "Just thinking."

"About?"

"I don't know. I guess nothing, really."

She shifts to face me, and I don't even hesitate when I open up to her. "I met someone."

"Really?" she says, completely surprised.

I laugh at her enthusiasm and shake my head. "Don't get too excited, Mom. I'm not even sure she notices me."

"Why's that?"

"I don't really know. She's hard to figure out."

"You meet her at the bar?" she questions.

"No. She isn't that type of girl," I say before taking a draw from my beer. "She's quiet. Reserved. She's studying dance at U-Dub." Looking over at my mom, she's smiling at me. "What?"

"Nothing. You've just never talked about a girl before."

"No girl has ever given me a reason to."

"So, have the two of you gone out yet?"

"No. Like I said, she's hard to read," I tell her as I look out over the water. "She's different than the chicks I normally go for."

"In what way?"

I turn back to my mom and respond, "In every way."

She sits back in her chair and asks, "What's her name?"

"Candace."

"Pretty name."

"She has these ticks though," I reveal.

"Like what?"

"She's awkward around crowds. She's close friends with a couple of guys I know, and they're really protective of her. I notice she stays the night with one of them a lot."

"Is she seeing him?" she asks, and I laugh.

"No."

"Why are you laughing?"

"'Cause they're gay, Mom."

"Hmm," is all she responds.

"I dunno. There're just these things I pick up on that she does, but she's so standoffish with me, and it's hard trying to get her to talk."

"Sometimes the things worth keeping are the things we have to work for," she tells me.

"Maybe," I sigh. "We'll see. I don't even really know her. It's just . . . I want to."

She reaches out and takes my hand as I look over at her and smile.

The house has been noisy and busy for the past couple of days. Every room is filled, and having the whole family here is always something I enjoy. I went for a run along the beach this morning, and when I came back, my mom and her sisters were already in the kitchen, preparing food for Thanksgiving dinner.

After getting cleaned up and heading downstairs, the kids are still lying on the floor, watching the Thanksgiving parade while my aunts are scouring the Black Friday ads with my mom. I swear, it's the highlight of the year for them. They take their middle of the night shopping seriously and always have a mission plan before heading out. I look over at the three of them, huddled over the paper, and laugh as I walk into the kitchen to make a pot of coffee.

"What's so funny?" my Aunt Carol asks.

Pulling a mug down, I say, "The three of you—plotting."

"Wanna be our driver?" she jokes.

"Sorry, ladies. You're on your own."

"Are you still heading out this evening?" my mom asks.

"Yeah. Even though the bar's gonna be dead, I let most of the staff take time off, so I need to be around."

I take my coffee and go sit with the kids as they watch with excitement when they see a cartoon character they know float by. I sit back on the couch and wonder about *her*, remembering what Jase told me the other day before I saw how upset she was after talking with her mom.

"Her parents are assholes to her. They treat her like shit and she doesn't deserve it."

I wonder how she's doing. I wonder how bad her parents really are. I wonder if they're the reason why she's so closed off. I wonder why I'm wondering so much, but I can't shake the fact that I need to know. For some reason, it bothers me, and I can't let it go.

I pull out my cell and go back and forth on whether or not I should take this jump. I don't know what I'm doing.

I've never done this before. I've never wanted to. But now . . . *Fuck it, I'm jumping.*

Punching out a text, I send it to Mark.

Can you send me Candace's number?

I sit and wait. No response. I'm hoping he's busy with his family, and not asking Jase what they should do to keep me away from her. *Fuck.*

My phone starts vibrating with an incoming call, and when I pick it up, I see it's Mark. I answer the phone as I step outside.

"Hey."

"Hey, man. How's everything going?" he asks.

"Good. You?"

"Really good. Jase is with my mom, cooking, so I wanted to give you a quick call."

"Okay," I respond, waiting anxiously for what he has to say.

"I just wanted to lay it out there for you. Jase loves Candace in a way that's hard to explain. He worries. I do too. She's had a hard time this school year, and I don't want to see her get hurt."

"I'm sure you've heard things about me—"

"So you know where I'm coming from," he interrupts.

"It isn't like that," I tell him.

"Good."

Before we hang up, I get her number and store it into my phone. When I go back inside, I don't text her. I hold off. Instead I distract myself with the kids. I spend most of the day putting together puzzles and playing dolls with Maddie and Bailey.

After we all eat and I'm lying in my bed, trying to nap off my food coma, I stare at my phone. Looking at the numbers that are my connection with her. It's a little after six o'clock.

The day is nearly over, so I fight against my apprehension and type out my text.

Got your number from Mark. Wanted to see how your Thanksgiving went. –Ryan

Lying there, I stare at the screen, waiting. I start questioning if that move was too bold for this girl. It's a move I've never had to question in the past. My moves have always been pretty blunt, so the fact that I'm worried about a text is unnerving. And then my phone buzzes with her reply.

I think we managed to fall into the universal tradition of holiday drama. :)

That bad?

I respond, naturally wondering what happened.

Kinda. Now I'm home with no food.

She's already back at her house. She wasn't supposed to be back for a couple more days, so whatever happened was bad enough that she bailed out early.

"Ryan!" I hear my mom call from downstairs. Setting the phone down, I go to the top of the stairs to see what she wants.

"What's up?" I call down.

"I need to run out and get some Pepto tablets for Connor. When are you planning on leaving?"

"I'll just head out now, if that's okay?"

"It's never okay," she teases.

I grab my phone and make my way downstairs. I feel like I'm rushing, saying goodbye to everyone, just so I can text Candace back. But once hugs are exchanged, I walk out with my mom.

"What are the plans for Christmas?" she asks.

"Same as always. I'll be here on the twenty-third."

"You drive safe, you hear," she tells me.

"I hear."

"Call me so I know you made it okay."

Nodding my head, I tell her I love her before hopping in my car and pulling out of the driveway. Before I'm even at the main street, I have my phone out and text her back while I sit at the red light.

Sorry, saying bye to everyone. About to head home myself.

Did you have a good time with your family?

Yeah, I did. Ate way too much. Feel like I need to hibernate.

LOL. Drive safe. Is it pouring where you are?

Not too bad. Try and have a good night.

Thanks.

I toss the phone onto the passenger street and drive the four hours that it takes to get home, all the while thinking about her.

chapter thirteen

I'm up early and just got off the phone with my mother. They haven't even made it home yet. They've been out shopping all night. It's almost embarrassing. I find myself rummaging through my kitchen, and something about eating so much yesterday has me craving another heavy meal.

I jump into the shower to get ready and remember what Candace texted me last night.

I'm home with no food.

When I get out of the shower, I take a shot and send her a text.

I am heading out for breakfast. Wanna join?

I pull some clothes out of my closet and get dressed when I hear my phone buzzing.

Sure. Where?

I'm a little shocked that she so easily agreed, but I go with it and don't even question her.

The Dish Café. 9:00?

See you then.

After another cup of coffee, I head out and make my way to the local dive. I'm there first, so I go ahead and order her a tea while I wait. I pick up the menu to give it a lookover, and when I shift my eyes up, I see her walking in. I notice her leopard rain boots peeking out underneath her jeans, and laugh to myself. This chick obviously has a thing for leopard.

"Hey," I say as she shrugs off her coat and sits down.

"Hi, thanks for inviting me. I literally have no food at the house."

"So, what did you wind up doing last night?" I ask.

Slumping back in her chair, she says, "I ate an old bag of popcorn and passed out on the couch."

"That's pathetic," I laugh.

Widening her eyes, she agrees, "My thoughts exactly."

When the waiter stops by and brings us our drinks, she eyes the tea he sets down in front of her and I say, "I ordered you a hot tea."

She looks a bit surprised when she replies, "Oh, thanks," before picking up her menu. I watch her and notice her eyebrow give a slight twitch, but she distracts me when she suddenly asks, "So, how was your Thanksgiving?"

"It was good. We did the typical family thing like we do every year. Mom and her sisters being loud and gossipy, cooking all day. I hung out with the guys and watched football while the kids ran around screaming and playing. My head was pounding by the end of the night."

She keeps a serious face when she says, "That actually sounds nice."

"Yeah, it is," I agree. "It's not too often that everyone can get together, so when it does happen, it's fun. Crazy, but fun."

"What can I get you guys this morning?" the waiter asks when he drops by again.

"Um, I'll have the two blueberry pancakes," she tells him as she hands him the menu, and then I place my order.

She takes a sip of her tea and then asks, "So how many nieces and nephews do you have?"

Setting down my coffee, I say, "Three nieces and four nephews all under the age of five." I smile when I add, "I'm not lying when I say it's loud and crazy."

When she doesn't say anything in response, I ask, "So, you're an only child?"

"Yeah. I have a pretty small family. My grandparents on my father's side died when I was in high school, and I have never met my mother's parents or her sister. My father is an only child as well, so it's just the three of us."

"Quiet."

"Hmmm . . ." is all she replies before switching the topic back to me. "Is your mother out with the crazy Black Friday crowd today?"

"God, you have no idea. She and my aunts go bat-shit over the sales."

When the waiter stops by and drops off our food, Candace lets out a satisfied sigh that I find humorous as she inspects her pancakes. She picks up her fork, and she must be hungry by the look on her face.

"That's a shitload of food. You gonna be able to eat all that?" I ask.

Eying me, she cuts a huge piece off and for such a sophisticated looking girl, she shoves it in her mouth, giving me a gratified nod, and I literally laugh out loud at the scene she's putting on.

"So, is all of your family in Oregon?" she asks while she eats.

"Yeah. I grew up there."

"Why didn't you ever go back after you graduated?"

"Because I bought out the bar. It was too good an opportunity to pass up. But honestly, Cannon Beach is a small town. I love Seattle and had already been here for four years and felt pretty settled. So I stayed," I explain. "My mom had a hard time though. She had hoped that I would eventually move back, but it's been ten years since I've been here, so she's accepted that this is my home."

"You two sound close," she says before taking another bite.

"Yeah," is all I respond when I take a sip of my coffee and continue to eat.

When Candace tosses down her fork and leans back, almost painfully, in her seat, she closes her eyes and lets out a groan that I laugh at.

"I can't believe you ate all that. You sound like you're about to die," I tease.

"You have no idea," she says as she opens her eyes.

"You gonna be able to walk, or will I have to carry you?"

Shifting around in her seat, she tells me, "Honestly, I really need to walk this off."

"Come on, let's get outta here," I say as I stand up, not wanting to become a victim of a missed opportunity. I toss some cash onto the table and reach my hand out for her to take, and she does.

Walking her out into the rain, I nod my head over to where I'm parked for her to follow.

She stops in her steps and asks, "What?"

"I know you don't have shit to do today, so come on," I say as I walk over to my Rubicon. When I look back at her, she's still standing there. "Come on," I repeat.

"Where are we going?"

"I'll figure that shit out when you get in."

Wanting to keep Candace around for most of the day, I took her to the aquarium. I knew we could easily burn a few hours there, and I was right. She seemed relaxed and had fun, but now I'm sensing tension from her. We just left her house after grabbing a few groceries from the store. I could tell she was uncomfortable with me being there.

As I'm driving her back to her car that's still at the restaurant, she watches the rain out the window and quietly says, "Thanks."

"For what?"

"Today. I had fun hanging out," she responds as she looks over at me.

"You should say yes when I ask you to go running with me tomorrow morning."

"Is that you asking me or telling me?"

When I look over at her and give her a smirk, she starts to giggle as she says, "Okay then."

Satisfied with her answer, I repeat her words, "Okay then."

Feeling a little more comfortable talking with her after spending the day together, I decide to ask her about what happened with her parents. So when I turn into the parking lot, I put the jeep in park and sit for a moment. The rain is coming down hard, beating against the steel. Turning to face her, she looks at me when I say, "I didn't want to say anything earlier, but I can't help but wonder about what made you come home yesterday."

She shifts to face me and lets out a sigh, leaning her head against the headrest. "I got into a fight with my parents. Some pretty nasty things were said, so I just left."

"You guys fight a lot?"

"My whole life," she tells me. "My mother is a difficult woman to be around. She doesn't approve of the way I want to live."

"What do you mean?" I can't imagine what this girl could possibly be doing wrong to earn her parents' disapproval.

"My parents are more concerned about their social standing than my happiness. So, having a daughter who wants to be a dancer and isn't engaged to be married is not a good look for them."

"That's pretty shitty."

"I'm used to it," she mumbles, and I hate the fact that this has been going on so long that she expects it.

"No one should be used to that," I tell her softly. "They should be proud of you. I've only just met you, but you're pretty great from what I know so far."

She fidgets with her hands, seeming uncomfortable with my words, but I needed to say them.

She keeps her focus on her hands when she speaks again. "I had always hoped that somewhere beneath their hard exterior that they would be proud of me, but after last night, I now know that they aren't." When she looks back up at me, she looks abashed as she tells me, "My mother actually said she was embarrassed by me."

Jase was right; her parents are pieces of shit. I can't even help myself when I lean into her, and slide my hand over hers. I want to do so much more, but I leave it at this. She stares at our hands, and I can sense her tensing up at the contact.

She sits up and pulls her hand out from under mine— flustered—she grabs for the door handle, but it's locked. I hit the switch when I see her panic.

"Thanks," she whispers before abruptly getting out of my car.

I watch her and wonder what's causing her to flip moods

in a mere instant. Fumbling with her keys, she finally gets in the car and starts it up. She quickly glances over at me, embarrassed, and I hate that. All I can manage to make sense of is that her parents have fucked with her head so much that she's become removed from feeling emotions. I get it. That's been me my whole life, but now, with her, I find myself wanting to feel instead of running away from it.

I was nervous about meeting up with Candace this morning to go running. I was a little unsure of how she would react to me after what happened yesterday in my car, but she didn't seemed fazed by it, so I moved past it, and we spent a good hour running around campus and her neighborhood. She kept up with my pace, and I really enjoyed working out with her. I don't even think she noticed how distracted I was though, trying to sneak a peek at her whenever I could. She's small but there's no doubt that this chick is in extreme shape. Her legs are insane, and in her tight running pants, I couldn't keep my eyes off of her.

And now, sitting up here in my office, I can't keep my mind off of her. I start packing my things up to head out early. It's Saturday night, but being the holiday weekend, the place is dead.

"Hey, man," Gavin says when he bursts into my office. "You leaving?"

"Yep."

"We going out?"

Standing up, I start heading out when I tell him, "No. I'm gonna go home and just chill."

"Are you serious? Dude, you avoiding me?" he asks as I make my way downstairs.

"No. I just have other shit going on, that's all," I explain. He wouldn't get it if I told him, so I don't.

He continues to follow me to the back door, but before I can open it, he steps in front of me and snaps, "Seriously. What the fuck is going on?"

"Nothing, man. Don't take it personally."

"Kinda hard when I'm the one you're avoiding," he says.

Taking a moment, I explain without telling him too much. "Gav, I'm almost thirty. I'm sick of going out all the time to just fuck random chicks. I'm tired."

He doesn't say anything. He's the same age as me, and I know he's perfectly happy doing the shit that he does, but it doesn't make me happy anymore. It never did make me happy; it only made me numb. Stepping to the side, he walks away, throwing a, "See ya," over his shoulder before I walk out to the parking lot.

Heading home, I decide to stop and grab a pizza and some beer to take back to my place. When I get back into my jeep, I start driving home, but quickly find myself taking a few new turns. I'm not ready to go home just yet as the urge to see her again takes over, and I wind up pulling into her driveway behind her car.

I wonder if she's gonna be irritated that I'm just dropping by unannounced, but it's too late now that I've rung her doorbell. She appeared to be less skittish about having me in her house when she invited me in after our run this morning, so I try and let that worry go.

"What are you doing here?" she asks, completely taken off guard.

I don't even let her see an ounce of my uncertainty when I give her a playful grin and step inside. "I ran out to grab some dinner and knew you weren't doing anything tonight, so I drove here instead of back to my place."

"Oh . . ."

"That a problem?" I ask as I head into her kitchen.

"Ummm . . . no. I just . . ." she mumbles.

"Just what?" I ask, looking at her, cute as hell in her pajamas.

"Just surprised that's all. Why didn't you just text me?"

"Because I figured you would probably tell me you were studying." I start rummaging around, opening drawers, until I find a bottle opener. Popping the caps off the beer, I hand her one as she nods, agreeing with my last statement, and I shoot her a wink before taking a sip.

"So, how was the rest of your day?" I ask as I move around her kitchen, grabbing plates and a few napkins.

"Good. I got a lot done actually," she says as she watches me.

"Great, let's eat then. Do you mind grabbing the beer?"

"No problem."

Walking into her living room, we set everything down on the coffee table and make ourselves comfortable on the couch.

She opens the pizza box to grab a slice, and then turns to me, asking, "How did you know I like pineapple on my pizza?"

"I didn't. Like I said, I got this for me before deciding to come over."

"Oh."

Leaning forward I take a slice and sit back to eat as I watch her do the same. The thought of being out with Gavin right now just doesn't even compare to this—sitting here, with this girl I'm getting know. I'm enjoying it. It satisfies me in a way I never would have expected.

"So, you know what I did with my day. What about you?" she asks.

She told me this morning that she was spending the day studying then going to the studio to rehearse. "After our run, I went to the gym to do some lifting. Then later, I went to the bar to work. Had to sign off on a bunch of paperwork and inventory orders. That's pretty much it," I tell her.

Nodding her head, we continue to eat our dinner when I suggest, "Wanna watch something on TV?"

She picks up the remote and hands it to me. Flipping through the channels, I already know she's a fan of MTV, so I decide to go for one of my channels. When I land on TCM and they're playing one of my favorite movies, I set the remote down, get comfortable, and wait for it. Knowing she's gonna tease me, I find myself already enjoying her reaction when she says, "What the heck is this?"

"You don't know this movie?" I ask, mocking a serious tone, playing right into her.

"Does anyone know this movie?"

Smiling, I say, "Candace, it's a classic." Seeing the blank look on her face, I continue, "It's 'Double Indemnity' from the 1940's. It's a great movie."

"You watch a lot of these movies?"

Shaking my head, I tell her, "Sit back and just watch. You'll like it."

When she sits back with me, I start to explain the movie. "See that girl? Her name is Phyllis and that guy is an insurance agent that she is trying to seduce."

"Why?"

"Because she wants him to murder her husband so she can collect the money from his policy."

"Oooh, I like her already," she playfully says, and gets me laughing.

"Just watch."

Kicking our feet up on the coffee table, we lean back and

watch the movie. After a while I feel her head drop onto my shoulder. Looking down, her eyes are closed. I don't move for a while, scared of how she'll react. After what happened in my car yesterday, I make sure she's sound asleep before I slip my hand under her head and lower her onto my lap.

She curls up into a ball, and I take this moment to really look at her. Her skin is light and flawless. I gently run the back of my hand down her cheek and along her jaw. She's soft. I knew she would be. My heart begins to beat faster at the subtle contact.

I sink down into the couch, getting comfortable, and observe the stark contrast of her dark, thick lashes as they fan across the tops of her cheekbones. Leaning my head back, I relax with finally having her close to me. The warmth of her against me is something I've been craving. Even though she isn't giving this to me—I'm taking it right now— it appeases me for the time being, hoping that one day she'll want to give this to me. That simple thought alone is enough for me to know that I'm falling hard for this girl, and that worries me, because I know better than to allow myself to feel like this. But with her, all my logic seems to dissipate.

I let her sleep for a while, but when I begin to grow tired myself, I know I need to wake her. She's out cold when I lean over and whisper, "Candace."

When I run my hand down her arm, she starts to stir. "Candace . . . Candace, wake up."

Her eyes slowly flutter open and when she looks up at me, she locks them to mine. I can tell she isn't fully awake as she continues to stare. Out of nowhere, she startles me when she lurches off of the couch, finally coherent and free from her haze.

"Are you okay?" I ask when I stand up, and as soon as I step towards her, she shoots her hands out, wanting me to stay away. She's scared of me, and I hate that. Whatever it is she's dealing with, whatever is causing her to react this way, I just want to comfort her, but there's no way she'd let me if I tried.

"I'm sorry," I say as calmly as I can, not wanting to freak her out any more than she is. "I didn't want to leave you without you locking the door behind me. You fell asleep, and I didn't want to wake you, so I let you sleep for a while."

"I'm sorry," she breathes out.

"For what?"

Lowering her hands, she looks a little mortified when she explains, "Startling easily. I didn't know I fell asleep. I'm just . . . I was just disoriented."

"Candace," I quietly say, not wanting her to feel uncomfortable with me. I step toward her, and when she doesn't move away, I take my hand and brush aside a lock of her hair that's fallen across her forehead. I feel her stiffen, and I quickly pull back.

"I'll lock the door behind you," she says.

"Let me help you clean this up."

She looks at the mess and tells me, "I'll do it. It's all trash anyway."

"You sure?"

"Yeah."

She follows me as I walk to the door. Before I leave, I turn back and she's right next to me. She has to tilt her head to look up at me, and when I see her from this angle, she looks so fragile. When her eyes shift up to meet mine, I softly tell her, in all seriousness, "I want you to feel comfortable with me."

I notice her shallow breaths when she whispers, "I know."

"Okay. So, we'll talk later?"

When she softens her face and says, "Yeah," I feel better about leaving.

chapter fourteen

When I pull into the parking lot of the gym, I spot Jase's 4Runner already here. He got back in town a couple days ago, and the three of them have been busy with school as the quarter is coming to an end, so the two of us arranged to get together to do some lifting.

"Jase, hey," I say as I walk in and see him mixing his Gatorade.

"Hey, man," he says as he turns around. "You ready?"

"Yeah."

We head over to the free weights and pick up our dumbbells to start our bicep workout.

"So, how was Ohio?" I ask him, knowing it was the first time he met Mark's family.

"Better than I anticipated. Never had to meet parents in the past, so I was uneasy going there."

Jase told me that before Mark, he was a lot like me. Random hook-ups. But he seems to really love Mark, so I'm glad everything is working out for them.

"His family cool?"

"His sisters are a little wild," he laughs. "But yeah, his parents are great. Much different than mine."

"How so?" I question.

Taking his weights over to the bench, he sits down and says, "I'm pretty nonexistent to them. And when I told them I was gay . . . they were done."

"That's fucked up."

"Before Mark came along, all I really had was Candace. She's been my family since I moved here."

"You guys seem really tight," I respond as I set down the dumbbells and start racking the weights on a barbell to do some bench presses.

"We've always been that way," he tells me, walking over to spot.

As I lift the bar out of the rack, he stands over me, saying, "Thanks for checking in on her. I didn't even know she had that blowup with her parents until I got back home."

Pushing out the last of my reps, he grabs the bar from me as I sit up.

"Yeah, well, I was home with nothing to do, so it was nice to have someone around to hang out with," I say, downplaying the whole situation. I'm not sure how Jase would react if he knew how I'm starting to feel about his best friend.

"Well, for what it's worth, it's good to see her hanging out with someone else besides me and Mark."

"Is she really that closed off?" I ask. I know what I've seen, but it isn't much.

"Lately? Yeah."

That's all he says when I lie back down to pump out another set, and I wonder what he means by 'lately.' Was she not always like this? Then I make the connect—I wasn't always like this either. Never really. Not until her. But it was before that—it was that night that got me thinking so differently. That night that messed with my head so much that I started drifting away from old habits, old friends.

My mind goes back to the alley, and I get a flash of Candace on that rainy night in the coffee shop. *Fuck.* Why am I thinking about that? I thought I let it go, but it's back—the question. Ripping through my reps, I force that sick thought out of my head.

There's no connection there. It's just your mind trying to put an end to what was left unresolved. I repeat this silently to myself a few times, knowing that my subconscious is just screwing with me. *There's no connection . . . is there?*

I spend the next hour distracting myself, talking with Jase about football and how the season is going so far for the Huskies. Anything to keep my mind away from that night. After we finish up and say our goodbyes, I head out.

When I'm not around her, my mind seems to drift, so I selfishly pull out my phone and text her, knowing when we hang out, I'm too consumed with her to think about the other shit that tends to creep up in my head.

You hungry?

I start driving home, which is only about ten minutes from the gym, and it takes about that long for her to reply.

Can't eat. Have a 2-hour dance studio today.

Well shouldn't you fuel up?

Not if you want me to barf. :-)

I laugh at her text as I sit in my jeep that's now parked in my driveway.

I'd love to see that.

That's disgusting.

More for having something to tease you about and less for the actual barf.

Can we stop talking about barf? LOL

You free for a run tomorrow morning?

Yeah.

Happy to spend more time with her, I type out my last text.

Be at your place around 7.

"You sure you wanna go?" I ask as we walk out to her front porch. She looks exhausted, and by her bloodshot eyes, I can tell she didn't get any sleep last night.

"I'm sure," she says with her head down as she walks past me.

We start with a light jog through the mist that fills the chilly morning. I look over at her as she stares straight ahead.

"Bad night?"

"What?" she questions when she looks over at me, and then responds, "I was up late catching up on school work. It's the end of the quarter."

I don't buy her lie. I know this chick wouldn't be behind in school, but I don't push it 'cause if she's choosing to give me an excuse, then she doesn't want me to know what really kept her up last night.

Going along with her, I ask, "You ready for the break?"

"Mmm hmm," she hums, and we're back to closed-off Candace.

I pick up the pace when we get close to campus, and she strides along with no problem right beside me. I wish she would talk to me, but even if I'm with her in silence, it's better than not being with her at all.

"I'm sorry," I hear her say softly, and when I look over at her, I ask, "For what?"

"I'm just tired, that's all," she explains.

"Candace," I say, and when she turns her head and

catches my eye, I continue, "You don't need to be sorry."

I see the corner of her mouth turn up before she looks away.

"So what did you do yesterday?" she asks, and I'm glad she's talking now.

"Not much. Hit the gym with Jase and that's about all."

"I think he mentioned that to me," she mumbles.

"What about you?"

"After studio, I had to work. Jase came up there and hung out for a little while," she tells me. "It was pretty dead, and Roxy left early."

Because the curiosity is killing me, I go ahead and bring up Jase. "You guys seem really close."

She looks over at me and narrows her eyes, like she's questioning what the real meaning is to that statement, but she goes ahead and gives me a response. "We've always been close. He's like my family."

"It's good that you have someone like that."

She doesn't speak as we continue to make our way through campus, jogging up the stairs as we leave the quad. We take the rest of the run through the surrounding neighborhoods with nothing more than random small talk before I drop her off back at her house and head home.

Something was clearly bothering Candace yesterday when we met up for our morning run, so when I call to see if she wants to grab a bite to eat before I head into work tonight, I'm surprised when she easily agrees.

I meet up with her at the sushi-go-round restaurant close to my loft. She looks a lot better than she did yesterday morning, and I smile as we sit down.

"You ever been here before?" I ask when we start picking our plates off of the carousel.

"A couple times. Mark likes this place."

"You coming to see him tonight?" I ask, knowing that she's never come to the bar to hear his band play.

She shakes her head as she plucks her sushi up with her chopsticks and takes a bite. When she's done, she says, "I'll see him after."

"After?"

"I'm staying with Jase tonight. So I'll see Mark for a little while before he goes home."

"You spend a lot of nights with him?" I ask, and when she looks up at me, she defends, "It's not weird or anything."

"I didn't say it was."

"We've always been this way," she tells me.

"What way's that?"

"Close."

I'm a little confused as to why she spends nights with him, but I don't push the subject anymore. It's not my place to question, so I drop it.

Changing the subject, I ask, "Are you free tomorrow?"

"Why?"

Grabbing another plate of sushi before it passes, I tell her, "Didn't know if you wanted to get in another run."

She doesn't say anything as she turns her attention to her food and starts eating. She's uncomfortable, so I add, "Wanna?"

"I have to work in the morning."

"After?"

Looking over at me, she nods and says, "Yeah. I'd like that."

Satisfied with her response, we grab a few more plates and finish up our dinner.

"Sorry I've gotta run, but I haven't been working much lately, and I need to get a few things done," I explain as we head outside, and I walk her to her car.

"It's okay," she says as she unlocks her door and then turns to face me.

I want to touch her, hug her, anything, but nothing about her is telling me that it's okay as she turns back around to open her door, and before I can even try to do anything, she's in her seat.

"I'll see you tomorrow," she says, and I wonder if I'm ever gonna get her to let me in.

When I walk into Common Grounds, I don't see Candace, but quickly notice her boss eying me. She's obvious and doesn't even try and hide it. I walk over to the counter where she's standing with her indigo hair, and for some reason, it totally works on her.

"Candace here?" I ask.

"Mmm hmm," she playfully hums as she turns away from me and walks into the back.

She pops back out after a couple minutes and says, "She said to give her ten minutes and she'll be out."

I nod my head and scan the tats on her arm, asking, "Who does your work?"

"Place next door. My boyfriend works over there."

"That's convenient," I tease.

"My thoughts exactly," she says with a hint of indecency, and I have to laugh at her vibrant personality. "You got any?"

"Yeah," I say as I lift the sleeve of my t-shirt to show her the half-sleeve I got a few years back. My mother's favorite flower is the peony, so I have an almost cryptic interpretation of one surrounded by shaded water with the words, 'Struggles are not identities,' woven through the art.

"Nice," she says as she moves her eyes over it, noting the details. "Any others?"

"No," I lie. I have another, but I keep it private and don't ever mention it to people if they ask. "How long did it take you to get all those?" I ask about the full colorful sleeves that run down the length of her arms.

"Here and there for a few years," she says when I notice Candace out of the corner of my eye.

"Hey."

"What are you guys talking about?" she asks as she walks over to me.

"Your friend, Ryan, was asking about my tattoos," Roxy tells her.

Walking towards Candace, who is already in her running gear, I ask, "You ready?"

"Yeah, I just need to put my bag in my car."

I take the bag out of her hand, and she turns to Roxy to say bye as I start heading out.

Candace is quiet while she listens to me talk about work. She asks a few questions along the way, and I end up venting about some of my aggravation with a couple of the staff that I had to get rid of the other night. But when the conversation shifts to Mark and his band, we start talking about music. When I ask her what some of her favorite bands are, I'm surprised to hear that they sync right up with mine.

We eventually weave into my neighborhood, which is only a couple blocks from her house. We both live right outside Fremont, which Jase's apartment is in the heart of. Candace stops talking for a while, and when I look down at her, I can see she's struggling a bit with her breathing.

"You okay?" I ask.

"I'm thirsty. We forgot water."

"No worries," I tell her, knowing that my loft is at the end of the street we're on. When we get close, I slow down and start walking up my drive.

"What are you doing?" she asks, and when I look back, she's standing in the middle of my drive—anxious.

"Getting you some water. Come on," I say, trying to act like her being here shouldn't be a big deal, but by the way she's hesitantly walking towards me, I can tell that it is for her.

Pulling out my keys, I click the fob and open the garage.

"Do you own this building or something?" she asks, not registering that this is my place, and I guess I can't blame her because it's a three-story loft—much bigger than one person should need.

"This is my loft. I live here," I say with a grin.

"Oh," she breathes and then stops in her tracks, no longer following me. She doesn't want to be here, but I want her here. She shifts uncomfortably before walking into my garage and following me up the stairs to the door.

When we walk inside, she stays in the living room while I head straight to the kitchen to grab a couple bottles of water.

"Here you go," I say as I walk back to her and hand her one.

She takes a big gulp before saying, "This is a great place. How long have you lived here?"

"About five years." I watch as she moves her eyes around my space, taking it in.

My phone begins to ring, and when I see it's Max, I answer.

"Hey."

"Ryan, Michael's a no-show. Said he has shit going on at home."

"Hold on a sec," I tell him and look over to Candace. "Make yourself comfortable. I need to take this call really quick. I'll only be a few minutes, okay?"

She smiles at me, and I head back to my office, closing the door behind me.

"Okay, I'm back," I tell him.

"Where are you at?"

"My place. Why?"

"Who are you telling to get comfortable?" he inquires, implying I'm trying to get laid.

"Candace," I tell him honestly.

"Who?"

"That girl I told you about," I explain.

"What's going on with you?" he asks, knowing damn well that I don't ever hang out with girls and that I have never even been interested in anything more than a passing screw.

"Nothing," I shrug off, not wanting to leave her in the other room alone for too long. "I'll be there in a few hours, okay?"

"Sounds good," he says before hanging up.

Walking back out into the living room, I find Candace kneeling down, looking at some of my mattes that are stacked against the wall. Stepping next to her, she looks up at me.

"I'm sorry," she says as she puts the mattes down and stands up.

"For what?"

"I wasn't snooping or anything, I just noticed these and was curious," she nervously explains.

"Candace, I have nothing to hide. I told you to make

yourself comfortable, and I meant it." I take a seat in one of the overstuffed leather chairs and drink my water.

"Where did you get those?"

"They're mine," I tell her.

"Yours?"

"Yeah. Sometimes I get bored and like to mess around with my camera."

"That's pretty amazing for just messing around," she says as she continues to stand against the large panoramic window. "You only shoot people?"

"For the most part, yeah." I get up and walk over to the photos and pick up the one lying on the top. It's the shot I took of Gina. It's a nice photo, but makes me almost feel guilty for having it. For spending so much time working on it, only to have Candace admire it.

"She a model?" she asks as she looks at the photo with me.

"No, just some chick I used to know." I toss the matte down and motion for her to sit with me on the couch, and when she does, she continues, "So, when did you get into photography?"

"When I was in college I took some art classes. So, one day I just decided to buy a camera and started taking pictures. Like I said, I pretty much have no clue what I'm doing. Just a little hobby of mine I mess around with every now and then."

"You ever do anything with them?" she asks.

"No."

I watch her as she begins to relax, getting more comfortable the longer she's here. Having her here in my space—I like it.

"Maybe you should," she encourages, and when I look into her eyes, I'm at a loss for words, so I simply repeat hers,

"Maybe I should."

We sit here for a few moments without speaking. I don't pull my eyes away from hers, and when I see the nervous shift in her, I cut the intensity and ask, "You sure you don't want to come out to the bar tonight to see Mark play?"

Taking a deep breath and looking down, she says, "I told you, I have to work."

"I just picked you up from work."

"I know, but I have to go back. One of the girls quit and Roxy hasn't hired anyone to replace her, so I've been picking up extra shifts," she explains. "Plus, I'd probably be tired and no fun to be around."

"I can't imagine it not being fun to be around you," I admit much too honestly, and when she shifts her eyes to look out the window, I take her cue and ask, "You ready to finish the run?"

Standing up, I reach out for her hand. She doesn't take it at first, but when I smile down at her, she slips her hand into mine. I keep a strong hold on it as I lock up and we head out.

When we get outside and to the end of my driveway, I still have her hand. This is the longest she's ever let me touch her.

"Wanna make it a long run, or are you ready to head back?" I ask.

She takes a moment, and then looks up at me, saying, "Long."

I give her hand a soft squeeze before letting it go, and something about the way she's looking at me right now makes me feel like I'm finally having an effect on her.

chapter fifteen

Leaving now. See you in two hours?

I read Candace's text as I'm working in my office at home. She's been really busy this past week, but we managed to grab another run a few days ago. We decided to meet up after her dance practice today before I have to go into work.

I'll meet you in the parking lot.

OK, catch you later.

Before I can type another response I get an incoming call from my mom.

"Hey."

"Hi. What are you up to this weekend?" she asks.

"Not much," I tell her as I stand up to go get a drink from the kitchen. "I'm supposed to meet up with Candace in a few hours then go to work."

"Really?"

She's surprised, knowing that I have never shown interest in a girl before.

"So . . . you really like her?" she asks, not even skating around the subject.

I grab a water and flop down on a chair in the living

room. "Yeah," I sigh as I lean back and stare up at the exposed beams.

"Have you told her?"

"It isn't like that," I tell her. "She's slow to warm up to people. Well . . . at least with me."

"But you've known her for over a month. Seems like enough time."

"Not with her."

"So what are the two of you going to do later?" she asks.

"She's at the dance studio now, so we're just gonna grab a coffee afterward."

"And how's work been going?"

"Same as usual. What about you?"

When she starts talking about some fundraiser that she went to with her sister, I lose focus as my eyes shift to the stack of mattes that are still lying on my floor. The photos that Candace had been looking at last week.

"Well, I better let you go. I just wanted to check in," she says as she pulls my attention back to her.

"I love you, Mom. I'll talk to you soon."

"Love you too, dear."

Shoving my phone into my pocket, I walk over to the photos and grab them. It seems like forever ago when I shot these when really it was only four months back. I was so distracted then, but now . . . now I feel focused. I'm not quite sure if anything will ever happen with Candace, but I love spending time with her regardless. But, God, I do hope that something will happen. I've never had to fight for a girl's attention or affection, but this one . . . she makes me work, and I find myself liking it.

I take the photos back to my office and shove them inside my credenza, not wanting to think about that time—about all those women. Sliding the door shut, I turn to get some work done—anything to kill time while I wait to see Candace.

Pulling into the studio lot, I park next to Candace's car. Stepping out, I take a moment to enjoy the chill in the December air. The dark clouds roll through the misty sky.

My eyes dart to the doors when I hear them bang open and see her storming out. She's upset—frustrated—and when she looks at me, she freezes, startled to see me, with tears streaming down her cheeks. When I rush over to her, she quickly wipes her face with her hands, trying to hide what she knows I already see.

She drops her head, but I catch it with my hands, cupping her cheeks as I tilt it up for her to look at me. "What happened?"

"Nothing, honestly. Just a tough rehearsal." Her voice trembles as she speaks, and seeing her this upset has something panging inside of me that I'm not used to— protectiveness.

I look down at her as a few tears seep out of her eyes, and I wipe them away with my thumbs. When I do this, I feel her tension melt, and she falls into my chest, wrapping her arms around my waist. This unexpected affection is like a reward I've been waiting so patiently for. And here it is. Sliding my arms around her, I hold her close, and she doesn't flinch away from me. I can feel her body relax, and when this happens, I lean down and rest my cheek on top of her head.

She sniffs and I know she's crying. Having her like this, in my arms, is an intimacy that's completely foreign but comfortable. I'm sure she can hear my heart pounding, but I need her to hear it. I need her to feel it as it thuds in my chest because I need her to hear me falling for her, 'cause that's what's happening here—I'm falling. I never wanted to before, but with her, all I want to do is fall. Fall into her. Fall so deep inside of her heart so that I never have to be without her. That's what this girl does to me. That's how powerful she is even when she thinks she's at her weakest. She's broken. I see it clearly, but whatever it is that's haunting her, I wanna make it fade. I wanna make it fade and make her fall too—with me.

When she begins to pull away from me, I selfishly want to tighten my hold on her and keep her like this for a little longer. I worry this was just a random need for comfort from her, that I won't get this again, that she doesn't feel what I know I'm starting to. *Fuck, this hurts.*

She looks up at me, and I ask again because I need to. "Are you sure you're okay?"

With no words, she simply nods. Unwilling to take my hands off of her, I step to her side with my arm around her shoulders and lead her to my car. She doesn't question me as I help her up into the seat. When I get in, her eyes are closed, so I don't turn on the stereo. I let her relax and drive her to my place, wanting her in my space. I watch her at every red light I hit. I turn on the heater because I know she has to be freezing, wearing nothing but long, baggy black pants with her pale pink leotard. Her hair is pulled into a tight bun and everything about her is screaming that she's way out of my league. Way too refined for me.

Her eyes open when I pull into my drive. She rolls her head towards me, and we watch each other for a moment before I get out of the car and open her door.

When we go upstairs, she gets comfortable on my couch as I grab a water for her from the kitchen. Walking back, I sit close to her while she gulps the water down.

"Feeling better?" I ask as I take the bottle from her and

set it on the coffee table.

"Yeah, I'm sorry. After being yelled at for two hours, I just . . ."

Needing that affection back, I wrap my arm around her and pull her in tightly next to me, and again, she allows it. "Don't worry," I tell her because I want her to show me this side of her—a side I know she hides.

"No . . . It's embarrassing."

"Don't let it be."

As she shifts forward, she turns to look at me. "Can I ask you a huge favor?"

"Anything."

"Do you have a dry shirt I can change into?" she asks with a coy smile. "I've been dancing for the past few hours, and I'm sweaty and stinky."

I laugh and say, "You don't stink at all actually."

"Liar." I catch her dimple when she says this with a slight grin.

"I'll be right back," I respond and then head upstairs to my bedroom. I pull out a pair of my long pajama pants and an old UW shirt.

"You need socks?" I holler down to her.

"Please. It's cold."

When I walk back downstairs, I hand her the clothes and show her to the guest bathroom.

"Thanks. Just give me a few minutes."

"Take your time," I say as I close the door and return to the living room.

Sitting back on the couch, I turn on the TV and start flipping through the channels. When I hear the bathroom door open, I watch her walk towards me. She's gripping the fabric of the pants, trying to keep them from dragging on the floor. My pants and t-shirt swallow her up and hang on her, but she's adorable as hell.

Seeing her in my clothes—I like it. And in this moment, I pretend that she's mine because I want her to be. I can't figure out why. Why this girl? All I know is, when I'm not with her, I want to be.

She sits down on the couch with me, but not close enough. Her hair is still in a bun, and I grab it, wanting to make her laugh, and tease, "This is cute."

Ducking her head, she says, "Whatever," as she swats at my hand, and gives me what I want—her smile.

"Come here," I say as I lean back into the couch and she follows, settling herself in my arms when I wrap them around her. "So, what happened?" I ask, wanting to know what made her so upset earlier.

"I have this tough piece of music," she starts to explain. "I'm having a hard time connecting with it. My instructor keeps telling me what I need to fix, but I don't really know how. It's frustrating. I can perfect my moves, but I don't know how to get into this piece."

"So she just bashed you the whole time?"

"It's how she is. But the fact that she even came in to work with me is unheard of. She's extremely stern, but she's only trying to help me."

"I didn't like seeing you upset," I admit to her.

When she looks up at me, she says, "It's not a big deal, really."

"I didn't like it," I repeat, wanting her to know that I feel for her in a way that seeing her like that bothered me. I keep my eyes on her, and when I sense her feeling uncomfortable, she looks away from me and I ask, "You want that cup of coffee?"

"That'd be great; I'm still really cold."

"There are some blankets in the trunk by the fireplace," I

tell her as I walk into the kitchen. I watch her move around the room as I quickly brew her a cup of coffee. "How do you take it?" I ask as she wraps herself up in one of my blankets and sits back down on the couch.

"One sugar and really blond," she responds from across the room.

"You getting warm?" I ask when I walk back in and hand her the cup of coffee.

"Trying too." She cradles the mug in her hands and takes a slow sip. When she turns to see what's playing on the TV, she laughs softly under her breath.

"What's so funny?" I question.

"You." She looks at me when she continues. "I don't know anyone who watches the classic movie channel, aside from you."

"You want me to change it?"

"No, it's fine," she says as she shifts back on the couch, allowing me to drape my arm around her. "I'm only teasing you."

Kicking my feet up onto the coffee table, we watch 'The Blue Dahlia' with her head resting on my chest.

She's still in my clothes when I drive her to her car that's back at the dance studio. As I pull up next to her car, I ask, "Why don't you come up to the bar and hang out with us tonight?"

"I can't."

I nod my head at her response, which never changes every time I invite her to Blur.

"I'm sorry," she tells me. "But I'm just really tired and will probably go to bed early. Plus, I have the early shift at work tomorrow."

"Your boss doesn't strike me as the type who would mind if you came into work a little hungover," I joke.

"You're probably right about that," she says with grin. "But I've never drunk enough to have ever been hungover."

"Never?" I question, shocked that this girl is so innocent that she's never been drunk.

"Don't act surprised," she defends.

"I'm more relieved." I love that she's pure in a way. That she's good and not tarnished like me—like all the others.

"I'm not even going to ask why," she laughs as she shakes her head. "But thanks for today."

"Anytime."

"Tell Mark and Jase I said hi when you see them tonight, okay?" she says as she opens the door and gets out. When she turns to look back at me, she adds, "Thanks again for being there today. It probably would have ended up being a crappy day if I just went home."

"Thanks for letting me be there."

I watch as she gets into her car and drives off before backing out and heading to work. When I walk in, I make my way over to the bar and spot everyone hanging out while Mel works the bar. I'm a little surprised to see Gavin since our last run-in wasn't all that pleasant.

None of them see me as I watch them interact. I look at Jase and Mark and see how they're so happy. They have a direction in life that I've been missing. They have a close relationship with each other and even with Candace, something I've spent my whole life avoiding. I shift my focus over to Gavin who's putting the moves on some random chick and I see me. I see the person I've been for so many years, and from this angle, it doesn't look good. Drifting. That's all I've been doing.

My life has been empty, but I never really saw it so clearly until seeing Candace, Mark, and Jase. I see their connection, their focus, and it makes me realize how unfulfilling my life has been up to this point. Up until her. The draw is there; it always has been, but it's beyond the pull. She's filling me with an awareness I never saw before. She's made me take a step back to see my life for what it is—disconnected and stagnant.

Before any of them sees me, I turn and walk up to my office. Pulling out my phone, I call Tori. I need assurance, and I know she'll help me.

"Ryan, hey."

Sitting at my desk, I ask, "You busy?"

"Not at all. Trevor's putting the kids to bed. What's up?"

"Are you happy?" I ask, remembering the flipside of this conversation when we had it back in the summer at my mom's house.

"What's going on?" she asks, picking up on the seriousness in my tone.

"Just tell me. You and Trevor, are you happy?"

"Yeah," she breathes. "I'm happy. We have our issues. Everyone does, but I'm happy."

I'm scared to fall any more than I already have for Candace, but I want to. God, I want to so bad. I want to connect. I want everything that I've been too afraid of.

My mom and dad used to be happy. There was a time when they really loved each other. She's told me about it, but it didn't matter. It wasn't enough, and that love transformed into a living hell. The hell is all I remember. The screaming, the fighting, the beatings, the constant turmoil and fear. Then I see Tori and her family. They're happy. They're okay.

I'm still scared though, but the thought of walking away

scares me more.

"Ryan, you there?" she asks.

"Yeah. Sorry."

"So are you gonna tell me what's going on?"

I've always been honest with Tori, so I go ahead and tell her, knowing my words are safe with her, "I met someone."

"Is this *that someone* you denied back at Thanksgiving?"

"Yeah."

"So what's bothering you about it?" she questions.

"I have a seedy past, and I've never done this. I've never wanted to. But she's nothing like anyone I have ever known, and she makes me nervous."

"You think she'll judge you for the choices you've made?"

"She's nothing like me. She's so green, and I've been fucking chick after chick since I was fifteen." Just saying the words is almost mortifying. Sickening. And what was once something I couldn't care less about is now something that I'm embarrassed about. Ashamed.

"I don't have a picture perfect record either. You know that. But Trevor loves me regardless of who I was before him," she tells me. "That's the thing about love . . . it's a pretty powerful force that can show a side of you that you never knew existed. Show you that you're capable of becoming someone you never thought you could be, and you do it for the other person because you love them, because you want to put them before yourself."

I don't say anything. I just let her words soak in. I don't know what the fuck I'm doing. All I know is, I want to—for her.

"Just a piece of advice," she adds. "Don't ever lie to her about who you are. If she ever asks, be honest."

"Yeah." When she says this, I begin to have doubts that it

will ever get to that point. I don't even know where this girl's head is at. Just because I want her doesn't mean anything. What if I'm just wasting my time? *Shit.* I see how she is with Jase. What if that's just how she is with her friends? I even see it when she's with Mark. All she has given me is exactly what I see her giving to the two of them.

Suddenly, I'm questioning everything.

chapter sixteen

I've been trying to shake my self-doubts about Candace for the past few days. We continue to chat on the phone and text back and forth, but I can't help wondering if any of this is different with me than it is with Jase and Mark.

Needing a distraction, I decide to get my Christmas shopping done for the kids today. I thought hitting the gym would help, but here I am, still doubting. My cell starts ringing as I'm grabbing my coat to head out.

It's her.

"Hey."

"Hi. You busy?" she asks, and something about the sound of her voice erases my questioning thoughts.

"No," I lie as I toss my leather coat onto the couch. "What's up?"

"Nothing. Jase and Mark left early this morning for Ohio, and I've just been sitting around the house. I didn't know if you wanted to hang out."

"Oh, I see. Second best since the boys aren't there to keep you entertained," I tease with a laugh.

"No," she drags out in feigned annoyance at my joke. "And you're not second best," she adds, and I'm happy she does because I like hearing it.

"What did you have in mind?"

"Anything. I just want to get out of my house," she says in a way that makes me think of her non-existent roommate. I know she lives with a girl, but in the past couple of months I've been hanging out with Candace, I've never seen or heard her talk about her roommate, but if she needs to get away, I'll take her away.

"You up for shopping?"

"Shopping?" she questions.

"Yeah, I need to do some Christmas shopping for my nieces and nephews. You in?"

"Um, yeah. That sounds good."

"I'll come pick you up," I tell her before we hang up, and just like that, my day got better.

When I pull into her drive, I see her walking down the steps of her front porch. She looks perfect with her leopard scarf wrapped around her neck and her hair down. When she gets into my car, she looks at me staring at her and asks, "What?"

Being honest, I tell her, "I like your hair down." She usually has it in a piled mess on top of her head, which always looks sexy on her, but I have to admit that it's cutest when she's in school, and it's almost always in a tight bun since she dances every day. But I rarely ever see her with her hair down like it is now.

She looks uncomfortable with the compliment and doesn't respond to it, instead asking, "Can we stop by Peet's and grab something to drink?"

Laughing at her deflection, I say, "Sure," before backing out and heading over to Fremont. As I'm driving, I notice that she seems a little absent as she stares out the window.

"Is everything okay?" I ask, and when she faces me, she questions, "Why?"

"You seem distracted."

"Sorry," she says and I can tell she's abashed. "Thanks for picking me up."

Not sure what's causing her mood, I intend to dispel it. Smiling over at her, I say, "Anytime."

We luck out, finding a parking spot right in front of Peet's, and the place is crowded when we walk in. Candace stands close to me while we wait in line. She's fidgety, absentmindedly wringing her hands together.

A burst of cold air floods in, and when the chime from the door goes off, Candace startles and turns to see an older couple walking in. Her face is nearly stone when I look down at her.

"Hey," I say as gently as I can, and when she turns around, I ask, "You sure you're okay?"

Fixing a smile on her face, she looks up at me and assures, "Yeah. Maybe I should just get a decaf tea or something," with humor I'm not buying, but I'm not questioning it either. I reach down and when I take her hand in mine, she grips me tightly as if she needs the comfort of my touch.

After we order our drinks, we walk out into the brisk air, and she finally seems to breathe easy. Crowds. I forgot for a moment that she doesn't like them, and Peet's was packed with people needing a hot drink to warm up.

Opening the car door for her, I help her up and then walk around to get in. We drive across town to a massive toy store that's my go-to spot for the kids. We listen to an old David O'Dowda album as we fight the holiday traffic, and when we pull up, we grab our drinks and head inside.

"So, what are you looking for?" she asks as she gets a cart and starts following me down one of the aisles.

"Don't know. These kids aren't too hard to please though," I tell her as I stop and flip through a few board puzzles.

"How old are they again?"

"Young. All under five," I say as I start wandering around. "Honestly, they'd be happy with a box of tissues and a stick."

She laughs at my words, and I turn back to her to get a glimpse. "That's nice," she says, teasingly.

"It's true."

When we turn down the next aisle, filled with pink . . . *everything,* Candace stops to admire a collection of dolls. I step up behind her and quip, "You want one?"

She looks at me over her shoulder, and mocks, "No, I don't want one," before looking back at them. "They're pretty."

"Grab a couple," I tell her and watch as she picks out two of the dolls and puts them in the cart.

We take our time, slowly strolling, grabbing toys here and there as she continues to ask about my family.

"So, seven nieces and nephews . . ."

"Yep."

"All cousins' kids?" she asks.

"I'm an only child, remember?"

Nodding her head, she says, "That's right. I forgot. You all sound close."

"I'm closest to my cousin, Tori. We spent a lot of time together while we were in high school. We lived in different towns, but would always get together on the weekends. Partying and surfing."

"You surf?" she asks as she looks over at me.

"I grew up on the beach."

"Jase surfs," she tells me.

"Yeah, he's mentioned that to me. Grew up in San Diego, right?"

"Uh huh. He goes to Westport every now and then."

"I've been there a few times, but I go back to Cannon Beach frequently, so I normally get my fill when I'm there," I tell her and catch her staring down the next aisle. "What are you looking at?"

"I always wanted one of those," she whines with excitement as she starts walking towards a huge wire bin filled with inflated Hop N Bounce balls. I laugh while I watch her grab one out of the bin and turn to me. "My friend had one of these when we were little, but she would never let me play with it."

"Why didn't you ask your parents for one?"

"I did, but . . ." she trails off, and when she does, I encourage, "Take it for a spin."

She completely surprises me when she doesn't even hesitate. Holding the ball by the handle, she walks over to me and hands me her drink. "Here. Hold this."

Taking her tea, I question, "You serious? That's a toy for an eight-year-old," I poke.

She sets the large ball on the ground and sits on top of it, saying with a huge smile, "In case you haven't noticed, I'm about the same size as an eight-year-old," before spinning around and bouncing away from me down the aisle.

I watch her, laughing as she bobs up and down, enjoying seeing her let go for a moment. She isn't worried about how she looks; she never has been. Not embarrassed in the slightest and I revel in this moment.

When she turns to bounce back towards me, I start cracking up at the laughter coming out of her. I've never seen her like this—so carefree. It's beautiful, and I just want to grab her off that stupid ball and kiss her. Just take her and make her mine, so I can touch her whenever I want—to have her.

She finally stops bouncing and stands up, still holding the ball in her hands. She continues to giggle while telling me, "Totally worth the wait."

"Must have been a good ride," I say. "I think the whole store heard you laughing."

She tosses the ball into the cart, and as I cock my head in question, she clarifies, "You have to buy that for the kids."

She takes her tea out of my hand, and I'm lost in her. Everything about her. I follow her lead as we continue to make our way through the rest of the store, thankful that she doesn't skip a single aisle because I need all the time I can get with her.

"Michael here?" I ask Mel when I walk into the bar.

"Yeah," she hollers over to me. "Upstairs."

The place is busy tonight as I head up to Michael's office. It's been a good day, although dropping Candace off at her house to come up here was the last thing I wanted to do, but I need to sit down with Michael. He's been dropping the ball on a few things, and shit needs to get back on track.

His door is open, so I go ahead and walk in.

"Ryan, hey, man," he says from behind his desk, which is a mess of papers.

I cut to the chase and say, "Talk to me."

While he sorts and stacks a few files, he asks, "About what?"

"Not showing up. Supply orders going in late. Schedules

not getting out on time."

He drops the files onto his desk and leans back in his chair. "Fuck, man," he sighs.

"You know I can't have this, so either we figure it out or I'm gonna have to let you go," I tell him honestly. No need to bullshit when it comes to my business.

"No, I'm getting everything in order. Things have been a little crazy at home, and I let it filter into work," he explains.

"Kids okay?"

"It's not the kids," he says and takes a pause before revealing, "I found out that Amber's been fucking around on me."

Seems Mel's eavesdropping skills don't suck.

"Shit, man."

"Yeah. It's fucked up," he tells me. "Don't worry about things up here though. I've got it under control."

Not too comfortable with chatting about this guy's issues, I leave it as is and let him get back to work, trusting that he's gonna get his crap together.

I make my way back down to check in with Mel, and as I pass along the edge of the bar, someone grabs on to my arm. Turning around, I'm face to face with my past.

"What are you doing here?" I ask, and when her hand lingers on me, I take a step back and out of her grip.

"Having a drink. Waiting for a friend, but he's running late."

"You should pick a different bar next time," I tell her, turning to leave and spot Gavin walking in.

"M.I.A.," he calls out to me while shaking his head.

I've found myself drifting from Gavin as well as most of my bad habits, so seeing him is a little awkward, but not as awkward as him walking past me and straight to Gina, kissing her.

Irritation causes my shoulders to tighten, and when Mel appears from behind the bar, I snap, "Back room."

She follows behind me as I head into the back stockroom, closing the door behind her.

"What the fuck did I just see?"

"He brought her in here the other day," she tells me. "Said he's been hooking up with her for a couple months now."

The door opens, and Gavin walks in, thankfully alone.

"You mad?"

"Mad? No. Disturbed? Kinda," I respond. "Dude, weren't you screwing her roommate?"

He gives me an almost proud smirk and boasts, "Yeah, man."

"Have fun with that one," I tell him.

"So we're cool?"

"I don't care who you're hooking up with, but that girl seems like trouble," I tell him.

"Maybe so, but she's good in bed, you know?" He laughs and then adds, "Yeah, *you* know."

Regretfully, I do know. I wanna forget, but that isn't gonna happen. It's my past, and unfortunately, you can't escape your past. I've dealt with that little piece of knowledge my whole life. But I do what I can to shut it out and tell him, "Don't bring her back up here again."

When he turns to walk out, not responding to me, I face Mel and say, "I'm serious. You see her in here, I want her out."

"Yeah, no problem," she says. "You okay?"

Switching the subject, not wanting to discuss it any further, I tell her, "Let me know if anything starts to fall through the cracks up here."

"Did you talk to Michael?"

Being irritated as shit, I don't want to go into this with her, so I leave it with, "Just let me know," before walking out and calling it a night.

chapter seventeen

Can you help me run an errand?

Yeah. What do you need?

I want to go pick up some firewood but I want enough to last and it won't fit in my trunk. Can you take me since you have the space in your jeep?

At gym now. Will you be ready in a couple of hours?

Yes. THANKS!!!

After I finish my workout with Max, I head home to grab a quick shower and a bite to eat before I leave to pick up Candace.

The night is colder than usual as I walk out to my jeep. I make the short drive through the neighborhood, and when I get to Candace's house, I run up to her door to get her. She's shrugging on her grey, wool coat when she answers.

"Hey," she says with a smile when she sees me.

"You ready?"

"Yeah." I watch her slip on her black gloves as we walk out.

As I pull away from her house, she tells me, "There's a tree lot on Holman, up from eighty-fifth street."

"How much are we getting?"

"I dunno. Probably just a fourth of a cord," she answers as she adjusts the vent on the dash.

"You cold?"

"Yeah," she says, and when I laugh, she turns and asks, "What's so funny?"

"Nothing. You just have no meat on you to keep you warm," I say teasingly. She's lean with defined muscles, but nothing that takes away from her femininity.

"Yeah, well, I can't do much about that," she shoots back at me.

When we get to the tree lot, Candace places her order with one of the attendants. After paying for the firewood, we find ourselves strolling the lot, looking at the Christmas trees as the guys load up the wood.

She stops in front of one of the trees and looks up at it, shivering. Reaching down, I take her hands and rub mine over hers, trying to warm her up. She seems a little apprehensive as she looks up at me, but she doesn't back away. When she starts to drop her arms, I reach down and hold her hand. It isn't the first time I've made a subtle move like this, and I hate the uncertainty of it all. Not knowing how she's feeling about this—about us.

"I miss Jase," she quietly says out of nowhere as she looks at the tree. She turns to me, and with an almost apologetic look, she explains with a shrug of her shoulders, "I'm not used to him being gone."

"Have you talked to him?"

"This morning," she says and then turns back to the tree. "We should buy this."

I look down at her, and even though she didn't mean it literally, I like that she said 'we.'

As she helps me unload the firewood and stack it in her garage, I ask, "What are you going to do for the next few weeks?"

"I don't know. This is the first year that Jase isn't here with me. We normally spend most of the break together when I'm not at my parents'."

"How's that going?" I ask, knowing that the last time she saw them it ended badly.

"It's not, really," she tells me. "I spoke with my father for the first time since Thanksgiving a few days ago, and he wants me to come over for dinner Christmas Eve."

"You haven't spoken with them for all this time?"

"No," she says as we walk back out to grab some more logs.

"So, you're going over to see them then?" I ask, already feeling like I want to keep her from going. I know I have no right to say anything, but I can't stand the thought of her being here alone if she winds up in another fight with them.

"Well, yeah, I don't really want to, but it's Christmas and all. I'm just a little scared about how it will all go. The last time I saw them, we said some pretty nasty things to each other, and I have never gone this long without talking to them."

"What are they so upset about?" I ask, confused by what this girl could possibly be doing that they don't approve of.

"Everything," she says as we walk into her house and into the kitchen. She grabs a bottle of wine that has already been opened and starts pouring a glass, adding, "Turns out I've been nothing but an embarrassing disappointment to them all along."

Taking a beer out of the fridge, I can't help the sigh of irritation that comes out of me. I follow her into the living room, and when we sit down on the couch, I wrap my arm around her, just wanting her to be close to me any way I can get it.

"I'm sorry, babe," I say softly and immediately catch the slip and hope she isn't freaked out by what I just said. But when she continues talking, I wonder if she even noticed that I called her 'babe' or if she did notice and is okay with it. *Shit, I really hate this grey area.*

"Honestly, it's nothing that I didn't already know deep down, but it was the first time that it actually hit me that these were their true feelings toward me."

I feel it. It's strong and causes a reaction I can't control, and I act on it, demanding, "I don't want you going over there." She looks up at me, and there isn't a hint on my face that I'm anything less than serious about what I just said.

"Ryan, I have to," she defends. "They're my parents."

"I don't care. I don't want you going over there for them to treat you like shit." My words are hard, but they come out before I can even think to soften them up for her.

She sighs and leans back into me, resting her head on my chest, and I enjoy the contact.

"I have to go," she whispers. "It's Christmas, and I really should be there. I'm only going for dinner. That's all."

"Then I'm going with you."

"What?" she says as she pulls away and sits up.

"I don't want you going alone, Candace," I tell her. "I'll go with you."

"I don't think that's a good idea," she says, but I'm not letting up on this.

"Well, I don't think it's a good idea that you're going. So we can argue about this, or you can just say okay."

Her eyes are locked on mine, stunned by my tone, but the feeling that I have to shield her from getting hurt again is powerful, almost uncontrollable. It takes her a moment, and I watch her brow twitch right before she turns and slowly leans back.

"Okay," she resolves with uncertainty.

Certain or not, I don't care. She said 'okay,' and I take it a step further, pushing her when I add, "And I don't want you spending Christmas alone either, so why don't you come home with me. I could use the distraction at the madhouse."

"What?! No. Thanks, but I'll be fine," she says in a high-pitched voice.

"I'm sure you will be fine, but I don't like the thought of you sitting here alone, so you're coming with me." I need her to come with me. I just need her . . . with me.

"Ryan, it feels weird," she argues.

"Why?"

"Because. It just does. I know you have a big family, and I just don't want to intrude."

"It's not an intrusion," I assure her as I move to face her. "My family isn't like that."

She drops her head and takes her time contemplating. Questioning. *Shit, did I go too far? Did I scare her?* As soon as I start to regret my words, she speaks.

"Okay, but no gifts. It makes me uncomfortable."

"Why's that?"

"I don't know. It just always has. Please," she says, almost begging, and I don't push it any further.

Excitement rushes through me, a feeling that's all too new for me. But I can't help it, knowing that I get to have her with me for a solid chunk of time.

"Okay. No gifts," I say with a smile.

We both sit back, and when she gets comfortable in my arms, she asks, "So when did you start making all the rules?"

"When you started making me worry about you," I respond, completely transparent.

Sitting there, I continue to hold her. We don't talk at all. It's quiet and peaceful, and having her warm body tucked in close with mine gets my heart racing. All I can think about is how I want to kiss her, touch her. Pick her up and make good use of her bed. But I know once that happens, I'll never want to leave that bed. The thoughts alone turn me on, and I need to get control of myself.

"Hey," I whisper, looking down at her. When she tilts her head and peers up at me, she's close. So close, that if I lean down slightly, I could kiss her. Maybe I should. But I know myself. I won't want to stop. I don't think I could with her, so instead, I say, "I should get going."

She nods her head, and feeling the movement against my jaw makes leaving so difficult, but that's what I do. I stand, and she walks me to the door.

"Thanks for helping me out tonight."

"You don't need to thank me," I tell her and then walk out to my car after she gives me another nod.

The drive home is almost painful because all I want to do is turn around and take her, claim her as mine, but nothing about this girl is telling me that I should handle her in that way. I'm holding back, and I've never had to do that before. The anticipation drives me crazy, wondering when I'll get to see her again, hear her voice when she calls, or read her words when she texts me.

I need to talk to her. Be honest and tell her how I'm feeling. But I just got her to agree to spend the holidays with me, so I'll selfishly take the time and won't mention anything right now. God, this is killing me.

When I wake up, I fix myself a cup of coffee before calling

my mom to tell her about the change of plans.

Taking my coffee over to the couch, I kick my feet up and call her.

"Hi, dear," she says when she answers the phone.

"Hey. You busy?"

"No. How are you?" she asks.

"Good. Um, I have a minor change of plans for Christmas," I tell her. "I'm gonna bring Candace with me." I say this, almost cringing at what her reaction is going to be. I've never brought a girl home with me—ever.

She's surprisingly understated when she says, "That doesn't sound like something minor. So what's going on with you two?"

"Nothing's going on."

"But you're bringing her here. Home. With the whole family. And nothing's going on?" she pries.

"She's alone, and I don't want her to be. That's all," I explain, but we both know that's not all.

"Alone? Where's her family?"

I take a long sip of my coffee before explaining, "She doesn't have a good relationship with her parents. The last time she saw them, they wound up in a huge fight and they said some pretty bad things to her. She's going back to see them for dinner on Christmas Eve, and I told her that I would go with her."

"Oh. So, when are you coming home?"

"We're gonna drive down on Christmas, so I won't be there in the morning with the kids," I tell her, feeling a little guilty that I won't be there when they wake up.

"They'll understand. I'll talk to them," she assures me. "I'm glad I finally get to meet this girl," she says with excitement.

"Mom, she can be really shy," I warn. "I know she's

gonna be overwhelmed with everyone at the house, and I don't want to make it any more awkward for her if anything was to be insinuated. It's just not that way with us."

"I'll be on my best behavior," she teases, and I know she will be. "Well, I should run out and get her a little something."

"No gifts."

"It's Christmas, Ryan," she says, annoyed by my demand.

"She made me promise. Told me that gifts make her uncomfortable."

"Ryan, how much do you know about this girl?" I can hear the uncertainty about Candace in her voice.

"Why?"

She lets out a heavy breath before saying, "It just sounds like she has some issues going on, and I wonder what you really know about her."

I take a moment because all I want to do is defend this girl. Truth is, I know she has issues. I'm not blind to the odd behavior I catch glimpses of and the couple of things that Jase and Mark have said about her. But whatever is going on, I don't think it could ever be enough to keep me away. So, I bypass my mom's concerns and leave it at, "She's special. I don't know what's going on with us, but she's important to me."

I can almost hear my mother's smile when she says, "Well, then she's important to me too."

"She's a good girl, but her walls aren't that easy to break down."

"Sometimes it isn't about breaking walls, dear. Sometimes it's simply about proving yourself to the other person that they're willing to just let them down."

My mom's support is a constant in my life, and I'm

grateful that I can depend on that from her.

"Thanks, Mom."

chapter eighteen

There's no doubt she's nervous when she gets into my car and I start driving up to Shoreline to her parents' house. She doesn't speak as she sits there, looking all proper in her plum, knee-length dress and black high heels. She hardly ever wears jewelry or makeup, she doesn't need to—she's perfect. But I don't like seeing her so worried.

"Relax," I tell her.

"Ryan. You need to know that—"

"Candace, relax."

"They're just very judgmental people," she warns.

"There is nothing that they can say that I haven't heard before," I tell her. If anyone can deal with people who degrade you, it's me. I spent my whole childhood listening to a father telling me, every way he could, what a piece of shit I was. I'm sure I can handle whatever it is I'm about to walk into. But it isn't me I'm worried about, it's her.

When I pull into the gates of The Highlands, an upscale affluent community, I look over at Candace and lay my hand over the two of hers that are clenched tightly together. I weave through the neighborhood and when she points to the house, I pull into the drive and shut the car off. She doesn't open the door or move in any way. She sits, and I let her take her time.

After a few moments pass, I ask, "You ready?"

"Yeah," she sighs and then opens the door.

Walking up to the large, two-story home that overlooks the Sound, she takes a deep breath before opening the front door. We walk in, and I take in my surroundings. I knew that she came from money—I do too—but there's a big difference between affluent and wealthy. This is wealth.

"Bunny," her father beams as he walks through the foyer with his arms out to pull her into a hug. From his demeanor, you would never expect the family drama that lies underneath the surface. My father was the same way. No one would ever suspect the violent man that he was behind closed doors.

He takes a step back from Candace and turns to me. He wears a tailored charcoal suit and has almost polished, silver hair. "And you must be Ryan. Thanks for joining us," he says to me, shaking my hand.

"Good to meet you, sir."

"Come in," he says as he leads us back through the formal living room and into the kitchen. He turns to Candace, and tells her, "Your mother is finishing getting ready. She should be out shortly."

She only smiles up at him.

"What can I get you two to drink?" he asks.

"A beer is good, Mr. Parker," I say to him.

"Please, call me Charles."

With drinks in hand we make our way back to their library that spans the two stories of the house with a large walk-in fireplace.

I sit next to Candace on the tucked leather couch as her father asks, "So, Ryan, what is it that you do?"

"I own a bar right off campus," I tell him as Candace shifts nervously at my side.

"Oh, how did you get into that type of work?"

I briefly explain how I acquired the business after I graduated from UW, and he follows along, nodding his head.

"What did you study in college?" he asks before taking a sip of his scotch.

"Finance."

"Now that's a respectable degree," I hear, and when I turn my head, I see a petite woman with shoulder-length, brown hair, wearing a dress similar to Candace's, only in navy. But where Candace is more reserved, there isn't a question about her mother's social standing by the way she carries herself in a much too proud manner as she walks across the room, almost demanding attention.

Candace stands to give her mom a stiff hug.

"Hi, Mom."

"Good to see you, darling," she drawls before turning to me. "And Ryan, welcome."

I step closer and take her hand, saying, "Thank you for having me."

"Of course. It isn't every day that our daughter brings a man home," she says in a patronizing tone, and I look over to see Candace rolling her eyes as we sit down.

"Ryan was just telling me about the bar he owns," her father announces.

"A bar?" she questions as if the words have a bad taste to them. She has no idea that the bar I own has afforded me an extremely comfortable lifestyle.

Before she can continue, Candace jumps in and changes the subject, asking about her parents' upcoming trip to Aspen.

Candace and I sit back and listen to their plans before her

father excuses himself and Candace takes me to show me around the house.

We walk outside to the backyard and look at the view of the Sound.

"I'm sorry about that," Candace says softly as we take a seat on one of the benches.

"About what?"

She looks at me with apology. "They can be a lot. They're pretty pretentious."

"Candace, no one has perfect parents. Everyone's flawed in some way."

I slip my arm over her shoulders as she tightens the scarf around her neck.

"So, you grew up here in Shoreline?" I ask.

"Yeah. In this very house. The Kelleys, who live across the street, have a daughter that's the same age as me. We used to be best friends when we were growing up."

"And now?"

"And now all I really have is Jase, Mark . . . and you," she tells me and knowing that she sees me as someone she can at least group with Jase and Mark gives me a little relief.

"What about your roommate?"

"Kimber? We used to be really close, but not so much anymore."

"So what happened to all your friends from high school?" I ask, curious as to why she secludes herself in a manner that prevents her from having more people in her life.

"They've moved on. Applying to grad schools, getting married, making a life for themselves. Most of the kids here wind up becoming people like my parents. More concerned about their image and what social circle they're in. It's not me, so I never cared enough to stay in touch with anyone."

I see how her parents could be upset that she doesn't

seem to follow suit with their expectations. That Candace would be driven enough to step out of that life to create a new one, a more comfortable one, for herself. She's ambitious in a way that's unique from her parents. Following a passion—dance—to build a life that she can find pleasure in.

"We should go back inside," she tells me, and when we walk in, her father calls from the other room, "Candace, could you come in here?"

"Yeah, just a second." She looks at me and says, "I'll be right back. Make yourself at home."

"Do you want me to come with you?"

"No, it's okay," she assures before heading back to the library.

I take this time to stroll aimlessly through the house. Walking into the formal living room, I scan the framed photos that are displayed on the black grand piano. Family portraits through the years. Candace as a young girl, wearing a frilly white dress with white gloves, searching for Easter eggs on the greens of a golf course. A picture-perfect family, but from what little I have picked up from Jase, she was miserable. But out of all the photos, none of her dancing.

I'm curious to know what she would look like dancing. She's so poised as it is, but to see how she would move intrigues me.

My attention shifts to the library when I hear Candace yelling. I don't miss a beat when I start walking through the house to where she is, concerned about what they're talking about and what has Candace raising her voice when she's always so quiet. I can draw my own conclusions about what kind of relationship she has with her parents and wonder if they are the ones she needs to be protected from.

When I step to the closed double doors, I hear her father

bark, "You have a name to uphold!"

"I just don't understand you," her mother snaps. "You should be thanking your father, not pouting," and the sound of her condescending voice irks the hell out of me.

"You are unbelievable, Mother! I'm not a child!" Candace's voice is strained as she yells, and I can't bear the pain in her words. I barge in and see the annoyance on her mother's face, so I lock my eyes on Candace, but she doesn't notice as she continues shouting at her mom. "You can't just step in and take away everything I have worked so hard for during these past four years! How can you call yourself a mother? You're nothing! You say you're embarrassed by me, well, it goes both ways."

I rush across the room to her side, and when she finally stops to catch her breath, she sees me.

"We're leaving. Now," I demand as I take in her tear-stained face.

"Excuse me, but this is a private matter," I hear her mother say, but I don't take my eyes off of Candace as she continues to cry, staring at me in shock. I'm pissed, and she sees it.

Holding out my hand for her, her mother doesn't stop when she threatens, "Candace, if you walk out, it's over. Don't come back. We refuse to sit back and watch you ruin your life."

When her mother says this, anger roils inside of me, and I want to slap the fuck out of her lily-white ass for threatening her own daughter.

"Daddy?" Candace says as she looks to her father, pleading, and it hurts to hear her so desperate.

"We're done letting you play games, bunny. No more."

She stands there, tears falling from her eyes while she looks at her parents. All I want to do is take her away.

Comfort her and get her out of here. And when she slides her hand in mine, that's exactly what I do. I grip her tightly and get her out of this house as fast as I can. I snatch up our coats and walk her out to my car.

When I open the door for her, she reaches out to grip the side of the seat, and I know she's about to break, so I grab her and pull her into me. Clutching my arms around her, I hear it. Painful sobs start to break through, and she clings to me, crying.

The tension in my body is heady with the urge to put her in the car and go inside to knock the shit out of her parents. I'm fueled by disgust for these people. That they would lash those words at Candace, leaving her broken in their driveway, falling apart in my arms. But at least they're my arms that are attempting to comfort her, because even though she doesn't know it, I don't think anyone could give her what I want to give her. I'd give her the fuckin' world if I could.

After a while, her body begins to shiver with chills as she starts to quiet down. She keeps her head tucked against me, and I feel her fingertips pressed into my back. Her breathing is staggered, and when she pulls back, she keeps her head down, not looking at me—embarrassed. I lean down and kiss the top of her head before helping her up into the car.

The drive back is somber. I look over to her as she stares out the window. She's sad, and my need to comfort her is overwhelming. She must sense me watching her when she turns her head to me. Her chin quivers, and she shrugs her shoulders, defeated, as fresh tears fall down her cheeks. I reach over and take her hand, pulling it onto my lap. I keep it there all the way back to her house.

Once we're inside, I go to the kitchen to get her a glass of wine, figuring she could use one. As I walk into the living room, she's curled on the couch with her heels kicked off on the floor. I hand her the glass and she swallows it fast before handing it back to me. Setting it on the end table, I sit down, leaning into the corner of the couch and pull her between my legs and on top of me. She lies there and doesn't move as I thread my fingers through her soft, thick hair.

"You okay?" I ask.

She doesn't answer, she just shakes her head and after a second begins crying again, wetting my shirt as she nuzzles into my chest. I strengthen my arms around her and let her cry without saying anything.

The hurt coming out of her is hard to listen to, but I do, and it breaks me. Breaks me in a way that even though I hate it, I find myself savoring it. The connection. Her need for me right now and the contentment I find in being the one to give it to her.

Time passes and she's fallen asleep on me. I can feel her steady breaths against me, and I'd hold on to her all night, just like this, if I knew she'd be okay with it. I want to be selfish and take it, but I know she wouldn't be comfortable with it. So as much as I don't want to feel her move off of me, I comb her hair with my fingers, and whisper, "Candace."

"Hmm," she softly hums as she stirs awake.

"It's getting late. You should go sleep in your bed."

Placing her hands on my chest, she pushes herself up, and I notice her bloodshot eyes.

"Are you gonna be okay if I leave?" I ask, hoping she'll want me to stay, but knowing that it's just a hope.

She nods her head and sits up. I move to stand and turn to take her hand, pulling her off of the couch and into a hug. She bands her arms around me, and I tell her, "We can stay here tomorrow. We don't have to go to my mom's."

Leaning her head back to look up at me, she says, "It's okay."

"Candace . . ."

"I could use the distraction. I'll be okay," she tries assuring me.

"Call me when you wake up. You might feel differently in the morning."

She walks me to the door and before I leave, she stops me, saying, "Ryan . . ." I look back at her, and she takes a pause before continuing, "I'm sorry . . . tonight just . . ."

"Don't worry about it. Honestly."

"Thanks," she says softly before I walk out.

Candace called me when she woke up this morning, assuring me that she still wanted to go to Oregon. I offered to stay here with her, but she told me that she really did want the distraction, so I didn't question her any more about it.

I finish packing my bag, and I think about how things with the two of us have shifted in the past couple of weeks. I'm falling for this girl hard, and I know I'm not gonna be able to keep this from her for very much longer, but I'm nervous that I might ruin what we have. Honestly, even though it isn't enough for me, I'll take it if this is all she wants to give.

I carry my bag downstairs, and decide to call Jase. I don't know if Candace has spoken with him this morning, but I call him anyway to let him know what happened last night.

"Hey, Ryan."

"Jase, hey. You have a minute?" I ask as I start making myself a coffee for the road.

"Yeah. What's up?"

"Have you talked to Candace this morning?"

"No, why? Did something happen with her parents?" he asks, sounding worried.

"It wasn't good, man."

"Tell me."

"Her parents are a piece of work. Pretentious dicks. I don't know the whole argument 'cause I was in the other room, but there was a lot of yelling, and when I went in there to get her, her parents threatened to cut her off. Told her they were done with her—threw her out."

"Shit," he sighs out. "How is she?"

"She didn't talk, but I didn't ask either. She was just really upset. I stayed with her for a while last night, but I wasn't sure if she had called you, so I wanted to let you know," I tell him as I screw the lid on to my travel mug and walk over to sit down on the couch.

"Thanks. I'll try giving her a call. I hate that she's stuck there."

"She's not. I'm about to go pick her up."

"Where are you guys going?" he asks, and I'm surprised that he doesn't already know.

"Has she not told you?"

"Told me what?" he questions.

"She's coming home with me to my mom's for a few days."

"What?" Yeah, he had no clue by the shock in his tone. "I can't believe she didn't say anything to me."

"Sorry. I figured you knew."

"No."

All of a sudden, I feel the need to talk to him about Candace. Knowing that the two of them are like family and that he's really protective of her, I need to know if I should be pursuing her. As awkward as this is, I go ahead and lay it out there.

"I need to tell you something."

"Yeah . . .?" he responds.

"Look, I know the two of you are really close, so I feel like I should let you know that . . ." I pause briefly before admitting, "I really like her."

"I figured as much," he lets out with a chuckle under his breath. "Have you told her?"

I'm relieved that he's being so relaxed about what I just said.

"No. I don't know where her head is at. I'm not sure if she'd even be interested in anything."

"I think she is," he says, giving me hope, and then adds, "Look, I get that she's closed off, but she wouldn't be hanging out with you like she has been if she didn't trust you."

"She's the hardest person I've ever had to read," I admit with a laugh.

"I probably shouldn't say this, but you need to know that she's been going through a lot this year. It's been rough, and I'm just gonna leave it at that. So if you're anything less than serious about her, then don't go there."

He tells me this, and I try not to wonder too much about what's going on with her, though I'm beginning to think that there could be a lot more to her parents than what I've seen.

"I hear you," I tell him.

"I'm serious. She isn't like most girls. She's really innocent, so don't push her," he warns.

"It's not like that with her."

"I don't mean to sound like an ass or anything."

"Jase, man. It's fine. I get it," I tell him, and a part of me is glad that he's being this way about her, that she has someone like him there for her.

"Mark and I are hanging out with his family, so I've gotta run. I'll try giving her a call though."

"Okay. Thanks, man. I'll talk to you later."

Hearing him assure me that I'm not wasting my time soothes some of the anxiety I've been having about Candace. This girl has woven herself into my life, and for a change, I want to keep her there.

chapter nineteen

Candace was a little antsy when I picked her up this morning. We're running later than what I told my mom because I didn't want to rush her. She didn't get much sleep last night, so she just wasn't herself, worrying about how she looked and wondering if my family would think she was rude since she tends to be quiet. I've never seen her so uptight, so I let her move at her own pace.

She fell asleep about halfway into the drive, and as I look over at her, she's still sound asleep, sitting there in her modest black dress. She looks beautiful as she sleeps, but it bothers me to think that at this moment, she's probably happier in her dreams than she is when she's awake.

When we start getting closer to the coast, I decide to go ahead and wake her up. Trying not to startle her, I run my knuckles up and down her arm until I see her eyes start to blink open.

"How long have I been asleep?" she murmurs.

"A couple of hours."

"Really?"

I smile over at her. "Really."

She adjusts the seat and sits up to look out the window.

The canopy of trees that hide the sky on the winding road through the mountains makes it dark.

"How much longer do we have to go?" she asks.

"About twenty minutes. Are you feeling better?"

"Yeah. I was really tired."

"Music?" I ask and when she agrees, I tell her, "You pick."

She takes my cell phone since she likes all my music and syncs it up with the stereo, selecting 'Ride' by Lana Del Rey. She sets my phone down and sits back as the music fills the car, and I enjoy the doleful, limpid melody of the song.

"You're quiet over there," I say after a while.

"Just a little nervous," she tells me as she continues to watch the mist collecting on the window.

I give her knee a squeeze and say, "Don't be."

Seeing the unconvincing grin on her face, I decide to just let her be for the rest of the drive. When we arrive, I park the car and walk around to open her door. She's not quick to get out, so I take her hands to help her down, encouraging, "Don't be so nervous. Just relax."

I laugh under my breath as I watch her fidgeting with the skirt of her dress, smoothing it down.

"Why are you laughing at me?"

"Because I've never seen you so wound up before."

I take her hand and start walking her to the front door, but when she tugs back and stops, I turn to hear her say, "Ryan . . . I don't do well around a lot of people."

I try to coax her with my words, telling her, "My family will love you, but if you feel that uncomfortable, we can go. Just say the word."

"No, I want to meet them, I'm just . . ."

"Hey, I'm right here. No worries, okay?"

"Okay."

Holding her hand, I lead her inside as two of my nephews run through the entryway, chasing each other. I laugh and walk her back to the kitchen.

"Finally, you made it," my mom says excitedly and rushes over to hug me, but I keep my grip on Candace.

"Mom, this is Candace," I introduce, and my mom pulls her in for a hug as well.

"I'm so glad to finally meet you, dear," my mom tells her, and she's not even trying to hide that she's thrilled with the fact that I brought a girl home and she isn't some barfly.

My Aunt Carol brings me in for a hug, excited to see me, and before I know it, the kids all start flooding into the kitchen, screaming my name. I spot Sophie, one of my nieces, and pick her up as Tori and my other cousins' husbands come in to say hi. Tori and my other cousin, Jenna, give me curious looks, and I try to ignore them, knowing they are just waiting to start digging into my business about Candace. I told my mom to discreetly tell my cousins to keep a tight lip so they don't embarrass Candace, but I know Jenna and Katie, and those chicks are nosey.

When Sophie starts poking her finger in my ear, I catch Bailey, toddling over to me. Bending down, I scoop her up in my other arm, ravishing her neck with playful kisses as she squeals and giggles.

"You weren't kidding," Tori whispers to me as my cousin, Jenna, comes over to take Sophie out of my arms.

"What?" I question, trying to keep my voice under my breath.

She laughs, "She's *way* out of your league."

"Thanks," I say with mockery.

"You know I'm teasing. She's just . . . polished."

"Tell the girls not to interrogate her."

"Donna already said something, but you know how Katie is."

"Where is she by the way?" I ask.

"Upstairs with Maddie. She had an upset stomach earlier."

"My room?"

"Yeah."

"Why is my room always the hot spot for everyone's spawn when they get sick?" I joke and then turn to look at Candace, but she's no longer in the kitchen, and I quickly realize, that in the madness of saying hi, I left her alone.

"Mom, where's Candace?" I ask.

'Ladies' room,' she mouths to me, and I walk down the hall to wait for her, feeling bad, and wondering if all that was too much for her. Who am I kidding? Of course it was. My family is big and loud, and Candace doesn't even like being in a crowded coffee shop.

When she doesn't come out after a few minutes, I gently knock on the door.

"Everything okay?" I ask as she opens the door. "When I looked up you were gone."

"Yeah, just needed a moment to myself."

"Sorry about that."

"It's okay. I'm just not used to . . ."

"I know." I see that she's a bit rattled, so I step closer to her and run my hands down her arms. "Do you need a few more minutes?"

"No, I'm fine."

When we walk back into the kitchen, the kids are watching their movie, and the chaos has dissipated. I pour her a glass of wine, and hand it to her, whispering, "Come on," in her ear. I lead her through the house, showing her around as I take her to one of the back rooms that looks out over the water.

We're alone, and it's quiet as we stand in front of the large picture window.

"Better?" I ask, and she smiles as she looks at me.

"I guess I didn't realize how big your family actually is. I mean, you've told me, but . . ."

"It can be a lot," I tell her. Having twenty of us here can be overwhelming. It's more the women and kids. The guys are always laying low, trying to dodge the madness.

"This is a great view," she says. "Have you always lived here?"

"Yeah."

"Small town."

"You have no idea," I say with a hint of humor. "I used to spend most of my time in Seaside or Astoria. That's where Tori's from."

"Is there even a school here?" she asks with a huge smile, finding it funny. Not a whole lot of people are permanent residents of this area. It's mostly vacation rentals, but we're one of the few that actually call it home.

"No," I tell her. "The schools are in Seaside, but I went to private school."

"Me too."

We chat for a few more minutes, and when she seems more at ease, we head back. Tori and Jenna are sitting in the dining room when we pass through.

"Candace, come join us," Tori offers, and when Candace hesitates, I tell her it's fine, letting her know that I'll be in the other room with my mom. I know Tori is curious about her, and I also trust her enough to know Candace will be fine.

I find my mom in the kitchen, working on dinner. It's just the two of us, and she stops what she's doing as we lean against the counter and talk.

"How did this morning go with the kids?" I ask, a little bummed that I wasn't here.

"Anarchic," she laughs.

"I bet."

"They missed you."

"I have all their presents outside," I tell her. "We can open them later."

She takes a sip from her glass of water, and then asks, "Where's Candace?"

"Dining room with Tor and Jenna."

She nods her head with a smile, and I know she's biting her tongue, so I tell her, "Just say it."

"What?"

"Whatever it is that has you looking at me like that, Mom."

When she sets her glass down on the counter, she reveals, "She's different than I was expecting."

"How so?"

"Just . . . different." When I narrow my eyes at her, she grins and assures, "It's a good thing, dear. Relax," before patting my arm a couple of times and walking away.

"Where are you going?"

"Dining room to visit with the girls."

I let her have her time with Candace, even though I feel like I want to go in there and check on her. But I don't. Instead I busy myself with Connor, helping him out with a puzzle on the floor. When I look up, I see my mom and Candace passing through the kitchen. She catches my eye, and I give her a small half grin as they walk through, heading to the study. I like seeing her here, with my mom, in my familiar surroundings, mixed in with my family.

Candace is now in the kitchen, helping Mom cook while I drink a beer and hang out with the guys. I can't keep my eyes off of her as I watch her laughing with my mom while they get everything ready for dinner, and I know instantly that I want to see this again. Have her here again.

She makes me nervous because she has this power about her that is dragging emotions out of me when no one in the past has been able to. She has no clue what she's doing to me, and that's a scary thing when I think about admitting how I'm feeling about her.

After a while, I unload the gifts and let the kids open everything. My mom was right—they're much crazier than they were last year, but they're another year older, and I'm sure next year will be even wilder. Candace sits on the couch with Tori while they laugh at me being overtaken by the little ones.

When dinner is done, Candace excuses herself to go upstairs to relieve Katie from mommy duties. Her daughter, Maddie, hasn't been feeling well all day, and Candace told me that she needed some quiet time, so she's up in my room with Maddie, and Katie is finally getting to eat dinner.

My aunts are cleaning up, Jenna and the guys are getting all the kids ready for bed, and Tori and I band off into the study to talk.

"I got a job," she tells me as we sit down.

"What made you decide to go back to work?"

"After you and I talked this summer, I decided to just be honest with Trevor. Told him pretty much what I told you," she says. "He suggested the same thing. Thought I should get out of the house, get back into a routine. So I called my old boss, and it was as easy as that."

"When do you start?" I ask.

"Second week in January," she says with a little uncertainty.

"You ready to leave Connor and Bailey?"

"Yes and no." Tori is a great mom and is very attached to her kids, so it makes sense that this transition would be hard for her since she's been a stay-at-home mom for the past four years.

"It'll be fine," I say. "So you and Trevor are on the same page?"

"He never got off track. It was me. I think I've been miserable because I've been lost. I wasn't doing anything about it, and it made me start questioning everything. But he's supportive. Always has been. He just had no clue how I was feeling. Once I was honest with him, things started to change. So yeah, we're good."

"Good."

"What about you?" she questions.

"What do you mean?" I ask, not understanding what she's asking.

"Being honest," she starts, "Candace told me that she thinks you brought her here because you feel sorry for her."

"She said that?" I feel horrible that she would even think that.

Tori nods her head and then questions, "How long do you plan on avoiding telling her how you feel?"

Letting out a deep breath, I tell her, "She makes me nervous." When Tori smiles, I say, "I'm glad you're enjoying my discomfort."

"I'm just enjoying seeing a girl have this effect on you," she admits before she stands up. "I'm heading to bed, but for what it's worth, I really like her."

I follow her out, and the house is quiet. I see my mom in the kitchen, turning everything off.

"You going to bed?" I ask her.

"Yes. It's getting late. Is Candace still upstairs?"

"Yeah, I'm gonna go up there and get her. I think we'll just crash down here and let Maddie take my bed."

"Well, tell her that I'll see her in the morning, will you?"

"Okay, Mom."

We say good night, and I go to the hall closet to pull out some blankets and pillows. I toss everything on the floor, making a makeshift bed for me to sleep on and lay out a blanket and pillow on the couch for Candace. We had planned on her taking my room, but since Maddie is sick, I figure this is a fair alternative.

I pick up Candace's bag and head upstairs to my room. Quietly, I open the door to see Maddie passed out, lying on top of Candace. When she rolls her head to the side and looks at me, I walk in and laugh. "Are you stuck under Maddie?"

"I didn't want to move and wake her up. What time is it?" she asks.

"Past eleven. Everyone has gone to bed. I told Katie that I would check on you and Maddie."

"I wanted to thank your mother before she went to bed."

"Don't worry about it. Here's your bag," I tell her as I set it next to the bed. "I made a big pallet of blankets and pillows downstairs in the living room. Since Maddie is in my room, we're just going to sleep down there. We can watch a movie or something if you want."

"Oh . . . umm . . ." she stutters, and I know she's uncomfortable with the change in plans.

"Don't worry. I'll take the floor, and you can have the couch." I walk over to my dresser to pull out a pair of pajama pants for myself and let her know, "I'll be downstairs. You can use my bathroom to change," before walking out and heading back down.

It doesn't take too long before Candace is walking down in a black sleeveless top and a pair of pajama pants. She has no clue how sexy she looks right now, and I have to look away. I open the fridge to grab a bottle of water.

"You mind if I take the floor?" she asks.

"You sure?"

"Yeah. It looks more comfortable anyway."

"Okay."

She sits down and slides herself under the pile of blankets as I walk over and sit next to her. The thought of sleeping, even in the same room as her, has me on edge. It's like dangling a piece of meat in front of a starved animal. It's life's sick revenge for taking things way too easily and now making me restrain myself in the worst way possible because I've never wanted anything more.

"TCM?" I ask as I flick on the TV.

"It's all we ever watch," she teases, and I like it. "Why switch now?"

"I think you're starting to like my movies."

"Maybe."

We sit back and start watching a movie before I ask her, "Were you okay today?"

"I was. You're really lucky; you have a great family."

"Well, everyone really likes you, especially my mom."

"She's really nice. We had some time to visit earlier."

She starts to grow tired as she inches herself under the covers and lays her head on the pillow by my side. When I look down at her, she has her eyes closed. Knowing she's still awake, I don't let that stop me from running my fingers through her hair.

I continue to do this as I zone out on the TV. My mind can't even focus, and when I hear her breathing steady, I slip my hand under her head and gently move her to my lap. When I do this, she unconsciously wraps her one arm around my waist, and with greed, I savor the contact.

She seemed to enjoy herself today, and I'm grateful that I was able to give this to her since yesterday went horribly wrong, having to walk away from the only blood family she knows. The reactions she sparks in me are intense, and I know I need to heed Tori's advice and be honest with her—soon. But I take this moment and just relish her being so close to me.

I don't want to fall asleep, but when my eyes grow too heavy for me to fight, I reluctantly slip myself out from underneath her, laying her head back down on the pillow, and find myself alone on the couch. I lie there, across the room, the only hint of light coming from the last sparks of fire in the fireplace. It's enough of a glow that I can still watch her, so that's what I do—I watch her as she sleeps until I finally drift off.

chapter twenty

My eyes shoot open when I hear a hard gasp of air. Candace is panicked, trying to catch her breath as her body thrashes awake. I lurch off of the couch, and I'm by her side in an instant, pulling her into my arms.

"You okay?"

Her body is stiff with tension as she shakes under my hold.

"What happened, babe?"

"Bad dream," she quietly whispers through her erratic breaths.

"Slow your breathing down, okay?" I tell her as I hold her against my chest. I'm slightly disoriented, still in a haze as my head catches up to my body's sudden alertness. When she wraps her arms around my waist, I begin to rub her back, trying to soothe her from her nightmare. She scared the shit out of me, yanking me out of a deep sleep.

I can start to feel her breathing slow down, and when it does, I ask, "Wanna talk about it?" curious as to what she was dreaming about that caused her that much panic.

She shakes her head no against me, and I keep her folded in my arms as I lower us down and pull the blankets over us.

Face to face, her eyes shift up to mine. I have her tucked tightly to me as she begins to get her breathing under control and relaxes. I don't want to think about what's in her head that's clearly tormenting her because looking at her as she peers up at me with her hazel eyes is all I want to focus on. I can't read her expression, but right now, I try not to decode her. I just take her in. I feel the build-up beating inside of me, and I can't keep it in any longer.

I want her.

I run my hand over her forehead and down to her cheek where I keep it. I study every detail about her, and her breathing increases slightly along with mine. I know she feels it. Feels what I want. I don't even need to say anything because the attraction is *that* palpable. Her brow twitches when she slides her small hand over my cheek and rests it there. Wrapped up in each other—close—I scan her face for a sign. Permission. For anything that tells me this is okay.

I can tell she's scared. I can tell she doesn't know if she wants this—wants me. God, I just want to kiss her. But more than that, I want her to kiss me. I want her to want it as badly as I do, and when my eyes find hers again, she gives me the slightest nod of her head, and I've never felt so relieved in my life.

She wants me.

Knowing that I'll want more than she'll give me, I move slow, needing this to last for as long as she'll let it. Her eyes fall shut and she begins to tremble. I hate that she's scared of this when it feels so right to me, but I'm determined to take her apprehension about this away as I softly press my lips to hers.

I'm gone. I knew I would be.

My heart thuds hard as I tighten my grip on her, needing her as close to me as I can get her. I kiss her slowly, and when she finally relaxes and begins to move her lips with mine, I take more. I can't help myself. I drag my tongue across her lip, smooth, soft. She's the sweetest thing I've ever tasted. Threading my hand in her hair, pressing her body into mine, she wraps her hands up from underneath my arms and braces them tightly on my shoulders.

A soft whimper breaks from her, but she never takes her lips from mine. She has me, and I'm fuckin' lost in her right now. I've never had the ties of emotion with a girl, so to say this one has me bound would be an understatement. What she gives me is something I never even knew I needed, so I never even looked for it.

Moving us off of our sides, I roll on top of her, and I feel her soften beneath me. She runs her hands down my shoulders and grips my forearms tightly as I gently nip her lip before she allows me to dip my tongue inside of her mouth. I linger, moving slowly, needing to feel as much of her as I can. She caresses my tongue with hers, and having her like this, giving this to me like she is, I know I have to make her mine because I'm never gonna want to let her go.

But when she pushes her hands against my arms, everything is questionable again as she pulls away from me.

"I'm sorry," she whispers, eyes still closed.

Tucking my arm underneath her, I speak quietly. "Look at me, Candace." I brush the back of my fingers along the soft skin of her face. When she finally opens her eyes and looks up at me, I say, "I don't want you to feel sorry for that."

She lets out a small hum as she slowly nods her head, but it's when she slides her arms around my back, holding on to me, that I begin to calm. I rest my forehead on hers and breathe her in, taking all I can. I feel her head shift as she tilts her chin up, and this time, I don't have to take. She lifts up and melds her lips with mine, and I slowly fall into her touch as she holds my face in her warm hands, keeping me close to her.

When I finally drag my lips off of hers, she stays close, and I keep her that way until she falls asleep. I watch her; I can't help myself. I have her arms around me and spend a lengthy amount of time stroking her back, touching the bare skin along her neck, her arms, her jaw, before falling asleep with her.

I'm awake. She's doesn't know it because I'm greedy and don't want to move away from her. She woke up a few minutes ago, but I lie here with my eyes closed, arm around her, legs tangled with hers. It feels too good to disrupt, so I don't.

I wonder how she's feeling after last night. A thousand questions start to rack my brain, and now I fear that I'll never get that again. So for now, I pretend to sleep.

"Night night over," I hear Bailey's voice declare, and I know the pretending is done.

"It's not over, Bailey," I mumble, just wanting a few more minutes with Candace. I feel her shift, but I keep my eyes shut, and I know I'm busted. I don't care though.

"I eat bweakfast. Night night over."

"Okay," Candace whispers and begins to slip out from my hold, but I tighten my arm around her and pull her back to me.

"Where are you going?" I ask, finally opening my eyes.

"To go get her something to eat."

She slides out of the blankets, and I can only hope that I'll be able to get her in my sheets again. That I can continue to have her like I did last night.

I roll over and watch as she settles Bailey with a bowl of cereal. Getting up, I make my way into the kitchen to start a pot of coffee while Candace busies herself with Bailey, peeling a banana for her.

"Want some?" I ask as she walks back into the kitchen.

She keeps her eyes down and gives me a nod. *Fuck.* She doesn't want to look at me. She's embarrassed. Nervous. Not what I was wanting.

"Umm, I'm gonna sneak upstairs and get cleaned up," she says as I rip open a packet of sugar for her coffee.

After I stir in the cream, I hand the mug to her, and she finally meets my eyes. Timid. She quietly thanks me and stands there for a moment, staring at the steam floating off of the coffee. I'm scared to know what she's thinking so intently about, but I ask anyway.

"Hey. You okay?"

"Yeah, I'm fine. I just want to get ready before everyone wakes up."

"Okay."

I know she just really needs to get space from me, and I have no choice but to accept it as I watch her head upstairs to my room.

I wander over and sit down next to Bailey at the table as she smacks on her cereal. Nursing my cup of coffee, I decide that I'm not gonna let her shut down. I don't want her feeling uncomfortable, so I'll get her out of the house and take her to one of my favorite places. I need to talk with her. Be honest. Let her know where how I'm feeling because if I don't, then she's just gonna continue to feel awkward for the next couple of days that we're here. I try to not think about what she's going to say. None of this is in my control and not having that power is unsettling.

Looking up, I see Tori walking in.

"What are you guys doing up?" she asks as she pulls down a mug.

"Your little rugrat was hungry and snuck downstairs," I tell her as I give Bailey a wink before I stand up. "I'm gonna go get ready."

When I walk upstairs, Maddie is still asleep, and I can hear the shower running as I grab some clothes out of the dresser and closet and then go to one of the downstairs guest bathrooms to shower.

She still isn't downstairs when I'm ready. I pass by the kitchen, which is loud as everyone is making breakfast and visiting. When I spot Maddie, I decide to go up and check on Candace.

The bathroom door is closed and the smell of her shower fills the room, intoxicating me, making this more agonizing. But I suck it up because I don't want to make her uncomfortable with how strongly I'm feeling about all of this.

When I knock on the door, she says, "Come in."

She stands there in a pair of jeans and one of her college sweatshirts, hair stacked on top of her head, applying her lipgloss. I slide up next to her, leaning back against the counter, and watch. *Grab her. Touch her. Kiss her.* I shake my scrambling thoughts as she tosses her things into her small bag, and avoids acknowledging me. But when she moves to walk past me, I grab her by the waist and pull her to me, asking, "What's wrong?"

"Nothing. Really," she lies, shutting me out.

Looking at her, watching that tick of her brow, I ask, "You wanna get out of here for a while?"

She doesn't miss a second when she nods her head. Relief. She doesn't want to stay away from me.

I slide my hand down her wrist and hold her hand, but this time, I lace my fingers with hers, holding her differently—needing to—and head out.

It's rainy this morning as I drive through the narrow, winding road in Ecola Park. I've always loved this area, dense with lush, tall trees and deep cliffs. I try to focus on the surroundings, but I can't escape my nerves. This is all new to me. I've never done this before, and I don't know what the fuck I'm gonna say. All I know is that I want her.

I park the jeep and grab one of my raincoats from the back seat for her to put on.

"Here, wear this," I tell her as she takes it from me, and starts slipping it on.

We get out, and I hold her hand again as I walk her down the old wooden stairs that lead down to Indian Beach. The wind is hitting hard as it mixes with the rain. It's cold, but I love this type of weather. Walking along the packed, wet sand of the beach, I hold on to her as we step over the piles of smooth, black rocks to some logs of driftwood that sit back from the water. We sit down on one of the logs, and I watch Candace as she takes in the view. She has the hood popped up over her head. I like seeing her in my clothes, even if it's an oversized raincoat.

I wrap my arm around her, and when I do, she speaks.

"This is amazing."

"Yeah, I love it out here. I used to surf here a lot growing up."

She looks out at the hard-hitting waves, her cheeks already pink from the chill. My heart is racing, and I know it won't stop until I talk to her.

"Candace," I say as I turn, kicking my leg over the log to face her straight on. "What's bothering you? And don't say 'nothing' because I know something is."

She looks away, back out at the water. Her hands fidget, and I know she's deep in her head, but I need her here with me.

"Candace," I urge, bringing her focus back.

She faces me, brows pinched together, worried. "I just don't really know what we're doing."

"Tell me what you want." *Tell me that's it me. That you want me. So I don't have to keep pretending.*

"I'm not good at this stuff, Ryan."

Neither am I.

"Come here," I say as I grab her leg and move her to face me.

Time to get honest.

"I've wanted to kiss you since the night of the concert," I confess. "I don't know where your head is at, but whenever I'm not with you, I want to be."

I watch as she drops her eyes. Shy.

"Talk to me, babe." *Tell me you feel it too.*

"I just . . ." she starts, trying to find her words and settling back on, "I don't do this well."

"Do what?"

"This . . ."

I can't take her shyness, so I hold her head in my hands, angling her to look at me when I finally admit, "Whatever *this* is, I want it. I just need to know if you do."

My tone is intent because I know what I want here. Her eyes don't move from mine, and I wait for her response. For anything. I put it out there, and now my heart is racing with nerves, uncertain of her response. Then finally, she gives it to me, and I wanna fuckin' cling to her when she nods her head yes.

Keeping my hands on her, I guide her to me and kiss her. I've never wanted anything as much as I want her, and when she slides her arms under my coat and around my waist, my heart finally starts to settle. I have her.

Her lips are cold and wet with rain, and I squeeze her to me. I move slowly because the thought of rushing anything with her, to quicken the pace of her touch, would be stupid. So I take my time as I graze my tongue along her soft lips, and when she relaxes, allowing me to take more, I pass her lips and taste the warmth of her mouth.

I'm relieved that she's giving me this, that she wants what I want, but I'm anxious because I've never done this before. Never have I had feelings like this for anyone. Not even close to thinking that I could.

She presses her fingers into me, tightening her hold, and I keep my hands on her jaw, marking her as mine like some pathetic puppy, but I do it anyway.

She moves with me, sliding her tongue along mine—gently—without any sign of urgency, and I love that about her. That she would want the time the same way I do.

When I feel her move her hands out from under my coat and wrap around my wrists, I pull back and ask, "Should we get out of here?"

"Let's stay."

"Come here," I say as I slide her on top of my lap, and she slips her arm around my neck, steadying herself on me.

"Can I ask you something?" she says quietly.

"Anything."

"I never asked before because I didn't want to intrude, but . . . where's your father?" she asks with a hint of trepidation.

I don't talk to anyone about my dad. Never have. I hide it, bury it, and mask it with vices that make it easier to deal with. But I know she's hiding something too. I wish I knew what it was, so I go ahead and break off a piece of me and give it to her. "He died about ten years ago."

"I'm sorry," she says and drops her head away from me—abashed. "I shouldn't have asked."

"Candace, you can ask me anything," I tell her as I lift her chin up. "I don't want you to feel like you can't, okay?" I don't know what else to say, but I do know I want her to start opening up to me.

"Yeah," she breathes softly.

"My dad was an asshole," I tell her, wanting to be honest with her. "He drank way too much and was never around, but when he was, he was a total dick. So, don't feel bad for asking, because I don't feel bad that he's dead." I know my words come out hard, but they come out in truth.

She scans my face for a moment. She knows there's more behind my words, but I don't elaborate because what I just gave her is more than I've given anyone. So I leave it.

I clutch her waist and hold on to her when she looks over my shoulder and asks, "Is there a trail up there?"

"Yeah, it's a pretty decent path if you want to go up there."

"Yeah, let's go," she suggests, and I eye her leopard rain boots, asking, "Those have enough traction?"

Laughing, she says, "We'll see."

Stealing another kiss from her, enjoying the freedom of being able to, I stand and smile down at her before scooping her up and over my shoulder. This chick weighs nothing, and she begins to laugh as I haul her up the stairs. The giggles and squeals coming out of her are beautiful, and she never complains. I adore this side of her.

chapter twenty-one

After hiking in the rain for over an hour, I didn't let the fact that we were rain-soaked stop me from taking Candace into Seaside to the Broadway Strip. We took our time, walking in and out of the shops and grabbing lunch.

We came home and had an early dinner before everyone said goodbye and headed back home. It's just the two of us and my mom, so we've made no plans for the night. After Candace gets cleaned up, she makes herself comfortable on the couch downstairs, reading a book, while I take a quick shower.

I was surprised with how easygoing she was after our talk on the beach. We fell into the laidback feeling we have built up to in our friendship, but now there's no more grey.

Toweling off, I throw on a pair of pajama pants and dry my hair. I hear my mom's voice when I walk out of the room, and I start making my way down the stairs, spotting Candace and my mom sitting on the couch.

"No child should ever have to hear that," I overhear my mom telling Candace and I ask, "Hear what?" curious as to what they're chatting about.

As I walk across the room, I notice Candace's splotchy

face, and I know she's been crying. She keeps from looking at me as she faces my mother, so I take a seat next to her on the couch and slip my arm around her when my mom answers me.

"Candace is telling me about what happened the other night."

"Mom." I've been avoiding asking Candace how she's been feeling about the whole situation to keep from upsetting her.

"It's fine," Candace assures me, so I stay quiet and listen as they continue to talk.

I watch my mom take ahold of Candace's hand when she asks, "Do you have any other family at all?"

"No. It's only ever been the three of us since my father's parents passed away."

"What about your mother's family?"

"I've never met them," Candace tells her. "I have never known them to speak. I'm not even sure they know about me." Her voice trembles as she says this, and I run my hand up her back, wondering why she would have a side of her family that she's being kept away from. But before I can question it too much, my mother leans in and takes Candace in her arms, hugging her. We both have her in our hold when she begins weeping.

I feel horrible, but glad that she's here with me and that she would open up to my mother, who's nearly a stranger to her. I think of how long it took Candace to show me even a hint of this side of herself, but I know my mom has a way about her that can make anyone want to open up. She's always been that person for me, so seeing her provide Candace a little of that when I know she's probably never gotten it from her own parents is a good thing.

My mom pulls back, telling Candace exactly what I'm

feeling as she wipes the tears from Candace's cheeks.

"I'm glad you're here with us." Candace only nods when my mom says, "I'll let the two of you be," before walking out of the room.

I pull Candace to me, resting her back onto my chest as I lean against the armrest. She continues to let out soft whimpers.

"Don't cry, babe," I say quietly.

"I'm tired," she tells me. "I don't want to talk anymore."

So I don't say anything else. Taking her hand, I lead her upstairs so that she can lie down. It's late, and I'm sure she's exhausted from our busy day.

I let go of her hand when we hit the doorway and watch as she walks into the bathroom. I wait, listening to the faucet run, and when she returns, she doesn't say anything as she looks at me and gets into my bed.

Her back is facing me, and I'm not sure what she wants me to do. I know what I want to do, so I swallow the questioning thoughts and decide to not leave her in here alone. I walk over to the edge of the bed, pull back the covers, and slide in behind her. She's curled into a ball, so I wrap myself around her, tucking her into me, when she wedges her hand underneath mine for me to hold. This small move is all I need to assure me that she wants me with her tonight, so I stay.

Waking up with Candace is something that I can get used to, and I want to. So much so, that when I dropped her off at her house after we drove back to Seattle today, I asked her to stay at my loft tonight. She didn't want to at first, hell, even after trying to talk to her about why she's so apprehensive about it, I still don't think she wants to, but she wound up agreeing anyway.

I know that Jase told me that she was inexperienced, but I'm not quite sure *how* inexperienced he meant. After seeing how shy she was when I told her I wanted her here tonight, I'm pretty sure this girl is more innocent than I thought. But I want her here, and I want her in my bed. I've never wanted anyone in my bed. I avoid it. Always have. Always keeping everyone I've ever brought here downstairs. But her . . . I want it with her.

Getting a drink of water, I see headlights shine through the windows as her car pulls into my drive. She had to work the closing shift tonight, so it's a little past midnight as I watch her get out of her car. I head over to the door and wait for her to knock, but when I hear nothing, I wonder if she's having second thoughts. Hell, I'm surprised she came in the first place with how hesitant she was earlier. I startle her when I open the door.

"What are you doing out here?" I question with a tilt of my head, knowing all too well what she was doing—worrying.

"Umm, nothing. I was just about to knock." A clear lie, but I find myself liking it.

I take her bag as she walks in, setting it at the foot of the stairs. When I turn, I see her fidgeting her hands as she stands awkwardly in my living room. Needing her to relax and not feel this way when she's with me, I go over and take her in my arms. She accepts the touch willingly and clasps her hands behind my back, leaning her forehead against my chest. When she lets go of a deep breath, I give her head a kiss, asking, "Better?"

Her hum is soft when she says, "Mmm hmm."

"Good. I'm wiped. What about you?"

"Yeah," she breathes.

I take her hand, leading her upstairs. Walking her into my room, I aim her past the large closet, saying, "The bathroom is right over there."

She looks up at me, smiling, before taking her bag out of my hand and closing the bathroom door behind her.

I change clothes while I hear her taking a shower, and just knowing that she's naked in there—in my shower—starts a swarm of thoughts I know I need to get under control before I get her in my bed. Heading back downstairs to grab a bottle of water for her, I hang out in my kitchen, giving myself a few minutes before I go back up.

She's stepping out of the bathroom when I return, wearing a similar tank and pajama pants as she has the past couple of nights. I watch her hop up onto the tall bed, and I have to laugh at her as she slides under the covers. Sitting next to her, back against the cool leather headboard, she settles herself into my hold. When I look down at her, she's looking at the tattoo that's inked on the side of my ribs. I know she's gonna ask me about it when she lays her hand on top of it, so I decide, on the fly, to just tell her. She was so scared to be here with me earlier. I told her she could trust me, but I know my words aren't enough, so I'll give her a reason to try.

"What's this for?"

"A reminder," I say as I take her hand off the tattoo that covers my scar and hold it to my chest. "Like I said, my dad was an asshole." Her eyes shift up and meet mine when I continue, "He was a drunk and liked to take his anger out on me and my mom. I took more of it than she did. The drunker he was, the worse it would get. He was like that for as far back as I can remember. It was all I knew. Then one night, I beat the shit out of him when he was wasted, and when he got in his car and left, he never came back. His car was found wrapped around a tree, and that was it. He was dead."

The look on her face is beyond disbelief, so I pull her in tighter, knowing that was probably the last thing she expected me to say. It was a couple months after the funeral that I didn't attend when I got the words *Pain is a reminder you're still alive* tattooed over the scar that he gave me. But after all the hell he inflicted on me, I'm the one that's still breathing.

I don't know how else to show this girl that she can trust me and not be so closed off like she's always been with me. I need her to know that I trust her, so I let her know, "You're the only one who knows that, outside of my mom and me."

"I feel really stupid," she mumbles as she closes her eyes. "I'm so sorry about complaining about my parents."

"Candace, you're far from stupid," I say when I run my hand along her jaw to urge her to look at me. "Your parents treated you like shit. They filled you full of misconceptions of yourself and fucked with your head. Anyone would be devastated. Don't dismiss your pain because you don't think it's worthy. It is."

She takes a moment after I tell her this and looks at me. I know she acknowledges my words when she reaches up and threads her hands in my hair, drawing me in to kiss her. I slide down to meet her face to face, and I take her lips with mine. Bracing my body over hers, I soak in the heat of her as I run my mouth down her smooth neck, taking my time, nipping her gently along the way. When I start taking little sucks across her collarbone, she uses her hands to guide my face back up to her lips.

I know she's scared to move fast, she told me this earlier, so I go at her pace. Taking one of her hands off my cheek, I slide my fingers between hers and hold her hand as I move past her lips and explore her mouth. I grip her hand tightly, pressing it into the mattress, and I'm finding it hard to not want to take her, feel her breasts, run my hands up her thighs. My thoughts intensify, and I slow down, pulling back. Her face is slightly flushed, and I finally notice how strong her hold is on my hand.

"I could do this all night." I lean my forehead against hers, and she closes her eyes, keeping them shut until I say, "Look at me, Candace."

It takes her a second before she opens her eyes and peers up at me.

"Tell me why you're nervous with me."

"Ryan," she whispers and turns her head to the side to break the contact.

"Tell me," I say, needing her to just give me a small piece of what's going on inside of her head.

She moves to look at me again and starts, "Because . . ."

"Because why?"

"Because this is new for me," she finally reveals.

I don't respond, I simply smile down at her, and I can feel her start to relax.

The smile on her face is perfect, and when I catch her dimple, I finally take what I've been wanting and lean down to kiss it before I lie next to her and band my arms around her.

I watch as she begins to wake up. She clutches the blankets around her, eyes still closed and shimmies herself further down into the bed. She did the same thing yesterday morning at my mom's house. I reach down and pull her back up to me, and she starts blinking her eyes open when I begin to run my hands up and down her back, attempting to warm her up.

"Hey," she mumbles as she scoots in closer to me.

"Why don't you wear something warmer if you're always so cold?"

"I've tried, but it's hard for me to sleep when I wear heavy clothes," she says.

"I'm not gonna lie," I tell her. "I think I would prefer you cuddling into me like this every morning."

Tilting her head away from my chest, she questions, "Every morning?"

"You know I'm gonna want you back here."

When she leans her forehead against my chin, she begins to nervously mutter, "I'm not . . . I mean, I don't know if . . ."

"Candace," I say to get her to stop. "I like having you next to me at night. I won't push, if that's worrying you."

She doesn't move her head away from me when she says, "I'm not sure what you're used to, but—"

"Just give me a couple days a week," I tell her to calm her nerves about moving too fast.

She nods her head, and I don't say anything else. We lie together with no words, and I enjoy the touch of her body against mine until we finally decide to crawl out of bed.

We spend a slow morning downstairs, drinking coffee and hanging out. I want to ask her about how she's feeling with her parents, but I decide to hold off because I don't want to upset her. So instead, I flip on the TV and we kick back on the couch. Just another excuse to have my arms around her.

chapter twenty-two

Candace stayed over with me a couple more times this past week. Jase is back in town, so she's been spending time with him and a lot of time at the dance studio to get in some solo rehearsals before classes start back up next week. Work has been a little busier with the quarter break ending and students coming back into town, so Candace and I have been snagging time together for a few morning runs. Jase picked her up earlier today to hang out, so I'll stop by his apartment to pick her up after I get off work tonight.

When I walk into the bar, I spot Mel and Max and head over. The other bartenders have everything under control, so I take a seat next to Max to catch up since he took the past week off.

"Good to see you back up here," I tell him. "How was your Christmas?"

"I got to meet all of Traci's family."

"Yeah? How'd that go?"

"Cut the small talk and just tell him," Mel pipes in as she leans her elbows on the bar.

"Tell me what?" I ask.

"She's pregnant," he says to me with a straight face, and

I can't tell if he's happy about this or not.

"Is this good news or bad news?" I ask him.

Setting his drink down, he admits, "I don't know. It's shocking news."

"How does she feel about it?"

"Scared. It wasn't something we had even talked about, and now here we are, not sure what this means for us."

"You two just need to talk and be honest with each other," Mel tells him.

"Like you talk to Zane?" he responds with a chuckle.

She smiles and holds her hands up, surrendering, "Hey, I never take my own advice, I just dish it out."

"Have you heard from him?" I ask her.

"He came home for a couple of days, but it was awkward. All he can talk about is how happy he is in L.A. How happy he is to finally be recording an album. He's my husband, and I'm clueless to what his life is like out there."

"You're choosing to be clueless," Max tells her. "You could easily pack your shit up and be with him."

"He doesn't want me to be. He told me that before he moved there."

Max looks over to me, surprised about that little fact that Mel had told me about when it happened. I haven't talked to Zane since he left, so I don't have any idea what's going on with him.

"Enough of our shit. How did everything with Candace go?" Max asks and immediately Mel's eyes widen. I've never mentioned anything about this to her.

"Who's Candace?"

"A friend," I cautiously tell her, but my words are deceived when I see the look Max is giving me.

"You lie," she says to me. "I'm your only female friend. Have been for the past four years."

I keep a straight face, not sure what to say about Candace, and she picks up on my seriousness when she says, "I knew something was going on."

"What do you mean?"

"Just been noticing your moods these past few months. You're quiet. Well, more than usual," she laughs softly. "Your distance with Gavin, girls . . ." she shrugs her shoulders and adds, "Everything really. So who is this chick?"

"A friend of Jase and Mark's," I tell her and then turn to Max to answer his original question. He knew I was taking her home with me for Christmas, so I tell him, "It went better than expected."

"It wasn't too awkward?"

"What are we talking about?" Mel questions.

"I took her to Oregon."

"What the hell have I missed? You took her to meet your family?" she nearly squeals.

"And no," I say as I turn back to Max. "It wasn't awkward."

"So things are good with you two?" he asks.

"Yeah, man. Things are perfect."

Laughing, Mel says, "How ironic, out of the three of us, Ryan is the one without any hang-ups." She turns to grab a bottle of beer and then says, "I need a drink," before walking away.

I spend most of the night in my office going over supply orders and inventory, double-checking Michael's work to make sure he's handling his shit. I'm not seeing anything out of place, so I call it a night around ten o'clock and head over to Jase's.

When he opens the door, I see Candace lying on his couch.

"She's passed out," Jase tells me. "She's been tired all night."

"What did you guys do?"

"Mark came over for a while and we had dinner. Just hung out though," he says as I walk around the couch to see her sleeping under a blanket.

Sitting down next to her, I lift her head into my lap and run my hand through her hair, telling Jase, "I haven't seen him since you guys got back from Ohio."

He sits down in the chair and watches my hand in her hair before shifting his eyes to me, explaining, "He's been working on some new songs, so he's been busy. Why don't you meet up with us tomorrow before we head up to the bar?"

"I can't. I've got to be there early, but I'll catch up with you guys later," I say as Candace begins to stir and wake up.

Her eyes open as she rolls her head to look up at me. "What's going on?" she mumbles as she sits up.

"Nothing. Just got here."

She lets out a yawn and lazily leans into me, asking Jase, "What're you guys talking about?"

"Mark's gig at the bar tomorrow."

Giving her arm a soft squeeze, I suggest, "You should come."

"Umm . . ."

Jase laughs at her and says, "Just come. You still have never heard Mark play. It'll be fun."

"I don't know."

"We'll all be there," he says, trying to convince her.

She keeps her eyes on Jase, and when he gives her a nod

and says, "Come on. One night," she gives in to him.

"Okay. Fine," she sighs, and I watch as Jase gets an almost victorious smile on his face, not understanding why it's such a big deal for her to go out.

"Wipe that smile off your face, Jase," she scolds with humor. "You're embarrassing me."

Before their banter can continue, I say, "Come on, babe. Let's go. It's getting late," as I stand up and take her hand.

"I'll pick you up tomorrow," Jase tells her and she walks over to hug him goodbye. "I'll call you."

"Night, Jase," she says.

"Bye, guys."

We take the elevator down and she asks, "Why is Jase picking me up and not you?"

"I have to be there early to get some work done so I can take the night off and not have to worry about going in too much this next week. But I'll be there when you and Jase get there."

When the elevator opens, we step out to go back to my place for the night.

"Ryan, how've you been?" Mark says when he walks in with Chasten, the drummer of the band.

"Good, man. How was Ohio?"

"Great. We got a ton of snow, so we were stuck at the house for a couple of days, but we survived," he chuckles.

"Survived?"

"If you knew the women in my family, you'd be scared to be cooped up with them during a snow storm. Luckily, my sisters are like a fresh new toy for Jase, so he just sits back and laughs at their shit while I try and find a way to escape it."

"So I take it you're glad to be back then," I tease.

"Yeah. Oh, hey, Jase said Candace was coming up here tonight. Is that true?"

"Is there something I should know about Candace that I'm not getting?" I ask as I follow him over to the stage so he can start setting up with the guys.

"What do you mean?"

"Why don't you tell me why you're so surprised by the fact that she's coming here?" I question. Maybe I shouldn't, but curiosity gets me.

He sets his guitar down and then turns to me. "Candace likes to avoid crowded places."

"I get that. I just can't figure out why," I tell him, hoping he'll throw me a clue, but he doesn't.

"She's slow to open up, but I'm sure I don't have to tell you that," he says.

"Yeah, I know."

"Just be patient with her." He leaves it at that, and I accept the advice because that's all I can do. I wanna get into my girl's head and unfold everything inside. Patience isn't my strong suit, but it's the only hand I have to play with her.

I go upstairs to get a few files from Michael's desk, and when I walk in, I look out his large window that overlooks the back lot and see Jase's SUV as he turns in. I find the files I need and then watch as Candace steps out of the car. God, I'm falling for this girl. I'm wound up just thinking about getting to spend time with her tonight.

Her back is to the building, so I can't see her face, and I wonder what she's staring at as she stands there. Jase says something to her but she remains standing next to the dumpsters. When she finally moves, her heel catches on the pavement, and she takes a hard fall onto her bottom. As soon as she hits the ground, I watch, numb, trying to make sense of what I'm seeing. She's freaking out, frantically stumbling back on her hands. Jase rushes over and huddles down in front of her, picking her up, and I can faintly hear her screaming.

I snap out of my trance. Tossing the files, I run down the stairs and fly out the back door to see the both of them back in Jase's car. Candace is crying and screaming, and I stand there in near shock, confused as hell by what just happened. As her eyes find mine, she throws her hands against the dash and yells at him hysterically as he peels out of the parking lot.

"Candace!" I yell after her as the car pops the curb when Jase hits the main street.

She's gone, and I don't have a clue what the hell is going on, but I'm freaked out at what I just saw. I don't even think about going back in, I just take the keys that are in my pocket to go to the one place I know she'll be.

While I drive to Jase's apartment building, hitting every damn red light, I replay what happened and try to figure out what she saw that triggered her like that. I pull up to the building and throw my car in park when it hits me.

Holy shit.

Chills prick my arms, and I swear my gut hollows out when the memory of that night floods me.

Oh my God.

She was standing right there. She's small. She's timid. Scared.

No. Get your shit together. It's not her.

My mind is racing faster than I'm able to keep up with. I feel like I'm out of my body and can't decipher reality from my fucked up head-trips. If Candace was *her,* I would know.

I would know, right?

I sit in my car as I feel my emotions swarm into a rotation of visions I wish I could just forget. All I can see is that girl. Her beaten face, her naked, bloody body.

"Fuck!" I slam my fists into the steering wheel, desperately trying to rid the memories, but they're too vivid. I don't even want to think about that girl being Candace. It's too fucked up. Pressing my palms against my forehead, I attempt to pull myself together. I know Candace is with Jase, and I just want her to be with me.

Pressing my head back against the seat, I squeeze my eyes shut and attempt to refocus on the fact that Candace is upset and that I need to get my shit together and quick. I take a few moments and sit here in silence before I finally get out of my car.

On the elevator ride up, I take some deep breaths, and calm myself before I knock on the door. When Jase opens it, he immediately tells me, "Man, it's not a good time."

But I don't care. I just want her. "Where is she?" I ask as I move past him and start walking to his bedroom when I see she isn't in his living room.

"Ryan, just give her space," he yells out to me, but I don't even acknowledge him when I open the door to his room and see my girl sitting on the edge of the bed sobbing.

The sight of her slows me down—stops me. She looks up, and her face is soaked with tears. I feel like the slightest move on my part could snap her, so I gently shut the door behind me and walk over, kneeling on the ground in front of her. I brace my hands on her knees, and I'm at a loss with her. Confused. But she doesn't let me dwell on it when she opens her mouth and begins to cry out, "I'm sorry. I'm sorry, Ryan. I'm . . ."

I reach my arm behind her back and drag her off of the bed and onto my lap. "What happened, babe?"

"I'm so sorry," she continues to say with her hands masking her face.

I hold on to her while she cries, and I'm desperate for answers. Wrapping my hands around her wrists, I move her hands from her face so I can see her. I hate that she's hiding from me. "I need you to talk to me."

She avoids my eyes when she tries explaining, "I just . . . I got myself too worked up and had a panic attack. I know you wanted me there tonight, but I couldn't."

She's still hiding from me, and I'm unsure of how much I should push the issue, so I simply ask, "Why couldn't you just tell me?"

"I was embarrassed," she says when she finally looks at me. "This has happened a few times in the past, but only Jase knows that I have these."

My gut is telling me not to believe her. That she's lying to me. But hearing the pain in her words makes the lie okay in a way. She's not opening up to me, and I need her to so badly. Have her trust me. Have her run to me instead of Jase. So I tell her that because I don't know what else to say to her.

"You could've come to me. Jase isn't the only one you have, you know? I need you to trust me enough to talk to me. I understand you and Jase, but I know how I feel about you." I tell her this because watching her run away from me like she did hurt. Like I'm not enough for her to want me like that, and I need her to, for me.

"I want you to need me more than him," I finally tell her, hoping I didn't just sound like an ass for saying it, but I have to say it.

"He's all I've ever had."

When she says this, I know I have a lot to prove to this girl who clearly doesn't trust so easily. I take her hand and press it against my chest, needing her to know how serious I am when I say, "You have me now too."

I know my words get through to her when she fists my shirt in her hand and slings her other arm around my neck, hugging me close. I feel her tears running down my neck as I hold on to her, so I sit here with her on the floor until she calms down and relaxes under my arms.

Brushing her hair behind her shoulder, I kiss her below her ear before whispering, "Let's go home."

She pulls back and looks up at me. I wipe her cheeks and cup her face in my hands when she says, "I don't want to hurt you."

Hearing those selfless words does something to me. And I'm becoming more aware, every day that I have with her, just how much I'm feeling for her.

I press my lips against hers because I don't know how to respond to her words. So I kiss her, but I don't move, I just take in the warmth of her lips against mine, and it's all I need right now. This is enough.

chapter twenty-three

Coming back to my place, Candace is still being very quiet, but I'm not saying much either. I watch as she walks up to my room, and I give her some space while I grab a beer from the fridge. When I do head upstairs, she's in the bathroom with the door shut, taking a shower. I'm noticing that she takes a lot of those, but figure that right now, she probably wants to be left alone.

I go back downstairs and flop down on the couch, mindlessly flipping through the channels before stopping on ESPN. I can't even focus because my head is still upstairs with Candace. I keep replaying what I saw from Michael's office over and over until I hear the creak of the wooden floor. Turning around, I see her standing at the foot of the stairs. As I walk over to her, I can see she's tired.

"You need anything?" I ask, and she shakes her head.

We walk over to the couch, and she lays her head against me as we sit here. Neither one of us says anything. I know she's embarrassed about what I saw, so I don't mention another word about it.

After watching the football highlights and catching the score updates, I say, "Let's go lie down."

Shutting everything off, we head upstairs and crawl into bed. I pull her onto her side, facing me, and hold her close. Her eyes are closed, and I'm sure she's tired, but I lean down anyway and brush my lips across hers, wanting to be close to her. She reaches up and runs her hand along my jaw as she moves with me. We lie there, no words, in the darkness, as we continue to kiss, and after a while, she shifts down on me, resting her head on my chest and falls asleep.

She keeps me up though. Her sleep grows restless, and I watch her as she begins to tremble. I rub her back, wondering, yet again, what's running through her head. She had a night like this just the other day, but I didn't say anything to her about it when she woke up. My need to comfort her overwhelms me, and I want to take her out of the dream that's haunting her.

I add pressure as I continue to rub her back, trying to wake her subtly, but she startles me when she springs out of her sleep, choking in a hard gasp as she abruptly sits up. I'm up next to her, holding on to her shoulders while her whole body shakes.

"Hey," I whisper. "Are you okay?"

Nodding her head, she takes in a deep breath and holds it for a second before slowly releasing it.

"Come here," I urge as I lay her back down with me, and she snuggles in close. Smoothing her hair back, I kiss her forehead. "Talk to me," I say on a hush.

"I'm okay," she tries to assure me.

"Babe . . ."

"I think I'm just stressed. That's' all."

"About what?" I ask.

"School. Dance," she says. Those seem to always be her go-to excuses for a lot of things, and I know she hides behind them. Uses them to distract her.

"You wanna talk about it?"

"Not really," she responds as she weaves her legs with mine.

Looking into her eyes, I encourage, "I want you to talk to me. I know something is bothering you, and I want you to talk to me about it."

She doesn't speak. I can tell that she's trying to think of something to say, but nothing comes, so I give her an out and tell her, "I just want you to try."

Nodding her head, she closes her eyes and after a while, she falls into another fit of sleep, keeping me up most of the night.

When I wake up, Candace is sound asleep, so I slip out of bed and let her rest since I know she didn't get much sleep last night. Looking down at her, she finally looks peaceful. Everything about her is soft and relaxed.

I head downstairs to grab a cup of coffee as my phone begins to ring. It's Sunday morning, so I know it's my mom. We talk for a while until I hear Candace walking down the stairs.

"Hey, Mom. Candace just woke up, so I'm gonna let you go."

"Let me say a quick hi," she says, and I know she's wanting to try to get to know her.

"Hold on," I tell her and then look up at Candace as I hold the phone out to her, mouthing, 'My mom.'

Probably feeling a little awkward, she takes the phone anyway, saying, "Hi, Donna."

I listen to Candace talking with my mom while I make her a cup of coffee. She talks about the solo that she's been piecing together for her audition next month. Walking over to her sitting on my couch, I hand her the coffee. She seems comfortable talking with my mom, and I like that she can have this with her, even if it is a random phone call. Both of these women are important to me, and to see Candace laughing at something my mom must have just said makes me feel like whatever it is that Candace and I are moving towards could be something special.

"What did she have to say?" I ask when she hangs up and hands me the phone.

"Just wanted to know what I had been up to," she says and then takes a sip of her coffee. "She's really nice."

We sit back and get comfortable when she starts, "Ryan . . ."

"Yeah?" I say as I slide my arm around her.

"Nothing," she mumbles, dismissing whatever was running through her head.

"Don't say 'nothing,'" I tell her, and when I do, she wraps her hand behind my neck and moves me in for a kiss before she nuzzles her head under my chin. Her instinct to avoid is strong, and I try not to question it because I've spent my whole life avoiding. I think about what my mom told me about not trying to break down her walls. Taking her advice, I don't pry. I'm gonna be what I think she needs so that she'll want to open up to me. I need her to want to do that for me.

Got out of class early. You home?
Yeah. Door is unlocked.

Classes at the university started back up this week, and I'm getting to see how busy Candace actually is with her dancing. She wasn't kidding when she told me that she lives in the studio. With her busy schedule, I've been trying to get most of my work done while she's in class so I can free up my time at night when she's typically not busy, unless she's working.

"Ryan?" I hear Candace call out when she gets here.

"Back in my office."

She taps on the door before walking in.

"Hey, babe. Come here."

She walks around my desk, and I reach out to pull her onto my lap. Brushing the hair off her shoulder, I ask, "How were your classes today?"

"Uneventful, but it's only the first week," she tells me. "Nothing but going over the syllabus for the most part."

"I'm glad you're here. I've missed you," I say and then bring her head down so I can kiss her. She looks good in her jeans and fitted sweater. She's always so pulled together, even when she wears her old college t-shirts. She always has a polished look about her that I find really attractive.

"So, don't be mad, but . . ."

"Oh, God," I interrupt because it sounds like she's up to something that I *would* be mad at.

"Just listen," she says as she pokes me in the ribs. "When I was on campus today I ran into Stacy Keets who works at the Henry Art Gallery. She was telling me that one of her pieces got picked up for a gallery show next month."

"So, you want to go?"

"Yes, but I was thinking that you could submit one of your photos."

There's the kicker. "Babe," I say as I shake my head. "Those are just a hobby that I hardly even take seriously. I'm far from having them displayed in a gallery of all places."

She rolls her eyes at me, dismissing my words when she

says, "Well, I happen to love the few photos I've seen. They're a lot better than you think they are."

"You're cute," I tease. The fact that she can view those pictures as something worthy of being displayed as art is a bit far-fetched for me.

"I'm serious, I think that you should at least submit something and see if it gets accepted. If not, nothing lost, right?"

"And if they are?"

A smile crosses her face as she says, "Then you can take me as your date for the showing."

"If I say I'll think about it, will that suffice?" I ask, but truth is, I'd take this girl anywhere for a date, so if that means submitting a few pictures, I'll do it.

"Yep." She looks like a kid who just convinced her parents to buy her an ice cream, and I can't help myself when I bury my head in her neck and start playfully ravishing it, knowing how ticklish she is in the spot I'm nipping. She squirms, laughing hysterically as she tries to wriggle her way off of my lap, and when she finally manages, she catches her breath and says, "Show me all your photos so I can pick out the ones for you to consider submitting."

Clearly I don't get any input in her little mission. Sliding the door to my credenza open, I pull out the stack of mattes and hand them to her.

"Here, boss," I say with a wink.

When she turns to head out into the living room, I follow and offer, "Want something to drink?"

"Yeah, anything hot."

I begin to heat up some water and pull down the tea she likes. She's been spending more time here, so we took a trip to the store, that way I could have some of her staples here at the loft. I love seeing pieces of her in my home, even if it's as simple as a canister of her Harrods Ceylon tea that she brought over the other day. As I dip the tea bag in the mug, I look up, and she has the mattes lying facedown on the coffee table.

"I'll be right back," she mumbles before rushing off to the bathroom.

Shit. She hadn't seen all the photos before, and I can only assume that she didn't like what she saw. They're mostly nudes, but she had to have known that by the few she had already seen.

I give her a few minutes, but when she doesn't come back out, I give the door a light knock.

"What are you doing?" I ask suspiciously, even though I have a pretty solid idea as I step into the bathroom with her. When I take a step toward her, she takes a step back, keeping the distance, and the gesture irritates me. "Babe, what's wrong?"

"Nothing." She's being evasive, and I wish she would just be honest with me.

I drop my head and let out a deep breath, trying to control my frustration with her.

"Is it the photos?" I ask, already knowing the answer, but I feel like I need to spell it out for her because I know how much she likes to avoid talking when she's uncomfortable.

She doesn't answer, but her brows are scrunched with worry, and it's all the confirmation I need.

"Candace, you asked to see them. You knew what they would be of."

"I know," she admits as she lowers her head and looks at the floor. "I'm sorry. I didn't think they would all be like that."

Leaning against the sink, I cross my arms around my

chest. I hate that I feel like I have to explain myself when I've been nothing but open with her, but I do it anyway. "They're just pictures, that's all."

She takes a seat on top of the toilet lid and says, "But . . . they just seem so intimate."

"Babe, don't." I drop my arms, hating that she feels this way because she's got it reversed. There was nothing intimate when I took those photos. I have no connection to them.

She looks up at me, and I see the hesitation in her eyes when she quietly asks, "Did you sleep with them?"

"Yes." I respond immediately, not wanting to bullshit her. Wanting to be completely transparent with her the way I wish she would be with me.

"How many have you . . .?"

"A lot."

"And you photograph them?" Her words are laced with disbelief, and she's got it all wrong, so I try to explain it to her.

"No. I've only photographed a couple of women. Most of those photos are the same person."

"Oh." Dropping her head, she tries hiding her insecurities that I can see right through. She's so opposite of what I know she is comparing herself to. She's modest and private. It's been three weeks since Christmas and she's never let me touch her, see her, anything.

Kneeling down in front of her, I grip her thighs and speak firmly when I say, "I know what you're doing, and you can stop. None of them meant what you mean to me. I never had or wanted a relationship with them."

"Then why?" she tries to argue, and I can't stand seeing her doubt herself, doubt me.

I take her hands in mine, holding them, when I look into

her eyes and give her another piece of me that only she gets to have. "Because for most of my life I've been lost," I confess. "I dealt with a lot of shit growing up, and I used women as a way to escape. But when I met you . . . you're just different. I wanted to know you, really know you. You're nothing like those women. Nothing. I've never looked at them or wanted them the way I do you."

"I don't know what I'm doing," she says, unsure of herself, but I feel the same way, so I tell her.

"I don't either."

"I mean . . . I haven't . . ."

"Been with anyone?" I ask, my words slipping out, wondering if that's why she's moving so slowly with me.

I know I've embarrassed her when she covers her face and doesn't say anything, but I'm not appeasing her this time by letting her avoid me. I need her to start talking and stop being afraid that I'm gonna judge her.

Grabbing on to her hips, I pull her down onto my lap, taking her hands away from her face.

"Talk to me."

She takes a moment before she finally exposes a part of herself to me. "Only once, but he was really drunk and it . . . well, it was pretty much over before it began."

God, this chick is practically a virgin, and the thought of some guy using her gets under my skin. Shit, just the thought of any guy, other than me, touching her makes me jealous as hell.

"Sounds like an asshole."

"He was," she responds. "But it kept my parents off my back. They really liked him and his family, so we would go out every now and then, but that was about it. So, I can't help but sometimes wonder what you're doing with me."

"Look at me," I demand because I hate that she would

belittle herself for even a second. "I don't give a shit how inexperienced you are. In fact, I prefer that because the thought of another guy touching you pisses me off. That guy was a dick for treating you like you were disposable. But don't devalue yourself because of that. I won't rush you into anything. You know that, right?"

When she nods her head, I try to make it even clearer when I add, "You're what I want. No one else, okay?"

"I just get scared, and I feel like you might start thinking you're wasting your time with me. I know you'd prefer that I stay here with you every night, but that's what scares me. I just need to move slow with this."

"You're not a waste of my time. You're worth every second."

If she only knew how I take in every moment with her, she wouldn't have to even question this. So when I see her nodding and letting out a sigh, almost in relief at my words, I take her face in my hands and kiss her. Slow. Because time doesn't matter to me with her. I don't even move; I just rest my lips on hers. It's only when she slips out a giggle that I pull back, and with a smirk, ask, "What?"

"Can we get off your bathroom floor now?" she says with a smile, and I have to laugh at her, happy to see that she's feeling better about this situation. At least I hope she is.

"Let's get out of here," I suggest and stand to help her up off the floor.

"Where are we going?"

"Let's go hang out at Zoca's and get some coffee."

"Perfect."

chapter twenty-four

Yesterday, after Candace got upset about seeing the photos, I took her to a local coffee shop where we ran into Gavin. I was nervous having Candace meet him, someone who knows way too much of my past, after she had just gotten a glimpse of it. Oddly, he wasn't as brash as he normally is, and the two of them seemed to get along for what small talk they wound up having, which wasn't much.

I've definitely put space between us, but I've known him for nearly ten years, and it's strange not having him be more of a presence. He stops by the bar on occasion to listen to bands and grab a drink, but it's not like it used to be.

I turn around from my desk, sliding the credenza open to take out a few files that I need to run up to the bar, when I see the mattes that I had thrown in here last night. I hate that Candace had to see those. I didn't consider her reaction then, but now, I regret ever showing her. I don't blame her for being so upset, having to see images of women from my past, knowing that I had slept with them. It's something we haven't done with each other, haven't even come close, and I tossed those images out there for her without thinking about how hard it would be for her to see.

I don't even want to think about her kissing another guy, touching another guy, but to see images like that . . . I know I would have lost my shit, so I can't hold her reaction against her. She has every right.

These photos are my past, a past where I never considered meeting a girl like Candace. A past full of masks, trying to hide from the person I was scared to be. A person that I am now realizing I might be able to be—because of her. Because she is the one I want to take care of—protect. No girl has ever made me feel that way, but she does, and wanting to love her is so much more powerful than my fear of loving her.

Grabbing the mattes, I head downstairs to my garage and don't give it a second thought when I toss them in the trash. They have no meaning to me, and she doesn't need reminders of my past lying around my home. I don't need the reminders either.

When I go back upstairs, I grab the files and my keys and head over to the bar. When I get there, I run into Max out in the parking lot, and he follows me up to my office.

"How's everything with Traci?" I ask as he shuts the door, and I sit down at my desk.

"I'm freaking the hell out, man," he says, running his hand over his head.

I chuckle under my breath. I've never seen him this tense. "You've gotta relax."

"Relax? Dude, we're talking about a fuckin' baby."

"You asked her to move in with you. You were all ready to have her there to share your life with, so what the hell?"

"Yeah, we shared all of, what, five months?" he says.

"But you guys have been together longer than that."

"Yeah, but I never really considered the whole kid thing," he says and pauses before adding, "We went to a

217

doctor's appointment this morning."

"How'd that go?" I ask as I watch him lean back into the chair, fully stressed.

"She's fourteen weeks pregnant."

"I don't know what the hell that means."

"Don't you have like twenty nieces and nephews?" he overstates, and I laugh at this guy's jest.

"Dude, that doesn't mean I know shit about pregnancy."

He sits up and rests his elbows on his knees when he states, "Baby will be here in June."

"It's so weird to think about," I say. "You with a baby. You spend your days barking and intimidating people." We both laugh, and I know he sees the same image I see in my head.

"Ugh," he groans. "Can we talk about something else, like you and your very unpregnant girlfriend?"

I shake my head when he continues, and asks, "When am I ever gonna meet this chick? You should bring her up here."

"I tried."

"What does that mean, 'I tried'?"

I've always been honest with Max about Candace, but I also know how private she is, so I just tell him what she's told me, which isn't much. "She has a thing with crowds. They make her uncomfortable. She tried coming, but it was too much for her."

"What's up with the crowds?"

Shrugging my shoulders, I admit, "I don't know. She doesn't say anything beyond the fact that she doesn't like them."

"Have you asked?"

"I don't feel like I can."

"I don't get it," he says, but I feel like I'm saying too much at this point, so I cut it off.

"She's doesn't like crowds; it's probably as simple as that."

He catches my intent and backs off, not saying anything else about it.

Hey! You home?

On way now. Leaving gym.

Mind if I stop by?

Not at all. Be there in 10.

See ya!

After I left work the other night, Candace came over and she spent yesterday here as well. I didn't want her to leave my bed this morning, but she had to go into work since one of the guys quit unexpectedly, so I decided to hit the gym with Jase and Mark to kill some time.

I leave the door unlocked when I get home and run upstairs to grab a quick shower. After throwing on some clothes, I leave my hair wet when I think I hear Candace downstairs.

"Hey, babe," I say while I walk down the stairs and see her riffling through the drawer in one of the end tables in the living room.

"Hey."

Walking over to her, I cradle her face and give her a kiss before asking, "What are you scrounging around for?"

"Your mattes. I can't find them."

"That's because they're not here," I tell her and then claim her mouth with mine again, taking my time and not backing away, but that doesn't stop her from mumbling over my lips.

"Where are they?"

"I tossed them."

She pulls back and breaks the kiss when she questions surprisingly, "What?! Why?"

"Because they made you uncomfortable."

"But I was looking for the photo of the woman's back so I could submit it to the gallery."

She looks disappointed when she says this, and I tell her, "I don't have it. I threw them all away."

She's frustrated when she falls back into the large chair. I move to sit on the edge of the coffee table in front of her and lean forward, asking, "What's wrong?"

"Nothing, I was just excited to submit that photo." She leans her head back and looks up at the ceiling, saying, "Maybe it was a stupid idea."

"Is it that important to you?"

"I just thought if you saw one of your pieces in a showing, that you would see the art in it."

Thinking about how I could just photograph her, I smile when I say, "It wasn't difficult to capture or enhance. I can recreate it if you want."

"We don't have time for you to find someone to pose. It needs to be submitted tomorrow by the end of the day."

"We don't need to find anyone," I tell her, already excited about being able to get photos of her. "Let's go upstairs. I'll shoot *your* back."

She immediately blushes. "No."

"No, what?"

"I'm not taking my top off for you to photograph me."

"You don't have to take anything off, promise. It's an extreme close-up; you only need to hike it up a little," I try to assure her. Her inhibition is nothing that I'm not aware of, but I also want her to be comfortable enough with me so that we can start to move forward.

"What?" she questions when I stand up and take her hand.

"We're going upstairs."

"Ryan, no."

She tugs her hand out of mine, and I ask, "What's wrong?"

"It feels weird to me."

"Don't let it."

"You just can't say that and expect me to be okay. I'm not like the girls you took those pictures of. I'm . . ."

"No, you're not. You're nothing like them, which is why I threw them in the garbage." I move to kiss her, needing her to just relax, knowing it's just the two of us and no one is judging. When I pull back, I look at her and affirm, "I only want you. No one else. The only photos I want are ones of you."

She hesitates, but then she nods. I want her to do this, so I don't say anything else as I walk her upstairs. Letting go of her hand, I leave her in the center of my room as I go into the closet to get my camera, and when I return, she's still in the same spot. I let her be while I pull the drapes shut, blacking out the room before taking her hand and leading her to the bed.

"Just lie on your stomach," I gently instruct and watch as she climbs up and lies down, folding her arms underneath her head.

Her eyes stay on me as I crawl onto the bed next to her. Her body flinches when I take the hem of her shirt between my fingers.

"I'm just going to lift it up a little."

It's just her back, but she always keeps herself covered up, and I can't help myself when I drag my knuckles along her spine as I lift her shirt up and then tuck it under the strap of her bra. Her skin is milky and flawless. Perfect.

She takes a deep breath and I ask, "You okay?"

"Mmm hmm."

I notice her eyes are closed when I get off of the bed to kneel beside it. Picking up my camera that I haven't used in months, I begin to adjust the settings for the lack of light in the room. I shift my eyes to see she's watching me, and I give her a small smile then bring the camera up to my eye to set the flash.

"I'm gonna take some test shots to get the shutter speed right, okay?"

Resting my elbows on the mattress, I move in close to her back and capture a few images to make sure the lighting isn't distorting her lines. When I look at the shot, I notice that there isn't much curve to her back, so I take a pillow from the bed.

"Here, lean up." She pushes her chest up from the mattress, and I wedge the pillow under her as I explain, "I just need a little more curve to your spine. Just lie down and relax."

Kneeling back down, I aim the camera close to her back and softly murmur, "That's perfect," and I begin to shoot. I only take about ten quick shots when I set the camera down because everything about this is turning me on.

I've never felt anything when taking pictures in the past, but this . . . this feels intimate. Looking at her lying on my bed. I know she feels exposed, and I can see how tense her body is. But for the first time, I feel like we're connecting in a way that we haven't before. That she's starting to trust me.

I pull her shirt out from her bra and lower it back down, covering her again before I lean over her, bracing my hands on the bed.

"Thanks," I whisper, and she rolls to her side as I lower

myself next to her.

I move in and lightly graze my lips across hers, just wanting the feel of her before I cover her mouth with mine. She tangles her hands in my hair, and everything about her touch makes me want her. And even if this is all she'll give me right now, it's more than the meaningless sex I've had with all of those other women. Everything is so much more with her, and I can't help but think about what it will be like when we finally get there. If just kissing her feels like this, I can't even imagine what I'm in for.

I roll her onto her back, finding it hard to control myself. I run my kisses down her neck and across her collarbone. She grips my arms, and her hold is tight on me when I reach down and grab on to her thigh, needing more of her as I run my hand slowly up her leg. Burying my head in her neck, she clamps her hand around my wrist, stopping my hand from moving between her legs.

Pulling back, I look over her face, but she keeps her eyes down and then whispers, "Sorry." But there is nothing about this that she needs to be sorry for because I can feel her trying, and that's all I need from her.

"You don't ever have to be sorry," I tell her as she looks up at me. "God, you're beautiful."

She doesn't respond when I tell her this, but it's okay. I've never ached for anyone like this. I've never ached to touch someone so badly before. So to hold back with her hurts because it's the last thing I want to do. But I know I'm falling in love, so I do it.

Taking her hand in mine, I hold it as I run my other hand through her hair.

"Stay with me," I tell her, not wanting to spend the night without her.

"I told you, I can't."

"You mean you won't," I respond. She's spent the past two nights here with me and told me this morning that she was going to go home tonight. I get that she doesn't feel comfortable being here every night, but I don't want her to go either.

"Ryan," she breathes out. "Don't make me feel bad."

"I don't want to make you feel bad; I just want to keep you in my bed," I say with a sly grin to lighten the mood because I really don't want to make her feel bad for wanting a night in her own bed.

She shakes her head at me, then pulls me down to her and kisses me, holding me close. We continue like this for a while and it makes the anticipation so much worse when I keep thinking about what it would be like if she would just let me touch her. So when she finally does leave, I take that anticipation to the shower.

Turning the water on hot, I let it wash over me as I allow my mind to run free. God, I want her, and the more time I have with her, the harder it is to control myself. Having her stop me when all I wanted was to keep running my hand up her thigh. To know what she feels like. To let myself go with her.

I can't hold back when I fist myself in my hand, imagining her soft skin against me. Fantasizing about having her naked in my bed and how she would look. My mind begins to lose itself in a myriad of thoughts when I finally zone in and see her so clearly.

She lies underneath me, running her hands along my chest, with a sated look on her face while I move inside of her.

The intense vision causes me to catch my breath, and I have to brace my hand on the tile wall, dropping my head.

Her legs wrap around my hips, pulling me in deeper,

gripping my hair in her hands. Her body is warm against mine while she moves with me. She's into it, losing herself.

The hot water runs down my back, and my shoulders tense as I begin stroking myself faster.

I drag my tongue over her nipple and suck it into my mouth, making her breathe my name for more.

Tightening my grip, I work myself through my heady breaths.

Sitting back on my knees, she rocks her hips into me, bowing her back off the bed as I run my hands up her torso and between her breasts. She's completely exposed to me. Her naked flesh, smooth, damp with sweat.

My muscles tighten, and I feel myself swell as I'm about to go.

She's moaning.

I'm panting.

Running my hands inside of her thighs, I slide my thumb over her wet core as she throws her head back into the pillow.

"Uhh, fuck," I moan out when I finally feel the pulses of release I've been needing from the eagerness that's been building up inside of me. I let it go as my head falls back while I ride out the images that are still reeling in my mind. The air is thick with steam, and when I'm able to stand without the support of the wall, I turn the heat down on the water to cool off before I get out.

After my shower, I get ready for bed and slide under the covers, replaying our evening together. Thinking about how she looked when I was photographing her. Realizing, that in her own way, she was finally opening herself up to me with her trust. It wasn't obvious, but I saw it anyway.

I grab a pillow from her side of the bed, and smile at the thought that I've allowed a girl to claim a side of my bed.

But I have and I like it. Rolling onto my side, I wrap my arm around her pillow and can smell her on the fabric. She smells so good; I know I'll never grow tired of it, so I lie there as she finds a way to flood my mind again.

Fuck, I need another shower.

chapter twenty-five

Candace stopped by a few days ago to pick up the photo after I finished enhancing it. I think she was surprised to see herself like that. Even if it was just the sway of her back, the photo was beyond sensual. For some reason, she's really uncomfortable with exposing herself. She's confident in her body—it would be odd if she wasn't, being a dancer and all—but being comfortable with herself in a sexual way doesn't seem to come easily for her. It could just be that she's never been that way with a man, but I see her starting to try with me.

The whole thing got me thinking about how I spend my time. Candace keeps herself busy with work and school, but mostly with dance. She loves it; it's her passion in life, and I admire her focus. I don't have a focus like that in my life, and although she takes it a step beyond most people, I feel like I need to find something outside of work and Candace to do with my time. I talked to her about this yesterday on the phone, and she encouraged me to spend more of my time working on my photography.

I've always enjoyed the editing aspect of it, but never took a whole lot of pleasure in the actual shoots until last weekend when she let me shoot her. She made me a very loose promise that she would let me photograph her again, and I plan on holding her to her word.

I hear my phone chime in the next room, and I'm surprised to see Gavin's name when I open his text.

You at work?

Home. What's up?

In the area. Mind if I stop by for a while?

Come on over.

After the random run-in that Candace and I had with him the other week, I didn't think I would actually hear from him when he said he would be in touch. But when he gets here, he says he just wanted to stop by and catch up. So we crack open a couple of beers and flip on ESPN, hanging out like we used to do, simply killing time.

"So I ran into Max and his girlfriend the other night," he tells me.

"Oh yeah, where at?"

"Lakeside," he says and then takes a pull of his beer before adding, "Did you know she's pregnant?"

"Yeah, man. I knew."

Shaking his head, he says, "I couldn't believe it when he told me that shit. We used to have so much fun before he got tied down with that chick. Speaking of chicks, who was that girl you were with the other day?"

Looking over at him, I don't even know why I'm even gonna waste my time telling him, but I do. "We've been seeing each other."

He gives me a smirk and says, "Nice, man," mistaking my word *seeing* for *hooking up with*.

"No, I mean we're together," I clarify.

Giving his head a questioning tilt, he says, "She doesn't seem your type."

"She's exactly my type."

"You sure about that?"

"Yeah, man. I'm sure about that," I tell him, annoyed with his almost condescending tone.

He takes my hint and changes the subject, asking, "You gonna be at the bar tonight?"

"Yeah. I've been going in on Friday nights to free up my weekends lately."

"A few buddies of mine were gonna hit up Monkey Pub, but we'll stop by to hang out if you have time for a drink."

"Yeah, come by. I think Mark and a couple guys from the band are gonna be there too," I say when there's a knock on the door.

I'm surprised when I open it to see Candace standing there. "Hey, babe! What are you doing here?"

"I wanted to see you before you left for work," she says with a smile before I pick her up off the ground in my arms and give her a kiss, appreciating the unexpected visit.

"I've missed you this week," I tell her when I set her down.

"Sorry. Auditions are in a few weeks, and then I won't be living in the studio."

"Candace!" Gavin says from behind me.

"Hey, Gavin. What are you doing here?"

"Just stopped by to bullshit with Ryan."

She looks up at me, saying, "I'm sorry, I should have called before stopping by."

Before I can respond, Gavin takes her hand and pulls her inside. "Wanna beer?"

"Um, no."

"I'll get you a water," I tell her as I walk by, knowing she just got out of a two-hour studio.

"Thanks."

She takes off her coat, and the two of them sit on the couch. When I return with her water, I hear Gavin making fun of her bun, saying, "What's with the hair, grandma?"

"Don't be a dick," I tell him when I sit down, pulling her to my side.

"I was in the dance studio all day," she says and then takes a long drink of water.

"How'd that go?" I ask.

"It actually went pretty well. My instructor complimented me on my solo."

"Really? That's great, babe."

Candace's instructor has been continuing to ride her ass a lot, so I'm glad today was a good day for her because she's been really upset about it.

"Well, actually all she said was 'That's better,' but coming from her, that's huge."

"You coming out with us tonight?" Gavin asks her.

"Umm . . ." She turns to look at me, and I explain, "Gavin's just coming by the bar tonight with some friends, that's all."

"Oh. No, I've got plans," she tells him.

"What are you doing?" I ask, not remembering her telling me of any plans for tonight.

"I'm going to Jase's to hang out. We haven't had a lot of time to see each other lately."

Wanting to be alone with her for a moment because I need more than the short kiss I got when she walked in, I stand and say, "Come with me to my office before you go."

We start walking down the hall when Gavin snarks, "If you guys are gonna fuck, I'm out."

"Dude!" I snap, pissed that he would say shit like that in front of my girl who already has enough insecurity about this shit.

230

Shrugging his shoulders, he says, "What? It wouldn't be the first time."

I see the way Candace is looking at him. She's embarrassed when he adds, "Just sayin'."

Taking her back to my office, I know she's upset when I close the door and brace my hands on either side of her, caging her against the door, and I see it. It's all over her face. The doubt.

"Sorry about that. The guy has no filter," I tell her lightly. But she isn't looking at me, and she isn't talking.

"Candace," I quietly say as she lowers her eyes to the floor, and I hate that she has to know that side of me. A side I'm ashamed of because I want to give her so much more than what I am. I'm embarrassed that she knows how much I used to use people.

"I'm sorry," I breathe out.

"Did you really do that?" she asks with a shaky voice when she looks at me.

Mortified to have to admit this to her, I nod my head and answer, "Yes."

I watch as her eyes begin to fill with tears, and I instantly hate all my choices before her. She blinks and the tears roll down her cheeks.

"Is that what you want?"

Taking her head and cradling it in my hands, I try to assure her with everything I have when I say, "No. I was miserable then. None of them ever gave me what you give me."

"That's the problem, though. I can't give you what they could."

"You give me everything," I say, trying to convince her of the raw truth as I use my thumbs to wipe the tears from under her eyes. I feel my chest constrict when I try to make her believe my words. "You have more of me than any of them ever had. And when you're ready to move forward, I can promise you that it won't be like what I had with them. It was just empty with them."

I rest my head against hers, wishing I could take back all those times I gave myself away to women I never even cared about. Wishing that it could have always been her because she's all I want. She's all I have ever wanted, and she doesn't deserve to feel like shit because of my past choices.

"I shouldn't be upset. I didn't know you then," she rationalizes.

"You have every right to be upset."

Her next move is much too forgiving, more than I deserve, and I'm not sure how she can be so understanding about all this when she wraps her hands around the back of my neck and draws me down to her lips. I feel like I don't deserve all of the good that's inside of her, and I let out a sigh as she moves her lips over mine and holds me close. Gripping her waist in my hands, I keep my lips on her when I say, "I've missed you."

She seals her lips with mine, kissing me intently as we both cling to one another. The taste of her on my tongue is intoxicating and there's no doubt. There's no question. She has a part of me that I never knew was up for grabs, but she has it.

Parting our lips, I ask, "Stay with me tonight?"

"I can't."

"Why not?"

"I promised Jase I'd stay with him."

I haven't had her in my bed since last Sunday, and it frustrates me to know that she'll be in Jase's tonight and not mine. That she'll be in his arms and not mine. I respect Jase, and I understand their relationship, but I want to be the only man that she shares a bed with.

"You have to work anyway," she says.

"I want you in my bed when I get home."

"Ryan . . ." she whispers, and I know she doesn't want me to push it, so I drop it—for now.

She cups my jaw in her hands and kisses me slowly before saying, "I should go."

After I walk her out and say goodbye for the night, I close the door and turn back to Gavin. "Don't ever say shit like that around her again."

"You really like her, don't you?" he asks, taking in my severity about the matter.

"Yeah, man. I do. And that shit just hurt her. She knows about my past, but she doesn't need you throwing it in her face."

"Dude, I'm sorry. I didn't know you were that serious about her," he says as I walk over and sit down in a chair next to him. "I'm just a little shocked. I've known you for years and never thought I'd see you like this."

"Me neither, but shit changes, Gav."

When I got home from work last night, I found it hard to sleep, thinking about Candace over at Jase's when I just wanted her with me. But it's more than that. She runs to him for everything, she always has, and until I came along, he's all she ever had. But I don't like the feeling that I have to compete, that I have to convince her to let me be that guy for her when she should *want* me to be that guy.

She needs to realize that she can trust me enough to come to me for anything. That she doesn't have to hold back from me. But I also know how I feel about her, and I don't think any guy would like the idea of their girlfriend sharing a bed with another man, gay or not. Having her in my arms at night is special, and I want her to only share that with me.

I don't know how she's gonna react, but I need to tell her how I feel about this because I don't like losing sleep over it. So I don't even call her to let her know I'm stopping by her house. She's happy when she opens the door and sees me, giving me a hug before taking me back to her room. She's got books everywhere and she gathers them up and shuts down her laptop before joining me on her bed. When she sits down, I decide to go ahead and cut to it.

"I need to talk to you about something."

"Okay," she says curiously as she folds her legs in front of her.

"Look, I get your relationship with Jase, and I haven't ever had any issues with it, but I don't like that you guys still sleep together," I tell her honestly, laying it out there.

"But, it's not like that."

"I know," I tell her, completely understanding their relationship. "But I still don't like it."

"But . . ."

I turn to face her straight on, placing my hands on her knees when I explain, "I know it isn't like that with you two. I get it. But I don't like the thought of you in bed with another man holding you. I want to be that guy. I want you to want me to be that guy, not Jase." My voice cracks when I say that last part because it hurts me to even have to ask her to want me like that.

"I want you to be that guy, but I don't know how," she tells me, and I'm glad she isn't shutting down, but instead, opening up. "Jase is so unthreatening to me because he's just my friend."

"Why do you think I'm threatening?" I ask, bothered that

after all this time together, she's still scared of me.

I notice her nerves hitting her when she begins squeezing her hands together, but she continues to talk when she admits, "Because you could easily walk away from me."

"You think it would be easy for me to walk away?" I ask, dumbfounded that she can't see right through me to know how I feel about her. "It wouldn't be easy, babe. And I doubt there is anything you could say, or do, that would make me want to walk away. It kills me that you're so scared of me."

She takes a moment before she locks her eyes with mine, and finally gives me a piece of her that I've been dying for when she reveals, "You're the only person I've ever felt this way about, and I don't want to lose you."

Her words hit hard, and I just need to be close to her when I shift to my knees and lower her onto the bed, kissing her. Slowly. I hold her head in my hands, and I can't go another day without exposing my feelings to her, so when I break away, I give it to her.

"You're not gonna lose me, babe. I love you too much to let you go."

She's doesn't even need to say it back to me. I don't need the verbal affirmation because the tears that spill out of her eyes and down her temples are all I need to know that she loves me too. She nods her head, telling me in her own way before I lean down and cover her sweet lips with mine. She opens her mouth and I take more of her, caressing her tongue with mine. When I do this, she grabs my hair and pulls my weight on top of her.

Shifting slightly to the side, I drag my knuckles along her bare skin between her shirt and pants. Her muscles tremble under my touch, but she does nothing to slow me down. I pay attention to her cues, cautious to not push her too far when I slowly slip my hand under the hem of her top and begin running it up the span of her stomach. Her breathing grows heavy, and her grip on me tightens when I hit the bottom of her bra. I stop my hand, waiting for her permission, and it's in this moment that I realize she has her head buried in the crook of my neck.

"It's okay," she breathes against my skin, and suddenly, I feel too much.

Dropping my mouth onto her shoulder, I kiss and gently suck along the curve of her neck. When I slide my hand over her breast, she lets out a soft whimper, and I hold her in my hand, feeling the lace against my skin.

"God, you're perfect," I whisper against her lips.

When I graze my thumb over her hardened nipple, she pushes her head harder into my shoulder, and I need to see her.

Pulling my head away from her, I say, "Don't hide from me, babe."

She's timid when she lowers her head onto the pillow and opens her eyes. I watch her as I run my fingers along the edge of the lace, touching the smooth skin of her chest. I can see the tension in the crease between her eyes as her brows pinch together. She's in her head and not here with me. Wanting her to stop thinking so much, I gently squeeze her small breast in my hand, and when I do, she grabs my face and pulls me down, kissing me.

Her legs tangle with mine, but her body is stiff as she keeps still beneath me. Hearing the way she's breathing though is hot as hell, and I want to feel more of her. So I hook my fingers under the seam of her bra and tug the fabric down, but when I do, her whole body instantly locks up.

"Please, don't." Her words come out quick, and I immediately slide my hand out from under her top, and move it to her head, threading my fingers in her hair. "I'm sorry."

I hate hearing those words from her. I hate that she feels like she's doing something wrong.

"Look at me," I say, and the words come out strong. "When we're together like this, I don't ever want you to be sorry for anything, okay?"

She nods her head, and I soften my tone with a kiss before telling her again, "I love you, babe."

I never thought I would say those words to a girl. Never thought I would be able to open myself to being vulnerable enough to feel those emotions, but with her, it comes so easily. I realize now that the hard part was keeping myself so far removed, seeking the disconnect, but with her, I crave the connection. It's all I want with her.

chapter twenty-six

"What are you doing?" I ask when I see Candace walking down the stairs still in her pajamas. "Get that cute, little ass of yours upstairs and change into your running gear. It's already after seven."

She walks into the kitchen to where I am and says, "I'm gonna pass," as she pulls down a coffee mug from the cabinet.

"You passed a couple days ago too. What's going on?" I ask. Candace loves running, so I don't get the sudden aversion.

"Nothing," she says while she stirs the sugar into her coffee and takes it to the living room.

"Not buying it," I call her out. "What's up?"

"I can't tell you," she says coyly when I sit down next to her as she leans back, propping her legs across my lap.

"You can tell me anything. Now spill it," I say while I run my hand up her calf and behind her knee. I love these legs.

"Uh uh," she says with a shake of her head. "You'll make fun of me."

"Now I've *got* to know," I respond with a much too curious grin.

"You can't tease me. I get enough of that from Mark and Jase."

"I can't promise you that, babe. Come on. Out with it. Why won't you run with me anymore?" I question.

"Because I'm scared," she says and then quickly takes a conveniently long sip of her coffee.

"Scared of what?"

"We're almost out of creamer."

"That's because you use a crap-load of it. Stop trying to distract me. Scared of what?" I ask again.

She takes a moment, and I can tell she's trying to hide her grin when she admits, "I'm scared I'm gonna break my leg or something."

"From running?" I ask as a chuckle slips out under my breath.

Nudging me with her foot, she says, trying to defend, "Yes, from running. It could happen."

"From running?" I repeat. "Candace, you're not gonna break your leg. That's ridiculous."

"Okay, maybe not a break," she says when she sets her mug down on the table. "But something could happen. Pulled muscle, strained ligament. That would ruin everything. My audition is in a few weeks, and getting this solo could be the difference between having a job after graduation or not." Although I find her seriousness amusing, she is, in fact, completely serious.

"Okay, so no running. Well, I'm proud of you for walking down the stairs this morning without any assistance. That was a big risk," I joke with complete mockery, and this time, when she nudges me, I grab her ankle and shift to move between her legs. "You're putting your tiny feet in a dangerous situation when you nudge me like that," I say and then kiss her along the ticklish spot on her neck.

She begins to giggle and squirm underneath me when she tries to throw out a firm tone as she says, "Are you threatening me, Ryan Campbell?"

"You're cute," I continue to tease as I devour her neck with my mouth, and she can't seem to manage to get any words out around her fit of laughter. When I pull away, she has a wide smile, but it fades with her laughter. She stares up at me and doesn't say anything.

"What is it, babe?"

"Nothing," she says softly.

"Tell me."

"It's just . . . You give me butterflies. That's all."

Looking down at that pretty face of hers, I tell her, "Fuck butterflies. I feel it all when I'm with you," before kissing her. She grips my shirt in her hands, and I decide to forego the run to spend the morning making out with her.

I haven't seen Candace much in the past couple of days now that I'm losing out on my morning runs with her. So when she texts me that one of her lectures got cancelled, I jump on the opportunity to snag some time with her even though I'm hanging out with Gavin.

In Fremont. Do you have enough time to meet me?

Yeah. Where are you?

The Barrel Thief.

In the middle of the day?

The Barrel Thief is a well-known wine and whiskey lounge that works with one of the distributors that Blur deals with. The owner called me this afternoon to swing by and sample some of the new ales he got in, and when Gavin called to hang out, I invited him along.

Think of it as a work thing. ;) I'm here with Gav.

I'll be there in 10.

When she walks in and takes off her raincoat, she slides into the booth next to me with a big smile on her face.

"What's that smile all about?" I ask.

"You two are the only ones in here. Are they even open?"

"Ryan has good connections," Gavin says, and when I kiss her temple, I tell her, "The owner is a friend of mine. Wanted to show me what one of his distributors was able to get him."

"Where's he at?"

"Had to take a call. Here, try this," I say as I slide the glass over to her.

She takes a sip and says, "That's surprisingly good. What is it?"

"Maudite. It's from Chambly. Good, huh?"

"Yeah."

"Figures she would like it," Gavin says with a smile.

"Why's that?" Candace asks him, and he responds with, "'Cause it's the most expensive."

She laughs at him, saying, "You're cheap."

"With girls? I tend to be," he jokes with her.

"I feel bad for them," she shoots back, and he agrees with a chuckle, "Me too."

I watch their banter, and I'm relieved that what happened at my loft last week isn't playing into Candace's attitude towards him.

"Are you drinking your water?" she asks me, and I hand it to her.

"So how long do you have?" I ask.

"About an hour before my studio begins. It's my three-hour day and then I have to work the late shift tonight, so I won't be over till after eleven."

"Okay," I say as I reach over to hold her hand.

"Hey, Candace," Gavin says, and the next words out of his mouth come as a shock to me when he tells her, "Look, I feel bad for the shit I said the other day. I'm sorry if I embarrassed you."

Never have I seen Gavin own up and apologize to anyone. It's out of character for him, and I appreciate that he would do that.

"Thanks, Gavin," she says to him, and I can see that she appreciates the gesture as well.

"It was a dick thing to do."

"Don't worry about it. Really," she tells him.

We spend the rest of our time chatting about nothing in particular, and then head out after making plans to stop by Gav's place in a few days.

When I pull up to Candace's house to pick her up, I see her roommate's car sitting in the drive. Candace has been trying to avoid her for the past couple of days after Kimber upset Candace when she told her that she wanted her to move out after graduation. I couldn't get a clear answer when I asked about the rift between them, but I hated seeing her so upset when she told me about the conversation.

"Hey, babe. You ready?" I ask when she opens the door and steps out into the cold mist.

"Yeah."

I help her into the car, and when I get in and start driving to Gavin's place for the party he's throwing, I ask, "How's everything with Kimber?"

"She's been in her room all evening. There's just nothing to say."

"You could at least try talking to her," I suggest, but it doesn't surprise me when she shuts down the idea.

"It wouldn't do any good," she says softly as she looks out the side window. I reach over and pull her hand into my lap, deciding not to mention it anymore.

Pulling up to Gavin's house, I park along the curb that's lined with cars. It's been a while since I've been over to his place, but the past couple times we've hung out since that awkward day at my loft with Candace, it seems that he's been trying to make an effort, so I'm here, reciprocating.

I take Candace's hand in mine as we walk inside. There aren't a ton of people here yet, and she doesn't seem to be affected as I start introducing her to a few buddies of mine. I think I'm more uncomfortable than she is, but I know what they're thinking about her—about what I'm doing with her—and I'm already regretting bringing her here. These people know my past all too well, but for them, my past is still my present because I don't talk to them all that often, aside from the infrequent run-ins when they drop by the bar.

"It's about time you guys showed up," Gavin says when he walks over to us. "Help yourself to whatever is in the kitchen."

"Hey, Gav," Candace says.

"Hey, gorgeous. I can't believe you haven't left this ass-hat for me yet."

Smiling at him, she pokes, "If it weren't for your delicate language, I might consider it."

"Leave her alone," I tell him, feigning irritation, before taking her to the kitchen to get a couple beers. But as soon as we walk in there, my gut confirms that this was a bad idea. Gina is standing with a group of women, and the wink she shoots me makes me very nervous. I hand Candace her beer and send Gina a message when I lean down and give Candace a kiss before taking her back into the living room.

I don't want to say anything because I don't want to draw any attention and embarrass Candace. Plus, last I heard, Gavin was still fucking her, so I'm just hoping that for Gavin's sake, she'll stay away from me.

We take a seat on the couch with one of my old college buddies, and after introducing him to Candace, we begin catching up. I keep my hand on her knee while I talk to my friend, but my mind is elsewhere. Bringing Candace here was more for her than for me. She had expressed to me that she was curious to get to know my friends since I'm now a part of her small circle with Jase and Mark, already knowing so much about the three of them. But these friendships here are superficial. None of them have a clue about Candace, and probably just assume she's a random chick I'm banging. There was a time that I would hang out with these people on a regular basis, but it's been a while.

The evening wears on, and eventually Candace leans into me, saying, "I'm gonna go get another drink. Want one?"

"Yeah, babe. Thanks."

When she heads into the kitchen, Gavin flops down next to me.

"What the fuck is Gina doing here?" I ask under my breath.

"Dude, relax. She's chill."

"You still seeing her?"

Cocking his brow at me, he says, "First off, you know I don't *see* anyone. But I haven't hooked up with her in a while. Between you and me," he says when he shifts himself on the couch, "she was only fuckin' me to get to you."

"What?"

"Yep. Her roommate told me, and that's when I backed away from that crazy bitch," he says with an exaggerated shudder.

"That's sick," I tell him and then add, "And you're trying to tell me she's chill?"

Gavin starts to respond, but I'm no longer listening when Candace walks back into the room, fuming mad. She doesn't even stop when she passes me and snaps, "Take me home," and then heads out the door.

Grabbing her coat, I don't say shit to Gavin or even look back when I go outside.

"Candace," I call out, and when she gets to my jeep, she turns, and I see the humiliation all over her face as she yells at me, "Did you sleep with that girl in there? Gina?"

I release a hard breath, hating that I have to do this to her, but she cuts me off before I can even open my mouth.

"Forget it. Just take me home."

She opens the door and hops in. She's pissed and rightfully so. I knew it was a mistake to bring her to Gavin's. Why the hell would she want to see what I'm trying to forget? I don't know what the fuck Gina said to her, but I hope I never run into her again.

As I start driving back across town, Candace is silent, staring out of her window.

"I didn't know she was going to be there," I start to tell her, needing to clear the air because I can't stand her being upset like this. "When I saw her, I didn't want to say anything to draw attention."

She doesn't speak. She only pulls her one knee up to her chest and turns to face out the window, giving me nothing but the back of her head. I don't know if she's crying or not, but the fact that she won't talk to me hurts.

"Candace, say something."

But she doesn't. I know she wants to go home, but I'm selfish and don't want her to run from me, so I take her to my place. Pulling up to my loft, she quietly says, "Ryan, I really just want to go home."

I don't respond when I get out of the car and walk around to open her door. Holding out my hand for her, she doesn't protest when she takes it and follows me inside and up to my room.

"Ryan, what are you doing?" she finally asks when I drop her hand to grab her some clothes from my dresser.

"You're not going home. Here," I tell her when I hand her a pair of my boxers and a t-shirt.

She takes them and makes her way into my bathroom, closing the door behind her. I quickly change, not enjoying a second of this tension, but I'm not letting it go unresolved.

"Ryan," she calls to me when she cracks the door open. "Can you bring me my purse?"

Picking it up off the bed, I go hand it to her before she shuts the door again. It bothers me that I've never seen her undressed. That she always hides herself in my bathroom to change. I've never been so in the dark with a girl before, and I don't know what to make of it.

I turn the lights off but leave the shades on the panoramic windows open so that I can watch the rain that is now falling hard. The moon must be full with the glow of the clouds that casts a faint bluish hue throughout the room.

When she finally comes out of the bathroom, I watch her as she pads across the wooden floor and climbs up onto the bed. I never get tired of seeing her in my clothes, and when she slides in, I instinctively pull her into me, face to face.

"Talk to me," I tell her softly.

She lets out a slow breath and is so forthcoming with me when she says, "I'm sorry. I'm not mad at you, and I shouldn't have snapped at you. I just . . . I don't like feeling the way she made me feel. It's embarrassing."

"She was nothing to me."

Looking down, she hesitantly asks, "When did you . . . I mean . . . How long ago?"

"August or so," I give her honestly. I brush her hair back when she closes her eyes and quietly say, "They were only there to distract me, but when I saw you, you faded everything I needed distracting from."

"Did you love any of them?" she asks when she opens her eyes and looks at me.

"No."

"Do you love me?"

"I've only ever loved you," I assure her, not even wanting to think about the absurdity of her question.

When I roll myself on top of her, she doesn't miss a beat when she pulls me down and kisses me. It's strong and sure. It's the first time she has ever kissed me this way, and I feel like I need it right now. The confirmation that we're okay. I return her intensity when I dip my tongue inside of her mouth and start running my hand down her neck, over her shirt, and between her breasts. She fists my hair, and I'm gone.

My desire for closeness takes over, and I need to feel her skin against mine. Slipping my hand under her shirt, I notice she's still wearing her bra when I take her in my hand. Her nipple hardens as I slide it between my two fingers, and when I press them together gently, her body arches up into mine, and I can't control the moan that comes out of me.

"God, I want you," I whisper when I sit back on my heels and pull her up to me. I can see it in her eyes, the want, so I don't ask as I slowly start peeling her shirt off when she lifts her arms up.

Tossing the shirt aside, I look at her as I gradually run my hands down her sides. She's perfect in her purple lace bra. She doesn't have large breasts, but fuck, she's sexy as hell, and I just want my hands all over her.

I peer into her eyes when she cups my face in her hands, and my heart starts beating in a way it never has before. "Babe . . ."

As I lay her back down, I drag my lips along her neck as she holds on to the sides of my head while I keep trailing down. I suck her nipple into my mouth, dragging my tongue over the swollen bud. Heat courses through me, and I need to feel more of her when I begin to run my fingers along the underside of her waistband. Hooking them under the fabric, I sit back, and when I slightly tug down, I see it.

No.

Suddenly, reality stabs into my chest, and I feel everything I never wanted to be true pour out of me. Time freezes. I can't breathe, and the panging inside of me is unbearable. I know I can't deny what I see, but I want to. Because it can't be. It just can't.

God, don't let it be.

Slow motion. Everything moves in slow motion as I bring my hand to her hip, and with a trembling thumb, I drag it across what I can no longer blame on head-trips. I brush it again, not wanting to believe what my eyes see. A thin black outline of a tiny heart. *That* tiny heart from *that* night.

The thudding of my chest is painful; it's the most painful thing I've ever felt in my entire life, and before I know it, she slings hers arms around me, but I'm in shock. I can't fuckin' move. I'm too scared.

It can't be her.

Not her.

Not that girl.

Not *my* girl.

Squeezing my eyes shut, it's all I see now. Her bloody thighs. Her beaten face. Her shredded nails.

"God, please! Stop!"

I hear it. Her voice. Her shrieking, desperate voice. Opening my eyes, I'm jittery. She has to feel it. Her body is clung tightly to mine, and I realize that I'm not touching her. I feel like I can't touch her. Like I don't know how, but I force myself to. And when I cautiously wrap my arms around her, I feel her shaking too. And now everything is clear. I can't pretend that I don't know exactly why she's shaking. I'm such a fuckin' dick, rubbing up on this girl because I can't fuckin' control myself around her.

God, what the hell is wrong with me?

Her body begins to soften into mine, and I don't know what to say. How do I tell her? Do I tell her? Do I say something?

Say something.

"Candace."

"Please, don't say anything."

Her voice is pleading, so I don't. And now, I'm scared to take my hands away from her. Like she would break if it weren't for my arms. I keep her close when I lie us down and pull the sheets over us.

She's doesn't say anything else, and the silence rings in my ears. My head is loud. It's a maniacal filtering of memories, flashes weaving together to form a solid image that's undeniable. But I denied it. How could I have done that when it all makes sense now? Every panic, every startle, her fear of crowds, her night terrors, her constant hesitation with intimacy. And fuck. That dumpster. How stupid could I be? She stood *right there.* She panicked . . . in my parking lot. My bar. That's why she's never come back.

I can't be with her.

I have to be with her.

God, I love this girl so much. I can't let her go even though I know I should. But with me, I have the guarantee that she's safe. And I need her. Because it's only with her that I'm finally realizing that I can be the man I never thought I could be, and I don't think I could be this way with anyone else but her.

Lifting up, I scoot back so that I can lean against the headboard, bringing Candace with me and tucking her head under my chin. I don't want to lie to her, but do I tell her who I am? Does she even know that someone was there? This girl has been hurt so much, and by too many people, that I can't have my name added to that list. I can't do that to her. And for what? What difference would it make, if any at all? For this, I resolve to not say anything. I just can't do that to her.

This shit hurts. Bad. And now, every time I close my eyes, I see her lying there naked, raped in the alley of my bar. It's like someone's slowly gutting me. And for the first time in years, I let myself break. Candace has long fallen asleep in my arms when I feel the first of many tears roll down my cheeks and into her hair.

When I release the pain, I see that I hold so much of the blame. I heard her from inside. I heard the banging around, and I ignored it. If I would have just gone out there, I could have saved her. I could have done so much more than I did because I dismissed the ruckus for a couple of drunken guys. She was being raped when nothing but a brick wall separated us. How could I be so irresponsible?

We've taken our slow time getting to know each other, but now I feel like she's different, and I don't know what to do with that feeling. I always knew she was hiding something. Jase even told me that she was going through some tough shit, but *this*? I don't know what to do with this. I feel like an ass for all the times I've tried to touch her in ways that were too much for her and she had to stop me.

I'll never be able to tell her how sorry I am. There aren't enough words. There isn't enough in this world that I could give her to show her how truly fuckin' sorry I am. So I sit here and cry for her because I don't know what else to do. I love this girl beyond anything. Love her from a place in my heart I never knew I had.

So now . . . now she sleeps in my arms while I stay up, because sleep isn't strong enough to take me out of my head tonight. When I close my eyes, it's August, and I'm hovering over my Jane Doe. The girl I spent weeks wondering about. The girl that kept finding her way back into my head, only to realize that I've had her in my arms for months now.

chapter twenty-seven

My head is pounding, and I'm tired as hell. Now that she's awake and moving around my loft, I suddenly don't know how to act. I don't know what to say. This realization has flipped a switch for me, and I don't know how to respond, so I stay quiet.

I'm in the kitchen, fixing her a cup of coffee when she walks over to me and asks, "Did you not sleep last night?"

Screwing on the lid to her mug, I'm evasive when I tell her, "Not much," before handing her the cup and walking into the other room to grab our coats so that I can take her home. I feel like I can't touch her. Like I can't be the same with her. I want to scream and punch my fuckin' fist through the wall. Why did it have to be her? And what piece of shit would do that to her? She's the sweetest thing I've ever known.

Handing her the coat, I ask, "You ready?"

"Yeah," she says shyly as she keeps her eyes down.

She slips it on, and I know that my attitude is making her uncomfortable, so I take her hand in mine as we head outside into the bitter cold.

It only takes a couple of minutes to drive to her house,

and when I pull up and park the car, she turns to me and says, "I'm sorry about last night, and I get that you're mad, but—"

"What?" I interrupt, not understanding what she did that she would need to be sorry for. "Why would I be mad?"

She shakes her head, unsure of herself when she tells me, "Because I keep pushing you away. You've hardly said two words to me this morning. So, I just figured . . ."

Fuck. I've been so wrapped up in myself that I didn't realize I've been a total dick to her this morning. Getting out of the car, I walk over to her side, open her door, and unclick her seatbelt, grabbing on to her hips to face me. I don't know what I'm doing, but seeing the look on her face snaps me out of my fears immediately. I feel like I can't be the same with her, but I have to be. I want to be, because I love what we are together.

I'm firm when I declare, "Everything you give me is perfect. You have to stop feeling like this. I'm here with you, and I'm not going anywhere." Needing her to believe me, I don't hesitate when I take her lips with mine. It bothers me that she doubts herself so much with me. My thoughts are all over the map, but one thing is certain, as hard as this is, I know I can't let it change us. I can't allow it to filter in and affect me because I can't give her any reasons to doubt that I love her from the purest part of me there is.

When I break our kiss, I softly tell her, "I'm sorry if I've been a dick, I just didn't get much sleep."

"It's okay. I overreacted."

But she isn't overreacting because her observations are astute and this is my fault. Taking her hand, I help her out of the car and shut the door, leaning her back against it when I take her face in my hands and look into her eyes, trying to connect in a way so that there is no doubt within her when I tell her, "I never thought I needed anything in this life until I met you. Everything you give me is exactly what I have always needed, and you do it perfectly."

I don't give her a chance to respond when I pull her into me, pressing my lips into hers. Her hands around my back are firm as she holds me close, and I wish she didn't have to go to school because I want to keep her wrapped up in me like this all day.

We say goodbye, and when she's inside, I start driving to work. When I pull into the lot and park, my phone buzzes with a text from Candace.

Can I stay with you?

I've never been so sure of anything when I type out my response.

Of course, babe.

I don't know what happened in the past ten minutes since I dropped her off, but if she needs me, she has me. Sitting in my jeep, I go ahead and call her so that I can make sure everything is all right.

"Hey," she answers apprehensively.

"Did something happen?"

"I'm sorry. I don't want to impose, but I just . . ." she trails off when I assure her, "You're nothing close to an imposition, babe."

"Kimber is here, and it's not good. I just think I should give her some space."

The comfort of knowing that she ran to me, and not Jase, shows me that she's in this, and I love her even more for that. "When do you get out of class?"

"I'm going straight to work after I get out of school, so I won't be home till a little after seven tonight."

"I'll meet you at your place and help you get a couple bags together, okay?"

I hear her release a sigh before she says, "Thank you, Ryan. Really."

We hang up, and when I get out of the car, I can't help myself when I turn to the back of the alley. I walk over towards the dumpster and can see that son of a bitch on top of her again. Shoving his hand between her legs. Slamming his fist into the side of her head. The images unleash a rage inside of me when I think about what happened to her, and the guilt that I was right fuckin' here and didn't protect her from it.

Questions storm inside. Is she a different person now because of it? What did she go through after it happened? What is she going through now? I know she has to be masking the pain because I'm pretty certain that I now know what it is that's constantly causing all of her restless sleep at night. Is that what she dreams about? Fuck! Is that the shit that fills her head when she's in bed with me?

Raking my hands through my hair, I drop my head and spot a small crate of empty bottles. When I can no longer stand the rapid banging of my heart against my chest, I fume as I pick up the whole crate, smashing it violently against the side of the dumpster. Screams grit through my lungs, and the explosion of glass shattering echoes in the quiet morning air.

"What the hell are you doing?" Max yells out from behind me, but I keep my eyes on the shards of glass that are scattered on the ground. The same ground where some fucker . . .

"Ryan, man," Max says and knocks me out of my thoughts when I turn to face him, and the anger inside of me is blatant. It's a force that I can't push down when I yell, "It was her!"

"What are you talking about?" he questions as he moves closer to me, glass crunching under his boots with each step.

"The girl that was raped . . . It's her."

He shakes his head, not piecing it together while my muscles tense up in frustration with everything.

"It's Candace," I breathe out because the constricting of my throat makes it painful to speak.

His face drops, stunned when he asks, "How do you know?"

"Because that girl, she has the same tattoo that I saw on Candace *last fuckin' night*!" Those last words seethe out of me as I pick up a bottle from another crate and barrel it into the dumpster, creating another spray of glass after it smashes into a splattering of pieces. My breathing is heavy as I press my palms to my forehead and admit, barely holding myself together, "I don't want it to be her, man." I can barely choke out the words, but I had to hold my shit together quietly last night and now . . . now it bleeds out.

"Fuck," I hear him mumble before he asks, "What did she say?"

Looking up at him, I tell him, "She doesn't know. I couldn't tell her." When I see the way he's looking at me, like I'm an idiot for not telling her, I shout at him, pleading, "What would I fuckin' say, Max?! What should I have said to her?!" I pause, catching my breath before I continue in a calmer tone. "I love her," I tell him with a defeated shrug of my shoulders. "I can't hurt her like that."

"Has she even told you that she was . . . you know?"

"No," I respond. "I don't think she ever intends to either." I start walking away, not wanting to talk about this shit anymore, and when I pass him, I stop and look over at him. "We're never gonna mention this again. Got it?"

"Yeah, man," he whispers to me. "Got it."

I'm not talking about this shit with anyone. Max knows and that's where it stays. It won't come up again. I won't talk about her like that. Whatever happens, it's private and stays between Candace and me.

Candace's roommate wasn't home when I went over to help her get a few bags packed. Most of her belonging were all ready to go by the time I got there, so it didn't take us too long before we left, which was good because she was really upset about the whole thing.

We spent a while moving things around in my room to make space for her. She didn't want to go through the hassle, but I wanted to make sure that she was comfortable and that all her things had a place in my home. She didn't say how long she was staying, and I told her to play it by ear. I'm just happy that I don't have to say goodbye to her at night anymore. That she will be here every day with me.

Getting into bed, I sit back against the headboard and watch her as she ties her hair up on top of her head.

"Come over here," I tell her as I wrap my arms around her.

She slips her arm around my waist as we lie here. It feels good to have her close after the shit day I've had. She's always has this effect on me, and I've never needed it more than I do now.

When I kiss the top of her head, she runs her fingers along my scar, asking, "How did you get this?"

"My dad."

"Sorry," she says as she looks up at me.

"Why?"

"Because I don't want to bring it up if you aren't comfortable talking about it."

"Babe, I'd tell you anything." She keeps her eyes on me

when I open up to her and show her the side of me that no one else gets to see. "I came home from a party one night and walked in on my father beating the shit out of my mom in our kitchen. He smashed a coffee mug into the back of her head, and I lost it. I started whaling on him. Eventually, he managed to get his hands on a butcher's knife."

"Oh my God," she whispers. I know it can't be easy to hear, but I give her this, knowing that I hold what is probably her darkest secret.

"That's the night he died. He left, and my mom called 911, so we were taken to the hospital by ambulance. The next morning, we were back home, and two cops showed up at the front door to tell me about the car crash."

"I don't know what to say," she quietly admits.

Running my fingers up and down her arm, I tell her, "There's really nothing to say. I hated him. He had beaten the shit out of me my whole life. He didn't even need a reason. Sometimes he would just come home from work and knock me around for the hell of it."

"But why?" she asks, and when she looks up at me, her eyes are rimmed with tears.

"I don't know," I admit. "But I do know that he couldn't stand me. He hated me just as much as I hated him."

"What could anyone possibly hate about you?"

Her words are sweet, and I lean down to give her lips a quick kiss before she continues, "So . . . nobody knew?"

I shake my head.

"How did you deal with all of that alone?"

"Vices. In high school I used to do a lot of drugs, but I stopped shortly after my dad died. I felt like what happened to my mom that night was my fault. I was wasted and passed out at a party when I should have been at home with her."

"That wasn't your fault though," she tells me.

"I know that now. But it got me to give up popping so many pills. In turn, I just traded one vice for another. I was searching for a way to numb myself. I'd been doing it since I was a little kid, and by the time he was dead, it was all I knew to do. So I kept looking for ways to escape."

"I can see that," she responds. "The need to hide."

I shift us down so that we're lying on our sides. She hides behind her dance and school. She busies herself when there isn't anything to really keep her busy. She's an overachiever, but I don't point out her vice, instead I reveal, "I don't want to hide from you though. You're the only one I can say that about." She runs her hand along my cheek, when I go on, "I've always been scared to connect with women."

"Why?"

Giving her my fear, I let it all out there. "Because I'm afraid I'll wind up just like him."

Keeping her hand on my face, she whispers softly, "That won't happen."

"How can you be so sure?"

"Because you're the kindest person I know. Because you've never put yourself before me. You're a genuine guy, Ryan."

"You're probably the only woman who would say that about me."

"But how well did they know you?"

"They didn't. Nobody does except you."

"Can I ask you something?" she says coyly.

"Anything."

Closing her eyes, she lets out a slow breath and then asks, "If you never wanted to connect with those girls, then why sleep with them?"

"Because they offered me an escape. If even for a few minutes, it was my way of disconnecting." Tucking a loose piece of hair behind her ear, I lean my forehead against hers and tell her, "I was too scared to feel because I hadn't ever done that before. I don't know what it's like to care more about someone other than myself."

"But why me?" she breathes.

"You've always intrigued me. You aren't like any girl I've ever known. Without even trying, you get me thinking about myself and what I want out of life. You're everything I never thought I wanted, but when I met you, you were everything I needed."

She rests her hand on my jaw, and slowly runs her thumb along my lips when she says, "Somehow, you make up for everything I was missing before you. I have a hard time opening up to people; I know that. But I don't want you to doubt that you have me, because you do."

I know she struggles, and I'm still waiting for the day she will drop that wall with me to feel safe enough to tell me she loves me, but this . . . this lets me know that she's trying.

"God, you are so much more than I deserve," I breathe against her mouth before I kiss her.

I take what I learned last night and refuse to let it stand in the way of what we have together. I'm not gonna beat myself up because I want to touch her, because I know that each touch I want is because I love her. And that's the only reason. I simply love her.

chapter twenty-eight

"What are you doing?" I ask when I walk through the front door and see Candace bent over in my kitchen, wrapping her thighs in Saran Wrap.

Peeking her head up, she tells me, "Helping my muscles recover," as if this image isn't anything out of the realm of normal.

I start laughing at her while she continues to wrap her legs. "Explain this to me because I'm dying to know."

She rips the plastic from the roll and sets it on the counter before defending, "I swear it works. I've been doing it for years."

"Wrapping yourself up like leftovers?" I tease.

"No," she drags out. "You see, I use Tiger Balm," she says as she hands me a tiny brown jar that can't hold any more than an ounce. "Then, I seal it in with plastic wrap. It traps in the vapors, which allows for maximum absorption, bringing more relief to my muscles."

Setting the jar down, I say, "Are you not worried about a chemical burn or some shit like that?"

"It's never happened before," she says as she walks out of the kitchen and into the living room.

Watching her, I laugh at the image . . . and the sound.

"Candace, this is some crazy shit you do, you know that right?"

She takes a seat on the couch as I move to join her.

"Yes, I know, but I swear it helps. Look, I have my audition in two days, and I'm freaking out because I keep getting these cramps in my legs. I've upped my calcium and potassium, but it's still bothering me."

"Give me your legs," I tell her and she shifts to lie on her back, kicking her feet onto my lap.

"What are you doing?" she asks when I turn to the side to face her.

"I'm gonna give your calves a solid rubdown."

She smiles as I start to knead my fingers into her muscles. I can't get enough of her legs, even wrapped up like she has them. They are solid and sexy, and I take my time, thoroughly enjoying myself, as I give her calves a deep massage. She closes her eyes and relaxes while I make good use of the next thirty minutes.

When I'm done, I take her up to my bathroom where she begins to unwrap her legs.

"God, that shit stinks," I complain as she wads up the wrap and tosses it to me.

"Be nice," she scolds playfully. "I'm gonna take a quick shower. I'll come to bed in a few minutes."

"Okay," I say when I lean down to peck her lips before I leave and close the door behind me.

I run downstairs to plug my cell into its charger in my office before locking up. Candace has her dance bag by the front door with her toe shoes lying on top of a towel. Walking over, I kneel down and run my finger over the dirty, torn pink satin. You can see the burn marks on the ribbon where I can tell she has used a lighter to stop them from fraying.

It's ironic how these shoes mirror Candace. On the verge of falling apart. Barely holding together. Yet they do. She's strong even though she's breaking. I don't see her doing anything to heal; she's hiding and masking what I know is eating away at her. And these shoes, as worn as they are, they're still strong and beautiful.

Turning off the lights, I head back upstairs and lie down. When Candace is done drying her hair, she crawls in next me, and I curl myself around her. We don't talk as we both drift off to sleep.

When I stir awake, I'm alone in bed. Sitting up, I lean over to her nightstand to check the time on her phone. It's after two in the morning. I roll out of bed and walk out to the top of the stairs and see her. She's downstairs, sitting on the couch in the dark, watching the rain fall. The past couple nights since she's been staying here, she hasn't slept well. I haven't said anything to her, but she spends most of her nights in a fit of restless sleep, keeping me awake while I hold her and just watch.

Quietly, I walk down the stairs and across the room. As I round the couch, I see her wrapped up in a blanket, and she's crying. My heart is so heavy, and I don't know what to do. All I want is to take it all away, but I don't know how to do that.

She senses me and turns to look. I see it all over her face—the pain. She's so tired. Without any words spoken, I sit down next to her and wipe the tears that stain her cheeks.

"I can't sleep," she whispers to me.

I look over her face, searching for words, but my own sadness wells up inside of my chest, and I can see the pleading in her eyes. She doesn't want me to question why she's crying, so I don't. I already know. Pulling her closer to me, I hold on to her as she draws her legs up to her chest, cuddling into me. She turns her head and continues to watch the rain while I sit here in a painful silence. All that fills my head is the sound of her shrieking cries from that night, and I do everything I can to keep my emotions intact. Eventually, she dozes off and I scoop her up, carrying her back to bed.

I've been sitting here, anxiously waiting for Candace to get back. She left a couple hours ago for her audition at Meany Theater. I wanted to go with her, but she made me stay, saying that she didn't want anything to distract her. I wouldn't have been able to go into the theater to watch, but I wanted to at least be there to support her, but I understand.

She was a jittery mess all morning, and I did what I could to relax her, but she was too distracted to focus on anything, including me. Her determination and the neurotic behavior that comes along with it make me smile. She even broke out the Saran Wrap again when she woke up.

As soon as I hear the front door open, I walk out of my office to see Candace running down the hall. She jumps into my arms, wrapping her legs around my waist, and I've never seen a more perfect smile. She's elated, and her joy is infectious, making me laugh, saying, "I take it you kicked ass?"

"I totally kicked ass. It was amazing!"

Her legs are clutched so tightly around me that I don't even have to hold on to her, so I take my hands from her hips, move them to her face, and kiss her smile. She crashes her mouth with mine, enthusiasm controlling her. Taking her, I press her back up against the hallway wall, and before I can go in deeper with our kiss, she pulls away and starts laughing, telling me all about her audition. She spews out a bunch of French ballet shit, and I have no clue what she's talking about, but she's excited and happy, and that's all I need to know. My smile is big as I stand here and watch her.

"I'm so proud of you, babe. I wish I could have seen you."

"I know. I'm sorry," she says as she combs her fingers through my hair. "Auditions are always closed."

"When will you find out?"

"March first."

"Next week?"

"Yeah, Friday," she answers excitedly before pulling my head back to hers to kiss me, but I've got something to tell her as well.

Mumbling over her mouth, I say, "I've got news too."

Not willing to take her lips from mine, she mutters, "What's that?"

"Thinkspace Gallery called."

Her head pops back. "And . . .?"

"They accepted your photo."

"Your photo?!"

"No, *your* photo, babe."

She smiles. She knows that picture is all her, and I refuse to take the credit for it.

"Congratulations," she tells me, and I slow her down, wanting to really feel her against me.

I kiss her softly, gently sucking on her bottom lip as I graze my tongue along it. She tangles her hands in my hair when I band my arms around her. We move like this, taking our time, and when she pulls back, she peers into my eyes. There's a look in her eyes that I can't peg, so I ask, "What is it, babe?"

She takes her hand and runs it slowly down the side of

my face, and I see the wall crumbling.

"I love you."

Every part of me awakens, and I've never felt so alive. I didn't think I needed to hear those words as much I did, but the trust that comes with them was what I craved the most.

"You'll never know what those words just did to me," I tell her and then carry her over to the couch so that I can show her, in our own way, how much I love her.

I lie on top of her, and she begins to lift up my shirt, so I reach over my head and pull it off. Sliding my hand down her leg, I lift it and wrap it around my hip.

"I'm sorry you had to wait so long," she breathes.

"Don't be," I tell her. "You don't even know how much you have already given me. When I met you, I found me."

She smiles, saying again, "I love you."

"I love you too, babe."

We move slowly and spend the next hour making out the way we tend to do. I want more with her. I'll always want more, but for now, I enjoy taking my time with her and savor every piece as she gives it to me.

"Ryan?"

Her soft voice pulls me from my sleep as I roll over and drape my arm around her from behind.

"Yeah, babe?" I whisper with my eyes still closed, but she doesn't answer, so I let myself begin to drift back to sleep.

"Ryan?"

She calls my name louder, almost panicky, and when I open my eyes to look over at her, she's still sleeping. I watch her for a second and then she screams, "Ryan!" as she flips onto her back, her hands clenched into fists.

"Baby, wake up," I say as I hover over her, scared to touch her.

She begins trembling, pleading in a strained voice, "Please, not again."

Fuck. Knowing exactly what her dream is, I panic. "Candace, babe. Wake up."

"Get off of me!" she yells, frantically kicking her legs.

Quickly straddling them, I grip her upper arms as she thrashes herself against my hold.

"Get the fuck off of me!" she shrieks, and when she opens her eyes, tears fall freely down the sides of her face. She looks at me, but there's nothing there. No focus. Her eyes are completely glazed over, scaring the shit out of me. "God, please stop!"

"Candace, wake up!" I bark at her, desperate for her to snap out of her nightmare.

She's in a frenzy, screaming hysterically. Crying. I let go of her, and when I do, she desperately shuffles back and away from me, falling off the bed and hard onto her hip. I hop off the bed and kneel down in front of her as she's huddled in a ball against the wall, sobbing.

"Don't fuckin' touch me!" she screams when I hold her shoulders with my hands, but I don't take them off of her.

"Candace, open your eyes," I beg as she covers her face with her hands. She's so loud, and my mind is overwhelmed with anxiety.

Her breathing is rapid and she's terrified, but I need her to know she's safe.

"Candace, please. Look at me. It's only me here with you."

I take her wrists to move her hands from her face, and she turns her head to the wall as she cries.

"Babe, please don't hide from me."

She struggles to breathe through her tears, and when she begins to gasp, I tug her between my legs and her body gives in, falling limp into my arms. I hold her tight. Tighter than I have ever held anyone. She has to get this secret out of her. It's agonizing to see how this is tormenting her. I just need her to get it out.

I rub her back while she has her head tucked into my chest. She's no longer screaming, but the crying continues.

I don't want her to hide from me, so I tell her, "You have to look at me. Please." With my hands, I move her head up to face me. She opens her eyes, and I hate the fear and embarrassment I see in them.

"You okay?"

She simply nods.

"What happened?"

Lowering her head, she takes a couple deep breaths before asking, "Can you please call Jase?"

"What?" I hate this shit. That she would run to him in a heartbeat like I don't exist. Like I'm not enough for her, but he is. "Shit, Candace, no," I tell her, refusing to allow her to run from me. She told me she loves me, I just need her to trust me enough to be here for her.

"Please." She begins to cry again.

"Candace, no. You can't always run to him. Need me for a change," I beg. "Talk to me."

"I can't."

"Yes, you can," I urge. *God, just talk to me. Tell me. Get this out of you so that you can start dealing with it.*

"No, I can't. Please. I just can't," she strains through her sobs.

"But you can with Jase?" I question in disbelief. I thought we were past this.

"I want you to need me," I plead, tightening my hold around her. I feel desperate.

"I do."

"You don't," I say. "You cling to him for everything. Look at me," I demand and then hold her hands, pressing them hard against my chest, and beg, "Cling to *me*. Love me enough to *need me*."

"I can't . . . I . . ."

"Why?"

"Because . . . you'd leave me."

"Not happening, babe."

"Ryan, please."

"I'm not leaving you," I assure her. She can tell me this; I know she can, and I need her to. "Nothing you could say would make me want to leave you."

"I'm just too fucked up." Her face is covered in tears that I just want to kiss away. I wanna take all of her pain away, but I resist the urge to give in to her. So I keep encouraging, knowing that I'm guiding her to a painful place.

"We're all fucked up," I tell her. "I want you to let me in."

Her body is shuddering as the sobs wrack her. I'm powerless, and it fuckin' sucks.

"I can't! You'll never look at me the same. You'll run away."

She says this and I want to cry for her. Take her pain and shove it deep inside of me. I'd take her misery as my own in a second.

Wrapping my hand behind her head, I hold it close to my heart when I vow, "I promise you, nothing will change the way I look at you. Nothing will change what you do to me when you're next to me. You make my heart beat in a completely different way—nothing will ever change that."

"I'm so embarrassed," she cries into my chest as she slips her arms around me, clinging to me like she's about to fall—maybe she is, but I need her to.

"God, babe." I'm fighting my own tears so hard. "Please, don't be."

I strengthen my hold on her, and when I do, she falters with a whimper when she releases it.

"I was raped."

Those words. I already knew it. I even saw her body afterwards. But hearing those words. I can't take the pain and guilt any longer. It's like a knife to my lungs, and I can barely breathe. I take a hard breath in when the tears slip out and fall.

I'm helpless. I don't know what to say to her, but I knew that she had to tell me. To stop hiding it away, but what have I done to her? She's broken in my arms right now, sobbing, and I don't know what to do to help.

We sit, clinging to one another as we both cry. Time passes and she begins to tire, now softly weeping as I continue rocking her and planting kisses on top of her head.

"I've been lying to you," she mutters quietly.

"I don't care. It doesn't matter."

"I feel horrible."

"Candace, don't do this," I tell her. "You have every right to lie."

"I can't go to see you at work because . . ."

"Shhh . . ." I want her to stop because she doesn't need to apologize for shit. She shouldn't feel bad for trying to cover this up. I get it. Understand it.

"Because it happened in your parking lot. By the dumpster," she tells me, and I figure she simply needs to get it off her chest, so I don't say anything. I just listen as she relieves herself of whatever guilt is weighing on her as she continues. "That's why I freaked out. I didn't know where I was until I saw the dumpster."

Hearing her say this to me is hard. It's hurts to think about her trying so hard to hide this from me and what that was doing to her. My breath catches, and when a small noise cracks, she pulls back to see my tears falling. Her face scrunches up as she begins to cry again.

"I'm so sorry," she chokes out, and I've had enough of her apologizing for shit that doesn't matter.

"Don't ever fuckin' say that again," I tell her when I cradle her cheeks in my hand. "Don't ever be sorry for anything again."

"I'm just so far from what you thought."

"You're not."

"I am. Every day is a struggle. Everything. I'm scared every day," she admits as she drops her head from my hands.

I've always wanted to know what she was hiding, but I couldn't have imagined this. And that she lives with this every day. Terrified. The fact that she has held herself together around me so well is shocking.

Candace finally looks back up at me, pained when she tells me, "I'm fading." I shake my head at her, hardly able to stand the misery in her voice. "He took all my light, and I've been fading ever since."

Giving her nothing but the core of my intentions, I tell her, "You're not fading. I won't let you."

Her words beat at me. In disbelief because she's brought so much to my life in such a short amount of time. The mere idea that she would see her life in such shambles that she would fear fading ignites a fight in me to do everything I can to pull her out of this darkness. To show her just how bright she is. How amazing and powerful she is. She's nothing but heart, and I'm going to make sure she sees every bit of it.

That there's no way for her to fade in my eyes.

She tucks her head down and leans into me as I fold her securely in my arms, vowing to myself that I will do everything I can to show this girl how strong she really is.

"That's why Kimber is mad," she says as she continues to talk. "I didn't go home after it happened. I stayed with Jase and never told her why. She knows I'm lying."

I listen. That's all she wants from me, so that's what I give her.

"I've been taking sleeping pills, but I stopped last week. That's why I haven't been sleeping." She pauses before revealing, "I dream about that night—about him. All I see are his eyes. He made me watch him."

A new bout of sobs courses through her, and anger courses through me, but I keep my cool for her. I take myself out of this and focus on her when she adds, "So, I take pills to keep him away."

"Babe, why did you stop taking them?"

"Because every night when I take them, it's only a reminder of what happened. I just want to forget, but I can't."

"Have you told anyone?" I ask as I brush her hair behind her shoulder.

"No. Only Jase and Mark. Jase was with me in the hospital. Mark only knows because he walked in and saw my face. I was pretty banged up."

"Your parents?"

"God, no. It was because of them that I went out with that guy at all."

"You knew him?" I ask, not expecting that she knew the fucker. "But you didn't do anything?"

"No."

"I wanna fucking kill him," I spit out, anger swelling

inside of me. I swear to God, I'm gonna kill that piece of shit. My body tenses up, and I do everything I can to bring myself back down—for her. It takes a while, but I begin to focus on Candace and what she needs out of me. I know she's afraid I'm gonna run, but she's wrong.

Looking at her straight on, I assure her, "This changes nothing for me. Okay? Nothing. No one will ever love you like I do." I kiss her. I feel it's all I can do right now to show her that I'm here and I'm not leaving her. When I do finally drag my lips away, I give her more of me when I say, "You are the only reason there's light in my life. Before you, there was nothing but darkness."

As the tears linger on her cheeks, I lean in and kiss them, tasting the salt of her secret that's been eating her up. But now it's out there, and she doesn't have to find ways to hide from me anymore. She trusts me enough to allow me to see the darkest side of her, and I love her for that.

chapter twenty-nine

I didn't want to leave Candace the day following her nightmare. I felt like being close to her, but she told me that it would have made her feel uncomfortable if I cancelled work to stay with her, and even though I didn't like it, I understood it. She's afraid things have changed between us, and just because I assured her that they haven't, I need to show her. So I went into work, and she went to Jase's where she managed to drink way too much wine, and for the first time in her life, got wasted.

Candace is still sleeping when I finish my shower and get dressed. Bringing her home last night was an adventure. She's gonna feel like shit when she wakes up today, but seeing her drunk was about the cutest thing I've ever seen.

I woke up in the middle of the night to find her fighting sleep. She said she was scared of having another nightmare, and it was tearing me up inside, so I stayed up and talked to her so that she could fall asleep. After she was out, I found myself wanting to stay awake to watch her, make sure she slept peacefully. Her nightmare scared the crap out of me, so I can't imagine how scary it was for her.

The past few weeks have drained me emotionally, so

while she sleeps, I decide to head up to the bar before anyone gets there to get a little space from everything. I write Candace a note before I leave, letting her know where I went and to call when she gets up.

Walking into Blur, I leave the front door unlocked while I busy myself filling bottles behind the bar. I spend a good amount of time staying occupied, but my mind is elsewhere. It's in that alley, and my stomach won't seem to unknot itself to buy me any relief. I grab a bottle of scotch and take a seat at the bar, filling my glass.

I don't take a sip; I just sit and stare at the burnished liquid. It's placid, and I get lost as I zone out in the glass. I'm so deep in my head that I don't even hear the door open, but when someone takes a seat next to me, I turn to see Jase. His expression tells me that he knows I know. Candace must have told him last night. I focus back on my glass that's still sitting on the bar, cradled in my hands.

"I'm sorry," he says.

I can barely move my head up and down to acknowledge his words that take me out of my daze and bring me back to the mass of emotions.

Without looking at him, I talk. "I always knew she was hiding something, I just . . ."

"I know."

"She has these moments in her sleep . . . almost nightly . . ."

"It's a lot better now," he says, and I turn to look at him.

"Better?" He nods and I ask, because I want to know, "How bad was she?"

His head drops to the side, not wanting to tell me when I ask again. "How bad?"

"Don't do this."

"How bad?"

He takes a pause before he tells me, "Bad. It was like suddenly the Candace I had always known was gone."

I turn back to my glass and take a drink before setting it back down, relishing the burn in my chest. Warmth.

"So she was different?" I ask, wondering what she would have been like if only I'd met her before that night.

"Yeah, but like I said, she's better."

"Better," I repeat, not knowing what else to say, trying hard to keep the pain at bay. "How?"

"She used to have these hallucinations. It freaked me out. They were intense, and I'd always find her vomiting in my bathroom."

His words punch me in the gut. Thinking about her like that is almost too much, and I feel the tears return, but I fight to hold them back.

"She said she knew him." My words crack as they find their way out past the lump in my throat.

"Yeah."

I turn back to him and ask, "You know him too?"

Shaking his head, he tells me, "I met him once."

"Who is he?"

He releases a hard sigh when I press, "Who is he?"

He still doesn't respond when I question, "Did you ever do anything?"

"I wanted to. I still do." His breathing staggers as his eyes redden and gloss over. "But I can't. Candace made me promise, and I just can't break that promise. It would hurt her too much."

"Why didn't she do anything?"

"She was scared. Embarrassed. I tried talking to her, but she'd rather bury it, so that's what she did."

I shake my head, and when I do, he speaks up, "Look, man, I wanna kill that bastard. I do. I saw what he did to her, and he fucked her up . . . bad. But I love her. And as much as I hate that all she wants to do is hide this shit, I don't fight it because I don't want to hurt her." I watch his tears fall as he adds, "I know what you two have is completely different than what I have with her, but she's my fuckin' heart, man. I hate her choices, but I also know how fragile she is right now, so I let it be. Right or wrong, I just give her what she wants."

I can't speak even if I wanted to because the pain in my chest is nearly unbearable at this point. All I can do is give him a nod, and I know he sees the emotion on my face. How could a person hide it?

He stands up and grips my shoulder, saying, "I couldn't deal with this shit if it weren't for Mark. If you ever need to talk . . ."

"Yeah. Thanks," I respond on a breath before he turns to walk out the door.

When he's out of my vision, I drop my head in my hands and let it out. It's a haze of unrecognizable emotions beating through me. To look past this and let her continue to sit and do nothing is something that I don't think I'm capable of. But Jase is right. My girl is so damn fragile even though she's so damn strong. It's a paradox that's hard to deal with. She's gonna break one way or another.

Irritation boils inside, and the longer I sit here it starts to eat away at me until it takes over and I stand up, kicking over the stool, screaming, and smashing my glass against the brick wall behind the bar followed next by the bottle. The blast of glass shattering and sprinkling to the floor is all I hear through the ringing in my head. I grab my keys, leaving the mess, and head to my jeep.

I drive. Making my way back to my loft and upstairs to find Candace standing in my closet, slipping on a sweater.

"Why didn't you do anything?" I ask, unable to control my frustration.

She turns to look at me, confused, when she asks, "What are you talking about?"

"Don't make me say it."

"Ryan, please. Don't," she says and then walks past me to sit on the edge of the bed.

"Who is he?" I press, emotions getting the best of me.

She keeps her chin tucked down. Avoiding.

"Candace, tell me his fuckin' name!" I belt out because sitting around and not doing shit isn't gonna work for me.

"Please don't do this," she chokes out as she begins to cry.

"Why aren't you more pissed?"

"I am."

"You're not," I tell her as I stand in front of her. "I don't see it."

She doesn't respond, and I plead with her, needing to make sense of all of this. "Tell me why I don't see it. Make me understand because this shit is killing me."

"Because I don't know how to show it," she weeps as she looks up at me.

My heart is hammering hard in my chest. She's so locked up, and I don't know how to help her.

"I need you to show it. I need to see it," I tell her as I kneel down in front of her, gripping her legs.

"Don't."

"I wanna see you fighting. I wanna see you doing something since you won't let me do shit."

"Why? For what?"

"For you, Candace! It's for you," I say in a hard voice. "Show me that you're mad because my anger is beyond what I think I can handle right now."

Her breathing picks up as she cries harder.

"Show me," I push.

"I can't."

"You can. Use me," I urge. "Yell at me. Scream. Hit me. Punch me. Something! Just do something!" I shout as she sobs. "Stop crying and do something! Hit me!"

"Ryan, stop!" she screams, and when she tries to move away from me, I grab on to her wrists and she kneels down next to me, bracing her hands on the floor as she cries.

"I want you to fight. I want you to fight because I'm so fuckin' mad and you won't let me fight for you."

"You wanna fight?" I stand in the doorway and listen to my dad. "Come here," he says to my mom with a crooked finger, and she steps towards him. "Hit me."

"No."

"Hit me, you little bitch!"

She stands there crying when he pulls his clenched fist back and punches her in the stomach, forcing out a gush of air as she heaves and doubles over.

"Daddy, stop!"

He looks at me. "You want me to stop?" he asks before impaling her ribs with his boot.

Her screams are strained as I start to cry.

"Stop!"

He kicks her again as she lies there, lifeless.

"Tell me to stop again, you sack of shit."

I look at Candace doubled over on the floor—crying—and it hits me.

"God, baby. I'm sorry," I say, reaching out to touch her, but she coils back from me.

"It wouldn't even do anything," she snaps. "You want me to fight? Why? It's not going to change anything. It's not going to make it better. It's not going to take it away."

Realizing that I pushed her way too far, that I scared her by yelling at her, I reach out, and again, she resists my touch. "I'm sorry."

She doesn't hear me, she just continues, "I just wanna forget. I just want it to go away. But me fighting isn't gonna make that happen. The damage is done, and I can't go back."

"Baby," I say as gently as I can. "You can't pretend it didn't happen."

"Why not?" her voice a mere whimper. So desperate. "What's so bad about pretending?"

This time when I reach for her, she doesn't flinch, and I fold her up in my arms. "Because it *did* happen."

"Why?" she cries into my chest. "Tell me why this happened. Why me? What did I do to deserve this?"

There are no answers as she completely breaks and continues crying, collapsed in my lap. I feel like absolute shit for pushing her to this point, and all my fears are brought back to the forefront. I can't deny for one second that I don't resemble my father in frightening ways. That I could be so selfish to be screaming at my girlfriend as she's crumpled on the floor crying. I don't know what the hell is wrong with me, but I can't do that shit to her. Fuck, why did I just do that to her?

"I'm so sorry." I'm desperate as my voice cracks.

She grips her arms around me while I rest my cheek on top of her head. I can't believe I let my anger take control of me. Just knowing the thoughts of what I would do to that guy if I ever saw him scares the shit out of me. I can't let this happen again with her; I just can't because I know myself well enough to know that I'll never walk away from her, so I have to get my shit under control.

I rub her back until eventually she quiets down, taking in hiccups of breaths. She has the sleeves of my t-shirt fisted in her hands, and when she lifts her head up, she keeps her eyes closed. I kiss her forehead, and she presses her weight into my lips. She's exhausted.

"Hey," I say lightly, and when she hums in response, I encourage, "Can you look at me?"

She does, and when I see how red her eyes are, I feel disgusted with myself.

"I'm so sorry. I should have never raised my voice like that. I just feel so helpless, but how I feel isn't your fault. I don't want you to think that it is."

"You can say that, but the thing is, it's because of me that you feel this way."

I don't know how to respond to her words, but she doesn't give me time when she says, "I just . . . I don't want to lose you. I don't have very many people that . . . I mean . . . I don't even have a home anymore."

When she looks up at me and into my eyes I tell her, "You *are* home."

"Am I?"

Wiping under her eyes with my thumbs, I ask, "Is this what you want?"

Nodding her head, she whispers, "Yes."

"Then you're home," I give her and wrap her back up in my arms.

Candace wound up getting a bad headache and is sleeping again. Not only is she worn out from what happened earlier, she's also not feeling well after drinking so much with Jase last night.

I leave her be as I head down to my office. Despite the shit day, I need to call my mom because in Candace's drunken state last night, she revealed that her birthday is in a few days, and I want to surprise her by having my mom here. They have been talking more and more on the phone, and I know Candace would like to see her. Hell, after this month, it'll be nice to have her here for a few days.

"Hi, dear," she says when she answers my call.

"Hey, Mom. I have a favor to ask."

"Sure. What is it?"

"It's Candace's birthday on Thursday, and I was wondering if you can manage to get away for a few days and come stay here with us?" I ask.

"*This* Thursday?"

"Yeah."

"Ryan, that's in five days. Why didn't you tell me about this sooner?" she nags.

"Because I just found out last night. This was sprung on me too, Mom."

"Why did she wait so long to tell you?"

"I don't know, but it slipped out last night. I know she'd love to see you, so I was hoping . . ."

"I'll be there."

"Thanks. I'm not gonna tell her, so if you two talk before then, don't mention anything. I want her to be surprised."

"Lips are sealed."

"And no gifts," I remind her.

"Ryan."

"I have no problem with it, but I know how she is, so . . ."

"Fine. No gifts," she says with a faint laugh. "How has everything else been? I haven't talked to Candace in a few days; how did her audition go?"

"It seemed to go really well. She was insanely happy afterward. She should know if she got the solo on Friday."

"That's great. Is she around to talk to?"

"She's sleeping."

"Oh, okay. Well, tell her to call me when she has time."

"Yeah, I will."

"Everything else okay?" she asks, and although I've always been open with my mom, I know this thing with Candace will forever remain private, so I simply tell her, "Yeah, Mom. Everything's great."

We continue to chat for a few more minutes before we say goodbye. When I walk upstairs, I see Candace curled into a small ball in the center of my bed. Shrugging off my shirt, I crawl in to take a nap with her. I slide in behind her, and as I pull her into me, she rolls over to face me, eyes still closed. Draping my arm around her, she nuzzles her head in the curve of my neck, and finally, after all the tension of the day, I relax in the warmth of her.

chapter thirty

"What do you want to do for your birthday, babe?" I ask as she stretches before heading to the studio for rehearsals. I always enjoy seeing her like this—poised, hair up tight in a bun, leotard with an old pair of torn, baggy sweats. There's no doubt she was made to dance because she completely looks the part, and that look is doing things to me that I need to get under control.

"Nothing. I told Jase that the four of us could just grab dinner."

"We do that all the time."

She sits on the ground to roll her ankles when she says, "Please don't get any ideas. I really don't like doing anything for my birthday."

"Why?" I ask when I sit in front of her and take her leg in my hand to rub out her muscles.

"My mom would always throw me these over-the-top parties when I was little. Well, she threw them for her and her friends. It was all show with the moms, everyone trying to one-up the others. It was never what I wanted, and I would spend the whole day upset but forced to pretend to be their perfect daughter and behave as etiquette told me I should."

"So let me do something nice for you," I suggest.

"It makes me uncomfortable. It always has. I'm a year older; I just don't see the big deal in making a fuss over it."

"Candace."

Her only response is a shrug of her shoulders.

"So tell me then, what was it that you really wanted when you were a kid?" I ask when I move to massage her other leg.

Her hands rest in her lap as she sits on the floor and tells me, "Simple. It sounds trite, but what I really wanted was my friends to come over and play with me. Have a cheap cake from the grocery store instead of the fondant covered ones my mom would order from the bakery in town. That fondant tastes like crap, you know?" she says with her brows raised with exaggeration, and I laugh at her.

"I don't even know what that is," I admit with a smile.

"Well, it's gross. And I hated—*hated*—being forced to open all the gifts in front of everyone. I never got toys, but instead little trinkets and things. Like that bouncy ball," she exclaims. "I never got stuff like that."

"So that's why you hate getting presents?"

"It's just awkward for me, so I'd rather not deal with it."

"I'll call Jase. Why don't we just hang out here? Eat pizza, watch TV," I suggest.

She smiles, agreeing, "Sounds perfect."

She's simple in ways that I like, but for reasons that shouldn't be. I'll give Candace her *non-birthday* birthday party, but I can't *not* get her something to make it special. Because it is. So I'll find a way to do that for her without making her feel uncomfortable. My girl can be a challenge, but I like that about her.

While Candace is busy on campus all day, I head over to Fremont to stop by a couple vintage antique shops. Jase and Candace are always hanging out here, and I know Candace well enough that she doesn't buy most of her things from mass marketed retail shops. Yeah, she's simple, but she likes nice things.

I spend a couple hours roaming around, but nothing catches my eye, so I decide to walk down to Peet's and grab a coffee. When I pass by one of the little shops, the name stops me because Candace came home the other day with some shaving lather for me from here.

Stepping into Essenza, the place is filled with fine European perfumes, soaps, clothes, and jewelry. This looks like a place that she would shop. I'm the only one here and the lady behind the counter steps out and walks over to me, saying, "You look lost," with a friendly smile.

"That obvious?"

Her smile is warm and even though she screams elegance, she's quite relaxed when she offers me a glass of wine.

"I'm good."

"So what are we shopping for?"

"A girl. I know she's been here before, so I thought I would stop in," I tell her.

"What's her name?"

"Candace."

"The ballerina?" she squeals.

I nod my head when she adds, "She's been shopping here for years. We're the only boutique in the state that carries the perfume she wears, so she's pretty loyal."

"Why does that not surprise me? That she would've picked a perfume that was exclusive to one store in the whole state of Washington," I laugh as she joins in.

"You must be the guy she was shopping for last time she was in a couple weeks back."

I nod and introduce myself, "I'm Ryan."

I give her a friendly handshake as she says, "Well, I'll let you be. Please, I'm Viv, let me know if I can help you or if you change your mind about the wine."

Joking, I ask, "Does your boss know you drink on the job?"

"Please," she drawls and winks at me, adding, "It's a requirement."

I wander over to check out the perfumes, and sure enough, I spot her bottle of Flou. Next to the display there is an old antique wrought-iron table with a locked glass case that serves as the round table top. Looking down through the glass, there are a few pieces of handcrafted jewelry, most of them rings. There are a couple hand stamped pieces with various quotes. I eye one of the necklaces. It's the only one with a flat, rectangular bar at the drop that connects the thin, delicate chain. I stop looking at the rest of the jewelry when I read words that couldn't be more true, and I know I have to get this for her because *this*—these words—is exactly how I see her and how I need her to see herself.

Looking up to Viv, who is sipping her wine, I ask, "Can you show me a piece from this case?"

She hops up and comes over to unlock the glass, and I show her the one I'm looking at. She pulls it out and hands it to me.

"It's perfect," I murmur as I look it over. The stamped letters are rugged and uneven, a contrast to the polished silver bar and fragile chain.

"A Midsummer Night's Dream."

I look up and she clarifies, "The quote. It's from 'A Midsummer Night's Dream.'"

I run my thumb over the jagged impressions of the words, *And though she be but little, she is fierce.* "Was this here the last time she was in?"

"No."

"I'll take it."

When I hand her the necklace, I follow her over to the counter. "A gift?" she asks.

"It's her birthday."

"Shall I wrap it?"

"No," I say, and when she looks up at me, I add with a smirk, "She hates gifts."

She smiles as she takes my credit card. "Ryan, Ryan, Ryan," she tsks and then swipes my card before handing it back to me. "I like you."

"Not gonna lie, Viv, I like you too," I respond with a light chuckle before she hands me the bag.

I head out to my car, having one more errand to run, because I'm not quite satisfied yet.

When I get home later, I hear Candace in the shower, so I go ahead and stash my purchases. I walk into my closet, shoving them into one of the drawers and cover them up with a couple sweaters. My camera sits on the tabletop of the drawers, and I grab it, taking it with me as I flop on the bed and wait for Candace to come out. I scroll through the only pictures that are stored—the ones of Candace's back. I click on each one, zooming in on the preview screen to get a closer look.

The bathroom door opens, and I look up to see her walking out, towel drying her hair, wearing a t-shirt and a pair of my boxers. God, she's hot.

"I didn't know you were home," she says as she stands at the foot of the bed.

Ignoring her statement, I let her know, "I like it when you wear my underwear."

"Stop," she says in a nagging voice as I pop up to my knees.

"I'm serious. It's hot as shit."

When she laughs at me, I hold my hand out to her and pull her on top of the bed with me, twisting around and laying her on her back. Her skin is still damp from her shower, and I weave my fingers into her wet hair as I begin to plant slow kisses down her neck. She smells insanely good, and when I pull back to look down at her, I'm taken by how beautiful she looks right now.

Leaning over, I pick up my camera, and as soon as I bring it up to my eye, she covers her face, complaining, "No."

"What?"

"You can't just take my picture."

I laugh at her. "Don't be shy with me," I tell her and then sit back on my heels. "Let me see you."

She removes her hands from her face, and when she does, I say, "Let me photograph you."

Lying there, she doesn't respond one way or the other, so I bring the camera back up to my eye and snap a few quick shots of her. Hair splayed around her face, flushed cheeks, and a soft expression on her face.

"Thanks," I say when I'm done capturing her face and then shift to the side of her, holding the camera back to my face.

"What are you doing?"

"Giving myself something to work on," I mutter before adding, "Bend your legs up, babe."

She does without question, and I use my hand to maneuver them to my liking until they are at the perfect angle. The clicks of the shutter are the only sounds that fill the room as she lies there, watching me intently every time I shift my eyes to hers. I'm glad she's comfortable with this and not so tense like she was the last time we did this.

I move to set the camera on the nightstand and then back to her, easing my weight on top of her. She runs her hands along my face, drawing me down to kiss her. We let ourselves get lost in one another, moving in a way I have only done with her, and when her shirt hits the floor with mine, I drop my head to her chest. Her arms encircle my head as I cover her in my mouth, finding that the feel of her lace bras are a turn-on I never expected.

Her skin is soft beneath my hand as I run it down her side and to her leg as I tighten my grip because she feels that damn good. When she grazes her lips up my neck, she sends chills down my arms. Our breaths begin to run deep, and my need for her strengthens as I slide my hand in from her hips, over the waistband of her boxers, and down between her legs, cupping the heat of her.

"Stop," she snaps and jerks my hand away, startling me.

"Babe?"

"Just . . . don't," she whispers.

I accept all of her hesitations, but it still hurts when she rejects my touches. Her eyes are closed when I lie down beside her, pulling her hip over so that she's facing me.

"Please look at me," I urge in a hushed voice, and when she does, I go with transparent honesty and say, "I want to touch you."

"I know. I just . . ." I see the worry in her eyes and the lines in her forehead.

"You can tell me anything, babe. I'll never judge you."

She takes her time as I run my hand up her arm and into her hair. When she does speak, it's strained as she confesses, "He's the only one that's touched me there."

I work hard to not get upset. To stay calm so that I can talk to her about this because we can't keep avoiding it. I know this is the last thing she probably wants to discuss, but it has to be done, so I choose my words carefully, telling her, "You know that I would never hurt you."

"I know. It isn't that."

"Then tell me what it is. I need to understand."

She tucks her chin down, and when I lift it back up with my fingers, I explain, "I need you to talk to me about this because I need to know."

"It's embarrassing," she admits quietly.

"There is nothing for you to be embarrassed about, babe. But I'm gonna be honest with you—it hurts when you push me away because I don't want you to be scared of me."

"I'm not scared of you."

"Then what?"

After she lets out a slow sigh, she finally reveals, "It makes me feel dirty."

My forehead gently falls against hers, and I close my eyes, shaking my head. With my hands on her back, I feel the soft heaves, letting me know she's crying. It infuriates me that he did this to her. That this is how she views intimacy. The last thing I would ever expect or want her to feel when she's with me like this is dirty. Knowing that makes me sick to my stomach.

"Listen to me," I say when I pull my head back to look at her. "That guy was a piece of shit, we both know that. He's a sick fuck, and yeah, what he did and how he touched you was dirty. The disgust is beyond that. But that isn't what this is. That isn't us," I try to explain to her. I pull her in tight, continuing, "I want to touch you and feel you. He made that something ugly for you, and I hate him for that. That he could take that away from us."

"I'm sorry," she cries.

"You have nothing—*nothing*—to be sorry for," I scold. "He did this, not you. The way I want to touch you is nothing like that. I love you, and I want to touch you like this because it's a way for me to feel close to you. It's a way for me to love you and to make you feel that too."

The tears run down the side of her face as she responds, "I want to give that to you. I do. I feel awful that I can't, but I'm trying. I need you to know that I *am* trying."

Wiping her face, I say, "I know you are. I see it. I'm not blaming you, but we need to talk about this so that I can understand."

"I hate this," she confesses and then buries her head in my chest.

"I know you do, and if I could do something I would. I just don't know what that would be. But I love you, even the parts of you that you think are ugly. I love it all."

chapter thirty-one

"What the hell is this, Mark?" I call out from the kitchen when I open the box with the cake.

He's on the couch, drinking a beer with Jase, and responds nonchalantly, "You put me in charge of the cake, so I got her a cake."

"She's turning twenty-three, man."

"Yeah, I know. Trust me, she'll like it," he tells me with an exaggerated wink.

"There are fuckin' rats in tutus."

"They're mice," he corrects as I look back down at the cake that's fit for a five-year-old. "It came with a free 'Angelina the Ballerina' ring," he laughs as he holds up his hand to show me the pink plastic ring he's wearing on his pinky.

I shake my head and laugh with them as I grab a beer and join them in the living room.

"You gonna give that to her?"

He smirks, saying, "No way, man. This is mine."

We hang out and watch TV for a few minutes until Candace walks through the door. She gives Mark and Jase each a hug and kiss before I call her over and pull her onto my lap.

"I missed you," I whisper as I run my nose up her neck and then tease, "Mmmm . . . coffee."

She always smells like she's bathed in a latte when she gets off work.

"I'm gonna take a quick shower. I'll be back," she says as she hops off of my lap.

I watch as she goes up the stairs, and as if we had planned it, my phone buzzes with a text from my mom letting me know she's about fifteen minutes out.

"Did Candace find out about her audition yet?" Mark asks.

"Not yet. She should know tomorrow."

"So what are you guys gonna do this weekend?" Jase asks as he takes a sip of his beer.

"My mom is only able to stay through tomorrow afternoon, so we will probably just lay low."

We continue to talk about nothing in particular for a while when the doorbell rings.

"Hey, Mom," I greet as I open the door.

She steps in and gives me a big hug, saying, "It's good to see you, dear."

"Donna?" I hear Candace call out from behind me, and when I turn to see her walking down the stairs, the surprised look on her face makes me smile.

"Candace," Mom says, excited to see her.

"What are you doing here?" She is completely caught off guard, wearing her pajamas with her hair pulled on top of her head, as she gives my mom an excited hug.

"I wasn't going to miss your birthday. But I'm a little disappointed that I had to hear about it from Ryan when you and I talk every week."

I step beside Candace, shoot her a wink, and kiss her on the cheek.

"Sorry, I . . . I don't normally do anything for my birthday, but I'm so happy you're here," she says and then hugs Mom again. "I can't believe you drove all this way."

"It's a few hours, dear. Hardly a chore." I watch as my mom takes Candace's hand and walks over to Mark and Jase.

Candace introduces them, and I make my way into the kitchen.

"Mom, what do you want to drink?"

"A glass of wine will be good."

"Me too," Candace tells me, and I laugh at the memory of her drunk the last time she had wine with Jase, so I just have to tease her, asking, "You're not gonna get drunk, slap my ass, and tell me how sexy I am, are you?"

"Ryan!" she scolds, completely embarrassed, and shoots a look towards my mom.

I laugh at her, knowing that she has nothing to be concerned about when it comes to my mom. She adores Candace, and the two of them have become quite close in the past couple of months.

I take a seat on the couch next to Candace as the three of us chat. I wanted to do something more for tonight, but this was probably the best idea. As we spend the evening relaxing and visiting over pizza, wine, and beer, I take in the fact that I have never had this before. At least not here in Seattle. I'm close with my family back home, but never felt that connection here, until now—until her. I've always known from the start that Jase, Candace, and Mark were tight. Just the three of them. And before I realized it, I'd become a part of that.

I've never had friendships and connections like I have

with these people. I never wanted to. Even though they are all younger than me, when I saw the level of closeness and trust between the three of them, I saw what I had been missing. Candace made me want that—the connect. The commonality between us was something that was lacking in my previous friendships. For the first time since I moved here, the first time in the past ten years, I have people that I trust and care about.

It's unfortunate when I think about it, but in a way, it's Candace's trauma that has bonded the four of us. I know we all love her in our own unique way, and at the root, there's never been jealousy. Only three men that love this girl. And knowing that she has all of us gives me a level of security that I never expected to feel.

So we take this night, and like any family would, we laugh and eat cheap birthday cake straight from the box. Mom helps me clean up in the kitchen while Candace sits on the floor, cuddled into Jase, bantering back and forth with Mark, determined to get that plastic ring from him.

"I love her."

I look at my mom when she says this to me as we load the dishwasher.

"She's really something special," she adds.

"Yeah, she is," I agree as I watch her from across the room.

We finish up and wipe the counters down, and Candace asks as we walk back in, "Hey, you guys wanna watch a movie?"

"You all go ahead. I'm going to get some sleep so I'm rested for tomorrow," my mom says.

Candace walks over and gives her a hug, saying, "Thanks again for coming, Donna."

"How about we spend a little girl time tomorrow, just the two of us?"

"That sounds perfect."

"I love being ditched by the women in my life," I tease as I step behind Candace and wrap my arms around her shoulders.

"I'm sure you can find something to busy yourself with," my mom shoots back at me. "Good night, you two."

"Let me help you get settled in," I offer when she starts to head back to the guest bedroom. I stand there for a moment with Candace in my arms and then turn her around to face me. Tilting her head back to look up at me, I kiss her before saying, "Give me a couple of minutes."

When I return, the lights are off, and the three of them have made a pile of pillows and blankets in the middle of the living room with the fireplace going.

"You guys work fast," I murmur as I lie down next to Candace and tuck her into me.

We watch 'The Breakfast Club,' and about halfway through, Jase and Mark call it a night and head out, leaving Candace and I alone for the first time tonight.

She rolls over in my arms and weaves her legs with mine.

"Thank you," she says softly.

"For?"

"Your mom and the cake."

I kiss her nose, and she smiles as I say, "Anytime."

"I love you," she says before she kisses me.

When our kisses turn into more, I stop and sit up. "Come on." I grab her hand and tell her, "I want you in my bed, under my sheets," before taking her upstairs.

As expected, the girls woke up this morning and went out for breakfast and shopping. I decided to take the time and work on the photos of Candace's legs that I took the other day. I spent most of the morning in my office, working on the computer before going to the gym to grab a quick workout.

It's a little after noon by the time they get back. When they walk through the door, their hands are full of shopping bags.

"Damn, that was a long breakfast," I joke as I help them with their bags.

"Sorry, time got away from us. If I didn't have to go home, I would have spent the whole day with her," Mom says.

"Well, thanks for bringing her back. I'm sick of sharing her," I tease as I wrap my arm around Candace.

Nudging me in the gut, she playfully scolds, "Ryan!"

"Sorry, babe, but it's the truth," I remark and then go in for a nibble on her neck.

"Okay, kids. I've seen enough. I'm going to go pack," my mom says, heading down the hall.

"Ryan, that tickles," she laughs, trying to squirm out of my arms. Picking her up, I haul her over to the couch where I lay her down and start planting soft kisses on her. "Did you have a good time this morning?" I ask between my nips and then lick the hollow of her neck.

"Uh huh."

I continue to kiss her like this until she says, "Ryan, we should stop."

"Why?"

"Because your mom is about to leave, and you should go spend a little time with her before she goes."

Not wanting to stop, I let out a groan and tell her, "Okay, but I'm not done with you."

Candace takes her shopping bags and goes upstairs while I check in with my mom.

"Did you two have fun?" I ask, sitting on the edge of the bed as she gets her things together to leave.

"We did. She took me over to the coffee shop where she works."

"What did you guys talk about?"

"You're nosey," she quips, and I laugh at her, but she quickly straightens her face and comes to sit next to me on the bed. "She's worried."

"About what?" I ask.

"Have you given any thought to what's going to happen after she graduates?"

"Yeah, Mom, I have. Is that what's bothering her?"

"It would be odd if it weren't. Isn't it bothering you?" she questions.

"I try not to let it. But whatever happens, I'd never leave her."

"Sometimes girls need a little extra reassurance," she offers as she pats my knee and smiles.

I help my mom with her bag as I walk her out.

"Candace," I call to her upstairs.

"Coming," she responds, and as she's walking down, I see the sadness creep across her face. She doesn't say anything, going over to hug my mom. I feel bad as she starts to cry, knowing she wants to spend more time with her.

I reach out and place my hand on her back when she pulls away from the hug, and my mom says, "Come see me, okay?"

Candace nods her head, and I know that she hates the sound of her voice when she's this upset, so she stays quiet as I wrap my arms around her from behind.

"When is your next break?"

"She has the last two weeks of this month off before her last quarter," I answer for her so she doesn't have to speak.

"You and Ryan come visit, okay?" she offers as she looks at her.

We say our goodbyes, and she leaves to drive back home. Turning Candace around, I hold her in my arms and give her a few minutes to just be sad. I'm grateful for the bond the two of them have forged, but I don't like seeing my girl upset like this.

"You okay, babe?"

"I hate that she lives so far away," she says as I wipe her face. "I really like having her around."

"I know you do. We'll go visit her when you're on your break."

She rests her head on my chest and sighs before saying, "My parents never even called me." I grip the back of her head and hold her tight as she adds, "I mean . . . I knew they wouldn't, but it still hurts."

"I know it does."

And this is the shit I hate. Thinking about her mom and dad, wondering how they could turn away from their daughter so easily. I know it's possible because of my own dad, but thinking about everything Candace has gone through in the past several months cuts me deep, and all I want to do is protect her from anything that could hurt her.

"Come on, let's go grab something to eat before we go to the campus," I tell her and just hope to God that she got this solo because I don't want to see how upset she'll be if she didn't.

Seeing the look on her face was priceless. She was shocked

and giddy and couldn't control her enthusiasm when she jumped into my arms, squealing. She got her solo, and I couldn't have been more proud. This girl works her ass off, but it got me thinking more about what my mom said. I'm not ignorant of the fact that Candace will probably get a job that requires her to move. I've been taking a lot of time away from the bar these past few weeks, and I need to start considering what her moving means for me and my business.

When I walk into the bedroom, I notice that the door to the bathroom is cracked open. Slowly opening the door wider, I see her standing there in my boxers and a tank top, finishing up brushing her teeth. It's been a long day, and she's been through a string of emotions since this morning. I walk up from behind and slip my arms around her as I drop a few kisses along the curve of her bare shoulder. She holds on to my arms with her hands as we watch each other in the mirror.

She turns around, and I lift her up onto the edge of the sink and look down at her; she has a peaceful look about her tonight.

"You're fuckin' gorgeous," I tell her, and my words make her laugh as I lower my mouth to hers.

Sliding my tongue past her lips, she hooks her ankles behind my waist, burying her hands in my hair. Her touch excites me but in a soothing way. I pick her up, walk her across the room, and fall into bed with her. I stare down, and I know, that no matter what happens, she has me. I don't want to belong to anyone but her.

She runs her hands up my chest and around to the back of my neck, pulling me down, and we kiss. We kiss in a way that's different than all the times before. I can't explain it, but it takes over me, holding a new level of passion. I press her firmly to me, tasting the mint that still lingers in her mouth.

Lifting her back off the bed, I sit her up and watch her as she removes her top. I get caught up in her and press her back down onto the bed, situating my hips between her legs. She's so warm against me, and my chest begins to tighten with the effect this girl has on me.

I never gave my heart to anyone before. I never wanted to. I was scared. But maybe I was just saving it for her. And now, I want to give this girl more than my heart. I want to give her everything.

Realizing that I'm getting too carried away with myself, I pull back, nearly panting, "We should stop," as I rest my forehead on her sternum.

She runs her hands through my hair, whispering, "Don't."

Her words are unexpected, so I pull up to look over her face, to try and read what she's thinking.

"Babe," I breathe out, heavy.

She looks me straight in the eyes and tells me, "I don't want you to stop."

"I need you to talk to me," I respond with nerves coursing through me, unsure of what to do here.

"I don't want to stop tonight."

Fear. That's what comes over me when I hear her words. Closing my eyes, I drop my head to hers. My heart is racing when I urge, "Please tell me this is okay," because the thought of this scares me.

She nods her head against mine, but it isn't enough. "I need to hear you say it, babe."

I finally open my eyes when she cups my face and assures me, "It's okay. I want this, with you, I just . . . I don't know if I can."

But suddenly, I don't know if *I* can. I want to. I've

wanted to since I met her, but now . . . now I'm afraid, and I don't know what to do with her. I'm not sure if she sees my panic when she takes my hand in hers and places it over her breast, urging quietly, "Just touch me."

Her hand trembles against mine, and if this does happen, I can't have her feeling like this. So I do everything I can to push my anxiety away to focus on making sure she's relaxed. She's been taken advantage of by the two people before me, and I want to make this perfect for her.

I lower myself and kiss her. I take my time and *really* kiss her. Pressing my lips slowly into hers, grazing my tongue along her lip, and sealing my mouth with hers. My hand slides up from her breast and underneath the strap on her shoulder. As I move my hand down her arm, I take the strap with it, slipping it off, feeling the tension in the elastic releasing.

She's never let me see her naked. The closest, a bra and my boxers. So when I begin to reach around her, my anticipation is overwhelming. But then, in a moment, she nervously mutters, "I'm scared. I've never . . ."

"It's just you and me," I tell her. "You're all I'll ever want."

She faintly nods, and when I unclasp the hooks behind her back, she crosses her arm over her chest. Laying my hand over hers, I lift it up and drop her bra to the floor. I look at her. I've always wanted to but she's always been too shy. Then my eyes stop on a serrated, crescent scar on her left breast, and what I think it might be is confirmed when she shamefully bares, "He bit me."

I won't let that piece of shit filter into this moment. She's embarrassed, and there's no fuckin' way I'm gonna let that bastard claim another piece of her. Even with this scar, he can't take away from how gorgeous she is.

Leaning down, I kiss her scar and breathe into her skin, "God, you're perfect."

I take my kisses and drop them down her stomach before sitting back on my heels to remind her that she isn't alone. I bring her hand to my ribs and over my scar. We don't speak. There's no need. She gets it when she brushes her thumb across the jagged line and then pulls me down to her, hands trussed in my hair.

The feel of her naked body against my chest is gratifying beyond words. With no barriers, I run my tongue up the smooth skin of her breast and slowly across her pert nipple before taking her into my mouth. The pressure of her fingertips pressing into my shoulders strengthens when my hands find themselves at the band of her shorts. She lifts her hips when I begin to remove her boxers and panties at the same time. God, every inch of her is stunning, and I suddenly feel undeserving to have this girl who is far above what I could have ever imagined for myself.

She watches as I slip off my pants and then lower myself back to her, grabbing the sheets and covering us up. I lie here naked with her and have never felt so connected. She's warm against me, but as I trail my hands slowly along her soft skin, I can feel her trembling.

"Babe, you're shaking."

"What if I can't do this?" she says with an uneven voice, worry etched in the lines of her face.

"Then we stop."

Her eyes fall shut, and I assure her, "We'll move as slow as you need. You just tell me when to stop."

"I don't want you to stop," she says, opening her eyes.

She slides her arms around me and draws my body back to hers as she kisses me, caressing her lips with mine, taking her time as she runs her hands along my chest and down my abdomen, making my muscles cinch at the touch. Her lips drag along my neck and down my shoulder while I gently knead her supple breast in my hand and kiss her exposed neck. When my mouth finds her hardened nipple again, I roll my tongue over it and begin to gently suck, her body writhing in response.

"Ryan." The sound of my name on her lips is sexy as hell, and I need her to tell me again before we move any further, so I ask, "You sure?"

"Yes."

My anxiety is back. The rush of emotions swarms in my chest as I try to stay calm for her, but I just need to hear it. "Tell me that you want this, that you want me."

"I want you to make love to me," she says with her eyes pinned to mine.

I take a moment to slip on protection before I reach down and slowly begin to guide myself inside of her, but as soon as I touch her, she locks up on me. Pulling myself back, I look down to see the rapid rise and fall of her chest.

"Are you okay?"

Holding on to my shoulders, she nods. "Yeah."

I've never been so scared to have sex, but I know with her, that's not what this is. I've never been with a woman like this before. I know I'm gonna make love with her, and I want to do everything possible to make this perfect. 'Cause for the first time in my life, this isn't about me—it's about her. So when I continue to push myself inside of her, I can feel every bit of how tense she is. It takes me a while, but when I'm finally inside of her, the feeling is almost too much for me. My head drops to her neck as I moan, "Fuck, you feel so good, babe," unable to keep it in.

I hold myself still while her thighs tremble as she clenches them against my hips. I wrap my hands around her head and give her time to relax. When I pull my head back, I immediately feel like shit when I see her eyes clamped shut with tears falling down her temples.

"Open your eyes, Candace. Look at me," I tell her, concerned about what she's seeing if she isn't seeing me.

"Don't make me look," she pleads, but I need her to. I need her to not be scared of this. To not let her mind drift to that alley. To show her that this can be something amazing.

"Baby, please open your eyes. I need you here with *me*. It's only me."

It takes her a second, but she eventually opens them and focuses on me. When I feel her body soften against mine, I gradually begin to move. Being this close with her—inside of her—I never want this to end. I can't even imagine wanting to be selfish with her, so I move slowly, needing this closeness to last. To make her see this for what it is—love.

Banding my arms around her, she clings to me, and the sounds of pleasure coming out of her are all I hear. Sighs, breaths, quiet moans. They turn me on even more as our bodies begin to work together, moving in a way I know I'll always want with her.

"God, I love you," I release on a ragged exhale and slide deeper inside of her.

Moving to kiss me, she mumbles over my lips, "I love you."

I notice her hands are still clenching my shoulders, so I reach up and take one of her hands in mine, lacing my fingers with hers, pressing our hands into the mattress. She begins to sway her hips up to mine as she starts moving with me. Her body is so tight around me that it takes a lot for me to hang on and not let go. I watch her beneath me, her body against mine, completely exposed to me, and I don't think I could fall any more deeply in love with her. I'm not sure how that would even be possible.

We take our time with each other, making love, lingering in the moment. When she closes her eyes, she constricts her legs to my hips, and I know she's close. I also know that she's never had this before.

"Relax, babe," I tell her because I want her to feel every piece of what I'm about to give her.

She has her hand braced tightly around the back of my neck when her breathing falters. I kiss her, simply resting my lips on hers, as I continue to ease myself in and out of her, feeling every part of her around me. Her hand jerks in mine, and I lift my head to tell her, "Open your eyes. Stay with me," wanting to be sure that I'm all she sees.

Locking her eyes with mine, her body is damp with a sheen of sweat, and I give in to the intensity that has been building inside of me when I hear her let out a whimper. It doesn't take me long to get to where she is, so when I say, "Baby, let go for me," her hips buckle, and she clamps her hand strongly around mine as I watch her lose herself, face flushed, panting out soft moans. I can't hold on when I feel her walls tighten and spasm around me. Dropping my head onto hers, I moan her name as I come hard, feeling the impassioned throbs with my release, giving myself in a way I didn't know was possible for me.

We lie here, bodies pressed together, breathing labored, as we both come down. When I finally lift my heavy head to look at her, the tears are back. Afraid that this has had some negative effect on her, I ask in utter worry, "God, baby, what's wrong?" as I wipe her tears.

She takes a slow moment before giving me words that almost break me.

"Being with you . . . that's all I want."

This is a lot. My emotions are all over the place, but they all lie within her heart. I keep myself inside of her, never wanting to leave, and when I lay my head against hers, I quietly confess, "You're the only one I've ever done that with. You're the only one I've ever made love to."

I didn't think there was anything I could give her that would be new, untouched, and only hers—until now. She's the only one that will ever have me like this. And finally experiencing sex in this way, I'll never want it any other way.

chapter thirty-two

Watching her sleep right now, hair draped over the pillow, face soft, lips slightly parted—she's beautiful. I could stare at her for hours when she's this peaceful, but I know she's going to wake soon, so I go ahead and slip quietly out of bed and head into the closet. I knew I wouldn't give her the necklace on her birthday. She probably would have resisted, so that's why I held off. But we're alone now, and it's not her birthday anymore.

I take the necklace out of its box and go into the bathroom, shutting the door behind me. I set it in between the two sinks and then brush my teeth before I get back into bed. Wrapping myself around her, my movements start to wake her, so I feign sleep as she begins to stir awake. I lie there, still, as she slides out from under my arm, and I can hear her close the bathroom door a few seconds later. I roll over and wait for her to come out. Listening to the water run, I wonder if the gift is going to irritate her when she made it perfectly clear she didn't want me to get her anything.

The door opens, and Candace walks out with a sly grin, holding the necklace up in front of her.

"What's this?" she questions, knowing very well what it

is, but I play into her and say, "Well, it's definitely not a birthday gift, because that was two days ago."

Her laughter is a relief when she hops up into bed and hands me the necklace to put on her.

"I love it," she says as I clasp it on, and she doesn't need to say anything else about it. She's read the scribed words. She's accepted it without hesitation. That's all I wanted.

Crawling over her as she lies on her back, I drop kisses along the chain. "Do you know how beautiful you are?"

"Mmmm," she hums.

"You were amazing last night," I tell her when I start removing her clothes because I need her again. We were both so cautious last night, and now, seeing her naked and having her calm, I want to give this to her again, and she lets me.

As we remain wrapped up in each other after making love, I stroke my hand through her hair lazily, enjoying her as our breathing slows back down.

"How are you feeling?"

She's in a tranquil state when she responds with a simple, "Happy."

That one word makes me smile. That's all I ever want her to be—happy. I begin to laugh when I think about the other surprise I have for her.

"What's so funny?" she asks with a grin of her own.

"I have something else for you."

"Besides the necklace?"

"Besides the necklace," I say.

She squints her eyes at me, and I defend, "I promise, you're gonna like this better. It's not a trinket."

That smile of hers grows and she sits up, clutching the sheet to keep herself covered, and her modesty is adorable. Leaning over, I open the drawer to my nightstand and then hand it over to her.

"I don't know what to say," she says as she keeps her eyes on the Hop N Bounce box, which holds the deflated ball.

"I have a pump out in the garage if you wanna take it for a spin around the living room," I tease.

Setting the box down on the bed, she crawls to me, sheet still clung around her, and gives me a kiss.

"You'll never know how much I love you."

After spending most of the morning in bed with Candace, I decided to run into work so that I can take the night off. Candace called Jase and went to spend the afternoon with him and Mark. I told her I'd be back at the loft around six tonight, but that quickly changed when one of our vendors stopped by today with a shipment only to inform me that the bar is now on COD with them. When I started digging through the backlogged bills, I discovered that Michael has been missing payments.

This is the second time this guy has fucked up, and I'm done. Walking into his office, the place is a disorganized disaster. Digging through his files, I find the ones that I need, and I spend the next few hours scouring through all of our various vendors' invoices, checking them against the bank statements, and then having Mel double-check the inventory.

I can't be having things fall through the cracks like this. I need to seriously start thinking about what's gonna happen to this bar if I wind up moving after Candace is done with school, but leaving it in Michael's hands isn't gonna happen. I need someone I can trust.

"Max," I call out while Mel and I are buried behind the bar as I help her check the last shipment.

"Yeah, boss."

"Get Michael on the phone. Tell him to get his ass up here," I shout over the band. I've been so busy, I didn't even realize how late it is or that Mark is here with the guys, but they're already on stage playing.

"Ryan!" Max shouts, and the chaos around me right now is giving me a headache.

"Did you get ahold of him?"

"Yeah, he's on his way, but Candace is on the phone. Line two," he says.

Making my way through the crowd, I run upstairs to take the call in my office where it's quiet.

"Babe, hey."

"Hey, I didn't think you were going to be working this late," she says, and I feel bad that I'm still stuck up here when all I want is to be home.

I explain everything to her, stressed about the whole situation, as she listens and then let her know that I'll be heading home in a bit. Hanging up the phone, I start getting my things together, and about five minutes later, Michael walks into my office.

"Shit, that was fast," I say.

"I was on my way up here when Max called. What's up? You leaving?" he asks as he stands there watching me.

"Yeah, but we need to talk," I say as I take a seat, and he follows suit. "I found out today that invoices haven't been getting paid. Never, in the six years I've owned this place, have we missed a payment, and now we're on COD with one of our vendors."

"Ryan—"

"Look," I say, interrupting him. "I'm gonna cut to the

chase. This bar is my livelihood, and when shit starts going wrong, then that livelihood is compromised. Feelings aside, I gotta let you go, man. I can't trust you to handle things up here when I'm not around, and that's a problem for me."

"Ryan, man. Come on."

"Look, my ass is tired. Been up here all day trying to fix your mistakes, and I'm ready to go home," I tell him as I grab my coat and leave. My stress is through the roof, and I don't have time to dick around with this guy.

I find Max when I get downstairs.

"Hey, I need to talk to you."

"What's going on?" he questions as we step into the back storage room.

"I just fired Michael, so I want you to go up there and oversee him as he packs his shit up. Make sure we get his keys and everything—"

"Hey, I got it covered. No worries."

"Thanks. I'm getting the hell out of here. I'll be back in the morning. There's a stack of papers on top of my filing cabinet. Make sure he signs them before he leaves."

"Got it."

I don't waste any more time, knowing that Max will handle the Michael situation, and I head home to my girl.

Candace and I camped out downstairs with some wine and an old movie when I got home last night. We hadn't done that in a while, so it was a perfect way to end the stressful day. I did manage to talk to her about trying to come to the bar again. I wasn't sure if I was pushing too much, but I figured this morning would be a good time since it would only be the two of us. She took me by surprise when she said she would try. I know this isn't easy for her, and while I'm in the kitchen fixing her a coffee to take with us, I watch her sitting on the couch, wringing her hands together. She's a nervous wreck. I walk over and hand her the coffee, telling her, "Babe, you don't have to do this if it's causing you this much stress."

"I told you that I would try, so . . . I'll try."

Holding my hand out, she takes it and we head to the bar. The morning is cold and the sky is dark with cloud cover. Candace is silent, and I keep my hand on her knee as I pull up and park along the curb in front of the building like I promised her.

When I open her door, she finally snaps out of her zoned-out state and holds my hand as I help her out. We walk inside, and I show her around before I take her back to the stairs.

"My office is up here," I tell her as I lead her up.

I keep my hold on her hand when I walk into Michael's office to grab the papers I need. Taking a few steps into his office, she jerks around, stumbling over her feet and into me.

"Babe?"

"I want to go," she says with her head down, and as I reach around her to quickly grab the file, I see what she saw and kick myself for not thinking beforehand that Michael's office overlooks the back lot.

I tuck her under my arm as I quickly pull her out and walk her down the hall to my office, tossing the file on my desk, and turning to hold her.

"I'm sorry, I didn't think," I say as she shakes under my arms—panicked.

I back us up to the desk and lean against it as I pull her between my legs. She keeps her head on my chest, and I continue rubbing her back, trying to calm her down. She isn't speaking. I know she's trying hard to keep herself together, and all of a sudden, being here with her isn't something I want to be doing anymore. I hate that this was the first place I ever saw her. I hate the visions that are starting to play back through my head.

I hold her, but all I can see is her covered in blood and dirt, lying naked on the ground. My heart rate picks up as the guilt returns. I could have done so many things differently that night. If I would have just gone out there sooner . . .

I focus back on Candace when she lifts her head. Keeping my focus on her before I get too consumed, I ask, "You okay?"

She nods, placing her head back on my chest, saying, "I hate seeing that dumpster." I hold her closer when she says this because I hate it too. I hate everything about that goddamn night. "It's weird because I also love it in a messed up way. It's all I had to focus on."

"I'm so sorry." I think about what must have been going through her head, the sheer terror she must have felt, and my stomach begins to knot up.

"When I dream about that night, it's always taken away from me. There's nothing to distract me."

"I wish I knew his name." I would find him and destroy him if given the chance. I would kill him for everything he took away from her.

She looks up at me and cups my clenched jaw, lifting onto her toes, and planting a kiss on my lips. I pull her into me and take a deep breath, letting it out slowly. Being here with her, I'm starting to feel like I'm lying, and the guilt is eating at me the longer we are here. I never thought that deciding not to tell her about who I am would make me feel like it is right now. Deceitful.

I'm trying to keep the memories out of my head, but I

can't help the constant flashes I'm getting each time I close my eyes. I'm not sure I'll ever stop hearing her pleading screams from that night. It's a part of her that I'll always have to bear, but it'll never even come close to all that she has had to endure.

I shift my thoughts because this is huge for her, and I need her to know that. I tell her how proud I am that she came up here with me, but I can tell she wants to leave, and honestly, so do I.

Chapter Thirty-Three

I call Max as I drive to see if he can meet me at the bar after my workout. I've been giving a lot of thought to getting things settled at work since I fired Michael a couple weeks ago, and the one person who knows that place inside and out, the one person I trust completely, is Max. It only makes sense to me that he would be someone that I could have complete confidence in, and knowing that he has a baby on the way, he'd be an idiot to not take the opportunity I'm about to offer him.

After a couple hours of lifting and running, I head up to Blur to meet with Max. He's sitting at the bar, chatting with Mel when I walk in.

"Hey, man. Let's go to my office," I say, and he follows me up the stairs.

"So, what's on your mind?" he asks as we sit down.

"I'm gonna be honest with you here," I start. "Candace is graduating in a couple of months, and I doubt that she's gonna be staying here in Seattle."

"You think you'll go with her?" he asks.

"I can't let her go without me, but I can't let this place fold either," I tell him. "I know you have a lot going on with Traci, but . . ."

"Look, you know I'll help out in any way I can."

"I was hoping you could help run this place," I say. "You know everything about the job, and you've always been loyal to me. Shit's been crazy since I let Michael go, but I'd like to bring you on as his permanent replacement, which means a sizable salary increase."

"Are you serious?" he says as he leans forward, resting his elbows on his knees.

"Completely. It's yours."

He stands up and I follow as he walks towards me and claps his hand in mine for a solid shake as he grips my shoulder with his other hand.

"So, you're in?" I ask.

"I'm in, boss."

"Great," I sigh in relief as I sit back down. "You know the drill, man, so let's get this going in the next couple days if you can manage on short notice?"

"Yeah. No problem. You still going out of town this weekend?"

"Yep. I'm not sure how long I'll be gone. A week, give or take a few days. It's Candace's last break before graduation, and I know she wants to spend time with my mom."

"You need an extra guy for the door?" he asks.

"I don't think so. Chase has been doing a good job at keeping everything under control in that department. Plus people are used to seeing you down there, so I think if you can keep that gig going when you have extra time, that would be great."

We finish up, filling out a few forms and going over some stuff I need him to take care of while I'm in Oregon next week. Having this situation settled takes a lot of stress off my shoulders, and even though Candace has yet to bring up school coming to an end, she has nothing to worry about.

When I'm all done, I head back to the loft, but Candace's car is still gone as I pull into the driveway. I grab a quick shower and get cleaned up. When she gets home a little while later we spend the afternoon listening to a few demos from local bands. Mark is graduating with most of the guys in the band, so I need to go ahead and find alternatives for when their gig is up with me in June.

I watch Candace in the kitchen, and when she walks back into the room, I tell her, "Something's been bothering me today." As she moves past me, I grab her and pull her onto my lap. "I've never seen you dance."

"Oh . . . yeah, I guess not," she says and then adds, "But you will in May when we have our production. You'll see me a lot. I have three ensembles plus my solo."

"It just bothers me that there is a huge part of your life that I've never seen." I see her nearly every day wearing her leotards, warm-up pants, and leg-warmers. I even watch her stretch and do her ankle exercises every chance I get. But I have yet to see my girl dance.

"Well, I can grab some videos at the studio of past performances," she offers. "They have also recorded some of our studios this year. Would that suffice for you, watching me on video?"

I grab her, flipping her down on the couch onto her back, and nip her neck before letting her know, "Nothing about you will ever suffice for me. I'm always gonna want more."

She laughs as we continue to kiss, and when she begins tugging my shirt up, I reach back and pull it over my head, tossing it onto the floor. Her smile is big and she keeps it on her face when I take her ankle and begin kissing and sucking my way up her leg. I love these legs.

I grip her behind her knees and go in for a slow kiss. The taste of her in my mouth is something I'll never tire of, so I take it as she runs her hands up my arms, my neck, and into my hair, fisting it in her hands.

She's playful with me as we take our time removing each other's clothing. My need to touch her is strong, but I know she's still really hesitant about being touched in that way, so I don't even try. Her light-heartedness right now is charming, and when she giggles and admits, "This tattoo is hot," as she grazes my shoulder with her hand, I smile down at her and laugh.

"Why's that?"

Pressing her lips together, she shakes her head, too shy to say what she's thinking, and I tease, "Don't let it fool you. I'm a private school prep just like you."

She laughs at me, responding with, "Your small town private school?" poking fun.

I run my hands down her small shoulders and take both of her breasts in my hands as I say with a smirk, "That small town has a lot of money running through it, and you love it there."

"I do love it there," she agrees and then runs her hand down the center of my chest, before adding in a more serious tone, "But I love it here—with you—more."

After I put on some protection, I make my way to the place I love the most—inside of her. She wraps her arms around my neck as we make love on my couch while the rain pours outside the windows. The beating of the rain mixed with our breaths fills the room as we take our time with each other, her eyes never straying from mine as I give myself to her.

I roll to the side, bringing her with me as I grab her thigh and drape it over my hip. Taking her bottom in my hand, I rock her into me as our heads are pressed together. Her eyes fully sated, green with golden flakes, her hands on my cheeks, sweet breath brushing my lips. Fuck, she's amazing at this.

Running my hand lazily up and down her bare back, we lie on the floor, wrapped up in a blanket together. With her head on my chest, she's been really quiet ever since we made love earlier.

"What are you thinking about, babe?"

"Hmm," she hums softly.

Laughing under my breath, I say, "That's a pathetic answer," and then feel her chest as she silently laughs.

"Seriously though. What's on your mind? You've been really quiet."

"I ran into Kimber today. She was leaving Jase's when I walked into his building."

"Did you guys talk?"

"She just asked where I've been, and I could tell she was hurt. Jase told me she reached out to him and that she's really upset."

"I'm sorry, babe. I know how much this bothers you. Have you thought anymore about talking to her?"

Now that I know what the issue is between them, I tried talking to Candace about reaching out to her roommate the other week, but she shut it down, telling me that the only way Kimber would talk to her is if she told her the truth, and she didn't want to do that. I know that she doesn't want to say the words. She told me that she never even said them to Jase; she made a nurse tell him at the hospital, and that I'm the only one she's spoken them to. When she explained this to me, I dropped it.

"I just can't. I don't trust her enough to not do something."

"I don't know what to tell you to do. Just try talking to her and see if you guys can move past this," I offer weakly.

She closes her eyes before saying, "I think it would help if I went back home."

"Candace . . ."

"Ryan, I was only supposed to be here for a week or two. I never intended on moving in like this," she tells me. "But, we are about to graduate, and I'd like to see if this is fixable. I can't do that if I'm not there."

"I still want you here," I let her know, not wanting her to leave.

"And I'll still be here. Just not *every* night."

Candace has been staying with me for a little over a month, and I love that she's here and that I get to come home to her every night. But I also know that this is important to her, and even though I don't like the idea of her no longer staying here, I won't be anything other than completely supportive of her.

"Okay," I respond. "We can go tomorrow and take some of your things back."

She smiles and says, "Thanks for understanding," and then gives me a kiss as I press her naked body against mine, fully savoring the rest of our night.

"Babe, you don't have to pack everything," I complain as I watch her pulling her clothes out of my closet. Truth is, I don't like this feeling in my stomach right now as she packs her stuff up. I like seeing her things in my space.

Getting off the bed, I walk inside the closet to where she

is and say, "Just leave a few things."

With an armful of clothes, she turns to me and says, "Ryan, I live less than five minutes away from you. I'll still be here."

I know I'm being a pussy about this, but I don't give a shit. I like her with me, here in my home, in my bed. So I repeat, "Just leave a few things."

She steps to me and looks up as I fold her in my arms. "I love you," she whispers, and I give her back the same words.

I carry her bags downstairs and out to the car before I drive her back to her house. Kimber's car is there when we pull up, and Candace lets out a deep breath.

"You okay?"

"I know I need to be here, but it's just so hard."

I get out of the car and walk around to her side, opening the door. "Call me or come over whenever. You don't even have to ask. You have the keys—use them."

She turns in her seat as I move between her legs, grabbing on to her behind her hips, and she takes my face in her hands and kisses me. I don't let up. I keep kissing her, taking in the feel of her soft lips as she melds them with mine. She has no idea what she's doing to me, and I have to pull back.

"Come on," I say. "I'll go in with you."

When we walk in, I take her bags back to her room and am helping her unpack her things when her roommate, whom I've never met, steps in the doorway and asks, "You're back?"

"Um . . . yeah," I watch Candace tell her nervously.

When Kimber doesn't respond, I try breaking some of the tension and introduce myself. "I'm Ryan, by the way."

She nods her head, saying, "I'm Kimber."

That's it for our exchange as she stands there. She's tall

with platinum blonde hair and has a look about her that's very different from Candace's.

"Well, Seth's on his way over, so I'll be in my room," she says before walking out.

Candace goes over and closes the door, keeping her hands on it as she drops her head. I step next to her and see she's crying.

"Babe," I whisper as I hold her face.

"I don't know what to do," she says as she hugs me.

There's nothing I can say because I honestly think there isn't much of a friendship to be mended at this point. Candace chose to keep this secret from Kimber, and I don't blame her. From what little I have heard about this chick, she's seems like a spitfire who would probably run her mouth. But regardless, Kimber's been out of the loop while Candace has been dealing with some heavy shit, and even Jase told me that she's a completely different person now. Kimber's missed all of that, so it's not so far-fetched to safely assume that what once bonded them is no longer there.

We lie down on her bed for a while, not ready to leave just yet. She's no longer crying, but I know she's still upset about the whole situation, so I tell her, "I don't want you thinking that you're the one to blame for what's happened with you and Kimber. This isn't your fault. You made the best decision that you could at the time when you chose to not tell her about what happened. Nobody holds that against you, and I don't want you too either."

"It's easy to say, but . . ."

"You haven't done anything wrong here. Sometimes life just sucks, and things fall apart. Not all friendships can last forever. People change, and whether you want to admit it or not, you've changed. And I don't want you thinking shit about yourself because I love every single piece of who you are—right now."

I watch as her face scrunches up and she begins to cry. "Baby, don't."

Looking up at me through her tears, she reveals, "I wish every day that you knew me before. That you didn't have to deal with this baggage. I think about how everything could have been so different than it is now. Better."

"Who says it would be better?" I question as I smooth her hair back.

"Because it never would have happened."

I shift to my side to face her, saying, "I wish, more than you will ever know, that this never happened to you. But there isn't one single part of you that I would change. That night is a piece of you, but it doesn't tarnish you. Not for me. I love us. I love what we have together and what you give me. Somehow you got inside me. No one has been able to do that before, but you did. You've seen shit that I've never let anyone see. Shit that I've masked for years, but with you . . . you made me want to take the mask off and in the process I fell in love with you. So I don't know how you think we could be any better than we are because I think we're pretty perfect." I run my thumb across her cheek, wiping her tears.

"I don't . . . I don't even know what to say."

"You don't need to say anything. Just know that you have me. I'm here because of you. I'm yours because I don't want to give myself to anyone else. No one could ever compare to you."

chapter thirty-four

I can barely focus on the road as I drive to Thinkspace for the gallery showing tonight. Candace looks amazing in the lace dress she's wearing. I never thought pencil skirts were sexy until I saw them on her. Most of her dressier outfits are of the same style and tonight, I would have rather stayed in with the dress tossed to the floor, but I have every intention of ending the night that way.

Candace hasn't stayed over with me since she went back home, and I've missed not having her there with me. I also worry. There is rarely a night when she doesn't have problems sleeping. Ever since that one horrifying nightmare, she's been back on her sleeping pill, but she says they only help control the really vivid dreams. She still wakes often from night terrors, and I don't like the idea of her dealing with that alone, but she insists that she's fine.

When we arrive, I help Candace down from her seat and lead her inside. She's been so excited for tonight, inviting Jase, Mark, and Gavin. I never took my photography that seriously until lately. I've been spending more time shooting, mostly Candace, and editing. I like the focus of having a hobby, and knowing that I can share that with her is a bonus.

"I'm really proud of you, you know?" she says as we walk inside.

"Babe, the only reason that photo is on display is because you're in it. You're perfect."

I take her coat and check it when I hear a lady call, "Candace!"

"Stacy, hi," Candace says and hugs a tall, slender woman who looks close to my age with short, raven hair.

"That dress is amazing," she says to Candace.

"Thank you."

"And this is . . .?" she asks as she looks at me.

"Ryan," Candace introduces.

"Ahh, 'Nubile.' Beautiful photograph," she says as I reach out to take her hand. "I'm Stacy Keets. I work at the Henry Gallery."

"Ryan Campbell," I say.

"Well, your piece is great. I saw a couple eying it a minute ago. Do you have more pieces?"

"A few," I tell her. "It wasn't ever something I intended to show anyone or have displayed, but Candace insisted," I add with a smile as I wrap my hand around her waist.

"I'm glad she did. I'd love to see more of your work," she tells me before looking at Candace and asking, "Do you still have my number?"

"Yes, I do."

"Give me a call," she says to me. "We have some wall space opening up soon, so if you're interested, we can discuss the possibility of displaying some of your pieces."

"Will do. I'll have Candace give me your number."

She turns back to Candace, telling her, "And I owe you a congratulations. I heard about your audition from Sergej."

"I hope it was all good."

She softens her voice when she says, "He thinks people will be fighting for you to sign with their companies."

"I can only hope," Candace responds with her modesty that I love so much. She's humble and gracious. She knows she's amazing but would never say it out loud.

"No hoping. I'm looking forward to seeing you perform in May."

"Thank you. I'll be sure Ryan calls you," she tells Stacy.

"Enjoy your night."

"You too, Stacy," I say and then head over to the bar where we spot Jase and Mark.

"Hey, man," Mark says when we approach.

We visit for a few minutes when Candace excuses herself to roam around the gallery with Jase. Art showings really aren't my thing, so I grab a beer and chat with Mark. I don't wait too long before I make my way over to the registrar.

Walking up to the desk, there's an elderly woman in a black cocktail dress who greets me. "Sir, how can I help you?"

Leaning my elbows on the counter, I say, "I'd like to inquire about one of the pieces being shown."

"Title?"

"'Nubile.'"

After a few clicks on the computer, she says, "It's been flagged by three interests, but no purchases yet."

"I'd like to purchase it then."

"Great! I have it marked for twelve hundred."

Shit. I had no idea my work would be worth that much. I had the photo canvassed in a large 24x40 wrap after it was accepted.

When I hand her my credit card, she begins to explain, "The piece is scheduled to remain on display until mid-April. At that time, preparatory will wrap it and have the piece delivered, unless you would like to pick it up yourself."

"Delivery is fine."

"Name?"

"Ryan Campbell."

She types it into her system and then looks up at me. "Ryan Campbell?"

"Yes."

She grins, asking, "Mr. Campbell, is this *your* piece?"

I respond with a mere wink as she continues to enter my information. There is no way in hell I'd let that photo of my girl hang in anyone's home but my own. Taking that photo was a huge deal for her, and I wasn't lying when I told her it was hers. She doesn't know I'm buying it. She'd probably be mad if she knew, but that's a memory I refuse to let someone else enjoy.

Once I finish with the purchase, I walk around and find Candace sitting on a bench with Jase.

"There you are," I say as I walk over to them. Jase stands and excuses himself, giving me and Candace time alone. "Where have you been?"

"Just walking around with Jase," she says as she leans into me.

"I heard someone bought your photo."

"Really?" she questions excitedly, and I get a kick out of her enthusiasm. But I'm done here tonight. I just want to be alone with her, away from everyone, because I've missed her.

I stand up and take her hand. "Walk with me."

When she slides her hand in mine, I lead her through to the back of the gallery, hoping I can come across a private area so that I can get my hands and mouth on her in a way that just wouldn't be appropriate in front of all these people.

"What are we doing back here? We're gonna get in trouble," she says nervously.

I laugh at her. "You're so cute."

We turn to go behind a wall, far from everyone else. I back her up against it, caging her in with my hands braced on either side of her. She knows what I want and gives it to me when she takes my face in her hands and draws me in, kissing me. I take over, eager for her. I want her right here, but I know my girl, and she's a private person. I'm shocked she's even doing this with me right now.

"We should go," she mumbles between kisses.

Pressing my hips against her, she grabs on to me, whispering my name.

I don't waste a second, taking her hand and leading her out the back, avoiding the time it would take to say goodbye to everyone. I just want to have her. Alone with me. In my bed.

Pulling up the driveway, I open her door, scoop her into my arms, and carry her up the stairs to the front door and then up to my room. I lay her on the bed and stand to look down at her. The light from the moon filtering through the clouds drapes a muted silvery hue on her fair skin.

I take my hands and run them down the length of her body, needing to feel the lace under my hands and the curve of her body beneath it. When I get to her legs, I wrap my grip behind her knees and trail them over her calves and down to her ankles, slipping off her heels, letting them fall to the floor. I toss my jacket over the chair and remove my shoes and socks before I climb into bed and back over her.

"I love you so fuckin' much."

"I love you, too."

I need her. The desire to have her is powerful. She looks incredible tonight, and I want her to give me another piece of her, so I make my request, saying, "Make love to me, babe."

By the look in her eyes, I know she understands what I mean. She's a little apprehensive every time we've had sex, so I have always taken the lead. But I need this from her— the certainty. I know she'd never do anything she didn't want to, but I also know that there is a level of fear about sex with her, and I want to give the control over to her.

She nods her head, and we pull up to our knees. As my lips land on hers, I fix my hands on her hips and slowly drag them up her lace-covered body before finding the zipper and sliding it down. She begins to unbutton my shirt, grazing the tips of her fingers against my chest while she works her way down. After she removes my shirt, she adjusts her shoulders, allowing the dress to slip off of her and pool at her knees.

She hangs on to my neck when I lower her down to the mattress and then pull the dress over her legs, tossing it on the floor with the rest of our clothes. My lips trail up her legs as I nip gently on her sensitive flesh, making her sigh, but she grips the sides of my head when I start planting soft kisses along her inner thigh. She clamps her hands on me, pushing me away before my mouth can reach her panties.

Patience is hard when I want her in ways I know she isn't ready for, but I move at her pace and allow her to lead me when she pulls my head up to her stomach. I kiss her heated skin as I start to shift her underwear down her legs. Sitting up on my knees, between her parted thighs, I run my eyes over her bare skin before she hitches her legs around my waist and pulls me down to her. But I pull back so that I can unhook my pants and kick them off.

Before I return to her, I slip on a condom and then reach around her back, shifting her on top of my lap as I sit with my legs in front of me. With her straddling me, I unhook her bra, slipping it down her arms. She rests her hands on my shoulders, staring into my eyes, when I move my hands to her hips. Lifting up on her knees, I reach down and help guide myself inside of her as she lowers herself on top of me.

Her head falls onto the curve of my neck when she slides over me slowly, and I let my head drop against her as pleasure radiates through my body. Her frame is so small, and she's so tight around me. My arms slide around her waist, and I hold on to her tightly when she finally lifts her head and looks into my eyes, foreheads pressed together. She rises up and takes her time as her body slowly falls back down over me.

"God, I love you," I breathe out.

Our bodies are pressed together, her arms wrapped around my neck, my head dropped to her chest. I needed her to give this to me, and hearing the soft moans coming out of her, I know I'm gonna need her like this again and again. Watching her take this pleasure from me is intoxicating as I begin to lose myself in her. The way she's moving, the way her skin smells with the light scent of her perfume, the way her hair feels as it brushes along the skin of my arms—it's a heady combination of elements that consumes my senses, but I still crave more.

Kissing her breasts, enjoying the feel of her soft skin against my lips, her body shudders as she rocks her hips into me. She's clinging tightly to me, and I can hear her unsteady breathing picking up. I'm able to read her body after all the times we've been together, so when her thighs tighten on me and her body grows more rigid, I know she's getting close, and knowing that she's giving herself this makes it all the better for me.

"Look at me, baby. I want to watch you come," I tell her as she leans her damp forehead against mine and opens her eyes.

She grips my hair in her hands, and I begin to feel her pulse around me.

"God, Candace," I moan, unable to hold on anymore, and she's right here with me as she rides out her pleasure, all the while giving me an intense release. Heat explodes throughout my body as she continues to move over me. I run my hand up her back and catch the sweat rolling down her spine. She lets go of a heavy breath, laced with a whimper, as she draws out the last of her orgasm with me.

My heart is pounding, and I can barely keep myself upright, so I hold her close and lie us down. Candace brushes the hair off of my forehead, and when she does, I tell her, "'I love you' will never be enough for what I feel for you."

She smiles, planting her lips on mine, and I keep myself inside of her as I pull the sheets over us and band my arms around her. This is the part I love. Having her completely content in my arms. Eyes closed and peaceful.

Candace scares me out of a deep sleep when she violently thrashes up, gasping for air. Her breaths hit hard as she fists the sheets, knuckles white, completely shaken.

"Babe, are you okay?" I ask as I pull the sheet up to cover her bare chest, knowing how modest she is. She clutches the sheet and begins to cry as she brings her knees up to her chest.

"Baby, it's just us," I assure as I pull her into my arms.

She's tucked in a ball as I move her between my legs and cuddle her against my chest. She hasn't scared me like this in a while, and I can tell that she's completely overwhelmed right now, so I keep her close, stroking her back as

I soothe her.

"I'm sorry," she mutters when her cries weaken.

"There's nothing to be sorry for."

Taking in a deep breath, she lets it out slowly while I ask again, "Are you okay?"

She nods her head and sits up in my arms as I run my fingers under her eyes.

"I forgot to take my pill," she says to me.

"Shit, babe. I'm sorry," I tell her, feeling guilty that I didn't ask her before we fell sleep. I brought her home and never gave her a moment before we made love and went to bed.

"It's not your fault."

"Where are they?"

"In my purse, but it's too late to take it now," she says, and when I grab my phone and touch the screen, it reads a quarter past three.

She's right. If she took her pill now, she'd sleep most of the day.

"What do you wanna do?" I ask.

"Nothing. It's fine," she tries telling me, but I know it isn't. I remember her last nightmare, and I worry if she falls asleep that it could happen again. "Ryan, I promise," she says, sensing my concern. "Let's go back to sleep."

I lay her down, but keep her tucked into me and wrap my body around her from behind. We spend the rest of the night in a state of restless sleep because she continues to toss and turn, and I find myself awake and watching her as she drifts in and out.

chapter thirty-five

When we arrive at my mom's the following day, it's late, and Candace is overly exhausted with a bad headache, so she goes to bed early while my mom and I stay up visiting. By the time I wake up the next morning, Candace is already out of bed and downstairs with my mom. While drinking our coffee, Mom mentions that she has to drive out to Portland for the day to take care of few things, leaving the day open for me and Candace.

While Candace is in the shower, I check the weather report, figuring I'll take her to Indian Beach to try and get her up on a board. When the bathroom door opens, she's wearing nothing but a towel and leftover drops of water, and suddenly, she has my full attention.

"Fuck, babe," I say as I walk towards her.

Holding her hand out to my chest to keep me from coming any closer, she says, "Don't start. Your mother is downstairs."

"I don't care who the fuck is downstairs when the only thing covering your wet body is that towel."

"That's why I'm getting my clothes," she says with a smile before running back to the bathroom, shutting the door behind her.

Once she's dressed and comes back into the bedroom, I start getting my things together and tell her, "Tori has an extra wetsuit in my closet that should fit you okay."

"What?"

"Surfing. You and me."

"I'm fine with trying anything new, but that water is freezing," she says.

"I promise, when you're in that wetsuit, you'll be fine. Tori loves to surf, so she has her wetsuit here and some swimsuits in my closet."

Grabbing Tori's wetsuit, Candace finishes getting ready before we hop into my Rubicon and head to Indian Beach.

Candace is such a sport about being outdoors, and it's great that we share that. The running, the hiking, and now, getting her up on a board—she's a natural and is taking her first wave in on her second try. I knew she'd be great at it, and she didn't let me down. We spend the morning hanging out in the water and having fun with each other. When we aren't surfing, she's fighting me when I try getting frisky with her.

After a few hours, we decide to call it and head back. She's freezing and wrapped up in blankets that I packed in the car. When we get back, she heads upstairs to take a hot shower and warm up. I unload the jeep, giving her just enough time before I go up to join her. I made a bet with her on the beach that if I got her up on the board, I would get a little action from her. I know she thought I was just kidding around, but when I strip off my clothes and walk into the bathroom, I take a moment to look at her through the fogged glass of the large walk-in shower before opening the door.

"What are you doing?!" she startles as I close the door behind me and wrap my arms around her.

"It's time to ante up, babe," I tease as I duck my head under the water and then push her against the glass wall. She gasps as the cold surface meets her skin, arching into me in response.

She doesn't push me away or make light in this moment. She stays quiet as I dip my head to kiss her. Gripping my hands behind her thighs, I easily lift her off her feet as she wraps her legs around my waist. My mouth runs down her wet neck, licking and sucking as she holds on to me, breathing heavily at my touch.

The water cascades down her naked body, between her breasts where my hand finds her, squeezing her soft flesh. When I press myself against her, she breathes hard, "I want you."

"I don't have anything with me in here," I tell her, but before I can set her down so that we can move this to the bed, she says, "It's okay. I've been on the pill for a while. I trust you."

"When did you get on the pill, babe?" I ask in shock, never knowing that she did this.

"I've been on it. I got it . . ." She hesitates before finishing, "I got on it after what happened."

Leaning my head on her shoulder, I sigh as she assures me, "It's okay. I just want you."

"I've never . . . I promise you I've always been safe," I tell her. "I've never been with anyone without a condom."

"You don't have to explain. I know you'd never do anything to hurt me."

She holds my face when I kiss her, water seaming between our lips as it falls over us. I focus on her mouth, exploring it with my tongue, tasting her slow and deep. Her arms stay slung around my neck, hands trussed in my hair as I begin to drag my kisses along her neck and down to her chest. Lowering my head, I circle her nipple with my tongue before gently sucking it into my mouth, pressing my tongue against the hardened bud.

Her body writhes in my arms, and I pull back to look at her when I move my hands under her bottom and lift her up, reaching down to hold myself for her. Slowly, with her head rested on mine, I lower her down. We take each other completely as our bare flesh meets, and I slide myself inside of her. She's so warm; she always has been, but to feel her like this, to have her give me this, I know it comes solely from our love for each other.

The air is heavy with steam, making my breaths ragged as I hold on to her. She clings her arms tightly around my shoulders, hugging me as I listen to her soft panting in my ear. I pull her off the wall and simply hold her. Feeling her naked body with mine. Savoring having her this close to me. Bared to each other with nothing but trust.

She draws her head back to look at me, and when she does, she brushes her lips across mine, breathing into me, "I love you."

With those words, I use my hands to move her, and when I do, I find it hard to stand with the pleasure that courses through me. Being inside of her like this, nothing separating us, it's an intensity that takes over my body. I turn so I can rest my back against the glass as I lift her back up and let her descend slowly down on me. Her legs are tight around my hips as I steadily maneuver her up and down.

It's hard to hold on to everything I'm feeling in this moment, and the pleasure moves us to the floor of the shower. I sit back against the wall as she keeps her legs wrapped around my body. The air is thick and she's all around me as I watch her. She's stunning with her soft eyes on me, her labored breaths escaping her lips, fingertips pressing into my back as we move together. Never in a rush, because I need this. Every piece of this.

"God, I want you," I say on a heavy breath, and she braces her arms around my neck, using the leverage as she sways her hips into me.

"You have me."

When her body begins to respond, she drops her eyes to mine. I don't even have to tell her, she just knows. It's my security of knowing that she's always with me in this moment. Never wanting her mind to drift. It shouldn't be the reason, but it is, and it's something that, even though it originates from such an ugly place, has become something I can redeem with her, because she's so beautiful when she comes.

My muscles tense up when I feel her spasm around me, moaning my name in the heat of the air as we both lose ourselves to each other. The pleasure she gives me radiates through my entire being, and I clutch my hands to her hips when our movements begin to falter as passion takes over.

She's incredible. She doesn't know it, and if I told her, she'd deny my words, so I don't speak. We just remain like this, together, on the bottom of the shower as our tired bodies collapse against one another.

We decide to stay the week here, so after Candace spends a couple of days with my mom, shopping and dining out, leaving me to fend for myself, I choose to steal her for the day.

We went to Astoria this morning for a late breakfast with Tori and the kids, and now I'm driving her up to Washington to take her to Long Beach to drive her along the water and spend the rest of the day together.

When we get there, I pull off the road and onto the sand, and she asks, "Are you sure this is okay?"

Laughing at her, I say, "Yes. Everyone does it." When I pass a sign that states the driving dates for the beach, I point, and tell her, "See. There's the proof," with a smile.

It's still cold this time of year, and today can't be any higher than fifty degrees, so aside from a group of guys hanging out, the place is pretty empty. We drive along the water, and I get a kick out of her laughing the whole time. The simple fact that driving on sand can make this girl so giddy is a trip, and I'm enjoying every giggle coming out of her.

Pulling away from the water, I find a spot back by the sea oats that's already set up for a fire. I pull the jeep up the beach and park.

"You wanna grab the blankets?" I ask as we get out of the car.

I open the back hatch and pull out the firewood to start a fire while Candace bundles up. Once I have the fire going, I sit next to her, wrapping the blankets around the both of us as she cuddles into me.

"I had fun at Tori's this morning," she says as she clutches the blanket to her. "She's really nice."

"Yeah, she is."

"So her mom is Donna's sister?"

"Uh huh."

She laughs quietly, saying, "It's hard to keep it straight."

"It's my mom and her two sisters. And then all my cousins are girls as well," I explain. "Tori and I always linked up because of our age, and she's really into surfing too, so we get together a lot to hit the beach."

When the wind kicks up, she turns her head and rests it

on my chest. "I was wondering something."

"What's that?"

"If that's the house you grew up in, why does your mom still live there?"

"I don't know. I asked her that not too long ago," I tell her. "She told me that she loves the house and that she chooses to remember all the good memories we had there."

"What about you?" she asks as she looks up at me.

Adjusting to pull her between my legs, I lean back against the log lying behind me before answering her. "It's hard for me to remember anything good. Being in that house is sometimes hard on me. I'll see things that remind me of a particular beating and stuff like that, and it dredges up a lot of shit for me."

She lets go of the blanket and wraps her arms around me, asking, "Why did she stay?"

"Honestly . . . I never asked her. Now that I'm older, I would just assume that she was scared. Worried about how she would support the two of us if she did leave."

She doesn't say anything, just leans into me as we hold on to each other. I stare into the fire when I continue to talk and explain, "My dad was a frightening man. I was terrified of him. Scared he was going to kill my mom one day. He would drink heavily and lose control. You never knew how far he would go. I used to sit and watch him beat her, scared if I left that he might go too far and I wouldn't be able to help her."

"So you watched?" she asks, horrified.

"I couldn't say anything because every time I would scream for him to stop, he would just go harder on her, making it worse."

"I can't even imagine. But what about you?"

"He hated me, Candace. At least with my mom, he had

once loved her. But never me. He didn't give a shit what he did to me. I was always walking around in pain. Broken ribs, concussions. That's mostly why I started using X. It just felt good."

She looks at me, and I watch her eyes puddle with tears that don't fall.

"And nobody ever knew? Nobody helped you?" she questions.

"The only other person who knows, beside me and my mom, is you."

"No one in your family?"

"Only you," I tell her.

"Does Donna know that I know?"

"No."

She shifts to her knees and faces me. I know she doesn't know how to respond to everything I just laid on her, so I take away the pressure when I hold her face and kiss her. She grips my wrists with her hands, and I keep my eyes open as I watch her tears finally fall.

I pull back and wipe her cheeks before I lie us down on the pile of blankets in the sand, the only heat from her and the fire. I've never unloaded this weight that I've been carrying for years the way she allows me to.

"You're the strongest person I know," she whispers against my neck.

"I'm not."

"You are."

"Before I met you, I hid everything. I was selfish and used people. I was weak."

"But you're not now. I don't see any of that in you," she says, and I know the only reason for that is her.

chapter thirty-six

After a few more days, it's time to head back to Seattle. I'm finishing packing our bags while Candace gets ready in the bathroom. Having this week away has been good for us. And having her here with my mom makes this connection that we have so much stronger.

Needing to grab a few things out of the bathroom, I don't knock when I see she has left the door cracked. When I open it, she startles as she pulls down on her sweatshirt.

"What are you doing?"

"Nothing," she says as she still has her top clutched in her hands.

I walk over to her and take her hand, lifting it up along with the shirt, and when I do, she says, "I don't like it," referring to her tattoo that is peeking over her pants that she has tugged down.

I lower her shirt and ask, "Why?"

"Because it's not me," she admits. "I was trying to be someone different, and it only led to bad things."

"What do you mean?"

"I got it in a moment of rebellion, I guess. It was stupid, really. I got it and started acting foolishly, which led to . . .

umm . . ." her words stammer off as she drops her head away from me. I know what she's trying to say, and it's insane to think getting a tattoo would result in her getting raped.

"I get it. But, babe, nothing you did led to that."

When she doesn't say anything and refrains from looking at me as she starts walking out of the bathroom, I grab ahold of her because I need to know that she agrees with me.

"Wait. You know that, right?"

God. She doesn't agree with me. I can see the guilt in her eyes. How could she possibly think this?

"Come here," I tell her as I sit on the bed, taking her hand and pulling her towards me. "Tell me you don't think that."

When she doesn't respond, I say, "Babe, there is nothing you could have possibly done to deserve that."

She turns away from me as I say this, and when I tug her back to me, she's crying.

Fuck.

How did I not know that she blames herself for this?

"Shit, babe. I had no idea this is how you feel."

"Please, don't," she says in a broken voice.

"I need you to talk to me about this. You have it all wrong. What that guy did was fucked up, babe, and you didn't do shit to deserve what he did to you."

She looks up at me and pulls her hands out of mine when she gets mad and yells, "You don't get it, Ryan! What I did was stupid, and I completely led him on. It wasn't right, and I knew it, but I did it anyway."

Infuriated that she feels this way when her logic is so fucked up, I raise my voice at her, saying, "What the fuck could you have possibly done? Because I know you, Candace, and I know you couldn't have led him on that much. But that shit doesn't even matter because you could've stripped down in front of him, and you still didn't deserve to be raped."

"Don't say that fucking word, Ryan!" she snaps and then begins to fall apart, sobbing.

Banding my arms around her, I hold her close. "Babe, I'm sorry. I just had no idea that this is how you think."

"I didn't even really like him," she begins to stammer out between her cries. "But I was stupid and lonely, so I would let him kiss me, knowing that I didn't like him. And I fucking hate my mother for this, because if it wasn't for her being such a bitch, I never would have gone out with him."

"Candace, please don't do this."

"You just don't get it. I did lead him on, and I pissed him off. I never should've acted like that. I should've just been honest."

"This isn't your fault." I tell her in a hard voice.

"Yes, it is!"

"It isn't your fault, Candace."

Facing me, she takes my shirt in her hands, fisting the fabric when she yells, "But it is!" and then falls into my chest. Her cries are loud, staggered, and strained. It's hard to listen to, but I do because I love her. I don't say anything else because I'm only upsetting her worse.

I can't argue her irrational thinking because she isn't seeing it with clear eyes. This guy screwed with her head so badly that she's been carrying the weight of the responsibility on her own shoulders. And here I am, blind to this fact. My girl has been holding fault when that son of a bitch is the only one to blame.

Moving her with me as I lie down on the bed, she tucks her head under my chin and continues to cry for a while. She's in so much pain, and I don't know how to make it any better for her. I've always questioned her choices for how she's been dealing with this, but now, knowing this piece of the puzzle, it's clear that she needs to do something.

We're face to face when she finally speaks. "It's been seven months, Ryan."

"I know, babe."

"I just want it to go away."

"I know. But it's never going to get easier if you keep blaming yourself. It kills me that you feel this way. It fuckin' kills me that I can't take this away from you."

Knowing that there isn't a goddamn thing I can do to lessen her misery frustrates me beyond anything I have ever dealt with. I want to take care of her, to be the person that makes this better for her, but that's what's so fucked up about this situation—that's what's so scary—because it all lies within her. She's the only one who can make this better, but she refuses to help herself. She figures if she just ignores it for long enough then it will fade away and everything will go back to normal. It's not a sane way to deal with this. In fact, I think it's just making it worse for her with every day that passes. The avoiding is catching up with her, and I'm afraid she's just going to—one day—crumble.

When her breathing begins to even out, she asks, "Can't we stay another night?"

"Anything you want," I tell her.

I lie here, and I can't shake my own guilt about this whole situation. I've always had it. I've always asked all the what-ifs, but the fact remains, this girl was outside fighting for her life while I was mere feet away. If only I would have gone out there, I wouldn't be lying here with my girl falling apart on me. She wouldn't be carrying this around with her every day. I was the only other person there, and I did nothing.

Noticing that her body has gone limp, I remember that she hasn't taken her sleeping pill. Slipping out of bed, I go to her purse to grab the bottle. I take out a pill and fill up a glass of water from the bathroom before waking her.

"Baby," I urge as she slowly opens her eyes. "Here, take this."

She does and then hands the glass back to me. I crawl back into bed and hold her until she falls back asleep. The whole time, my mind is just eating away at me. At everything. When she's finally asleep, I quietly head downstairs because I need a little space to get my thoughts together, but shit is just spinning more and more the longer I sit at the dining room table.

"Hey, dear," I hear my mom say softly when she crosses the room to sit with me.

"Hey," I sigh.

"Where's Candace?"

"She's sleeping. We're just gonna head back tomorrow," I tell her as I look at her from across the table.

"Are you okay?" she asks. "I heard you two fighting earlier."

Leaning forward in my seat, I rest my forearms on the table, saying, "We weren't fighting, Mom."

She shakes her head at me and questions, "Well, is everything all right?"

I normally tell my mother everything, but when I found out about Candace, I held it secret. But I feel like I'm in so deep with this girl, and the stuff I'm dealing with is some of the heaviest shit I've ever dealt with. I haven't had anyone to really talk to about it, and knowing how much my mother loves her, I trust her enough to make this confession that I have had locked up inside of me.

"No." I drop my head when I say this because I already feel the remorse building inside for betraying Candace by telling her secret, but it's breaking me, and I don't know where else to turn.

She places her hand over mine as she says, "Talk to me, sweetheart."

Staring at our hands, I take in a deep breath and begin, "There's something I've never told you about Candace."

"Okay."

"Remember the attack I told you about that happened this past summer at the bar?"

When she nods, I swallow hard and reveal, "It was her, Mom. That girl was Candace."

"Oh my God," she whispers as she removes her hand from mine to cover her mouth. She's in complete shock when she asks, "How did you . . .?"

"She doesn't know," I confess. "I didn't even know it was her for a while. I thought it could be, but I wasn't sure. I was so confused, thinking my head was just trying to make something out of nothing with her weird behavior. But I honestly didn't know."

"I don't understand. Where did you meet her?"

"I grabbed a coffee from where she works. And then I kept seeing her because she's friends with a couple buddies of mine. But there's this tattoo," I say as I fight to hold back the tears that threaten. "I saw it on that girl, and then after I had already fallen for Candace, I saw that same tattoo on her. I was scared, so I never told her."

"Ryan . . ."

"We weren't fighting earlier. She told me that what happened to her was her fault. I was trying to talk to her about it, and she got really upset." Pressing my palms to my forehead, I tell her, "God, Mom, you have no idea what that fucker did to her. What she looked like when I found her."

It's when I drop my hands that I see the tears running down my mom's face and that's what sends me over. I don't cry, but I feel it stabbing inside of me.

"Honey, you have to tell her."

"It felt like the right thing to do at the time. That I was keeping it from her for all the right reasons," I try to explain. "I didn't want to hurt her, but now . . . now it feels like a lie, and I'm scared. I'm scared I'm gonna lose her."

"But now things are different with you two, and she needs to know."

I can feel the heat of the tears welling in my eyes when I ask, feeling desperate, "Do you think she'll understand?"

She takes her time before responding with, "I think you have a girl that's been shown, in the most horrendous way a person can be shown, just how gruesome life can be. She's been stripped of her security and faith in people. It's awful, and people like that don't trust easily."

Dropping my head in my hands, I nearly beg, "What do I do? I love her."

She takes my hand and pulls it down when she looks at me and tells me to do what I'm terrified of doing.

"You have to tell her . . . You just have to."

But I don't want to. I can't risk losing her. All I want to do is keep her forever, so I selfishly go back upstairs, crawl under the sheets next to her, and hang on to the one good thing that finally came into my life and changed everything about me. I can't lose her.

Waking up with Candace just didn't feel right with the dread that has made its home in the pit of my stomach. And seeing how clingy she's been with me all morning, and now on the drive home, makes the thought of telling her that much worse.

She has kept a hold on my hand ever since she opened her eyes this morning. I don't question her about it; I just give her the closeness, the security that I'm here and I'm not leaving. I can't tell her. Not now. Not when she's vulnerable like this.

Thinking about what sparked the whole conversation with Candace yesterday, I say, "I hate that your tattoo makes you feel the way it does." I hate the way it makes me feel too. It's hard for me to look at because almost every time I do, I see the girl from that night, and I can't stand thinking of her like that, the way she looked lying there unconscious. There have been a couple times in the past where I've had to cover it with my hand while we make love because it hurts too much to look at.

"I thought about having it removed once."

"Have you thought about changing it?" I ask as I glance over at her, giving her hand a little squeeze.

"I just don't know what I would do. I don't want anything bigger than it is now," she explains.

"Did Roxy's boyfriend do it?"

"Jared? Yeah."

"When we get home, why don't we talk to him, see what he can do?"

"I guess," she says, unconvinced.

"I just think if it looked different, or you could add something to it that was meaningful to you, that you could associate it with something new, instead of what you're doing now. Give it new meaning."

"We can go talk to him," is her only response, and I don't say anything else about it because I know it's a difficult thing to talk about.

When we arrive back in Seattle, I take Candace to her house to spend a little time with her before I have to run to the bar to take care of some work.

Setting her bags down on the bed, Candace quietly says, "I don't want you to go to work."

I hate that she's feeling like this today, and that she doesn't want to be alone, but I tell her, "Baby, I have to. It's Saturday night, and I've been gone all week."

She leans into me, sliding her arms around my waist. She's needy, and I don't want her to be alone either, so I offer, "Come with me."

"What?"

"You don't even have to be around everyone. Stay with me in my office."

I'm not expecting her answer when she says, "Okay."

"Really?" I question, stunned that she would agree so easily, especially for a Saturday night.

"Just park in the front, okay?"

chapter thirty-seven

I was relieved to see Candace enjoying herself when she went with me to the bar. I was nervous because Saturday nights are really busy, but I had Max with her the entire time. Jase was there to hear Mark's band play and was able to talk her into going downstairs with him while I got my work done. Once I finished up, I hung out with her for the rest of the evening. Aside from meeting Max, she also met Mel. Candace has always been a mystery to them, so to have them finally meet her was nice since they know what a big part of my life she's become.

When Candace walks down the stairs, I ask, "You ready?"

"Yeah, I just need my coat," she says as she walks towards me.

"I got it," I tell her when I stand up and help her put it on.

We head out into another rain-filled night to go spend the evening at Max's place. He invited us over when he met Candace at the bar last week. Zane is back in town for a few days, so he and Mel will be there as well.

It's an odd transition to be coupled off and doing things like this tonight, but it's a welcome change that seems to better suit me now.

When we pull up to Max's place, I help Candace out of the car and then head inside and out of the cold. We walk in, and I introduce her to Zane and Traci, who is now very pregnant. We sit around and talk for a little bit until Traci takes Mel and Candace back to see the baby's room, leaving the guys alone in the living room.

"Dude," Zane says as he nudges me with a smirk.

"What?"

"Who's the chick?"

"Candace?"

He laughs when he says, "Yeah, man. What's going on?"

Last I spoke with Zane, I was still into going out a lot with Gav, so I clue him in when I tell him, "We started dating soon after you high-tailed your ass to L.A."

"What?!" he exclaims, nearly spitting out his beer. "What the hell have I missed around here? Seriously, I come back and you're settled down with some chick, and this guy," he says, pointing the neck of his beer bottle towards Max, "has his girl knocked up."

Max laughs at him and says, "That's what happens when you ditch town and don't check in."

"I guess," he says and then turns to me. "Just never thought I'd see you with a chick." Taking a swig of his beer, he asks, "Are you guys serious?"

"Yeah, man. Pretty serious."

Max butts in, and asks Zane, "Tell us what's going on with you and Mel."

"I have no idea. She refuses to come to California, but I'm not giving up this opportunity so that she can stay close to her family."

"Stop bullshitting," I say, calling him out. "She said you told her you didn't want her to go with you."

"Why would I?" he responds. "I mean, she has done nothing but bitch about all of this, so why would I want her to tag along with her piss-poor attitude?"

Our attention is distracted when we hear a burst of laughter coming from the girls in the back of the house. In this moment, I smile. I just can't help it. Candace doesn't have any girl friends aside from Roxy, so to hear her laughter spilling through the house is infectious, and I let out a light chuckle.

Looking back over at Zane, I tell him, "She was upset when you left."

"When I left? What about now?" he questions. "Seems to me that she's doing pretty well on her own here."

"God, you're hard to talk to," Max interjects.

"Can we not talk about my shit?" Zane says. "What about you?" he asks as he eyes Max. "I can't believe you're gonna be a dad. How are you not freaking the hell out right now?"

"I did when I found out, but it's all good now," he states simply.

We continue to catch up for a while until the girls eventually join us again. Candace has a smile on her face when she sits next to me on the couch as she continues to talk with Traci and Mel. Max and Zane are in their own conversation while I find myself focused on Candace. She's happy and light-hearted tonight in this new circle of people. She's so tight with Jase and Mark, but I'd like to see her widen her group of friends. She needs it even though she doesn't see it.

On the drive home, I look over at her and ask, "Did you have a good time?"

"Yeah, Mel's pretty funny."

"She definitely keeps things entertaining at work," I say with a grin. "So what did you talk about? We kept hearing you all laughing."

"Traci was just talking about her pregnancy. I was a little shocked with some of the things she was telling us," she says with a dramatic shudder.

Laughing at her, I ask, "Like what?"

"Stuff I had no clue about," she tells me in a high-pitched voice, reeling with disbelief. "She told us that she has hemorrhoids!"

"What?!"

"Yes!" she squeals.

"I don't wanna know about that shit," I say, disgusted.

"Well, I don't either, but I do now, thanks to Traci!" she says as she begins to laugh, and I join right in with her. "She said that most pregnant women get them! It's so gross!"

"Shit, are you serious?"

"Mel said it was true too."

We both continue laughing as she fills me in on more than I ever wanted to know, and the theatrics of Candace telling me all of this and freaking out is completely entertaining when I'm not cringing at the unwanted information.

Once we have quieted down and composed ourselves, I look over as we're stopped at a red light and ask, "Do you think that's something you want?"

"What? A baby?" she asks.

"Yeah."

"I don't know," she says softly. "I've always been scared to be a mom."

"Why's that?"

When she leans her head back against the seat, she tells me, "Because I'm not sure I know what it is to be a good mom. I mean . . . how would you know if the choices you were making were the wrong ones? I wonder if my mom thought she was making the right choices with me."

She says this and I understand her fears. I get it because they're my fears. Scared to become what we are products of. But I know that she would have nothing to worry about because she's the most non-judgmental person I know.

"But I don't have to think about that for a long time," she adds.

"Why's that?" I ask, when I pull up to the loft and park the car.

"Because dancers don't have babies until they are done with their professional careers. Your body changes too much, so the likelihood that the way you dance would be impacted is high. It's just not something you toy with if you want longevity," she explains. "What about you?"

"Me?"

"Yeah," she says as she shifts herself to face me.

"I've always wanted what my cousins have, but never saw it in the cards for me," I tell her. "But when I really think about it, it scares the shit out of me too."

"Because of your dad?"

I nod my head and when she smiles up at me, she says, "I don't think you have anything to worry about."

I lean over and kiss her before giving her sentiment right back. "I don't think you do either. You're amazing at everything you do."

Making our way inside, she turns to me and asks, "You wanna camp out and watch a movie?"

"Anything you want." I tell her as we head upstairs to change clothes.

When we return to the living room, I get the fireplace going while Candace tosses a bunch of pillows and blankets onto the floor and flips the TV to TCM. I love sharing my black and white movies with her, and lately, I'm finding that she's starting to get into them as well.

Lying down, pulling Candace into my arms, we relax and watch 'Bank Holiday.' I lazily comb my fingers through her hair, and we fall asleep before the movie ends.

Waking up in the middle of the night, Candace is sleeping along my side, and the fire is almost out. When I pick up the remote to shut the TV off, the screen reads that it's almost two in the morning. Setting the remote down, I roll over to look down at Candace, and my shifting causes her to stir awake.

It takes a moment, but when her eyes flutter open and she focuses on me, we stay silent as we watch each other in the faint glow of the firelight. When I lean in to kiss her, she runs her hand behind my neck, pulling me down to her. I slide my tongue across her lower lip before sucking it into my mouth, and she grips my neck tighter. Her body is flush against mine, and I begin to lift her shirt so that I can feel the warmth of her on my skin. Discarding her top, I reach back and remove mine as well before bringing her back to me. The room is silent as our bodies begin to move as the haze from our sleep dissipates.

When I roll on top of her, I drag my head down the center of her body, letting my lips move along her smooth skin. Licking and sucking my way down, her hands are holding the sides of my head, and when I hit her pants, she lifts her hips, allowing me to pull them off, keeping her lace panties in place.

Taking her leg in my hand, I kiss my way back up, giving her soft sucks behind her knee before I lower myself down on her. I want to feel every part of her, but she has always been so skittish with some of my touches. Needing the closeness in the moment, I break our silence and whisper, "I want to touch you."

I see the reluctance when she looks at me, and I reach my hand back to hold her knee as I say, "Let me touch you."

I catch her faint nod and take my time as I let my hand fall along the inside of her thigh, but as soon as I reach the edge of her panties, she clamps my wrist with her hand and jerks her hips away from me. I want to show her that it isn't disgusting and that she doesn't have to be scared of my touch, so I move my hand back to her knee as I rest my body on top of her. With my forehead against hers, I take her lips with mine. Her hand rests on my cheek while she keeps her other locked around my wrist, not letting go. I stay close to her when I move my hand back down her leg, and this time, she doesn't startle.

Her breathing is shaky when I touch her and cup her in my hand, holding still as her legs are clutched to my sides. My lips continue to move with hers as I take in the warmth of her before I gently run my hand up the edge of her panties then tuck my fingers under the lace of the fabric and run them back down.

She lets out a whimper as I feel her smooth skin under my fingers.

"Just relax, baby," I breathe as I drop my head to her shoulder.

Keeping my wrist clutched in her hold, I bring my hand to the top of her underwear and then slip it under the fabric, moving the back of my fingers down the seam of her. I know this is hard for her, but I also know that no one has ever touched her like this, without hate and force, so I keep my touches soft as she gives me this. After a little time, her body begins to respond to me, and I feel her relax as she grows hot in my hand. Her forehead becomes damp when I sink my fingers inside of her, breaths heady, and bodies on fire as we move in this new way together.

We spend a good amount of time like this before we make love in the darkness of the room. The only noises are the ones that are products of the pleasure we give each other and eventually the moans that come from us losing ourselves completely to the other.

chapter thirty-eight

"You okay?" I ask while I drive us to the tattoo parlor. She's fidgety and a bit vacant. Placing my hand over hers, I question, "Were you this nervous when you did this the last time?"

"No . . . well, kinda. I dunno. It was different then."

"You don't have to do this today. We can always call Jared and reschedule."

She shakes her head and then looks over at me. "No, it's fine. I'm sure I'd be just as nervous if it were any other day. Let's just get it done."

I hold her clammy hand for the rest of the short drive. When we arrive and walk in, Jared is the only one here. He came in early so that it would only be the three of us.

"You look like you're about to puke," he teases her and laughs. "You've been through this before. No big deal, right?"

"Right," she responds with a nervous smile as we follow him back through the shop and into his booth.

Candace takes a seat on top of the black table, and I stand next to her, still holding her hand.

"So, what are you thinking about doing?" he asks her.

"Umm . . ."

Jared squeezes her knee, and soothes, "Relax."

She looks over at me, and then looks back, telling him, "Can we just fill it in?"

"That's it? Damn, girl, by the way you're acting I thought you were gonna tell me to wrap a skull around it or some shit," he jokes, and it's just what she needs as she laughs with him.

Jared gets everything set up, and when he slips on his black latex gloves, he instructs her to lie back and shift her pants down.

"So, no more empty heart," he mumbles as he slips the paper cloth under the edge of her pants, and she laces her fingers with mine as I stand over her.

"No more empty heart," she repeats as she looks up at me.

We talked about what she was going to do with the tattoo the other day when she told me that she wanted to keep it small. She said that she wanted to simply fill it in, and I was worried that it wouldn't be enough of a change for her. But she assured me that it would be, and I know it holds a new significance for her. I'm glad she sees her heart in this way now—full—no longer empty.

Once the gun starts buzzing, Candace squeezes her eyes shut, and it takes less than a minute for him to be done. Jared and I both laugh when she opens them back up.

"You guys are evil," she tells us as she sits up after Jared applies a small bandage over the area.

"Let me know when you're ready for that skull," he says with smirk.

Candace hops off the table and says with joking aside, "Thank you."

He smiles at her, saying, "Anytime," followed by a wink.

"This one's on the house, so I expect a few hook-ups with those scones."

Returning his smile, she tells him, "Of course. See you later."

"Later, guys."

Walking outside, the mist still fills the air. When I open the door and help her up into her seat, I ask, "Happy?"

"Happy," she confirms with a kiss to my lips.

I hope now every time she sees that tattoo, she is no longer taken back to that night.

Three weeks have passed and Candace has been tied up at the studio almost daily, preparing for the production in May. She has the lead in all of the ensembles she's dancing in, plus a duet and her solo.

She's yet to mention what might happen after she graduates. It's nearing the end of April, so we only have a couple months until she's finished with school here. I know she doesn't know where she'll be, but offers should start coming in after her performance next month.

I don't want to stress her out with everything she has on her plate right now, so I haven't broached the topic, but I know it's on her mind. It has to be. I know she loves me, but I wonder what she's thinking and what she wants, because I'm so clear with what I want.

Max has really stepped up and gotten the bar under control since I brought him on as manager. I'm confident with leaving him in charge if I have to move. It's the best situation for the time being, but she has no idea that's the reason why I promoted him.

Tonight, Max has arranged for one of the bands Gavin

represents to put on a concert at the bar, and Candace agreed to come along. We met up this morning for a quick run, but then I had to spend the day up at work. I left a little while ago to go pick her up since she left her car at my place last night.

When I get to her house and walk into her room, my stomach drops. There are a few cardboard boxes packed up with her belongings. I wanna ask her. I wanna know where we stand in the mix of everything that is about to happen, but that's gonna be a long conversation that we don't have time for right now.

"Babe, you ready?" I ask, no longer wanting to think about any of this shit.

"Yeah, I just need to grab my jacket."

As she walks into her closet, I feel like I should prepare her for what the bar will be like tonight, so I tell her, "So, it's going to be busy. A lot busier than the past few times you've been. You sure you're okay with that?"

Walking out of the closet, she looks at me and says, "I mean, if it's too much then I can always go upstairs until you're ready to leave."

Grabbing her hand and yanking her flush against me, I suggest, "Or we could just stay here and break in your bed a bit more," remembering our sweaty sex session this morning after our run.

"I think we should go now and break in the bed later," she says with a blushing smile.

Leaning down, I playfully nip on her lips before we head up to the bar.

The place is packed when we arrive. We park out front, and Candace eyes the crowd of people waiting to get in. Walking to the door, Max sees us and comes to Candace's side, holding on to her as he walks us in. I keep her hand in mine, and she grips it tightly as Max leads us through the throngs of people. The band is already playing, and the music blasts through the building as we round the back of the bar and spot Jase, Mark, Gavin, and a few of our other friends.

"Hey, guys," Jase hollers and then takes Candace in his arms. I watch as he orders them some shots, and I call out to Mel for a beer.

We have this area cornered off, so Candace is relaxed with it only being our friends around her. I hang out and bullshit with Gavin and Mark while Jase and Candace take their shots and start goofing around with each other.

After a while, I turn to see Candace chatting with Mel who is working behind the bar. They've started talking on the phone, and the two of them have gotten together to hang out a couple of times. I know Mel is going through some shit, but Candace says that she isn't letting it take too much out of her. It's great that the two of them are starting to become friends and to see Candace coming out of her shell a little bit more.

A couple hours pass, and Max leaves us when the band takes a break. I catch Candace standing a few feet away from me, leaning over the bar, whispering something to Mel and making her laugh. She looks incredible in her dark jeans, fitted grey v-neck sweater, and her hair pulled up on top of her head from the heat of all the people in here tonight. She's simple and stunning. She doesn't even have to try, she just is. When she turns and catches me ogling her, she shoots me a smile before walking over to me and into my arms.

"What are you doing?" she asks.

"Staring," I give her blatantly as I lower my lips to hers.

She smiles up at me, and the band returns to the stage, playing their next set. It's loud when I tell her, "Hey, I need to run up to my office to grab some papers for Mel before I forget. Do you want to stay down here?"

"I'll go with you," she shouts over the music.

Max hasn't come back, so I grip her hand and pull her in close as I start pushing us through the crowd. She clings tightly to me as we bump shoulders with nearly everyone we pass, and I know she must be freaking out with the contact. I pull her a little when I feel her stumble, but then her body goes rigid and she starts shuffling back against my hold.

"What are you doing?" I holler over the crowd.

Her eyes are focused on something, but I can't figure out what it is in this chaos. She tugs against my arm, and when I turn, she falls out of my hold and onto the floor. Terror streaks across her face, and she panics, stumbling back on her hands. I grab her, and when she makes it to her feet, she turns and starts to bolt. Quickly, I link my arm around her waist from behind, leaning over her shoulder, shouting, "Babe, what's wrong?"

"It's Jack!" she yells in a panic, trying to pry my hands off of her to get away.

"Who?"

"Get me out of here!" she shrieks, thrashing to get out of my hold. "I can't breathe! Get me out of here!"

I don't even question her; I tuck her under my arm and rush her, as fast as I can, to the door. Spotting Jase through the mass of people, I call out to him, "Jase!" but I don't wait to see if he heard me or not because all I'm focused on is getting Candace out. She has her hands clutched to my arms that are holding on to her.

Making it past the door and outside, she's shaken and barely breathing when she breaks away from me and runs to my jeep.

"Babe, what the fuck happened in there?" I ask, when we

get to my car, her whole body shaking. "Who the fuck did you see?"

She falls with her back against the side of the car and grabs on to my shirt as she's crying, gasping for a decent intake of air.

"Jack is in there. We have to leave."

"Who's Jack?"

"Him! Jack is . . ." Her cries are strained when I see Jase approach, asking in shock, "Candace, what happened?"

"Jack's inside."

"Oh, shit!"

"Who the fuck is Jack?!" I scream, confused as fuck with what's playing out in front of me.

"The guy that attacked her," Jase tells me.

Everything stops.

Grabbing on to Candace's shoulders, I demand, "Get in the car. Now." I pull my keys out of my pocket and hand them to Jase, yelling at him, "Get her in the fucking car!"

Everything tunnels as I turn from everything good in my life and walk away.

One second. That's all it took.

Suspended in a false reality where actions and consequences no longer exist. Where rage boils so deep inside your veins that you'd do almost anything to drain them. I'd bleed it all out for her.

Chaos. I'm in it when I slam through the doors and bark out, demanding only the way a feral animal would, "Where's Jack?!"

When the guy to my left points him out, I come unleashed.

Without a conscious thought, I grab ahold of the hair on the side of his head and drive him with unrelenting force as I smash his face into the brick wall, blood splattering everywhere. The screams around me are nothing but hollow echoes as I keep my hand fisted in his hair and with one fluid movement, jerk him back and throw him to the floor, hearing the crack of wood as his head clips the edge of the table on his way down.

I watch his eyes roll back with heavy lids as I slam my fist into his face. Over and over. Blow after blow. I'm ravaged with hate, feeding this guy his own blood as I knock another punch into the side of his jaw, giving him only a small piece of what he gave my girl. I'm blinded by the rage that pounds in my chest. I'm gonna fuckin' kill this piece of shit as I ram my fist into him until I'm suddenly pulled back.

I can't feel anything besides the strain in my muscles, tense with fire.

"Breathe, man!" I hear Max yelling in my ear from behind me. His large hands are clamped to my arms, pinning them to my sides as I try to jerk out of his grasp. When I peel my eyes off of the sorry fucker lying there, spewing blood, I see Mark in front of me, hands against my chest, holding me back. Everything moves in slow motion around me when suddenly the noises start to filter in clearly. No more static. Everything in full force around me.

"Get the fuck off of me," I seethe at Max.

"What the hell is going on?"

Yanking myself out of his grip, I turn and lean into his ear, forcing out the words, "He raped Candace."

His head snaps up as he looks at me, and I see the fury in his eyes grow.

"Get the fuck outta here, man," he tells me in a low growl.

Looking down, the guy is starting to come to, when I say, "No way, man." I'm not even close to being finished with him. "This guy's dead," I spit out, and before I can propel myself on him again, Max pulls me back, and says, "You left her outside. Go!"

"Dude, she's outside, hysterical!" Mark shouts.

That's all he needed to say to grab me. To suck me out of this tunnel.

Looking at Max straight on, I give him my hard words, "Finish him off, and throw this piece of shit out by that dumpster." I feel my tears well up as he nods at me. "I'm not fuckin' kidding, man!"

"I hear you, boss," he says when I turn to Jack, draw my foot back, and kick the living shit out of him, cramming my boot into his balls. The pained shriek that rips through his throat is the last sound I hear as I storm out, fists still clenched when I spot my girl sobbing in the front seat of my car.

"Keys," I quietly demand as I pass Jase.

Hopping into the car, I keep my eyes to the front. I'm still fuming, and my racing heart is making it hard to take in a solid breath. I need to get the hell out of here before the cops show up, but all I want to do is go back and destroy every little piece of that sack of shit.

I know I'm scaring Candace; I know how sensitive she is, but I also know that if I open my mouth right now, I'll probably really upset her. So I stay quiet and focus on bringing my heart rate down and calming myself. I don't even realize how firm my grip is on the steering wheel until I feel the blood from my knuckles running down the back of my hand.

By the time I pull up to the loft, my breathing has slowed, and I'm in a daze with all that just happened. Everything that I never wanted to do in front of her, I just did. And without a single second thought. Completely shut down, letting my anger get the best of me. I wouldn't have been able to control it even if I wanted to. And the sick thing is, I'm still not satisfied.

Parking the car, I get out and walk around to her door. When I open it, I see her reddened face, soaked with tears. I grab on to her hips and turn her towards me as I drop my head onto her lap and cry. It hurts too much to keep it in, so I let it out. I feel her body as she leans down and drapes it over mine.

I hate every piece of me that I got from him. Pounding my fists into someone else to try and make myself feel better when all I feel is worse. It's as if I could stand in front of a mirror, and the reflection I'd see would be that of my father.

Candace holds on to me, hands threaded in my hair, but not even her touch can take this misery away. Knowing that I can't escape what's in my blood. I hate that I scared her, but I don't hate what I did to that guy. I'd do it again, and worse. I just hate that this asshole has infected what Candace and I have. That he holds this power over both of us and has the ability to stir up so much pain.

When her grip loosens on me, I lift my head up, and I can see the torment in her eyes as she wipes the tears from my face. There's blood on her fingers as I reach for her hand to hold, and I know it has to be Jack's, so I walk her inside and straight to the bathroom. As she cleans her hands in the sink, I hop into the shower and watch the muddled, red water running off of me, taking his blood down the drain.

I can hear Candace crying, and my heart just crumbles to have her so upset. I'm terrified to see what this has done to her. She's always been nervous of crowds because she's always feared running into him. Now that it's happened, I'm worried she's going to shut down. Worried about what this has stirred up and awakened inside of her.

I quickly finish up, throwing on a pair of boxers, and

slide into bed with her where she's curled up, crying into her pillow. I scoop her in my arms, and it isn't but seconds before I feel her tears running down my chest. Sliding us down in the bed and under the covers, I hold her close, and her loud cries begin to soften.

She draws her head back and then presses her lips to mine, but my stomach is in knots so it's hard for me to do much of anything aside from keeping myself still.

"Make love to me," she whispers before covering my lips with hers again.

I can't do this. Not now.

"Baby, you're crying."

"I don't care," she says when she tugs me in and starts kissing my neck, but I don't want to do this. It feels wrong, and she's so upset. Pulling back to look at me, tears still spilling out, she says, "Kiss me."

"Candace, you're upset."

"I need to be close to you right now. I want to get him out of my head, and you're the only one who can do that for me."

I roll on top of her, hating what I'm about to do because it feels so wrong when she's hurting so bad. "Are you sure, babe?"

"Yes."

The thought of making love to her in the shadow of him makes me sick, but if this is what she needs, I won't deny her. As soon as I slip my hand under her top and take her breast in my hand, she starts pulling my boxers down. Rushing.

"Candace," I plead, wanting her to slow down.

"Please, Ryan."

Hearing her desperate voice, I take off my boxers and then sit back as I remove her shorts. She quickly strips her top off and pulls me down to her, urging me, so I go ahead and slide inside of her. Nothing about this feels right. With her eyes closed, she grabs my hips, wanting me to move faster, so I do. As she clings to me, and I give her a part of me that I never wanted to experience with her. She won't look at me, and I don't feel like I could even ask that of her. Holding on to my hips, she encourages me to thrust myself inside of her. I never wanted it to be this way with us. So disconnected and too fast.

I watch as she cries. She's cried while we've made love in the past but for completely different reasons. It kills me to know that it isn't me behind her closed eyes; it's chaos mixed with me. It's *him*, it's that night, it's this night, it's everything I never wanted to bring into our bed.

Moving at the speed we are, it doesn't take long for both of us to come, and when I roll off of her, I pull her close to me and cling to her, hating what we just did. My chest is heavy, and my throat is achingly tight. I reach down and find her hand, locking my fingers with hers.

"I'm so sorry," she whispers on a broken voice. "I shouldn't have done that."

And even though I never want to do that again, I would if it was really what she needed, so I tell her, "Don't be. You take whatever you need from me," because I'd give it all no matter how much it hurt me just to take away an ounce of her pain.

Waking in the middle of the night, I open my eyes to see light filtering from underneath the bathroom door. Candace isn't in bed with me, and when I walk over to the closed door, I can hear her soft cries on the other side. Slowly, I open the door to find her sitting on the edge of the tub with her head in her hands.

Kneeling down in front of her, I rest my hands on her legs. She doesn't respond to my presence, she just keeps her face covered as she tries to control the sobs that are breaking through.

"Talk to me, baby. Please."

"It's . . . I just, I can't get it out of my head now." When she lets her hands fall, her eyes are so swollen and red. "I don't know what to do anymore."

Her wrecked voice penetrates me, and I feel my throat begin to restrict again as I fight my own tears back.

"I'm so sorry," I release on a hard breath. "I'm sorry I lost it like that and scared you." I pause for a moment, and then admit, "I scared myself."

She catches her breath and looks at me. She's worn out, but I continue to talk.

"I wanted to kill him." Those are the words that break me and cause the tears to escape. "I would have killed him if it weren't for Max pulling me off of him. I've only wanted to kill one other person in my life, and he's dead. And now I wonder if I'm turning into him."

When I drop my head onto her lap, she lifts it back up and holds my face in her hands as she says through her tears, "You're nothing like him. I don't have any doubt about saying that. And I'm not scared of you. I never have been."

"I completely lost control. Wasn't even fully aware of what I was doing."

She slides off the edge of the tub and onto the floor with me as we wrap each other up in our arms.

"I wasn't scared of you, Ryan. I was just so scared of losing you," she cries. "I was afraid you'd kill him and I wouldn't have you."

"Baby, I'm so sorry. But I'm here. I swear you're not gonna lose me," I assure her. "I promise you that he will never step foot in my bar again."

We cling to each other, and when we both calm down, she softly says, "I'm sorry about earlier. I just . . . I wasn't thinking."

"Don't be sorry, babe. I love you. I'd give you just about anything if you asked me for it."

"It was wrong. Selfish."

Brushing the hair off of her face, I tell her, "Do you know how much I love you?"

"Hmm," she hums.

"You don't ever have to worry about me because I've never wanted anyone the way I do you."

She kisses me, and I linger in it before picking her up and taking her back to bed. I can't help the worry that still consumes me. I wonder how she's going to feel about everything when she wakes up. I can only hope that tonight doesn't have a lasting impact on her because I feel like she was just starting to come out of herself. But all I can do tonight is hold on to her, hold on to my hope.

chapter thirty-nine

Waking up, I roll over to Candace but she isn't here. The bed is empty, and when I look over to the bathroom, the door is wide open and the lights are off. She's probably downstairs drinking her coffee.

"Candace," I call out as I sit up, still half-asleep.

When there's no response, I walk out of the room and see her cell phone lying on the floor at the bottom of the stairs.

What the hell?

"Candace," I call out again as my pulse quickens, wondering where she is. I rush over to the windows only to see that her car is gone. Panic and confusion start to tear through me. What the hell happened last night? Where is she?

I throw on a pair of gym shorts and a t-shirt before getting my shoes on and then I'm out the front door and in my jeep. I rush over to her house and figure if she isn't there then she must be at Jase's, but when I pull up, her car is in the driveway.

Thank God.

I knock lightly, and when no one answers, I check the handle to find it's unlocked. Worried about why she's here and not in my bed, I go ahead and let myself in, making my way back to her room. As soon as I open her door, she's in a frenzy, slinging the sheets from her bed across the room.

"Candace?"

She snaps around, and her face is worse than it was last night. Puffy with bloodshot eyes, and she's crying.

"Get out," she seethes, and my gut knots. I don't know what's going on, but the look in her eyes is freaking me out.

"Babe, what's going on?" I ask as I walk towards her, but she shoots her arms out at me, not wanting me to come any closer.

"Stay away from me."

"Baby, what happened?"

She begins to cry loudly as she backs herself against the wall, and I just want to know what the fuck happened and why she's acting so scared of me.

"You know exactly what happened. You know exactly who I am!" she screams.

I stand there, in the middle of her room, confused as shit while my mind races to find clarity in this.

Suddenly, it hits.

She knows.

But how?

She's freaking out, and I can't seem to find the right words to explain myself.

"How could you?!" she screams, and I don't know how I'm gonna calm her down. My heart is pounding, and the utter fear inside of me has me in a panic.

"Babe, let me explain."

"Explain what?! That you've been lying to me this whole time? That you've just been using me? Why?!"

"No! It's not like that. I didn't know."

"How could you not know? God, I'm so fucking stupid."

"I didn't know when I first met you. I didn't know until I saw your tattoo," I try telling her, but I see it in her eyes. She doesn't believe me, and I don't know what to do.

Fuck. What do I do?

"What?!"

"Babe, please let me explain."

"Get out! Get the fuck out! I don't ever want to see you again."

Her words pierce through me, and I choke in a breath as she falls to the floor, wailing, but I can't leave. My mind is racing, and I'm at a loss.

"Just leave me alone," she cries.

"I'm not leaving," I tell her because I don't know *how* to leave her. I can't. I've never seen her so mad and to have all that anger directed at me makes me terrified to walk away until I know we're okay.

I quickly move to the floor, kneeling in front of her, but she coils herself away from me.

I'm desperate.

"I fuckin' hate you," she throws at me, and it kills. "You made me fall in love with you, and it was all a goddamn lie."

"God, Candace. Please let me explain," I beg as I reach out to touch her.

"Get out! Get the fuck out!"

My head snaps back when I hear the door slam open.

"Get the fuck out and away from her before I call the cops," Kimber says as she stands in the doorway, but I don't give a shit about her as I look back to my girl who is falling apart on me.

"Babe, please. I love you so fuckin' much. Let me explain. Don't do this."

"I didn't do shit, Ryan! Just go. It's over!" She covers her face and won't even look at me. It's like a damn knife in my heart, and I feel like I'm drowning. I don't want to believe her words. She's just upset. She can't really want this to be over.

"I'm serious. After the shit from last night, you better get the fuck away from her and leave. Now!" I hear Kimber say from behind me.

I don't know how to fix this or what I can do. Every time I speak, I seem to only make it worse. So against everything I want to do, I stand up and walk away. It's like I'm losing her piece by piece with every step I take, but I love her too much to hurt her, and I'm so fuckin' mad at myself for lying to her.

Walking past Kimber, I can't even look back to Candace who's crumpled on the floor crying. It hurts too much to know I'm the cause of her pain. How could I do this to her? How could I have been so selfish?

"Fuuuck!" I scream, gritting it out of my lungs as I slam the door shut and walk out to my car. Getting in, I strike my palms against the steering wheel, pounding it over and over again, screaming. It hurts coming out, but I need to feel the pain because I feel like I just lost everything.

I've seen her cry and be upset in the past, but *this* . . . this is beyond just being upset. Instead of going back inside to be with her, comfort her, explain to her how stupid I am, I drive back home. I don't want to, but I do. I don't feel like I have a choice since I just ripped out my girlfriend's heart because I was too much of a coward to tell her the truth.

Walking through the door, I see her phone that remains at the bottom of the stairs and begin to wonder what the hell happened while I was asleep. How did she find out? I have a thousand questions swarming inside of me, but I'm just too far gone to concentrate to try to make sense out of all of this.

I don't know how to respond or what I should do. I figure

I'll give her space to calm down before I try talking to her again. She has to understand. She has to listen and believe me when I tell her how much I love her. I can't lose her, but what if she doesn't believe me?

The agony ripping through me hurts so much, and I can't control the unrelenting tears that begin to pour out of me, taking every bit of happiness with them, until I'm nothing but numb, sitting on the couch and staring out at the rain.

Time doesn't exist right now. Nothing does. I don't know how long I've been sitting here in a stagnant melancholy when I hear a knock on my door. I hope with everything I have that she's standing on the other side. When I walk over and open it, I barely get a glimpse of Jase before his fist barrels into the side of my face, clipping my jaw, causing me to lose my balance as I stumble back.

"I told you not to fuck around with her."

Looking up, he steps inside and slams the door shut. I wish he would come back and bury his fist into me again. I deserve every hit. When I straighten myself up and wipe the blood from my split lip, he's pissed and has every right.

"What the fuck, man?" he slings at me.

I don't even try to defend myself. I'm a piece of shit and know it.

"You better fuckin' say something and give me a reason to not beat the shit out of your ass."

"Is she okay?" I ask because that's all I care about.

"No, man. She's not okay. She's a fuckin' mess right now, and I don't know what to do for her. What the hell were you thinking?"

"I don't know," I say as I walk over and flop down on the couch. "I didn't know it was her."

"Don't bullshit me."

"I'm not bullshitting you."

"Did you just feel sorry for her?"

"Fuck no. It wasn't like that."

"Then tell me what it was like, because right now, my best friend is falling apart," he says, completely pissed, as he sits down in the chair.

His words hit me hard, and I lose it. I don't even try to hide my pain from him because at this point, I feel like I have nothing left. I give him the honest truth when I tell him, "I was the one who called 911 that night. But that girl was unrecognizable, so when I met Candace, the only thing that struck me about her and that girl in the alley was their small size. I swear I didn't know it was her."

"But you did eventually."

"She has this tattoo. The same tattoo I saw that night. I had already fallen hard for her when I saw it, and it fuckin' killed me. I didn't know how to tell her at that point. I couldn't hurt her."

"So you lied to her?"

"It didn't seem like a lie, man. Not for a while. Not until she opened up to me about the rape."

"So why didn't you tell her then?" he asks.

"I was scared I'd lose her. It was selfish, but I love that girl with everything I have. I just . . . I didn't know how to tell her."

"When I met you at the bar that morning . . . you hadn't just found out, had you? You already knew."

"Yeah, man. I knew," I admit. "It was just the first time she opened up about it."

Jase leans forward, with his elbows propped on his legs when he releases a deep breath and says, "You should have told me. We could have figured out a way to tell her."

The two of us have become pretty decent friends, and now I see that I deceived him as well.

"I'm sorry, man," I tell him, completely defeated.

He stares out the window when he says, "She's devastated."

I want to help her, but I'm not even sure if I know how. "What do I do?" I ask, desperate.

"I don't know. She feels betrayed and lied to. Like she was some project just to make you feel better about what you saw."

"She said that?"

He nods his head, and I ask, "You believe that?"

When he looks over at me, he says, "No. I know you love her. I get that you were trying to protect her."

"I just need to talk to her. I need her to understand."

"I don't know if that's gonna happen." He takes a pause before continuing. "You know how she is. She avoids and hides. I don't know if she's gonna want to deal with this pain."

Lowering my head, I choke out, "I can't lose her." I let the agony take over me for a moment before I sit up, and ask, "How did she find out?"

"She spoke with the detective this morning."

"What?" I ask in shock. "Wait. Is she pressing charges?" I ask.

"I think she was considering it, but now, I don't think so. I don't think she'd be able to deal with it right now. Not with how upset she is."

I had no idea that she was thinking about this. Enough to make a phone call. It's all I've ever wanted her to do. To take control and stand up for herself. Whether or not she wants me in her life, I need her to do this because I know it will help her deal with all of it, so I tell Jase, "You need to tell her to do it."

"I don't think it's gonna happen, man. Not now."

Guilt floods me. Knowing that I possibly ruined this for her. Ruined this opportunity for her to seek justice and to help herself fight through this. That my lie would take that away from her. I feel like I keep failing her. Hurting her because of my selfish decision.

"Talk to her. Tell her to not let what I did stop her from doing something about this. She needs to do something."

"I know that. Trust me, I do. But she's in a bad place right now, and I can't push her."

I take in his words, knowing that he's right, but it doesn't make it any easier.

Jase stands up and says, "She wants me to get her things."

His words take me by surprise. "Why?"

He doesn't say anything, but I can read his face. She's having a knee-jerk reaction, and I'm losing control. That she would be so quick to walk away from me. To want her things out of my house. The place she's been spending all of her time when she's not at school. How could she want me gone in an instant when I want to fight so hard to keep her? I want to throw him outta here. Not because he isn't a friend of mine, but because the longer he's here, the more I feel her slipping away. If he takes her things, he takes a reason for her to come back here. It's selfish, I know, but it's all I have.

"How much?" I ask, fearing the words that come next.

"Everything."

He follows me upstairs, and as I help him pack her clothes and dance stuff, it's like I'm packing up parts of me that she helped me find. Without her, I just don't know who I am anymore. I can't even wrap my head around what's going on right now.

I go into the bathroom to get her belongings, but I keep a few of her things, including her bottle of perfume. I can't let him take all of her away from me, so I leave them on the counter as I carry her other items out and pack them in her bag.

I watch as Jase zips it up and slings it over his shoulder. Before he walks out, he steps next to me and says, "I'm sorry."

Nodding my head, because I can't speak with the pain in my chest, he adds, "I'll try talking to her for you. You're a good guy and the only reason why she was able to be happy after what happened to her," before walking out of my room and out the front door to head back to where I left my heart—with Candace.

Turning to face the bed, I look at the mussed up sheets where I held her last night. I tell myself that she just needs time. That when she calms down, I'll be able to explain everything and we can work this out. Because we just have to.

Walking over to her side, I sit on the edge of the bed and see her necklace on the nightstand. She never takes it off, but here it lies. When I reach over to pick it up, I notice the chain is broken. I run my finger over the stamped words and wonder if we're broken too.

chapter forty

"Baby, please. I know you're upset with me, and you have every right. I fucked up, but I love you. Please call me back. Let me talk to you and explain everything. I miss you."

I hang up the phone after leaving another voicemail for her. I've been calling and texting for the past few days, but I get nothing in response. It kills me to think that I might not ever hear her voice again, but each day that passes without being able to talk to her confirms what I don't want to accept because it can't be over. This can't be it.

I went out yesterday to get her necklace fixed. I didn't like the idea of it remaining broken. I can only hope that she'll one day wear it again, but for now, it lies on the counter in my bathroom by her perfume.

I decided to come into work today because I'm going crazy at home. I need the distraction, and when I get here, I head upstairs. Max's office door is open, and when I stop in, he says, "Hey, man. Been trying to call you."

"Sorry. Things have been crazy," I tell him as I sit down in front of his desk.

"Dude, I don't even know what to say. Shit was insane when you left the other night."

"Yeah?" I ask, but that night feels like it was weeks ago instead of days. So much has happened, and my thoughts haven't been on anything but Candace.

"The cops came by later that night."

"What did you tell them?"

"Just that I didn't know who the fuck started the fight. That by the time I made it inside they were gone. There were so many people here that they weren't gonna waste their time asking around, so you're good."

"Thanks, man," I say. "What happened when I left?"

Leaning back in his seat, he tells me, "I dragged his ass out back and kicked the shit out of him before slamming him into the dumpster. He was fucked up. Bad."

I don't even know how to feel about all of this because it all just hurts. Every part of it. It all came crashing down so fast.

"How's Candace?"

"I don't know. She won't talk to me."

"Why? What happened?"

Dropping my head to the side, I rest it in my hand, telling him, "She found out about me being the one who found her that night. She bailed, and I haven't heard from her since the day after the fight."

He shakes his head, confused, and questions, "You told her?"

"No. I talked to Jase. He said she had spoken with the detective on the case, and he had told her who the witness was . . . *me*. She took the call while I was still asleep, and when I woke, she was gone."

"Fuck," he sighs out.

"I really fucked this up."

Leaning his arms on the desk, he asks, "What are you gonna do?"

"I dunno, man. I keep calling and texting, but knowing her, she's probably just deleting them."

"Maybe she just needs time."

"Yeah," I say as I stand up. "Maybe. I'll be in my office if you need me."

I spend the rest of the day buried in work that Max should be doing, but I need to keep busy, so I take it off his hands and work late into the night.

I finally talked to my mom last night after avoiding her calls. She was upset, hating that Candace had to find out from someone other than me. But I can't keep asking myself what if. It is what it is, and I can't go back because if I could, I would have done it all differently.

It's been two weeks—and nothing. I call her everyday—and nothing. I'm going crazy, practically living at the bar, hiding in my office, and doing what I can to keep busy. I wound up hanging out with Jase and Mark the other day when they came up for drinks.

They're my only connection to her, but they are also genuine friends and I don't want to let go of that. Aside from Max, they're friends that I've connected with on a more authentic level than I have in the past. I don't want to go back to what I had before I met them. Candace showed me what it was to connect, and I'm not going to trash that. I can't.

When there's a knock at my door, I open it to find Jase standing there.

"Hey, man. What's up?" I say as he walks in.

"Nothing. What are you up to?"

"Not a damn thing," I tell him. "Wanna beer?"

"Nah, I'm good," he says as he takes a seat in my living room. "How have you been?"

"How do you think I've been?" I respond as I fall back on the couch, kicking my feet onto the coffee table.

"I can't get her to talk to me," he admits.

"Join the club."

"I'm serious, man. She won't leave her house. I'm worried."

"Why are you telling me this?" I ask, because all his words do is hurt me.

"Maybe if she could hear you explain yourself . . ."

"You don't think I've tried? Dude, I call her every single day. She won't talk to me."

"Go over there," he says.

"If she's not returning my calls or texts, she's not gonna let me in."

"She needs to talk to you. Take my key and just go. She needs to hear you 'cause she's shutting us all out," he says. "You should see her. She looks awful."

I watch as he slides her house key off his key ring and then sets it on the table.

"I don't know, man. I don't wanna hurt her."

"She's already hurting. You're the only one who has ever really gotten through to her in the past. Just try?"

Staring at the bronze key lying there, I'd be an idiot to not take it. If only just to get a look at her. Anything. I'm desperate, so I take it.

"Thanks, man," he says before heading out.

Pulling into her driveway, I already feel my anxiety welling up. I don't know what I'm about to walk into, but I know she's inside, and I'm desperate to see her. When I ring the doorbell, it takes a moment before I hear that voice I've been missing so much, but her words are nearly lifeless when she says, "Go away."

"You won't return any of my calls, babe. Please, let me talk to you."

She doesn't respond, and when I use the key to unlock the door, she turns to me and yells, "What are you doing?!"

"Jase gave me a key."

She mumbles something under her breath before saying, "Ryan, please go. I don't want to talk."

Jase wasn't lying; she looks awful. She was small before, but I can tell she's lost weight by the way her clothes are hanging on her. And I know she isn't sleeping by the dark circles under her eyes. What the hell have I done to her? God, knowing she's hurting so much that she isn't taking care of herself is just another punch to my gut.

"I can't *not* talk to you. It's killing me."

"It's killing *you*?" she snaps. "What about me? Ryan, I can't do this. I can't even look at you. Please, just go." Her words are strained as she speaks.

"I can't stand to see you like this."

"Then go! I will do almost anything to make you leave."

"Just let me talk to you. Please, babe, just let me talk," I beg.

"Fine, say whatever you need to say, then leave me alone."

When she sits on the couch, I walk over and sit next to her as I watch the tears begin to fall from her tired eyes. I wanna touch her. I wanna pull her into my arms like I've done so many times before, but now I feel like I can't. Like if I tried, she would just reject me. I'm so close to her right now, but I've never felt so distant. I hate it.

"I'm worried about you."

"Don't," she says as she turns her head away from me.

"When was the last time you've eaten?"

"Ryan, don't. Just say what you need to say."

Reaching out to take her hand, she yanks it away from me. God, this is bad. Needing to get through to her, needing her to know, I just start talking—pleading. "I love you. I know you don't believe me, but I do. No one has ever affected me the way you do, babe. I swear to you . . . I swear I didn't know. I didn't, Candace. Not at first," I tell her when I start to choke up, and I just let it out. I let all the tears fall that I've been holding in because I feel like I'm losing everything I am at this point. She's all I have ever wanted in this life, and I'm losing her.

"When I saw you at the coffee shop, I thought it was you. I thought you were *that* girl," I tell her, nearly crying out the words because they hurt so much. "But then I kept thinking, 'What are the chances?' I didn't know because you looked so different than from that night. And then I found out that you were friends with Mark. Every time I saw you, I felt myself being drawn to you in a way I've never felt before. I had myself convinced that my head was playing games with me, and I honestly did not think you were that girl. It wasn't until I saw your tattoo when we were in bed. That's when I knew. When I found that girl, I saw her tattoo—*your* tattoo."

"Ryan, please," she begs, but I can't stop. She needs to hear this because I'm starting to wonder if I'll ever get this chance again.

She's trying to shut me out, so I continue, "When I saw it, I broke. I didn't want you to be her. I had already fallen so hard in love with you, and realizing that it was you fuckin' killed me," I explain through my tears as she sits there crying with me. "Everything started making sense to me.

How scared you always were with me when we first met, how afraid you were when I tried to touch you. Everything made sense. But, I didn't know how to tell you. And then you told me you loved me, and I know how hard that was for you. I just couldn't hurt you."

"But you did," she sobs out. "You lied to me. I let you see all the parts of me that weren't pretty, but you knew all along. And when I finally opened up to you, you already knew." She drops her head and begins to cry harder when she says, "You let me give everything to you. You had to have known that you couldn't hold on to that secret forever. I would've eventually found out, and you still let me fall for you like I did. I feel so stupid and used, like you just felt sorry for me or pitied me."

"I never pitied you, babe. I have only ever loved you. I just didn't want to hurt you."

When I try pulling her into my arms to hold her, she shoves me back and gets up from the couch, stepping away from me.

"I can't do this. You can't say those things to me," she says.

Walking toward her, I stop right in front of her and confess, "I know I fucked up. I fucked everything up so bad. I know all you wanted was someone you could trust. I wanted to be that for you, and I fucked it all up. But I didn't know what to say; I was scared. You'll never know how fucking sorry I am."

"I knew better. I knew I shouldn't have let you in like I did. But I can't see you anymore. You have to stop calling and texting," she says. Her words tearing me apart as she continues, "I need you to just not exist for me because I can't do this. It hurts more than I thought anything possibly could."

"Candace, please," I beg. I can't fuckin' do this. I can't *not* have her in my life.

"Just go."

I see it. She means what she's saying, but I can't move. I don't how I'm gonna turn and walk away from her. So I stand here, a broken man, in front of the only girl I've ever given my heart to and I cry.

"Please, you have to go. I can't do this," she pleads.

"You have to know how much I love you."

Closing her eyes, she whispers, "Please, Ryan."

I wait for her to open her eyes, but she doesn't. I'm always gonna want her, but reality hits me like a brick.

It's over.

I've never felt pain like this before. It's one thing to get the shit beat out of you by a man you don't even like, but it's another thing entirely when the person you love the most in this world doesn't even want to look at you. I'd go back and take a thousand more beatings just to have her open her eyes and look at me.

But she doesn't, and I can't bear the agony, so I take one last look and absorb everything I can before I turn away from everything I never wanted to. She gave it all to me, and now I leave it behind as I walk out of her house.

The finality of what just happened starts to sink in as I drive home. How is this over? Ending faster than it began. I'm not sure what else I could have said to save what we had. I would've kept her forever if she would've let me. But it's done, and I'm not sure where I go from here. In my head I've been thinking that I was going to give it all up for her. Move to wherever she was going. Maybe I was just in too deep.

There's a black van parked in front of my place when I get home, and as I'm getting out of my car, I see a guy opening the back doors and pulling out a large, wrapped item.

Walking toward him, he asks, "Mr. Campbell?"

"Yeah. What's this?"

"I have a delivery from Thinkspace Art Gallery for you."

Her photo.

"Would you like me to carry it up?"

"No," I tell him as I reach out to take the piece, which is covered in a brown paper wrap.

"You sure?"

"Yeah. I've got it. Thanks."

Before getting into his van, he turns and says, "It's a beautiful piece, sir. Enjoy."

I watch as he drives away, but I don't think I could ever look at this photo—her photo. How could I enjoy something that has been torn to shreds because of me? Carrying the canvas upstairs, I lean it against the wall as I go to the kitchen to get a beer. Popping the cap, I turn and rest my back on the counter and look at it, just sitting there—masking away my happiness, knowing that she's underneath the paper. But being the masochist that I am, I need to see her. I set the bottle down and rip the paper off, revealing the white line of her back.

As I step away, I keep my eyes on her. Her smooth skin. Nothing ever felt better on me, and the thought of never having that comfort again makes seeing her painful. It's tearing out my fuckin' heart, and I need it gone.

Picking it up, I take it upstairs to my bedroom and into my closet where I shove it behind one of the racks of clothes. I hide it because I don't want to look at it, but I don't want to let it go either.

The memories of that day start to run through my head. That rainy afternoon with her in my bed. She was jittery, lying in the dark while I snapped her picture. She trusted me. But now that trust is gone, and she can't even look at me. I just want to touch her. Have her lips on mine, her body warm against me. She was so good at everything she was willing to give. I took it all, and no amount of pain could make me believe that it wasn't worth the fall because falling in love with her was the best thing I ever did.

chapter forty-one

Sitting here, nursing my beer that has now grown warm, I watch as Gavin talks to some blonde who's wearing way too much makeup. I want to leave, but I don't want to go back home. Home and work, those are the only places I seem to find myself lately. But that's all it was before Candace, so why should I expect it to be any different after her? It feels different, but the routine is the same. I work, I go out with Gavin, and I go home—alone. I'm always alone. There was a time not too long ago that I liked it. Now . . . I hate it. So even though I sit here, miserable and bored in this bar, it's better than being alone.

Gavin keeps trying to sling girls at me, but the thought of touching anyone other than Candace is something that I just can't stomach yet. A part of me wants to. Desperate to do anything to get her out of my head, but then I get scared of losing her, even if my head is the only place she exists for me. I'm torn. Lonely, but unwilling to walk away from the girl who doesn't want me.

Another chick approaches, and as soon as she lays her hand on my knee, I'm out of my seat and walking away to go get another drink from the bar.

"Can I get another?" I ask the bartender as I set down my bottle.

"I don't understand why you keep coming out if you're just gonna be a dick," Gavin says when he slides up next to me at the bar.

Looking over at him, I ask, "Who am I being a dick to?"

"This place is loaded with chicks, but you're the biggest pussy in here."

"Nice," I say as I laugh with annoyance.

He turns to lean his side against the bar and gives me a serious look before saying, "She's gone, man."

When the guy from behind the bar hands me my beer, I take a long draw, but it hurts to swallow past the lump in my throat that reared itself at the mere mention of her. Setting the bottle down, I turn and say with irritation, "Yeah? And what if I don't want her to be?"

He sighs when he responds in a matter-of-fact voice, "It doesn't seem to be about what you want. She holds the cards on this one because you handed over that power when you fell for her."

He's right. I've always called the shots with chicks until Candace. It sucks to have someone else dictating your destiny, but with her . . . I wouldn't have it any other way. If this is what she needs, to be away from me, then I'll stay away.

"You wanna know what's gonna make you better? Make you forget?" he asks me.

"What's that?"

He lifts his arm, beer in hand, and points over the crowd of people as he says, "Take your pick." When he turns to look at me, he gives a smirk and adds, "Just like old times."

I might not know what my life is right now, but I do know that it isn't this. It vanished when I met Candace. She made me see this for what it is. She showed me a different version of myself—a version that I was happy to be. So this? This is nothing but a distraction that I no longer want.

Before taking a sip of his beer, he mutters, "I never understood what you saw in her anyway."

"What's your problem?"

"Nothing. Just being honest. She was just so different than your normal type. I didn't get it."

Tossing a few bucks on the bar, I get up and tell Gavin, "I'm going home."

"Ryan," he calls out as I make my way to the door, but there's nothing here for me. Who am I kidding? No matter where I am, my misery follows, so I might as well be home.

When I was hanging out with Jase the other night, he told me about his plans to go over to Westport for a day trip to get some surfing in. Needing the headspace, I decide to tag along. He met me at my place earlier this morning, and after several hours of driving, we unload my jeep and zip up our wetsuits before heading out into the water.

For the first time in a while, I feel good. If only for a moment, being out here in the water, my head finally settles as I simply enjoy the breaking waves as I ride them. The salt on my face and the sun that's starting to break through the clouds is freeing in a way. Being out of Seattle and away from the gloom that seems to follow, I take a break as I straddle my board and stare out over the endless water.

"The breaks are pretty decent today," Jase says as he paddles over to me.

"Yeah. The tide is starting to come in."

Shifting himself to sit up on his board, he asks, "You

doing okay?"

I nod my head, but I know he isn't just talking about surfing, and curiosity gets to me when I decide to ask, because I just can't avoid it. No matter what she says or what she does, I can't forget about her. I can't stop caring about her, so I go ahead and ask, "How is she?"

Running his hand through his hair, he says, "She's better."

"Yeah?"

"She started seeing a therapist a couple weeks ago," he tells me. "She's been going a couple times a week."

"That's good." It relieves me to hear that she's finally talking to someone, but at the same time, it's hard to not be there to support her.

"Yeah. She's been working really hard, trying to sort everything out."

When I don't respond, he questions, "What about you?"

"I don't know, man. I'm fuckin' stuck. Like I'm just waiting for something I'm not sure is gonna happen."

"With her?"

Nodding my head, I ask hesitantly, "Should I be?"

"Waiting?" he questions.

"Yeah."

Looking out over the water, avoiding having to face me, he breathes out, "I don't think so."

It's the reality I've been trying to hide from. I've been hanging on to a thread of hope, but hearing those words from Jase, they hold an honesty that there's no more hiding from.

"She's working hard on pulling herself together, to make sense of the madness she's been living in. Maybe you should do more for yourself too. I hate to see you stagnant, waiting for something that doesn't seem likely to happen at this point."

I hear his words, and they're hard to take. I don't want to accept them, but he makes it clear what I should do when he adds a hard truth to my reality, saying, "I think it's time you just walk away from it. She seems to have."

How do you walk away from someone that still occupies so much of your heart? To be so certain about something just to turn your back on it? And how can she move on so quickly when I'm still in pieces over here? It sucks to have all these questions that I can't get any closure with. To constantly be wondering and hoping.

"I've tried talking to her, tried telling her how you feel about everything, but she shuts me down. She said she just needs to be on her own."

"No, I get it," I mumble. "You don't need to say anything to her. If she's happy . . . that's all I've ever wanted for her."

"Sorry, man."

"It's life," I say as I lie down on my board and paddle back out.

"So, I'm planning on leaving here next Friday morning," my mom tells me as I sit in my office at home.

"Mom, I don't know if that's a good idea."

"It's your birthday," she exclaims, but we both know that's not her reasoning for wanting to come.

"You never drive up here for my birthday. I know you're coming to see Candace dance, but I just don't know if that's a good idea at this point."

"I told her I was going to be there. I would feel awful if I didn't show up. This is a huge night for her, and I've never seen her dance."

"I just . . ."

"Her family turned their backs on her; I'm not going to do the same. I want to support her. No matter what happens with you guys, I'd like to at least offer my support."

"Nothing's gonna happen with us, Mom," I tell her as I shut the lid to my laptop.

"How do you know that?"

"Jase told me last week that she's done, and I should just walk away. So that's what I'm trying to do."

"I'm sorry, dear. I know you love her."

Having her so close, blending so nicely with my mom and me, it was perfect. It's something I don't think I'll be able to find again. Something I'm not sure I want to open myself up to again.

"You still there?" she asks when I don't say anything.

"Yeah, I'm here."

"Are you okay?"

Taking a hard swallow, I admit, "I don't know how to be okay. I don't how she's moving on when I can't."

"Maybe she isn't. Maybe she's hurting just like you are."

"Then why isn't she coming back?" I ask as my voice slips.

"She could just be scared."

"It's been over a month, and I wanna run to her every day, but I know if I do, I'll only be hurting her. She lives right down the fuckin' street from me, but it's like she's across the world."

My mother is at a loss for words, so I cut the conversation short, not wanting to talk any more, but as soon as we hang up, Tori's name flashes on my phone when it starts ringing again.

"Hey, Tor."

"Hey, how are you? I talked to Aunt Donna earlier today. Why didn't you tell me what happened?"

"There's not much to talk about," I clip out.

"Well, what happened?"

Leaning back in my chair, I say, "You were right. I wasn't honest with her and fucked everything up."

"What did you lie about?"

"It doesn't matter. I kept something from her that I shouldn't have, and it's done." I'm tired and just need to blow this off so she doesn't keep me on the phone. "Look, it was over a month ago, so there's not much to say about it. Moving on."

"Got it," she responds. "You coming back here for Memorial Day weekend?"

"Maybe. Haven't thought about it. But, hey, I'm gonna hit the sack, so I'll talk to you later," I tell her so I can hang up.

I'm about to throw the damn phone across the room when it starts ringing again, but this time when I answer it, all I hear on the other end is panic.

"Ryan?"

"Hey, Max. What's going on?"

"Traci's in labor. We're heading to the hospital." His voice is rushed, and I can't help but laugh at the fear in him.

"So why are you calling me? Shouldn't you be driving?" I ask with a chuckle.

"Because I know when I get there it's gonna be us and her crazy-ass sisters driving me insane."

"You better watch it," I hear Traci bark at him in the background.

"Dude—"

"Okay. I'll admit. I'm scared shitless," he tells me when Traci butts in, saying, "You're scared? Are you serious? I'm the one about to have a baby here and you're on the phone with your buddy because you're scared?"

"Shit, you've got your hands full," I laugh, and the next thing I hear is Traci as she says, "Ryan? You there?"

"Hey, Trace."

"Tell your buddy to calm the hell down and to stop being a pansy."

The dramatics of this late night call are cracking me up, and I do not envy Max with having his girl fed up with him.

The phone muffles and then Max says, "You coming to the hospital?"

"You need to relax before Traci rips your head off, but yeah, I'll be there."

Seeing Max with a baby is a head-trip for me. Traci went into labor quickly, and by the time they made it to the hospital, it was too late for her to get any drugs, so now Max has some god-awful scratches on his arms where she took her pain out on him. But in the end, they have a healthy baby boy.

The sheer happiness splayed across his face is something that any man would envy. Max is content, and I couldn't be happier for him, but I'd be lying if I said I wasn't panged with a slight sense of jealousy. I never thought that settling down and having a family was in the cards for me, but with Candace, I was starting to believe that it could be a possibility. So in my attempt to move on, I hold his baby in my arms and shut my selfish emotions out as I sit here with one of my good friends as he gushes over his new son.

chapter forty-two

"How was your drive?"

"Long," my mom says as she hugs me. "It's good to see you."

"Come in," I tell her as I take her bag and set it against the wall. "Max called a little while ago. He said that Traci is feeding Bennett and now would be a good time to come over, so if you still wanted to see the baby, we should head out."

"Of course I want to see the baby."

Grabbing my keys, we leave and make the drive over to Max's place. My mother has gotten to know Max a little over the years, and she never passes up an opportunity to hold a baby, so when we arrive, she melts at the sight of Bennett.

We settle ourselves in the living room, and Mom doesn't even wait for me to introduce her to Traci. She is already sitting next to her, making her own introductions, and before I know it, they're chatting away. My mom just has this way about her that can put anyone at ease. Candace loved that about her.

"So, what's been going on?" Max asks as he flops down

on the chair.

"Just covering for you every day," I tease.

"Ha, nice, man."

"Got another band booked."

"Yeah? That's good. So what's going on with Mark and the guys?" he asks, and I'm momentarily distracted when I hear my mom talking gibberish to the baby.

Shaking my head and laughing at her, I turn back to Max and tell him, "They're gonna alternate Saturdays with the new band for the next four weeks, and then their contract is up."

"Is he staying here in Seattle?"

"Yeah. He and Jase had a few interviews at some firms in the city," I tell him.

"Nice."

"How have you been? You look like shit."

"Dude, this kid wakes up to eat every two hours. When we first brought him home he slept solid for the first few days, but now he's up around the clock."

"Sounds great," I joke when I turn to Traci and ask, "So how's this guy really holding up?" I laugh as I nod to Max.

She shakes her head and teases, "For such a big guy, you wouldn't think he'd be so squeamish."

"Don't listen to her. I've got this completely under control," he defends with a smile.

"Oh my goodness," my mother squeals as we all turn to look at Bennett when he lets out a massive fart.

"Holy shit!" I crack up, nearly doubling over at the insane gas that baby just released.

"Ryan!" my mom scolds. "Don't cuss in front of the baby."

"Are you serious, Mom? He's barely a week old. Little dude doesn't even speak English," I laugh out as she rolls her eyes at me.

"Speaking of having everything under control," Traci says to Max as she picks up Bennett and hands him over. "Why don't you take care of this issue your son has in his pants?"

"You think you're funny, don't you?"

She pats him on the back and mocks, "Try to control the gagging this time, huh?"

He plants a kiss on Traci's nose, and I follow him back to the nursery. I take a front row seat in the rocker as Max lays Bennett on the changing table.

"Dear Jesus!" he says in utter disgust when he peels the diaper off, and it only takes a second for the stench to hit me.

"Ugh! What the hell is that?"

Before Max can say anything, the baby rips out another rancid fart.

"For the love of God!" Max says, and I have to clutch my stomach because I'm laughing so hard at the visual of him being taken down by his own baby, one fart after another.

Max tries holding on to his tiny ankles, when he farts again.

"Dude," he snaps at me. "He's shitting everywhere. Traci!"

"Oh my God," I laugh out. "I'm dying."

"*You're* dying. This shit's right in front of my face."

"What is going on in here?" Traci exclaims when she walks in.

"Honey, there's poop all over me!"

"You boys are ridiculous," my mom says when she takes Max's place and starts cleaning Bennett.

"Donna, let me take care of that," Traci says.

"No worries. You go sit and relax," she tells her. "And you boys get out of here," she scolds as if we're kids and not grown men.

Once Bennett is cleaned up and changed, my mom returns to the living room and lays him on the couch between her and Traci. As she's rubbing his belly, Traci kicks her feet up on the ottoman and leans back into the couch, laughing.

"What's so funny?" Max asks when he returns with a clean shirt.

"You."

"Why is it that every time I change him, it winds up in a fiasco, but when you do it, it's just a simple pee diaper?"

"Payback for me having to be pregnant."

We continue to hang out and when Bennett falls asleep, we say goodbye and head out.

I've been anxious all day, knowing that tonight is Candace's production. I feel weird about going, almost like some kind of voyeur, but I couldn't miss seeing her dance on stage. I have only seen her in a couple of videos she had once shown me.

The whole time we were together, she was preparing for this night, so to finally have it here is bittersweet because I always thought I would be there with her. I should have wrapped her legs up last night in her crazy Saran Wrap. I should have been watching her walk around my loft all day, a neurotic nervous mess, helping her stretch and rub out her calves that had been bothering her, staring at her while she stood in the bathroom as she put her hair up in a bun with all those tiny hair pins.

This day should have been completely different; instead, I've been walking around with a knot in my stomach. I haven't seen her in a long time, and I'm not sure how tonight is going to affect me, but I have to see her.

"You ready?" my mom asks when she walks down the hall.

"Why don't you go on without me?" I suggest. I just think I should be alone tonight when I go. It's definitely not something I want to do with my mother right next to me.

Without a single question, she walks over and runs her hand down my arm as I stand, leaning up against the windows in the living room. "Of course."

When she turns to walk out, I stop her and say, "Mom . . ."

"Yes?"

"You look really nice."

"Thanks, dear. I'll see you later."

Leaning back against the windows, I look out at the darkened night sky and decide that after tonight, I have to be done. I can't keep questioning and wishing things were different. They aren't, and enough time has passed to know that she isn't coming back.

When I arrive at Meany Theater, most everyone is already in their seats, quietly holding their personal conversations. The theater is large with seating up in the balcony. The curtain is dropped, and I look at the program to see which numbers she will be in. She's one of the two featured dancers, so she'll appear throughout the night. I feel so disconnected even though we are probably closer tonight than we've been in a while, knowing she's in the same building as me.

She's in the opening number, so I quietly stand in the back of the room when the curtain draws up. The stage is filled with girls who all look the same, hair pinned up, short white tutus. It isn't until after the music has already started that I see her.

God, she's beautiful.

She's the only one wearing purple, standing out from all the others as she dances in front of the other girls. I've only ever seen her in leotards and tattered warm-ups. Never like this. She fits the part perfectly. Stoic and polished. Graceful and soft. And even on a stage filled with other dancers, she's all my eyes can see, captivating me in a way that only she can do. No one else exists in this room right now—it's only her.

But it isn't until her solo when it hits me. She stands center stage as the curtain goes up, and chills prick along my arms. She's perfection, wearing black with a short, full tutu, pale pink tights, and her pink toe shoes. Her skin is a striking contrast to the black, and she looks amazing. She isn't someone you simply look at; she's someone you admire.

I know her music by heart from all the times she played it at my place. It's a dark and intense piece that she struggled with for so long, but watching her work the whole stage, she's nothing but a natural as she bares her heart up there, making me feel the haunting pain of the piece. She gives it all, up on her toes, gliding through her movements. It almost hurts to look at her because I know this will be the last time I will probably ever see her. I can't take my eyes off her. I don't ever want to.

I'd hide back here forever if it meant I wouldn't have to stop looking at her. As tiny as she is, she made the biggest impact on me. I've never loved as hard as I did with her. I don't know how anyone could ever love her more. With everything we went through to get to the point we were at, knitted so tightly together, I never thought there could be a possibility of us unraveling like we did. But we did.

I don't blame her though. She hasn't made a wrong choice yet. I know she left me because it was the best thing for her. I talk to Jase often about her, and knowing how hard she's working in therapy, I know she wouldn't be doing that if she were still with me. She needed to be on her own. To do it for herself and not just because it was something I wanted. I'm proud of her, and even though it hurts me, I know she's doing everything right to try and pull herself out of the darkness that was consuming her.

The crowd is deafening when the music stops, and I finally see it. Her big, gorgeous smile with that cute dimple in her cheek. She soaks up the standing ovation, as she should, because she deserves every second of this. She's elated. I can see it in her eyes, even from this far away. Her instructor walks out with a huge bouquet of roses and hands them to her as she takes her final curtsey before the curtain drops, taking her away from me.

The pain hits hard as I blink back the tears. I'll never want to see her any other way than what I just did. That's the image I want in my mind. My girl, not a tormented thought in her head. Happy, free, and on top of the world. Filled with nothing but joy. She has a couple more numbers to dance, but I take what I just saw because nothing could possibly be better. She gave me perfection, and I decide to leave with that as I walk out, leaving a huge piece of my heart in that theater.

And now I start over because I can't look back. She's happy, and I have to be content with that, no matter how much I wish I could be a part of it.

I wake up the following morning to the smell of bacon and eggs. I lie in bed for a while before getting up to see my mom in the kitchen, fixing us omelets.

"There you are. I was starting to wonder when you would drag yourself down here," she says as she stands over the stove.

"Sorry. I didn't get much sleep last night," I respond as I walk over to fix myself a cup of coffee.

"Wait. Before you do that, you should open your birthday gift," she says with a smile as she nods her head to the dining table where a large box sits, wrapped in gold paper with burgundy ribbon. Tearing the paper, I note the store name on the box and question, "Sur La Table?"

"Just open it," she says as she fixes our plates.

Opening the box, I pull out the De'Longhi cappuccino machine. "This is perfect, Mom."

"Yeah? I figured you'd get good use out of it," she says as she walks past me and sets our plates down on the table.

"It'll give me something to do today, figuring out how to use the damn thing," I joke as I sit down.

"Happy twenty-ninth birthday, darling."

"Thanks."

As we start eating breakfast, she looks up and says, "So, I never saw you last night."

"Yeah, I crashed early. Sorry about that." After I left, I was too upset to even think about seeing my mom, so I spent the evening upstairs.

"Did you go?" she asks.

"I went."

"Do you want to talk about this?"

"No."

I get up and walk into the kitchen to fix my coffee, and when I return to the table, I tell her, "It's done with, Mom. I'm walking away, so there's no point in ever bringing her up again."

Nodding her head, she responds, "Of course, dear."

But I'm not completely walking away because her canvas is still in my closet, and a bottle of her perfume still sits on her side of the sink. It's pathetic, but even though I know I should, I'm not entirely ready to let her completely go just yet.

Another week passes, and while I'm cleaning up my home office, I come across the sheet of paper where Candace wrote down the information for the woman we met at the gallery showing. It's funny that I should run across this now because this past week, I started working more on some of the photos that were stored on my camera. Albeit photos of Candace, but the thought of trying to find someone else to photograph turns my stomach.

Needing to step out of the monotonous routine I have going, I pick up the phone and give this lady a call. She once mentioned being interested in seeing more of my pieces, so why not?

"Henry Gallery."

"Is Stacy Keets available?" I ask.

"One moment."

The line is picked up after a few seconds. "Stacy here."

"Stacy, this is Ryan Campbell. We met at Thinkspace a few months back."

"Yes. I remember. 'Nubile,' right?"

"Right."

"What can I do for you?"

"I have a few pieces that I've been working on if you were still interested in taking a look," I say.

"I'd love to. My time is a bit limited, and I'm about to go

on vacation, but I'm free this afternoon, if that isn't too soon?"

"No, that works for me."

"Great. How about three o'clock?"

"Sounds good, Stacy. I'll see you then."

After running up to the bar for a few hours, I head over to the Henry Gallery.

Sitting down in Stacy's office, she says, "I'm glad you called. We actually just had two wall openings become available yesterday."

I hand over my samplings and while she studies them, she keeps her eyes down as she casually says, "Your girlfriend was brilliant last week. You must be so proud of her, huh?"

She says this not having a clue that we're no longer together, but for the moment, it feels good, so I don't correct her, saying, "Yeah. She's amazing."

"She's more than amazing. Sergej has always considered her a prodigy," she says as she flips to the next photo. "Has she gotten many job offers?"

"Umm, I don't really know," I answer honestly, and when she looks up, she says, "Well, I have no doubt that she's gonna have quite a few companies to choose from."

"I'm sure she will."

"And these," she continues as she takes her sleek glasses off and sets them on her desk, "these are really beautiful."

"Thank you."

"Are you being displayed anywhere else at the moment?" she questions.

"No. Didn't really think all too seriously about pursuing anything with these photos until this past week, to be honest."

"Well, I'd be interested in these two, if you'd like to

discuss further," she tells me as she sets two of the samples aside and stacks the rest. "Are you optioning a sale?"

"No. I won't sell these," I respond. All these photos are of Candace, and I don't want any of them hanging in some random person's home. They're mine.

"Well, then. Let me look at something really quick," she says as she starts clicking away on her laptop. "I can do a six-week spot showing. It's a good slot because they will be on display during one of our invite-only showings next month. You'll have a lot of eyes on these that could help jumpstart some work if that's a direction you'd like to go."

"That sounds great."

"Perfect, then. Let me go grab all the necessary paperwork, and we can get everything secured for you right now."

Feeling like I've been needing to do something different, have a little more focus, this couldn't have come at a better time. Although I would never sell these particular photos, I'd love to have an opportunity to expand this and possibly take on some work. So we spend the next half hour getting everything set up before I head out, feeling good about this new door that could be opening for me.

chapter forty-three

After Stacy selected the two pieces for display a few days ago, I went to have them canvassed and just got back home from dropping them off at the gallery. The wall had already been prepped, and they should be up by tomorrow. It's a good feeling to be doing something that will hopefully bring me some opportunities.

When I start heading back to my office, there's a knock on the door.

"Are you Ryan Campbell?" a guy questions when I answer it.

"Yeah."

He hands over several papers and says, "I've got some legal documents here for you. Are you active military?"

"No."

"Okay. Well, there's no signature required. Have a good day," he tells me before walking down the stairs.

Closing the door, I unfold the papers to find that I've just been served a subpoena, and when I see who the plaintiff is, anger that I haven't felt in a while kicks up. This fucker has a lot of nerve, and I'm about to put an end to this shit, pulling out my phone and calling Jase, who's out of town with Mark right now.

"Hey, Ryan. What's up?

"I need to know where I can find Jack," I demand.

"What?" he asks as I take him off guard.

"I just got served a subpoena, man. Tell me, or I'll just get on the computer and find him myself."

"What are you gonna do?"

"What should have been done months ago," I tell him as my annoyance builds inside of me. "Don't make me ask again," I nearly threaten.

Jase huffs out a hard breath before responding. "He lives at the frat."

"Which one?"

"The Lambda house on nineteenth."

I hang up without saying anything else and grab my keys.

My heart is racing when I pull up in front of the large brick house. There aren't many cars around, and with classes over for the summer, everything is in my favor when I knock and he's the one that answers. The preppy son of a bitch stands there in his white polo as my fist clenches around the court documents in my hand. Looking at his face, you can still see the slight greyish-yellow bruising around his nose and muted pink rings under his eyes where I beat the shit out of him nearly two months ago. There is no doubt that I seriously fucked this guy up.

His eyes are wide as he looks at me in shock, and I don't say a word when I push my way inside, kicking the door shut before I fist his shirt and slam him up against the wall, pinning him with my forearm square across his neck.

I'm seething, and the fear in his eyes is prominent.

"Candace Parker, you know her?" I grit out in pure hate. My muscles tense as I keep him locked against the wall.

He doesn't speak as all the blood drains from his face at

the mere mention of her name.

"Yeah, you know her." Backing my weight off, I slam my arm into him again, causing his head to pound against the wall. "You're lucky I didn't fuckin' kill you at the bar."

"Dude," he faintly gasps out in distress, and his voice just adds to my rage.

"Don't think that I'm not still considering it because I'll kill you with my bare hands, and there's not a goddamn thing you can do to stop me because I know you don't want your dirty secret being exposed."

"I don't know what that bitch told you, but I didn't do shit," he spits at me.

Slamming him down to the ground, head smacking hard against the wooden floor, I grip his neck in my hand, yelling, "I was fuckin' there, you sack of shit. Who do you think beat your ass that night? I know everything you did to her, and there's a rape kit with your DNA all over it, so tell me again that you didn't do shit!"

Before he can respond, I pull back and hammer my fist into his nose as he screams out, blood running down his face.

"Don't worry, I'm not gonna kill you. But I am gonna let you go through your life every day wondering if that's going to be the day that I show up, because I'll never let what you did to her go. So you can live your life in fear just like she does every day, you piece of shit."

Striking my fist into his jaw, I stand and pick up the papers that I dropped. I step back over to him as he lies there, curled up in agony, and lean over as I smack the papers on the ground next to his face, telling him, "You're gonna drop these charges today and fuck off."

My veins are on fire with vengeance and knowing that I've got him by the balls on this, I ram my booted foot into his smug-ass face, listening to him heave in pain as I walk out. All my emotions about Candace that I've pushed down these past couple weeks flood back in a matter of seconds. I could kill that fucker, but it still would never feel like enough because even after all this time apart, the hard truth is, I still love her with every part of me. She's moved on, and I have been trying to do the same, but here I am, back in this.

Driving home, fueled by rage laced with sadness, I crack. I've never hated a single thing more than I hate that sick fuck for what he did to my girl. For what he did to us. I lost it all because he's the one that gave me the secret that I held from her. He's the one that inflicted himself on our relationship that no longer is. Without even trying, he continues to cause chaos in our lives.

After spending a good chunk of the day taking my lingering aggravation out at the gym, I'm finally able to settle my nerves and calm down. I have no doubt that the charges will be dropped, so I'll give it a few days before calling to make sure there isn't anything pending against me.

I've been trying to keep my mind occupied with anything other than Candace and what happened this morning, so when I'm completely burnt out from watching TV, I head upstairs to get ready for bed.

It's after one in the morning when I hear a knock on my door after brushing my teeth. When I make my way back down, I peek out the windows to see who could be here this late, but there's no car in the drive as the rain pours down. I unlock the door, and I swear to God, the whole world stops moving when I open it to see Candace. In an instant, she begins crying and falls into my arms. She's soaking wet from the rain, and I know she had to have walked here.

For this moment, I lose my breath in her as I feel the warmth I thought I would never feel again. A warmth that only she can give me. She clings to me as she cries, and I break for her, not knowing what to say because I'm afraid if I speak, she'll leave. She's here, and all I want to do is make sure that she stays.

God, just stay.

Reaching down, I slip my arm behind her knees and scoop her into my arms as I carry her inside. She keeps her head tucked into me, and I've missed this so much. Even with her hurting, for whatever reason, I miss it. The touch, the feel of her skin, the smell of her hair. I have it all wrapped up in my arms, and it's where I want to keep it.

I sit us down on the couch with her still in my lap, and I keep my arms tightly banded around her because I just can't let her go. I listen to her sobs as they begin to soften into whimpers, feeling the soft quakes of her body as she takes in tiny gasps of air.

"Baby, what happened?" I finally ask, and when she lifts her head and stares into my eyes, I fall for her all over again. It's in my heart, the heavy weighted emotion that's nothing but the love I have for this beautiful girl. Needing to touch her, I reach up and run my fingers down the soft skin of her cheek.

"Jack died tonight."

What did she just say?

Suddenly my heavy heart takes on a pounding as questions brew inside. What the hell happened after I saw him this morning? Fuck! Did I do it? Did I kick him too hard in the head? I could have easily killed him. Panic shoots through me, cold like ice, but the sudden rush of fear is diminished when she says, "Kimber called and told me he died in a car crash earlier today. Drunk driving accident or something."

A hard breath thuds out of my chest. Relief. Maybe I'm sick, but there's not a single piece of me that feels bad about this. But her? She's so upset, and I have to wonder where her head is at with this.

She's so close in my arms, tears still streaking down her face, and when I rest my forehead against hers, greedy to take every touch I can, she begins to ramble, an emotional mess.

"I'm sorry. I didn't know where to go. I'm so confused. I don't know what's wrong with me."

"Slow down, babe."

"Should I be happy? Or relieved?" she asks as she pulls her head back and looks at me, pleading for answers I don't have.

"Well, what do you feel right now?"

"Sad. And hurt," she admits honestly before dropping her head and adding, "I don't know why. It's like all I can think about is Jack when he was good. Or when I thought he was. But I know he wasn't. I know I should hate him. But, if I'm sad, does that mean I don't hate him?"

Lifting her chin to look at me, I say, "I think you're just in shock. I think you need a little time to sort this out in your head." She rests her head back on my shoulder, and I feel her body lightly shivering under my arms. "Let me go get you a towel. You're freezing."

She slips off of my lap as I grab a couple of large towels from the guest bathroom, and when I return, I wrap one of them around her shoulders and then pull her back into my arms.

"You need anything to drink?"

She sits up, and I lose her touch as she clutches the towel around her, shaking her head no. I reach to her again and slowly pull her back against me. I'm selfish, but I don't care. I've missed her so much. No matter how hard I try to give up on her, I just can't. I bury it and keep myself busy enough to where I don't think about her. But she's always there, lying beneath, deep inside of me where I'm starting to believe she will always be. It's like she's the other half of me. The half that would make life miserable if I didn't have it, so I've always kept it. It's not even a choice.

"Talk to me," I urge.

"I'm sorry. I didn't even realize I was here until I was in front of your door."

"I'm glad you're here," I tell her before I move to hold her face in my hands, trying to keep myself together when I let her know, "I've missed you so much."

My words hurt coming out of me, a confession that shouldn't be because she should just know, but I tell her anyway. The thought of her walking away from me now that I have her here in my home, in my hands, and so fuckin' deep in my heart makes it hard to breathe right now. But she gives me hope, a hope I thought was forever lost, when I look into her eyes that are rimmed red with tears and she touches me. She gives me her soft hand as she places it on my face and runs it down my jaw, and then she crumbles. With her eyes shut, she chokes on the sobs that break through.

"Baby, don't cry."

Leaning in, I kiss her forehead, simply resting my lips against her. I need every second of this as I feel her coming back to me, until she pulls away, shaking her head, and then the knife strikes when she whispers, "I can't."

"Babe."

"I can't. It hurts so bad, I just can't."

"I swear to you," I beg because that's all I have at this

point. "I will never hurt you again."

"But you swore you wouldn't hurt me before and you did."

Lowering my head to look her in the eyes straight on, I affirm, "I love you. God, I love you so much," as I move in, holding her face in my hands, and gently graze my lips across hers, tasting the sweetest thing I've ever had.

"I'm moving," she breathes against my lips, and her words echo in my head. A painful reality that I knew would come, but to have it here when I finally have her, is something I don't want to face.

I shift back to look at her, not wanting to accept her words, when she says, "I got a job. I'm moving to New York in two weeks."

Dropping my head, I feel the panic in me. The finality of this has never been more tangible than it is right now, and it's a sharp blade in my heart. A slow bleed that bears the agony of an unrelenting suffering.

"You can't kiss me," she says as a new slew of tears starts. "If you do . . . I'll never want to leave you."

"Then I'll come with you."

"Ryan . . . I just can't. I'm too scared you'll hurt me again. I just need to be on my own. I've been working so hard to pull myself out of the hell I've been living in."

"I know you have. I ask Jase about you all the time. He's told me how well you're doing. I just wish I could be around to see it, babe," I choke out around the knot in my throat that I can no longer fight as I drop my head and cry. Cry for what we once had. We were so good and happy. Completely in love and bound together in a way I never thought two people could be. But we were, and I don't think something like that comes around too often.

"All I ever wanted was for you to be okay, to be happy,"

I tell her.

"I'm okay."

She lets me hold on to her, so I do. Scared to let go of her because I know what it means when I finally do, and it's a pain I'm not ready to feel. So I let time pass as I keep her tucked into me, her head nestled in the curve of my neck, the feel of her damp hair against my skin, the smell of her soft scent that filters into my lungs . . . my senses consumed with her, and then comes sound as she finally speaks.

"Do you think you could drive me home?"

"Yeah," I whisper, wondering how you say goodbye to someone like her. But I find happiness in one thing, and that is, after all we have been through and all the time that has passed, she ran to me for the comfort that she needed.

I let my tears fall as I drive her home, and with each glance over, I see her own stained face. My gut is in knots, and with my eyes on the road ahead, I ask, as desperate as a man could, because I have nothing else, "Tell me how to fight for you."

"Please," is her only response, spoken softly, pleading for me not to push any more.

When I pull up to her house, I turn to her and ask, "Can I walk you in?"

"Ryan."

Nodding my head, I get it. I see the pain in her eyes, but when she turns to grab the handle, I give her my last attempt to let her know, "I'll never love anyone the way that I love you."

She looks back at me, tears streaming, and she nods. Without words I hear what she's telling me, and I hate that she's denying us something we both know is great. She feels my words too, and having the knowledge that she feels the same way about loving me makes this all the worse. With

419

the click of the handle, she steps out as I hear her crying begin to crack though, and the sound is excruciating.

And that's it.

She's gone.

chapter forty-four

"How is it that you're so good with Bennett?" Traci asks me as I lay him down on the floor on his blanket.

"Because for the past five years my cousins have been pushing out babies," I tell her.

Max returned to work this past week, and he wanted me to stop by and check on Traci. He told me she was freaking out about being alone with the baby, so I decided to bring my camera along to take some photos of Bennett for her.

"Can you turn off the light? I just need the natural light right now."

"Yeah, sure," she says as she flips the lights off.

The sun is shining today, making it perfect for these pictures. Bennett is asleep as I adjust him before bringing the camera to my eye and taking a few shots then moving him into a different pose.

"Thanks for doing this."

"No problem. I wasn't doing anything today, so I'm glad I have the distraction," I tell her because I feel like I just went back in time a few months, and I'm feeling the loss of Candace all over again.

"Max is worried about you," she says, and when I look

up at her, I say, "Is that so?"

Tilting her head at me, she adds, "Yeah, that's so."

"Tell him I'm fine. Life is full of shit. It's nothing that I'm not used to."

"That's a depressing outlook."

Sitting back on my heels, I scan through the photos I just took as I say, "Not everybody gets what they want, Traci."

"There's probably someone else out there that you're gonna want more; you just haven't met her yet."

"I'm not so sure about that."

"Ryan," Traci says to get my attention as she sits on the floor next to Bennett and me. "We've all lost someone we loved only to find that it wasn't as deep of a love as we had thought when we finally find *the one*."

"Is Max *the one*?"

She looks at her son and smiles when she says, "Yeah."

"And there's never been a question or hesitation about it?"

Turning back to me, she tells me, "No."

"And what about the others you thought you loved? Any hesitation there?"

When she nods her head yes, I add, "That's the difference here. Never was there a question or hesitation. And she wasn't just someone I loved."

She doesn't respond as I lie down next to Bennett with my camera to get some close-ups of his facial features. Traci and I have gotten to know each other better since the baby came along, and I started spending more time over here at their house. At first, I was just trying to keep myself busy, but in the process, I've connected with Traci, and Max and I have become closer as well. I have a good bond with Jase, and even Mark, but it's hard to be around them at times because it only reminds me of how it used to be. But having this with two people that don't have that connection with Candace gives me a reprieve.

I head up to the bar to give Max the prints of the photos I took of his son a few days ago, and when I walk in, I see Jase sitting at the bar, talking to Mel.

"Hey, Ryan. I didn't think you were coming in today," Mel says as I walk over to them.

"I just needed to drop some stuff off with Max," I tell her and then look at Jase, asking, "How are you doing, man?"

"Good. Just waiting on Mark to get out of an interview."

"How's all that going?"

"I got a job offer yesterday, so I'm good to go. Just hoping that Mark gets this one because it's the firm he really wants," he tells me.

"Congrats, man. That's great. So when do you start?"

"Next week."

Knowing that Candace should be moving soon, I ask because I guess I like to torture myself, "When does she move?"

I don't even need to say her name when he tells me, "Friday morning."

It's hard to imagine that she'll be in New York City, all alone, in three days. It's always been her dream to dance with the company that she signed on with, and I'm happy that she's doing this for her and no one else. It's something she's always wanted and to have this opportunity in life, to see your dreams through, is an amazing thing, and I'm so proud of her. I honestly never thought she would ever move away like she is, all by herself. It's hard for me to imagine her in a place where she's okay to do this on her own. The girl that was always so scared of crowds and going out. Timid and paranoid. I worry about her.

"Could you do me a favor?" I ask.

"Yeah."

"Are you taking her to the airport?"

When he nods his head yes, I ask, "Will you give me a call when she's gone?"

The pity in his eyes irritates me, but I expect it. There's no doubt that this girl makes me weak. She always has. She softened me up because she was so delicate, and I loved that about her, that she could do that to me.

"You sure?" Jase asks.

"I'm sure."

"Alright," he says as he stands up. "I gotta get going. Mark should be at my place soon."

As he walks out, Mel comes back over after giving the two of us space to talk.

"Mel," I sigh out on an exasperated breath.

"You look like you need a drink."

"When did life get so damn depressing?" I ask her with a slight laugh.

"You're asking me?" she responds as she hands me a beer. "All I know is, I'm over it."

Her expression mirrors mine, and I know something is weighing on her.

"Talk to me."

The place is dead with it being early in the day, so she takes a seat next to me.

"Zane wants a divorce," she tells me.

"What?"

She nods and says, "Yeah. I got the papers a few days ago."

"Shit," I mutter. "I'm sorry."

When she shrugs her shoulders, she tells me, "We just grew apart, you know? Maybe it was me. Music was always his life; I just never thought that he would make anything big out of it, so I never considered it in our path in life. But that's not the life I want."

"So now what?"

"I don't know," she mumbles.

Taking a swig of my beer, I say, "Yeah, me neither."

It's Friday, and I'm sitting around dreading the call that I asked for. *Why do I do this shit to myself?* I tried to keep busy by working on some photo editing from a shoot I was hired to do for a portfolio, but my head just wasn't in it. So now I'm killing the minutes, surfing around on the internet when my cell finally rings, causing a quick drop in my gut.

Seeing Jase's name on the screen, I take the call that I should have never sought.

"Hey," I say quietly.

"Hey, man. I just got back to my apartment. Sorry it took so long to call; I had to take Kimber back home."

"So you got her dropped off?"

"Yeah. She should be boarding now."

"How was she?" I ask.

"Nervous as expected, but this is what she's been working so hard for, so I know she's excited."

Feeling the welling of sadness, I rush off the phone, needing to just drown in this for a while.

"Thanks for calling, I'll catch you later," I tell him before hanging up and leaning back in my desk chair as I stare up at the ceiling.

I'm completely drained, and to finally have the book

closed on this may be what I've been needing. With her on the other side of the country, maybe I can finally let it go. Let go of the hope that died months ago when I woke up to find her gone. The hope I was determined to keep alive when it was already dead.

Needing to get out of the house. I start heading upstairs to change my clothes for a run, but as soon as I hit the top step, there's a ringing at my door. I look out the windows and see a cab pulling out of my driveway, and when I go back downstairs to open the door, all that hope comes back to life.

She's beautiful, even though she's crying, as she stands on my doorstep.

"What are you doing here? I just got off the phone with Jase. He said he dropped you off at the airport."

"I can't go. I'm so sorry. I can't do it," she cries and with each word I feel the ever-vacant part of my heart filling up.

"What do you mean you can't do it?"

"Because . . . I love you too much to leave. And I miss you. And I made a huge mistake by leaving you. I'm so sorry," she continues to cry, and I don't even waste a second, pulling her into my arms where she was always meant to be.

"Baby, you didn't make any mistakes."

"I did. And I know I hurt you. But, I'm so sorry. I can't go because I can't leave you. I don't want to leave you."

Pulling her inside and taking her to the couch, I feel the weight of what she's doing pile on, and tell her, "I can't let you give up on your dream. I can't."

"But, it's not my dream," she says in her unwavering confessions. "I was just hanging on to it because I was scared to see that it really wasn't what I wanted. It's you. It's always been you."

Covering her lips with mine, I hold on to her as she climbs onto my lap, straddling her legs across me, and gives me what I've been dying for. I kiss her hard, in disbelief that this is even happening.

"I've missed you so much, babe," I tell her when I pull back and look into her eyes. "You have no fucking idea."

"I love you. I'm sorry I've been so stupid and wasted all this time when all I really wanted was to be here with you."

"You have nothing to be sorry for. I fucked up. I hurt you, and you'll never know how much I regret it."

"I don't blame you, Ryan. I did, but I don't anymore. I just want to be with you."

Her words mend all that was broken inside of me, and I cling to each one, desperate for this, and tell her, "I don't ever want to lose you again."

"You won't. I'm yours."

That's all I need to hear. I don't give a shit that it took her this long to realize it because I have her.

She's mine.

This time when I kiss her, I bring her in slow because I intend on taking my time to make up for all that we lost. With her soft lips pressed against mine, I'm taken back to a place where the pain of losing her doesn't exist. With her hands on my face, I stand, picking her up with me as she loops her legs around me. When I get her upstairs, I lay her down on the bed, needing the smell of her all over my sheets—all over me.

Hovering over her, I slip off my shirt, and when I do, she slowly sits up as I rest back on my heels. I watch as she takes her hand and brushes her fingers along my scar. A scar that doesn't even amount to the pain I felt when I lost her.

She tilts her head back to look up at me, and I tell her, "I couldn't breathe without you."

"I need you."

And so I give her me, every little piece. She doesn't even

427

need to ask because I've always been hers, even when I tried so hard not to be, to move on and put her in the past. I could never do it because she's always had me.

Lying on top of her, I press the weight of myself onto her to feel her softness beneath me. She runs her hands from my wrists, up my arms, and to my shoulders before she lets them fall above her head. Comfortable, as if she's saying 'have me.' Taking the hem of her silk top, I slowly slip it off of her body and toss it onto the floor.

Everything about her is familiar, and I need the comfort of her as I use my hands to reacquaint. Sliding them down her neck, over her lace-covered breasts, and down her stomach. Her breathing quickens along with my pulse as I undo her pants and slide them down her legs. *God, her legs.* After discarding my pants, I return to her, pulling the sheets over us, needy to trap her heat to me. She slips her arms around my neck when I reach around to remove her bra.

The warmth of her naked body with mine, we linger in the moment, touching, kissing, and exploring what we've been missing with each other. I'd go through the ache of these past few months all over again just to be with her like this. Nothing compares to this feeling of peace that she's able to give me. She's the one who allowed me to find myself, and without her I didn't know who I was.

Dragging my head down the length of her, I kiss my way back up her stomach, underneath her breast, and I slide my tongue over her nipple before sucking her into my mouth, pressing my tongue against her pert bud. She releases a heady breath into the air, moving her body as the passion takes over us. When I reach down, needing to reclaim everything we had taken our time working up to, I gently run my hand between her legs, touching her intimately. She doesn't push me away when she lets go of a soft moan as I feel how ready for me she is.

Spreading her legs apart, I settle myself between the heat of her thighs. Gazing at her, naked beneath me, bared to each other and coming out of the agony that's loomed over us, I see all I'll ever want.

"God, you're so beautiful."

She pulls me down to kiss her, sealing her mouth with mine. Her kisses are deep and purposeful, laced with an intent that settles my heart in hers, filling up the joy that I've been without. She's my happiness. She's the light in my life and without her, I was lost, but now . . . having her giving this all back to me, it's elated every part of my soul. We're completely wrapped up in each other as I guide myself inside of her, never breaking our kisses. The connection is intense, both of us claiming the other as our own but in the most unselfish way a human can as we give ourselves entirely to the other.

Her grip tightens on me, and I push myself deeper inside of her causing her body to bow up into mine, head pressed into the pillow beneath her. As she rolls her head back, I drag my mouth up her exposed neck before I flip us over and sit up to keep our bodies close, with her legs draped on either side of me. Wrapping my hands around the back of her small shoulders, I press her down on me as she rocks her hips into me in response.

When she grabs my shoulders, she begins to slowly roll herself over me. My breathing is heavy as I drop my head down to her chest, kissing and sucking lightly. We move slowly, taking our time with each other.

Gripping her bottom, I guide her as she begins to stagger as emotions flood over. She tangles her hands in my hair and looks into my eyes as she begins to cry, but I have no worry because I know she's safe with me. Vulnerable, exposed, but entirely safe in my touch.

Our eyes remain locked as I feel her body trembling on top of mine. She rocks her hips over me as she's finding her release. And as my body parallels her, I reach the peak of my build.

"Let go, baby," I breathe out and she drops her head to mine, eyes hooded, tears falling, but they never leave mine.

Running my hand up her damp back, she falls apart in my arms. Body quaking against mine, and I explode into a thousand pieces beneath her as our moans fill the room, taking every bit of pleasure we can while we continue to move with each other, my fingers pressing into her delicate skin as she writhes against me.

Movements begin to slow and she kisses me, pressing her face, wet with tears, against mine. The beating of my heart is strong, and my emotions are in overdrive when I focus on what just happened. Making love to the girl I thought I'd lost. It overpowers me as I lay us down, keeping myself buried inside of her.

With my lips on hers, we continue to kiss as I hear her whimpers, and I know she feels it too.

"Babe."

Pulling back, she takes her time before choking out, "I never want to know what life is without you."

"You won't ever have to."

As I keep her folded up in my arms, she cries, releasing the pain we've been through to get here. I let her get it out, and she eventually grows tired, falling asleep in my arms, the only arms I ever want her to have around her because it's within them that she will always have a safe place to fall.

chapter forty-five

When I feel the bed shift, I begin to wake, and as I open my eyes, I catch a glimpse of Candace walking into the bathroom, wearing my t-shirt. I'm not sure what happened to make her heart shift back to me. The whirlwind of emotions when she showed up at my door a few hours ago are now replaced with sated contentment, but also questions.

I watch her flick on the light, but she doesn't close the door. She stands there, and it isn't until I step out of bed and walk up to her, that I see what she's looking at. I couldn't ever get rid of her things that I kept the day Jase came over to pack up her stuff. I had the necklace repaired, and it has always sat on the sink counter next to her bottle of perfume.

I slip my arms around her waist from behind and she stands there, running her finger along the etched words: *And though she be but little, she is fierce.* Her eyes meet mine in the reflection of the mirror before I tell her, "I could never let you go."

I take her necklace and clasp it back around her neck, where it's always belonged. Turning around in my arms, she rests her hands on my chest as she hangs her head down, saying, "I'm so sorry."

Not wanting her to regret a single choice that she has made, I tell her, "Come here," as I take her back to bed. I sit against the headboard and pull her next to me before asking, "What could you possibly be sorry for?"

"Leaving you. Hurting you." She takes in a shaky breath as her emotions get to her and she tells me, "I hated every second I wasn't with you. I wanted to come back . . . I was just scared."

"I'm the only one who has something to apologize for."

"But I get it," she says. "It took me a while to see it, but I understand."

We sit there for a moment, quiet, with her head rested against me when she finally says, "I feel like I have so many questions."

"I know, babe."

"I never knew we had so many holes."

"So let's fill them in," I tell her as she looks up at me.

"I don't know where to begin," she says as she shifts down, and I move with her as we lie on our sides under the covers.

With her face only inches from mine, I brush her hair back and whisper, "I love you, babe. I don't want there to be any uncertainty about anything between us. You can ask me anything, and I swear I'll tell you whatever you want to know, but I also feel like I have missing pieces of you that I need."

She nods her head and closes her eyes when she softly says, "I didn't know anyone was there that night. That anyone saw me like that." When she opens her eyes, she asks, "What happened?"

I know we both need to hash everything out, and as hard as this conversation may get, it's one that needs to happen. I'll spend days in this bed with her, filling in all the blanks, just so we can have nothing between us but fleshed out honesty.

"I was working late that night," I begin as I hold her hand that's rested between our chests because I know this is going to be difficult for her to hear. "I heard noises outside but ignored it. There are so many people who cut through the back lot, and I figured it was just some drunken college kids." I take a moment as the guilt creeps in and then confess, "I'm so sorry. You were out there the whole time, and I just ignored it." The pain of my words to her is something I don't think I will ever be able to get rid of.

She's silent as tears begin to roll off the side of her face. Wiping them away, I continue, "It wasn't until I heard you screaming that I ran out. I swear I moved as fast as I could, but . . . by the time I made it out . . ." I'm scared to continue because I don't know if I should say anything else, knowing how bad this will hurt her to hear. "Baby, are you sure you wanna hear this?"

"I feel like I need to." Her hand is tightly clenched around mine when she asks, "What did you see?"

Letting out a sigh, I reveal, "You were naked and covered in blood and dirt." I choke around the words, and she begins to whimper as she tries to hold in her cries. "He had his hand between your legs, and you were screaming, then all of a sudden, he punched you in the side of your head and knocked you out. It all happened so fast. In a second, I pulled him off of you and beat the shit out of him, but I couldn't hold on to him and he fled. I stayed with you—"

"While I was naked?" she asks out of embarrassment.

"I had covered you up with my shirt. But I saw your tattoo. That's how I knew the connection."

"But how did you not know before?"

"I thought it could be you, but I had such a hard time

after seeing what I did that I just figured my head was playing with me. Trying to trick me into thinking it was you," I tell her. "When I saw you the first time at your work, it was my initial thought. The girl from that night was so tiny, and so was the girl in the coffee shop. Max tried telling me my mind was just trying to put closure to everything."

"Max knows?"

Nodding my head, I gently tell her, "Yeah, babe, he does. I had told him about what happened at the bar because he was head of security and needed to know, and then I told him about the girl in the coffee shop because I was really screwed up about it. I never thought I'd fall in love with you; it wasn't like I told him behind your back, he just always knew everything. Then once I saw your tattoo and put it together, we never spoke about it again. And I swear we never have."

"God," she breathes out. "I'm so embarrassed."

"Babe, you have nothing to be embarrassed about," I try telling her, but I know my words are weak in comparison to her feelings about this.

"It's humiliating, Ryan."

Running my hand through her hair, I say, "You're the most beautiful person I've ever met. No one could even come close to how genuine you are, and I swear to you, that's all people see when they look at you, including Max."

"Does anyone else know?"

"Only my mom."

"Why would you tell her?" she cries, mortified.

"She heard us when we were at her house, and you were upset, telling me that you blamed yourself for what happened. She thought we were fighting. I was upset after you fell asleep, and we were talking downstairs. Again, she knew about what I saw before I ever met you, and I felt like I needed someone to talk to. I probably never should have said anything to her, but my own guilt about not getting to you faster was eating away at me, and then seeing how hurt you were, thinking it was your fault . . . it killed me."

I hold her close as she wraps her arm around my neck, clinging on to me as I continue to hold her hand.

"All I ever wanted to do was protect you, and the one moment you needed me the most, I let you down. If only I would have gone out there when I first heard the noises, but I didn't, and I'm so sorry, baby." I take a moment before I tell her, "I couldn't stop thinking about you and what had happened after the ambulance took you to the hospital."

She loosens her hold around my neck and wipes her face as she takes a deep breath.

"I know I shouldn't ask," I say. "But . . . what happened that night?"

"It was a mess," she quickly responds and then takes a pause before she continues. "I didn't even like him, and I had only gone out with him that night so that I could talk to him." Never letting go of my hand, she tells me, "There was a party at his frat house, and he had gotten mad at me for leading him on. He had thrown me into a wall and pinned me against it. We fought, and I ran out. But he drove me, and I didn't have my phone, so I . . ."

She trails off, and I suddenly feel bad for asking her. "You don't have to tell me."

"I need to."

"Why?"

She drops her head before she eventually brings it back up, telling me, "My therapist keeps telling me I should talk about it."

I don't say anything else. I just keep her tucked into me when she eventually starts to speak again, and I listen as she tells me how he chased her down, beat the shit out of her, and raped her. Hearing her tell me the hell he put her through is gut-wrenching. I don't know how anyone could ever come out of something like that without an insane amount of damage. Knowing how violent he was with her makes me want to hide her away forever, but I can't do that. So I lie here and cry for her. For everything that little shit took away from her.

"Were you going to press charges? Is that why you were talking to that detective?" I ask after a while.

"Maybe. I don't know. I never planned on it, but then when I was packing I came across his card he had given me in the hospital. I guess I was more curious than anything," she explains.

"After all of this, if he were still alive, do you think you would?"

"Would you think I was weak if I said no?"

"Baby, there's nothing about you that I find weak," I tell her. Of course I would want her to fight and press charges, but I'm not the one who was stripped of all my trust, so I understand the need to avoid it. Who'd want to go back and relive what she had to endure? She fights in her own quiet way. Most probably don't even see it. I didn't used to, but I do now.

I roll onto my back, and she shifts her head into the crook of my arm. "When did you start seeing a therapist?"

"A couple days after you came by to talk to me. I just . . . I was so miserable. I didn't know what else to do."

Kissing the top of her head, I tell her, "I'm glad you have someone you can talk to. You think it's helping?"

"I think so. I mean, she's helping me see things a little clearer. We've been focusing on my anxiety and pointing out my triggers. She wants me to put myself in situations that tend to make me panic. I've tried a couple of times, but it's hard," she says.

"It's gonna be, but it'll get easier, babe."

"She wants me to stop taking my sleeping pills."

I run my hand up her arm and around her shoulder, asking, "Are you going to?"

"I told her I wasn't ready. She said she wouldn't push it but that I should think about it."

"I know you're scared, but they're just dreams."

"Dreams that feel completely real. And stress always triggers all that stuff, and with everything that's been going on . . . graduation, packing, the production . . .*you*. It was all too much."

"I know. You don't have to explain. I get it," I tell her. "But what about New York?"

"What about it?"

Turning to look at her, I say, "You don't have to give it up. I'll go with you. It's not a big deal. I was already planning on moving anyway."

"What?" she questions, confused.

"It's one of the main reasons why I replaced Michael with Max at the bar. I figured you'd be moving and there was no way I wasn't going with you."

"Why didn't you ever say anything?"

"I didn't want to stress you out. You had so much going on. I kept waiting for you to bring it up, but you never did, so I just started getting everything worked out on my end," I tell her as she shakes her head.

"I had no idea."

I let out a light laugh and say, "You didn't think I'd let you leave without me, did you?"

"Honestly? I didn't know. I didn't bring it up because I was scared I *would* have to leave without you. I didn't know what I was going to do, but I knew I wouldn't be able to leave you," she admits. "But I'm going to stay here. I called Pacific Northwest Ballet. I had originally turned down their offer, but I called them when I left the airport, and the spot is still mine. I go in on Monday to sign all the papers."

"You don't have to do that. You can still have New York."

"I'm not ready for it," she says softly. "I thought I was, but I think I was just forcing it. To prove to myself that I could go there on my own and be okay. But I need to be here. This is my home, with you, Jase and Mark, and everything that I'm used to," she tells me. "I want to get better, and I want to do that here where I have the support."

"Are you sure?"

"I'm not saying no to New York, I'm just saying no for right now."

I finally let go of her hand to cup her face before bringing her to my lips. She holds on to my wrists as I move my lips over hers, giving her only a couple long and slow kisses before pulling back, and saying, "I love you so much."

She runs her hand behind my neck and whispers, "I love you too," before our lips meet again. But before I can lose myself in her, she pulls away. "Oh my God," she draws out.

"What's wrong?"

"All of my stuff—everything—is already in New York. I've gotta call the landlord from my apartment there. I shipped everything last week."

"Don't worry about it. I'll take care of all that. Did you have luggage?" I ask.

"Yeah, I had already checked it," she says with worry.

"I'll call the airlines. Don't stress about it. We'll get everything shipped back," I tell her, but I'm not letting her move back in with Kimber. I have her here with me, and I don't want any more space between us, so I add, "But babe, when I arrange everything, I'm having it shipped here."

She nods her head, not picking up on what I'm saying, so I clarify, "Here to my loft." When I see her pinch her brows together, I say, "I want you here. With me."

"Move in?"

"Yeah. Move in. I don't want to be apart from you."

The smile that grows on her lips is beautiful, and I can't help myself when I kiss her.

"God, I missed that smile," I say. "It's been too long."

"So that's it?" she questions.

"That's it," I give her. "I want this to be your home. Here with me."

She wraps her body around me, hugging me close when she whispers in my ear, "Thank you."

"For what?"

"Everything."

After talking everything out this afternoon, Candace was drained and had a headache, so I gave her some aspirin, and she's been upstairs sleeping for the past hour. I go ahead and make all the phone calls to arrange for her belongings to be shipped back here. Her luggage should be at the airport tomorrow morning, so at least she'll have her clothes.

It's amazing how quickly everything can change. One minute, I thought I'd lost her and the next, she's back here and agreeing to move in with me. But I don't want to waste any more time. I want to pick up where we left off, and it seems she wants the exact same thing.

When I notice the sun starting to set, I call in an order for dinner at the little Italian place down the street that Candace likes so much, figuring she could use a solid meal after the day she's had. As I set the phone down, I hear a ringing from Candace's purse that's lying on the coffee table. I pull out her phone and answer it when I see that it's Jase calling.

"Hey."

"Ryan?" he asks.

"Yeah."

"Sorry, man. I thought I was calling Candace but accidentally dialed you," he says.

"No, this is Candace's phone."

"Huh?"

"She's here," I tell him, and I know he's completely thrown off when he questions, "What do you mean she's there?"

"After you called me this morning, she showed up at my door. She didn't get on the plane. She's been here ever since."

"What happened? Is she not going?"

Sitting down on the couch, I tell him, "No. She's staying. She took the spot at PNB."

"Is she happy?"

"She's happy," I say before letting him know, "She's moving in."

"With you?"

"Yeah."

He takes a pause before saying, "I knew she'd make the right choice."

Laughing, I say, "She nearly destroyed me in the process."

He begins to laugh with me, and then asks, "Can I talk to her?"

"She has a headache and is sleeping right now."

"Just have her give me a call later, okay?"

"No problem."

"I'm really happy you guys worked things out. She wasn't the same without you."

"Thanks, man. You've been a really good friend to me."

"No thanks needed. You guys have a good night and give her a kiss for me. I didn't know what I was going to do without her."

"Me neither. Talk to you later," I say before we hang up.

Walking upstairs, I step into the bedroom and look at the only love I ever want to know, curled up in my sheets. She's peaceful and quiet as she sleeps. She needs this after the emotional day she's had. We spent hours in this bed, hashing everything out, filling in all the gaps, and settling all the questions. But it needed to happen, and finally, for the first time, everything feels whole.

chapter forty-six

Candace and I finally drag ourselves downstairs for some much needed coffee after making love all morning. I'll never get my fill of her, and I made sure she knew that.

She's a little needy this morning, but I like that. I've missed that—her need to have me close. It's to be expected with everything going on, so I hold her hand as we walk downstairs and into the kitchen.

"All I have is milk, babe. We'll have to stop by the store to get you your creamer and stock up on groceries."

"When did you get this?" she questions, and when I look over to her, she's checking out the cappuccino machine.

"My mom. She got it for my birthday."

"Birthday?"

Grabbing the milk to pour into her coffee, I say, "Yeah."

"When was your birthday?" she asks as I hand her the mug and head over to the couch.

"Last month. May nineteenth."

"Oh," she says with a twinge of sadness.

"Babe, don't let it bother you. It's really not a big deal."

Taking her eyes off of her mug, she looks up at me as she rests her back against the arm of the couch and says, "It does bother me. I feel like I've missed so much time with you."

"You weren't missing much. Nothing happened. Everything was literally in slow motion the whole time."

"I still feel bad that I wasn't here for your birthday."

Setting my coffee down on the end table, I take hers as well, setting it aside as I pull her over to me and fold her in my arms. "None of that matters, so just forget it, okay?"

"I can't just forget it."

"Would it make you feel better if I told you that I was with you on my birthday?"

She pops her head up and stares at me with question. "What do you mean?"

"I saw you the night before," I tell her. "I went to see you dance."

"You were there?"

"Nothing would have kept me from seeing you that night," I tell her and then kiss her forehead. "You were amazing. I couldn't take my eyes off of you."

"I didn't think you were there. I saw your mom afterward, but I had no clue."

"You saw my mom?"

"Yeah. I ran into her as I was leaving."

"She never told me that," I say, but then remember telling my mom that we weren't going to mention Candace again. I never gave her a chance to tell me.

"I felt awful."

"Why? What did she say?"

"All the right things, but it was hard to see her because I was missing her. She drove all that way and then I told her that I needed space. It just hurt too much," she explains.

"I know she wasn't expecting anything. She just really wanted to see you dance. I told her not to come, but she insisted."

"I miss her," she says as she rests her head on my shoulder. "I feel like I should apologize or something."

"For what?" I ask with a light chuckle. "You didn't do anything, babe. If anyone should be apologizing, it's me, so stop thinking that you did something wrong, 'cause you didn't."

She nods her head, unconvinced, but I don't push. Instead, I offer, "Why don't we go visit her in a couple of weeks for Fourth of July weekend?"

Her smile shows off her dimple when she says, "I'd like that."

"I'll give her a call later today."

"Speaking of calls, I need to call Kimber. My car is at her parents' house. We should probably go pick it up today."

"I'm gonna go grab a shower, so why don't you call her, and we can pick it up after we go to the airport to get your bags."

"I don't have any clothes," she tells me. "Maybe Jase can bring me some. Crap!"

"What?"

"I was supposed to call Jase when I got to New York last night. He doesn't know I'm here," she panics.

"He does. I talked to him yesterday when you were napping. I just forgot to tell you."

"You talked to him? What did he say?"

Giving her a smirk, I tell her, "He said he was glad you made the right choice."

She pokes me in the ribs as she whines, "No he didn't."

"I swear, he did," I laugh and then stand up. "Make your phone calls. I'm gonna go get ready."

Once I'm out of the shower and dressed, Candace walks into the room and says, "Jase is on his way."

"Did you get in touch with Kimber?"

Flopping down on the bed, she says, "Yeah. Her parents aren't home, but she gave me the code to the garage," in a dull voice.

Walking over to the bed, I look down at her and ask, "What's wrong?"

"She just doesn't get it."

"Get what?"

Candace sits up and tells me, "She said that I was throwing everything away. She was annoyed when I told her I wasn't gonna move back in with her. It's just hard because she doesn't know you. All she saw was how upset I was when we weren't together. She knows that you kept that secret from me, but she doesn't know how far I've come this year and that it was mostly because of you. She never saw how bad it was, and now all she has is this tainted idea of you."

"Maybe she just needs time to get to know us together."

"But I feel like she doesn't even know me. We used to be close, but so much has happened this year, and she wasn't around," she says. "I'm just . . ." She drops her head when she admits, "I'm not the same person. I wish I could be, but I'm just not."

"That's not a bad thing like I know you're thinking it is. The cause of it is the only thing that's bad. But it's like I told you before, there isn't a damn thing about who you are now that you should be ashamed of. You're perfect to me," I tell her, and I can see that she still struggles with this concept, but I'll keep reminding her every day if I have to.

We're interrupted when the doorbell rings, and Candace jumps off the bed, saying, "Jase is here," as she flies down the stairs.

When I make it to the top of the stairs, she is already in his arms. I smile at the sight of her as I start making my way down.

"So what the hell happened after I dropped you off?" he asks her as I take the bag out of his hand and set it by the stairs.

"I realized that all my worries about leaving were more about my fears of losing Ryan than they were of moving to New York," she tells him as she sits on the couch, and I walk over to join her.

"So now what?" he asks as he takes a seat in the chair.

"I'm gonna sign with PNB on Monday."

"So, no New York?"

"Not right now," she says. "I feel like I need more time here, where I'm comfortable. I just want to put the past few months behind me and have things settled again."

"You talk to Kimber?"

"A little bit ago. She didn't seem happy that I was moving in here," Candace responds as I slip my arm around her.

"I think she just feels left out of everything. All of us have been through a lot, and she wasn't around. And let's face it, she has a skewed perception of Ryan, and she barely even knows Mark. And now Mark and I are about to move in together, and you and Ryan are too. She's just kinda out of the loop."

"You're moving in with Mark?" I ask, having had no clue, and both Candace and Jase give me a look as if I should already know this. "Why are you looking at me like that?"

"I thought you knew," Jase says.

"How would I have known if you didn't tell me?"

"Sorry, I guess with everything going on, I just never brought it up," he says.

"That's great, man. I just didn't know, that's all."

Candace gives me a smile and then turns back to Jase and says, "Anyways, I'm just not really sure where we stand."

"I suggested that maybe we should all get together so Kimber can get to know me. You and Mark should be there too, though," I tell him.

"That's probably the best thing to do at this point," Jase says as he looks to Candace.

"Okay, then. I'll call her later and see when she's free."

Jase leans back in the chair and lets out a long breath, saying, "I'm relieved, girl."

She lets out a giggle when she asks, "Why?"

"Because I hated the thought of not having you here. I've been a mess, and Mark has been stuck dealing with me."

"Mark isn't stuck. He loves you."

"Still. I'm just glad that you're staying and that you're happy."

Candace looks over to me and then back to Jase, saying, "Me too."

After picking up her car and getting her luggage at the airport, we stopped by the storage unit Candace had rented to keep all the stuff that she wouldn't have had room for in her apartment in New York. She doesn't need much since I have everything she could possibly want already at my place, but we picked up a couple of boxes, and now we are shifting things in my room so that all of her belongings have a place.

She's in the closet, hanging up her clothes, when I hear, "Ryan!"

Rushing in, I see her sitting on the floor, pulling out the canvas from behind the clothes where I had been hiding it.

When she looks up at me, she says, "I thought someone

bought this."

I lean against the doorframe and tell her, "It was me. I bought it."

As she shakes her head, I say, "Did you really think I would let that hang in anyone's house but my own?"

"But why is it shoved back here?"

Walking over, I sit down next to her and look at the picture that I haven't seen in a long time and say, "Because it hurt too much to look at. It only reminded me of everything I lost." I look at her and slide the picture back against the wall before I kiss her, leaning into her as she lowers herself to the floor.

Grabbing on to my face, she pushes me back slightly when she says, "I can't believe you bought it."

I press my lips into hers, dipping my tongue in to caress hers as she fists my hair in her hands. Our lips move slowly together, as she pulls my weight wholly on top of her. She keeps me close, running her hands underneath my shirt and up my back. We move slowly as we lie on the floor of the closet, her clothes strewn everywhere in the midst of combining our belongings. Making this place ours.

We spend the rest of the evening situating her things, but before it gets too late, I tell Candace, "I'm gonna give my mom a call."

She acknowledges me as she continues to move things around, and I take a seat in the chair by the window while I call.

"Hey, Mom."

"How are you?"

"Actually, I'm really good," I tell her, and when I turn, I catch Candace grabbing her pajamas as she mouths to me, 'I'm gonna take a shower.'

I give her a nod as my mom says, "Well, that's good to hear."

"I have some news I think you'll like," I goad and she falls into it, saying, "Don't keep me in the dark. Tell me."

"Candace is back. She's moving in with me."

"What? How did that happen?" she asks in total shock.

"She showed up here yesterday, and we talked everything out."

"And she's moving in?"

"She *is* moved in," I clarify as I look at all of her things scattered around the room.

"That was quick."

"It feels like it took forever," I joke.

"You know what I mean," she says. "How is she?"

"Good. I think we're just both so worn out, but I was calling to see what your plans were for the Fourth."

"No plans really. Why?"

"Candace and I want to come down for a few days. I know she misses you."

"Of course," she exclaims. "I miss her too. Is she around for me to talk to?"

"She's in the shower, but I'll have her give you a call tomorrow."

"So . . . how are you feeling about all of this?" she asks in a more serious tone.

"Like this was how it was always supposed to be. Having her here with me. I felt completely lost without her, and now it just feels right again."

"I'm so happy for you, dear. For both of you."

When I hear the water shut off, I say, "Thanks, Mom. I'll talk to you later, okay?"

"Love you."

"You too."

I walk over and grab her empty luggage off the bed and take it downstairs to store it in the guest bedroom closet before heading back upstairs. Slipping into bed, I don't have to wait too long before Candace comes out and crawls under the sheets with me.

As she lets out a heavy sigh, she says, "I'm exhausted."

"It was a long day, huh?"

"Too long," she says with a breathy laugh.

"So, my mom said we could come out for a visit. She's anxious to see you. I told her you would call tomorrow."

"Oh . . . umm . . ."

Seeing the hesitation on her face, I ask, "What?"

She inches down and lays her head on the pillow, and I do the same as we face each other.

Reading her eyes, I ask, "What's going on?"

"It didn't feel weird to me until you called her."

"Is that why you rushed in to take a shower?"

I watch as her eyes drop and I ask, "Tell me what makes this feel weird?"

She moves her eyes up to mine when she says, "Because she knows."

"Knows what?"

"What you told her about what happened . . . to me."

Pulling her in close, I tell her, "Please don't let it make you feel weird. You know a lot of her secrets too, babe."

"But she doesn't know that. It's awkward because I'm aware that she knows this about me."

"I'm sorry."

"I hate that people know," she mumbles as she rests her forehead against my chest while I run my hand down her back.

Leaning down, I kiss the top of her head. "I'm sorry I told her, I—"

She cuts me off, looking up at me and saying, "Don't be sorry. I'm not mad about it, just embarrassed." She quickly moves her fingers to my mouth to keep me from talking, adding, "And I know you're gonna tell me to not be embarrassed, but there's no way around it. I just am."

I kiss her fingers and then take her hand, holding it against me. "She loves you. She has her own past that I know is embarrassing to her. She never wanted anyone to know either. That's all I'm gonna say," I tell her lightly and then put an end to all of the talking for some much needed kissing.

chapter forty-seven

"She's living with you?" Max questions before laughing and saying, "This from the guy who once gave me shit for Traci moving in with me."

"Go ahead, man. Get your laughs in, but I don't give a shit."

"I know you don't," he says. "I'm really happy for you. I was getting tired of your broody side."

Packing up my things, I let out a chuckle when I say, "Me too."

"You guys should come over. I know Traci would like the company. She's going a little crazy being at home every day."

"Yeah, that sounds good. I'll talk to Candace and call you. I gotta run though. She signed all of her contracts today with that ballet company, and I wanna be there when she gets home," I tell him as I start heading out.

"See ya."

When I get back to the loft, Candace's car is already there, and when I walk in, she's finishing up a phone call. I don't wait as I go to her and pull her in for a hug, lifting her off the floor.

"Okay, thanks. I'll see you then," she says and then hangs up before kissing me.

"How did everything go?" I ask when I set her down.

"Good. I start tomorrow."

"That soon?"

Smiling at me, she says, "Yeah. Auditions for the first performance run are in August."

"You're gonna have to explain how all this works, babe, because I don't know the first thing about what your job is going to look like."

We walk over to take a seat in the living room, and I reach out to set her on my lap as she explains, "Okay, so basically a season runs from September to June. I'll have typical rehearsals throughout the week with about five to seven performance runs that I'll have to audition for. Performance runs are around two weeks long with matinees and evening shows. Normally they have a two-month run around the holidays, but they cast two dancers for each role to divide up the schedule. So I'll have some time off for Christmas, hopefully."

"You seem excited."

"I am, but I'm mostly nervous. Most of these girls have done their apprenticeships up there and already know each other. I'm the only one coming from a university," she tells me.

"You'll be fine," I assure her. "I'm so happy for you, babe."

I kiss her dimple when she smiles, and then ask, "Who were you talking to when I came in?"

"Oh," she says as she sits up, looking a little flustered. "Um, that was Dr. Christman, my therapist. I needed to get back on her schedule. But . . . umm . . ."

"What is it?" I ask when she starts hesitating.

"Well, I told her what happened with the whole New York thing and moving in with you. She suggested that maybe you could come in with me for my next appointment, but you can say no," she says timidly, avoiding my eyes.

"Why would I say no?" I question. I've never done the whole therapy thing, but for her, I'd do anything.

"Because it's . . ."

"Embarrassing," I answer for her.

"I know you're sick of hearing that, but I can't help it."

"I'm not sick of hearing it, babe. I get it. You just tell me when, and I'll be there," I say, trying not to make too big of a deal about it for her.

Switching the subject, she tells me, "I invited Kimber to come over Friday night."

"Jase and Mark coming over too?"

"Yeah, if that's okay? I should have asked first."

"This is your home, Candace. You don't need to ask me if you want to have your friends over. It's fine," I tell her. "Max invited us over to hang out as well."

"What about Gavin?" she asks out of the blue.

"What do you mean?"

"You still talk to him?"

"I haven't seen him in a while. I think that friendship is dead. We're just on totally different wavelengths," I explain.

"When did that happen?"

"When he kept trying to sling chicks at me when all I wanted was you," I tell her as I run my fingers through her hair.

She looks uncomfortable when her only response is, "Oh," and knowing her so well, I go ahead and answer her unspoken question.

"No. I couldn't even bear to look at another girl. You were all I ever wanted even when I didn't have you."

She runs her hands along my jaw before she kisses me with an affection that only she can show. Slipping my hand under her knees, I cradle her in my arms as I carry her upstairs and lay her down in our bed. We move at a leisurely pace as we remove our clothes, feeling the need to connect with each other in this way. She normally keeps herself tucked against me, bodies close, when we make love, but to see her now, completely relaxed underneath me as I move inside of her, it's stunning. Her hair splayed around her face, her arms draped above her head, she's completely exposed to me as I move up to my knees and watch her.

Seeing her this comfortable with me, a level of comfort I'd yet to experience with her, is something I wasn't expecting. She's beautiful as I reach down and grab on to her hips, lifting them off of the bed and completely flush against me as I move deeper inside of her. She has her whole body bared to me, and I can't help but stare down at her and admire how perfect we look together like this. It's overwhelming, and when she grips my wrists and thrusts up to me, I let myself fall on top of her as we both come. Her hands never let go of my wrists, as if she needs them there for support as we both continue to move, greedy to prolong our release.

She holds my hand as we walk into the dimly lit office of her therapist and take a seat on the small leather couch. Pulling her hand onto my lap, I can tell she's nervous. Shit, I am too. I have no idea what to expect or what this lady plans on talking to us about.

"It's good to see you again," Dr. Christman says to Candace and then turns to me to introduce herself before saying, "It's nice to finally meet you. Candace has filled me in on a lot already about the two of you, but I wanted to take this time to not only talk with you, Ryan, but to hear from both of you together. First, Candace, tell me what happened."

"With New York?"

"Yes. Last we spoke, you were excited and happy to be moving on and starting something new. What changed?"

Her grip tightens on my hand as she adjusts herself, bringing her legs up onto the couch and folding them in front of her. I watch her as she begins to speak with Dr. Christman.

"I don't think anything really changed. I was sitting at the gate, about to board the plane, and all I could feel was sadness and regret. I was scared, but I realized that everything I was so scared about wasn't the fresh start, but what I was leaving behind. It was like I was trying so hard to focus on my dream of New York that I completely shut out my dream of Ryan. Like I was trying to switch one for the other. Somewhere along the way my dream of New York changed, but I never allowed myself to see it until I was about to leave."

It's a little strange for me to hear Candace being so open. I'm not used to her speaking so freely, so I'm taken aback by her candidness.

"So what did you do?"

"I left the airport," she tells her. "I felt like my world was spinning out of control, but in a good way. As soon as I got to his place and saw him, it was like all the happiness I lost when I lost him came rushing back. I just knew this was the choice I was supposed to make."

Dr. Christman turns to me, and says, "I bet that came as a shock to you."

"You have no idea," I tell her with a chuckle.

"So, Ryan, Candace and I have spent a lot of time talking about your relationship and how the two of you came to split. Have you had a chance to explain to her the reasoning behind why you withheld who you were?"

"I feel like I have. I mean, I hope I have. We spent a few hours talking the other day, unraveling all the questions we each had."

She looks over at Candace and asks, "Do you feel you got everything you needed from that conversation?"

"I think so," she says in a shaky voice, and when I turn to look at her, she's wiping her fingers under her eyes.

"Tell me why you're crying," she asks Candace.

"Because it was hard to hear. I've gone nearly a whole year without having to talk about what happened. And listening to him tell me what he saw that night . . . it's just hard to hear and to know that he saw me like that."

"Ryan, I'm curious. When you realized Candace was the girl you had seen that night, how did you deal with that?"

I wrap my arm around Candace while she dries her tears with a tissue and answer, "As soon as I knew, I wanted to tell her, but I didn't know how. Then I started thinking that if I did tell her, how much it would hurt her. She was in a really dark place at the time, and I was scared she would break. She hid a lot, but I always knew she was barely holding on. But it fucked with my head—a lot. I get these flashbacks. It used to only be of my childhood. I see something or whatever and my mind takes me back. But ever since that night she was attacked . . . it keeps playing back in my head."

"What do you normally do when that happens?"

"Nothing. I eventually just snap out of it. But it kills me that I have that in my head," I say before I turn to see

Candace staring at me in disbelief with what I just said.

"I'm sorry," I tell her.

"Were you aware that he has these flashbacks, Candace?"

"No," she answers and then asks me, "So that's how you see me?"

"No. I denied you were that girl for so long. I fell in love with everything I had in front of me. But when I found out you were that girl, the visions were just so conflicting because I don't see you like that at all. I know it's you, but I still don't want it to be."

She's crying now, and I take her other hand in mine when I affirm, "That is *not* what I see when I look at you."

"I don't want that in your head," she chokes out.

"I don't either, babe. But these aren't our choices, and I've told you before that I love you regardless."

"It makes me feel disgusting."

She takes a moment to settle her tears and take in a few deep breaths when Dr. Christman asks me, "What's the biggest thing you feel you struggle with about Candace's attack?"

Letting out a sigh, I tell her, "That I let her down."

"How so?"

"I was inside and heard the commotion in the alley. I ignored it, figuring it was just people passing through, which happens occasionally. If I had gone out there, then maybe none of this would have happened."

She sits back in her seat as she looks at Candace and asks, "Is it okay if I share some of the things we've discussed in our previous sessions?"

"Of course."

Focusing back on me, she says, "One of the issues I've been working on with Candace is her feeling of blame. She believes that her behavior led to her attack, and she continues to hold herself responsible."

"Yeah, I know."

"Do you see the parallel here?"

Looking at Candace, I see what Dr. Christman is trying to point out, something I guess I never really saw before. I've always thought it was crazy that she could think she was to blame, but in turn, she probably feels the same way about my thoughts.

"Yeah," I answer.

"Neither one of you are to blame, yet both of you are holding yourselves responsible," she says. "Did you know he felt this way?" she asks Candace.

I watch as she nods her head, saying, "Yes."

"Just as Candace and I have been discussing, there's no way you could have known what was going to happen that night, so you can't hold yourself responsible for that."

She says this, I get it, but I can't accept it . . . not right now.

"Well, I want to be mindful of our time together, so I'd like to focus on Candace, simply because she's the one who I have been working with. But going forward in your relationship, it's important that you're there to help support her as she continues to process and heal. Being aware of her triggers and knowing ways you can help her cope and push her are key."

"I know that she shuts down and avoids. I like to get it out and talk, but it's a challenge to get her to open up. I notice she's been more willing since we've been back together this past week, but . . ." I let my words fall, but she picks them up when she says, "It's very typical of trauma victims to shut down. Candace has expressed to me that when she opens herself up to emotions, she panics and feels like they're going to flood her, and the loss of control is scary."

I look to Candace and ask, "But what do you think is going to happen?"

She shakes her head before turning to Dr. Christman, and when she blinks, tears fall.

"Babe, I need you to tell me because I don't understand."

"Can you tell me why you can't answer him?" she asks Candace.

She shakes her head as I move my hand to her back.

"Go ahead and take a moment, but I want you to tell Ryan what you have told me whenever you're ready."

I feel like we sit here forever in the silence when she eventually turns to me and takes a deep breath before revealing, "It feels like I'm losing control and that I won't be able to handle it."

When I shake my head, still unsure, she tells me, "In the moment . . . it feels like I'm going to die."

I can barely handle her words and to know that this is how she feels. I pull her into my arms, thinking back to all the times she's been so scared. The day she saw that dumpster, her nightmares, our fight, and so many other things.

As I keep her folded into me, Dr. Christman says, "I've been asking Candace to try and put herself in situations that will generally trigger these emotions but in a place where she feels safe. Trying to help her cope with living inside the emotions, feeling them and not shutting down. Understanding that even though it's scary, the emotions will eventually lessen, and she'll be okay. I think it's important for you to understand how she's feeling during these episodes so that you can help push her through them, but to also be aware of her limits. Also, encouraging her to talk about her attack will help lessen the power it has over her."

I give her a nod of acknowledgement as Candace pulls away and sits back.

We talk a little while longer about how I can help Candace and discuss some goals as we move forward. Before we leave, we agree I will come in with Candace twice a month, but the rest of her visits will remain focused on her.

I was proud of Candace before, knowing she was doing this, but to actually sit next to her and listen to her makes me realize how much strength it must have taken her to do this on her own. Honestly, I don't think she would have ever done this if it weren't for us being apart. She had to do it alone and for herself. And just from that one session, I learned things about her that I never knew before. It helped me understand her in a way I wouldn't have been capable of on my own.

Instead of going back to the loft, we decide to take the rest of the afternoon to relax, and we head to Fremont to grab some coffee at Peet's before roaming around some of the antique shops. We don't talk about what was said. Although it seems Candace is feeling needy with me, I let her be. She never takes her hand out of mine as we drift aimlessly in and out of the different shops, simply enjoying each other.

chapter forty-eight

The past couple of weeks have been disappointing for Candace. She's been trying hard to include Kimber in our lives, but she continues to have a crap-ass attitude with me. I'd never say anything to Candace about it, but she sees it, and it upsets her that her friend has been shutting me out.

Candace realizes that too much has changed in the past year and they've simply grown apart. She's been sad, thinking about the what-ifs and wondering how it would have been different if she would've just told her about the attack instead of hiding it. But what's done is done, and people grow apart. I have with Gavin, but along the way we've made new friends. Candace now has Mark and has also been getting together with Mel and Traci, and I've befriended Mark and Jase and even become closer with Max, who I continue to spend more time with.

Now as we drive to my mom's, Candace is sleeping. We invited Mark and Jase to come as well, and they plan on driving down later this afternoon. We thought it would be fun for the four of us to get away since everyone has been so busy with their new work schedules, and we haven't spent that much time together.

Candace has been avoiding my mom's attempts to talk on the phone. I understand her apprehension about it, and I know she's a nervous wreck about seeing her, so I'm glad she's finding some relief from the stress as she sleeps. It's a good thing that Jase and Mark won't be there until later, giving the three of us time to talk privately and hopefully help ease Candace's embarrassment.

When I pull up to the house, I run the back of my hand down her arm. Rolling her head to me, she slowly opens her eyes.

"We're here," I quietly say, and she turns to look at the front of the house, letting out a soft breath. I hop out of the car and walk around to her side, helping her out. Placing my hands on the sides of her face, I tell her, "I love you."

I take her hand and walk her inside, calling out, "Mom." We head back to the living room, and my mom is already making her way to us.

"Candace!" she squeals, not even acknowledging me, and I have to laugh when she pulls my girl into her arms.

I'm relieved to see Candace smile. I went ahead and told my mom a few days ago that Candace is aware that I told her about the attack because she was starting to wonder why Candace wasn't returning her calls.

"I'm so happy you're here," she beams and then turns to me to give me a hug. "How was the drive?"

"Candace slept most of the time, and there was a ton of traffic." Cannon Beach is a hot spot for the summer, let alone the Fourth of July.

"Well, I'm glad you two made it safely. When will Jase and Mark be getting in?"

Candace lets me do the talking while she stands close to me, holding on to my hand. "Jase texted me a while ago, so maybe five hours or so with the traffic." Wanting to get

Candace alone for a moment, I tell my mom, "We're gonna take our bags upstairs. We'll be down in a couple minutes."

Closing the bedroom door behind me, I sit with Candace on my bed. "Babe . . ."

"I *hate* this," she lets out as she falls back on the bed, staring up at the ceiling.

"Just talk to her."

"What do I even say?"

"Come here," I tell her as I tug on her hand and draw her up to me. "Just like you and I have been doing, just talk. Clear the air."

When she nods, I offer, "You want me to go with you?"

"Yeah," she says, and then I pull her off the bed, not wanting her to stew on this any longer. I give her a soft kiss before taking her back downstairs.

Walking through the house, I find my mom in the study, sitting in one of the chairs, flipping through a book.

"Hey, Mom."

"That was quick," she says as she closes the book and sets it on her lap while Candace and I take a seat on the couch.

"I think we need to talk," I tell her and then look at Candace who's holding my hand with both of hers, keeping her eyes fixed on them.

"Has Ryan told you about his father?"

Candace looks up to my mom, answering, "Yes."

"So, I'm sure he also added me to that equation as well."

When she nods her head in response, my mom begins talking and opening up to her about things she hasn't even talked to me about.

"Richard was a horrible man who would beat me on a nearly daily basis. I have scars to remind me of it every day. When he drank, the fights would get even more violent. At one point, I had become pregnant, but I never told him. I was too scared," she tells Candace, and I stare at my mom in horror because I never knew this. "I saw what he was doing to Ryan, but at the time I was so terrified of the man, that I never defied him because I feared what he would do to me. But he eventually found out about the pregnancy. He was furious, dragging me by the hair all the way up the stairs and then kicking me in the stomach over and over."

She stops talking to catch her breath as she begins to cry, but I can't move because I'm in shock. It isn't until I hear Candace let out a shaky whimper that I turn and see her tears as well.

"After he was done with me," she continues, "I couldn't move because the pain was just so excruciating. And then he threw me down the stairs. I knew I couldn't go to the hospital. He never would have let me get away with it. It took almost four days for me to miscarry my baby."

Candace's grip on me is tight as I watch my mom wiping the tears from her face. I never knew that had happened to her. The secrets that these women keep are horrific, and I'm at a loss for words.

My mother keeps her eyes on Candace when she says, "We both have secrets, dear. And that's the secret I have always held on to . . . until now."

When Candace's cries start to break through, I wrap my arm around her as her tears roll down her face.

"Ryan told me that you were embarrassed, but you have *nothing* to be embarrassed about around me. I have your darkest secret, and now you have mine."

She stands and walks over to sit next to Candace, and I let go of her as she turns to my mom and hugs her.

"You are an amazingly strong woman," my mom says to her as she pulls back to look at Candace. "Watching you get through this year with everything you had to go through with the attack, your parents, and with Ryan . . . I don't know if I'd be able to come out of that with the poise you have. It's been eighteen years since I lost my baby, and it wasn't until just now that I was able to finally say it out loud. I've held on to it for all these years, and then I look at you . . ."

She takes a moment as she begins to cry again, before adding, "You are everything I wish I could have been. I see you with my son, and how you've opened your heart to him even after what happened to you. I've never been able to do that since Richard died almost eleven years ago."

Candace doesn't even need to speak, and I love my mom for what she just gave my girl. Gave it in a way that Candace didn't even have to talk because I know she was so nervous about what she would say. The two of them cry together, and at this point, I give Candace the space I feel she needs to spend time with my mom and talk without having me around. I kiss the back of her head before I leave the room and go outside to the beach to digest everything I just heard.

When Jase and Mark arrived later that day, we spent the evening grilling steaks out back and hanging out on the beach. Candace told me, that after I left, she and my mom were able to talk for a while. And seeing them now, in the kitchen, cooking breakfast, they seem closer than ever.

"Hey, Mom, where are your binoculars?" I ask after we eat.

"They're outside on the table," she says when I grab Candace's hand to take her out to the beach.

"Where are we going?" she questions.

"I wanna show you something," I tell her as we walk outside.

Picking up the binoculars, I walk her down towards the water, and when I look through the lenses, I spot what I want to show her. I hand them over and instruct, "Here. Look over there to that sea stack. I want you to look carefully for anything bright orange."

"Okay," she draws out slowly as she holds the binoculars up to her eyes. "There, I see . . . oh my God!" she squeaks out, and it's cute as hell, bringing a huge smile to my face. "Look! There's so many of them. What are they?"

Wrapping my arms around her from behind, I rest my chin on top of her head, telling her, "Puffins." She keeps looking at them as I say, "Every year around this time they nest over there on Haystack Rock. That's why we can't shoot off fireworks because they come here to mate, and it would scare them away. This is the only place on the coast where it's not legal."

"They are so cute."

I lean down and press my lips into her soft neck, taking kisses when she drops the binoculars and turns in my arms to face me. The wind kicks through her hair as the sun casts a glow on her face.

"Are you happy?" I ask. Her smile tells me she is, but I want to hear it.

"I never thought I could be this happy."

She runs her hands behind my neck and brings me into her, kissing me intently, but the moment is short-lived when we hear Mark say, "Break it up, kids."

"What are you guys doing?" Jase asks as they walk over to us.

Candace holds out the binoculars and tells him, "There are puffins out on that big rock."

"Give me those," Mark says as he snatches the binoculars out of Jase's hands and starts searching for the birds. "There they are," he mumbles before telling Jase, "We should totally get one."

Candace laughs while Jase says, "Dude, it's a bird."

Handing the binoculars back to Jase, he says, "They look like penguins. Haven't you ever wanted a penguin for a pet?"

I can't control my laughter as I watch the two of them.

"No," Jase answers in exasperation. "Who even thinks like that?"

"I do. People have that shit for pets."

"Who?"

"I dunno, just . . . people. I've seen it on TV," is Mark's pitiful explanation as the three of us laugh at him. He turns to Candace and tries to get her to back him when he says, "Why are you laughing? You once told me you wanted a pig for a pet."

"What?" I question through a burst of laughter.

Turning to me with narrowed eyes, she defends, "Not like a gross barn pig. A domesticated micro pig."

"What the hell is that, babe?"

"They're these tiny little pink pigs. They say they're cleaner and smarter than a dog. You can even litter train them."

She says this in complete seriousness, and she looks adorable doing it, but that doesn't stop Jase and I from laughing at her and Mark for their choice in pets.

Slapping my arm, she scolds, "Stop laughing at me," with a hint of a smile.

"Just so you know, we're not getting a pig."

"You don't even know what they are. You've never even seen one."

Looking over at Jase for support, I call out to him, "Dude, Jase, are you hearing this?"

"It makes more sense to get a pig than Mark's desire to snatch up a wild bird just because he's thinks they're *cute*," he says with a chuckle while shaking his head.

"Hey, guys," Tori announces as she walks out with Bailey on her hip, and Connor runs around her, straight to me.

Squatting down, I give him a big hug, as I say, "Hey, buddy. When did you guys get here?"

"Just now."

Picking him up in my arms, I watch as my mom follows Tori and Bailey, who just turned two, out to the rest of us.

"Candace, it's so good to see you again," she says as she gives her a one-armed hug while still holding Bailey.

"Can you say, 'Hi, Candace'?" Tori asks of Bailey, but all Candace gets in return is a 'hi' followed by babble.

The two of them laugh as Tori says to Bailey, "We're just gonna have to change her name, huh? Something a little more simple."

Looking at Candace, I tell her, "Don't worry. She can't even say my name." Setting Connor down, I reach over and take Bailey, as she says, "Wy-wy!"

"See? I'm Wy-wy," I say to Candace as I keep my eyes on Bailey.

"Tori, these are my friends, Jase and Mark," Candace introduces as they all hug and greet each other.

"Where's Trevor?" I ask.

"I'm here," he hollers as he walks out. "Had to unload the bags."

"Hey, man," I say when he gets closer. "You remember Candace, right?"

"How could I forget?" he says before giving her a hug.

Everybody meets Mark and Jase and spends a good amount of time playing with the kids before Candace and I take Connor down the beach a little ways to show him the puffins. I watch as she is on her knees behind Connor, helping him with the binoculars as he looks through them. She's relaxed and happy. I love that I could give this to her. This bond of a family we are beginning to form with not only my family, but with her friends as well. It's only because of Candace that I have this right now. She's the one who showed me what it was to open up. To connect to others. That I was capable of having meaningful relationships. And since having her in my life, my relationships with Tori and Max have grown to a new level, allowing for an even deeper friendship than before.

The shift that life has taken is one that I never would have expected, but one that I would never change as I watch her and then look down the beach to see Mark and Jase making a sand hill with Bailey and Tori while my mom and Trevor sit back and talk. And when Candace looks up at me with her beautiful smile, I know I have everything I could ever want.

Mark has taken a keen liking to Bailey over the past couple of days, which Tori has appreciated since he pretty much has taken Bailey off of her hands, giving her a much-needed break. She and Candace spent a couple of hours yesterday shopping at The Landing while the rest of us played outside with the kids on the beach. This time of year the weather is nice, so we take advantage and ditch the indoors.

On the Fourth, we take the kids down to the local parade in the morning and then over to Seaside later that night, for fireworks. We've had a good visit, and it was needed in more ways than one.

When I wake up the next morning, Candace isn't in bed with me, so I slip my pajama pants over my boxers and head downstairs to find her. The house is quiet with everyone still asleep, and when I walk through the living room, I look out the windows to see Candace sitting alone, down by the water.

Walking out, she has the binoculars up to her eyes, and when I get close, I ask, "What are you doing out here?"

She looks back at me when she says, "Watching the puffins."

I sit down in the sand next to her, wrapping my arm around her shoulders, teasing, "You want me to swim out there and get you one?"

"Mark may get jealous," she says with a quiet laugh.

"Yeah. You're probably right."

She sets down the binoculars and lays her head on my shoulder, saying, "I love coming out here."

"Why's that?"

"Because," she says, waiting a beat before continuing, "I feel like I'm part of a family. I never felt that way with mine, but I feel it with yours."

"Have you ever talked to your parents? Did they come to your graduation or anything?" I ask.

"No."

Not wanting to dampen this moment, I lift her chin up to me and tell her, "I love having you here. The first time I brought you here, last year at Christmas, I watched you in the kitchen with my mom, and I knew I wanted to bring you back. I had been chasing you for so long, nervous that I would scare you away if I told you how I was feeling, but bringing you home with me, I knew I had to make you mine."

She smiles, saying, "You never seemed nervous around me. I always thought you were so sure of yourself."

"There wasn't a second that I felt sure of myself with you. You're the hardest person I have ever tried to read."

"Is that a bad thing?"

"No. There isn't a single thing about you that I would change. I love every piece of you."

chapter forty-nine

The leaves litter the streets as I drive home in the rain. I've been on a job all afternoon after I was commissioned to photograph a model for a portfolio. The photography thing has really picked up for me, and I've been trying to get a few more of my newer pieces on display at a couple of galleries. The exposure has been great, and Candace is nothing but supportive, coming along with me to showings when she can.

She's been so busy with rehearsals lately for her first performance run that will start in a few days. The transition into the company has been a challenge for her. Most of the girls up there have been there for years, skipping the college route to go straight into their dancing career. Candace told me that it's not very common to go from a university to a company, but she did it mostly to appease her parents. It's been very competitive and some of the dancers haven't welcomed her into the program very easily, giving her a hard time at first, but my girl is determined and always keeps herself focused when she's dancing. It isn't until she comes home to me that she finally lets out her frustrations.

We've made a routine of having Jase and Mark over

every Thursday night so that Jase and Candace can watch the new episodes of 'Ridiculousness.' I just have to laugh at the two of them and their taste for trash TV, but she redeems herself each time we camp out downstairs by the fireplace to watch our black and whites.

Candace is already home when I pull into the drive, and when I walk up the stairs to the front door, I spot one of my bowls sitting on the ground. Picking it up, I go inside and set it in the sink then head upstairs. I stop in my tracks the moment I catch sight of her. She's securing felted green leaves around the bun on top of her head, wearing a puffy red strawberry costume with green tights.

"Baby, what's this?" I question with a smirk while I enjoy the view.

Taking out the hairpin from between her teeth and sticking it in her hair, she stands proudly on display for me, saying, "My Halloween costume!"

She's fuckin' cute, and I smile as I step towards her and ask, "Where did you get this?"

"Marilyn, the seamstress at the studio. She made it for me."

"I didn't know we were dressing up."

She looks down at her costume, running her hands down the fluffy red fabric and says, "I never do anything for Halloween, so I figured since we're gonna be with the kids, I wanted to dress up."

Wrapping my arms around the pillowy costume, I pull her close to me and kiss her. I love seeing her playful and happy like this. We decided to go to Astoria to take Tori and my other cousin, Jenna's, kids trick-or-treating next week. I felt bad that I didn't go last year, so I'm making it a point this year, and Candace is excited to tag along and see everyone. My whole family has embraced Candace, and

474

hearing Bailey call her Aunt Ce-Ce every time we video chat means the world to her.

"So you like it?" she questions when she breaks our kiss.

"It's adorable, babe."

I kiss her dimple before she says, "I'm gonna go take it off. I just wanted to put it all on to see how it looks. Give me a few minutes."

My eyes follow her green legs as she walks into the bathroom and shuts the door. Even after all this time, she's still modest with me, always shutting herself away to change and get ready. It used to bother me, but now it's just another thing I love about her. So I sit on the bed and wait for her to reappear, looking more sophisticated in a pair of black pants and a fitted sweater, hair still in a bun.

"You wanna go grab a coffee before our appointment?" I ask.

"Yeah. Can we go to Common Grounds? I haven't seen Roxy in a while, and I'd like to stop in and say hi."

"Of course," I respond as I tug her onto the bed and pull her between my legs before kissing her. "Oh, hey," I say when I pull back. "Why was there a bowl by the front door?"

"I put some food out for this cat I keep seeing."

"Babe, if you do that, we're gonna have a shitload of stray cats hanging around outside."

"She looked sad. I just couldn't let her starve," she defends. "She doesn't have tags or anything, and it's cold and rainy outside. The least I could do was leave out some food."

I laugh at her, but love her soft heart, so I don't say anything else about it.

Kissing the top of her head, I tell her, "Come on. Let's get out of here."

After we stop by and visit with Roxy for a while, we

head over to Dr. Christman's office for our appointment. We've continued to see her twice a month, and Candace has still been keeping her weekly appointments on top of what we do together. She's been working hard and talking more to me about the rape and how she's trying to process it. She still blames herself, but I can't get down on her for that because I still blame myself as well.

She did come off of her sleeping pill back in the beginning of September, but a couple weeks ago, she had another terrifying nightmare and immediately started taking her pills again even though Dr. Christman wanted her to continue on without them. I understand Candace's fear of her dreams. That nightmare freaked her out, and she wound up making herself sick, vomiting several times afterwards.

After seeing Jack at the bar, she was scared to come back there. I wound up telling her about the subpoena and going to see him. She was having a hard time believing that he was really dead, so I found out where he was buried and took her to show her that she didn't have to be scared of him anymore—but she still is.

Candace has been busy ever since we got back in town from spending Halloween in Astoria with my cousins a couple weeks ago. It was a short trip, but Candace had fun with the kids, and I had fun watching my strawberry go door to door with Bailey, helping her fill her bag with candy. Candace even got some candy herself at a few houses that just assumed she was a kid. We all teased her about her size, and she took it like a champ, but she's used to it from Mark. The two of them banter like brother and sister, and I'm starting to see that same connection building with her, Tori, and Trevor.

This past week has been crazy while Candace has been having costume fittings and dress rehearsals. But tonight is her first performance, and seeing her meddle around the loft, trying to keep her nerves in check, I think back to the last time—the only time—I saw her dance. I was alone, miserable, fearing I'd lost her for good. I watched her dance for the first time while I was hiding in the back of the theater, wishing I could have been with her, and now I am. This is the way it should have been the day of her performance in college, but I'm getting my moment now. And savoring every minute of it.

We ran out of bananas this morning, so she sent me out to grab a few since she worries about muscle cramps. When I get back from the store, a tiny white and tan cat greets me. No doubt, Candace's little buddy, waiting for her next meal. I walk past it and let myself in.

"Your friend's out front," I say as I walk through the room and into the kitchen to set the bag of bananas down.

"Who?" she asks from the couch.

"That cat you keep feeding all of our food to."

"Ryan, she doesn't have a home. She's been hanging around for a couple of weeks," she says as I walk over to her and sit down.

"We can take her to the pound."

"Oh my God! You're crazy!" she squeals at me. "We're not doing that."

Looking over at her, I already know what she wants to do, but I ask anyway, hoping she'll surprise me.

"So what do you suggest we do?"

In the most timid way possible, she suggests, "We could keep her."

"I'm not inviting a feral cat into my home."

Narrowing her eyes at me, she says, "You act like I'm

asking you to invite a vampire in."

As I laugh at her analogy, she defends, "And stop calling her a *feral* cat like she's some Dickensian orphan."

"Why do I have a feeling like this cat is going to become part of our family?"

She gets a huge grin on her face at the mere suggestion as I sit back and drape her legs over my lap. When she lies down, I ask, "You doing okay?"

She turns her head to stare out at the rain that's now beating against the windows, and says, "I've never danced for a crowd this big before."

"You'll be fine," I tell her as I start rubbing her calves.

"Hmm," she softly hums with her eyes shut as I massage her legs.

"When I finally got to see you dance the night of your solo, I never thought you could look so beautiful. You were all I could see even when the stage was filled with other dancers. You stole every bit of my attention as if nothing else in the world existed but you."

She looks up to my eyes when I tell her this, and then I say, "I know you work your ass off, but when I saw you on stage, it's like you didn't even have to try. That's how I know you'll be fine. You can't help but be captivating, babe."

Sitting up, she climbs into my lap, straddling my hips, and says, "I wanted you that day of my solo. I was a wreck, and I just wanted you there with me."

Tangling my fingers into her hair, I tell her, "You have me now, babe."

She leans down and kisses me, moving her lips slowly with mine while I tug her hips into me. Leaning my head back onto the couch, I guide her with my hands still trussed in her hair. I love the taste of her in my mouth, and we continue to make out for a while, just like this, before she drags herself off of me to get ready.

I spend a good amount of time sitting in bed while I watch her move around the room as she stretches and works her ankles, puts her hair up in her bun, and replaces the lamb's wool in her toe shoes. She's quiet, but flashes me a grin every now and then as I watch what I hope will become our routine. Tonight's her first performance, but she'll have two tomorrow and two on Sunday followed by a few throughout the week. This will last for the next three weeks, and I'm excited that I get to see her dance like this, performing for thousands of people every day. She's a star in the darkness that hovers over us—she always has been.

I say goodbye to her early because she has to be at McCaw Theater hours before production, so when I arrive, Jase, Mark, Traci, and Max are already there and seated. Candace was able to get them all tickets for opening night, which is nearly a black-tie affair.

Tonight won't be like the last time I saw her. With the company, she dances in what they call the corps de ballet, an ensemble of dancers that accompany the soloists. It could take a while for Candace to work her way up to being a soloist.

Dancing 'Les Sylphides,' my eyes stay locked on her throughout the whole night. She's the only one I see as she moves gracefully around the stage. Just like before when I saw her dancing, she gives me goosebumps. She's soft and stoic, taking each number with a focus that only she can make so effortless.

She loves this. It's who she is, and to see her take this passion and turn her dreams into reality is an amazing thing. She's known what she's wanted to make of her dancing, and she did it. I'm in awe of her. To see her suffer through so much, yet never lose her way with her goals is a determination you don't find all that often in people. But she has it.

I never thought a guy like me would be found at the ballet and actually enjoying it, but I like knowing that this is now a part of my life and that I get to watch my girl up on that stage throughout the year.

Once the curtain drops and the lights brighten, I visit with everyone for a while before saying goodnight. Candace told me to meet her in the dressing room afterwards, so as I walk out of the theater, I see the main lobby emptying out when my eyes catch a man with familiar silver hair walking towards me. As he approaches, I'm stunned to see it's Candace's father.

"Charles?"

He looks up and stops in his tracks when he recognizes me. I can tell that he can't place my name.

"It's Ryan," I say, reminding him.

"Ryan. How are you?" he says as he reaches out his hand, but I don't take it.

"What are you doing here?"

It takes him a moment, but when he lowers his hand, he shifts his weight, saying, "I came to see Candace."

"Does she know you're here?"

"No."

When I slowly begin to shake my head at the man who is sneaking out because he's too much of a coward to see his own daughter, he defends, "I love her."

"You don't know her."

He doesn't speak after I say this, and my need to protect her takes over when I continue, "I don't know what it is about her that you aren't able to accept or that you don't think is good enough. I've tried to understand, but I can't."

Taking a step closer, I pause for a second before saying, "I wish you could see the amazing girl that I do. The girl who has dreams that she's able to make come true. The girl who loves harder than anyone I've ever known. She's got a beautiful heart."

"I know."

"Do you know what you did to that heart when you turned your back on her?"

"I love my daughter," he says. "But I love my wife too. I won't stand here and make excuses for her. She has her faults, but in the end, I love her."

"So where does that leave Candace? Because I'll be honest with you, sir, I love that girl and seeing how the two of you hurt her is something that I would be willing to look past if it meant that you could repair things with her."

Shoving his hands into his pants pockets, he turns his head to the doors before looking back at me and resolves, "I just wanted to see her dance. Maybe you shouldn't tell her that you saw me," and then walks out the doors.

I've never wanted to protect anyone the way I want to protect Candace, but I won't ever hold anything back from her. As sick as it sounds, it's probably best that her parents walked out of her life. This is a girl who apologizes for herself more than anyone I know because she feels she is always making a mistake simply by being herself. She's someone who is so determined to succeed, but I know it's stemmed from growing up with parents who never thought she was good enough and made it their goal to make sure she knew it. And when she opens the door to her dressing room and I see her big smile, full of life and satisfaction, I know she's going to be better off without them.

"God, you're amazing," I tell her as I pick her up in my arms and hug her.

Her smile's infectious and after I kiss her, she beams in excitement, "That was incredible." Setting her down, she shuts the door behind me and asks, "What did you think?"

"I think you're gonna be seeing me here a lot."

"So you liked it?"

"There isn't anything I don't like about seeing you on that stage," I tell her and then move in to cup her face in my hands. "Do you have any idea how proud I am of you?"

She kisses me and then tells me, "You're the one that made me want to feel again. That helped bring me back to life."

I could easily give those same words back to her because she did the same for me, only on a completely different scope, so I let her have those words. I love that we can give each other so much. That we can have the best of ourselves with each other. We continue to hug and kiss for a while longer, celebrating Candace's opening night at the ballet in our quiet way.

She is already out of her costume, so I sit on the small couch as she powders her shoes and begins to pack up.

Spotting a vase full of pink roses, I ask, "Who are those from?"

She looks at the vase and then back to me, saying, "Your mom had those delivered before the show. She felt bad that she couldn't be here."

"Babe, I need to tell you something," I say and then motion for her to come sit next to me, and when she does, I turn to her and take her hands in mine. I know she'll be okay when I tell her about her father because she has such a solid support system in the people that choose to be a part of her life. "I saw your dad tonight."

Seeing her eyes open up with hope, she asks, "He's here?"

"He was," I say gently. "I ran into him as he was leaving," Her face falls when I tell her this.

"Didn't he want to see me?"

Her head drops when I shake my head.

"What did he say?"

We've been nothing but transparent with each other, so I give her that respect when I say, "That he loves you, but he loves your mother too. He didn't want me to tell you he was here, but I never want to keep anything from you again, and I need you to know that."

The tears in her eyes are hard to look at as she sits here. "Don't doubt for a second that you don't have a family full of people that love and support you because you do. They might not be your blood, but they are your heart."

She takes a second before she speaks on a soft breath, "So that's it?" referring to her parents.

"I think so."

Defeat washes over her as her shoulders slump.

"I know it hurts, babe, but I also know that you haven't done a thing wrong here. It's them, not you."

"Can you just take me home?"

"Yeah," I whisper and help her gather her things before I drive us home.

She's quiet, and I hate that I had to dampen her night, but I swore to her that there would never being anything that I would withhold from her again.

It's cold and rainy when I open the garage so we don't get wet. Walking into the house, everything is dark and quiet until a faint, "Meow," from outside filters in.

Cocking my head at Candace and giving her a knowing look, she knits her brows together, silently pleading with me.

"No."

"Ryan, it's freezing outside," she says.

"We're not bringing that stray cat in here."

"You're being mean. She's a nice cat. I've never seen her be aggressive," she defends.

Shaking my head at her, she pleads, "It's pouring out there."

Candace is giving me the most pitiful look, and knowing she's already feeling defeated tonight, I give in and sigh out, "Fine."

She tilts her head and questions, "Really?" for clarity.

"For tonight."

She doesn't waste a second when she runs to the front door and opens it, bending down and picking up the tiny cat who huddles in her arms. I smile at her as she coos and starts walking over to me.

"I'm gonna give her a bath."

"What?! No, you're not. The cat is gonna sleep in the garage," I tell her.

"She's filthy."

"You do know cats hate water, right?" I say, but she ignores me as she starts walking back to the guest bedroom.

Not trusting this animal in the slightest, I follow her back and proceed to help her grab towels and run a little water in the tub. This cat is terrified as shit, so I take it out of her hands and hold it while it squeals and writhes in fear as Candace washes her. But it's when she begins thrashing in my hands that she slips out of my hold, jumping out of the tub and tears through the house, no sound but her claws clicking against the wooden floors.

"Fuck!"

Chasing after her, all I hear is Candace laughing, still in the bathroom.

"Help me find her!" I call out while I make my way upstairs.

I follow the dreadful meows to the bedroom and find her under the bed. Getting on my knees, I peek my head under, and see her curled against the wall in the middle of the bed.

"Come here," I say in a singsong voice, mocking my liking for her. Giving the floor a couple light taps, I call again, "Come here," when I see Candace's head poke down from the other side, giggling.

"This shit isn't funny," I tell her.

She rolls her eyes at me, and then calls to the cat, but she still doesn't budge. "Great," she huffs out. "You've scared her."

"What?"

"She knows you don't like her."

"You're kidding me, right?" I say as we continue to go back and forth with our heads underneath the bed. "You're the one that tortured this thing because you just *had* to give it a bath."

"I didn't torture her," she argues.

Tapping the floor a few more times, the cat slowly inches to me, and I can't help but look over to Candace with a victorious grin as I reach out and pick up the cat.

When we reemerge from underneath the bed and get up, cat in my arms, she stands, hands on hips, miffed.

We manage to get the cat dried off, and after everything is cleaned up, we head to bed. Lying there together, Candace stares at the cat that is sleeping down by our feet, purring softly.

"She's so cute."

"You're so cute," I tell her, and when she looks at me, she smiles.

"I bet she was the runt of the litter," she says. "She's so small."

"Hmm," I hum as I pull her closer to me.

"I wanna keep her."

"I knew this was coming."

"What?" she questions when she tilts her head up to me. "You can't tell me that you don't think Tatiana is adorable."

Laughing, I question, "What did you just call her?"

"Tatiana."

"I'm not calling her that," I say firmly, refusing to call the cat a name like that.

"Why not?"

"Because it's way too girly."

Candace laughs at me when she says, "Well . . . she is a girl, Ryan."

"She's a cat," I say. "And where did you get Tatiana from?"

"She's a famous ballerina that I've always loved. I like the name."

"What's her last name? Maybe it'll sound better than Tatiana."

Candace answers through her giggles, "Riabouchinska."

"What the hell is that?"

"She's Russian."

Sliding down in the bed to face her, I kiss her lips before saying, "I'll call her Ana."

She gives me a sweet grin, asking, "So we can keep her?"

"No. She can stay here until we can figure out what we're gonna do with her. But we're taking her to the vet as soon as we wake up to get her checked out before we bring her back here."

I kiss her again, slowly, lingering against her soft lips when she begins to mumble, "I'm glad I had this with you."

When I pull back, she adds, "Everything about today . . . I'm glad it was all with you."

Rolling on top of her, I spend a great deal of time letting

her know, in my own way, how much I love her as I thoroughly kiss her.

chapter fifty

"Baby, make sure you leave enough food out for Ana," I call out to Candace who is upstairs.

The seasons have gone by fast and now we are packing up, getting ready to head to my mom's for Christmas. We were just there for Thanksgiving a few weeks back. I didn't get to spend a whole lot of time with Candace because she was too busy plotting Black Friday shopping tactics with my mom and aunts. It was fun to see her so into it, finding deals on toys she thought we should buy the kids for Christmas. She left me at home while she spent the whole night and half of the next day shopping just to wind up sleeping for the rest of the afternoon.

"Do you have everything?" Candace asks me as she walks down the stairs.

"Yeah, it's all in the car."

"Did you give Tatiana her new toy?"

"Yes, babe," I sigh. Candace insists that we buy that cat a new toy every time we leave her for a few days. Even though the cat has been living with us for over a month now, I still haven't fully agreed to letting it stay with us permanently. Life has just been crazy with Candace's performance schedule around the holidays; she's lucky she was allowed this time off to go out of town. Plus my photography has really picked up, and I'm now in several galleries in the city. Needless to say, trying to contact vets and whatnot hasn't been high on the list of things to do. I know she loves that cat, and it's so funny to see how they mirror each other. Tiny, quiet, and both very timid. I can't lie, the cat is adorable, and when Candace isn't around, she spends a good amount of time in my lap. But I love teasing Candace about my loathing relationship with Ana, so I keep up the charade because she's so fuckin' cute when she gets all defensive over that cat.

Picking up Candace's coat, I help slide it over her arms before we head out into the blistering cold. Once I help her into the car, I hop in, blast the heat, and start heading down to Oregon.

"Jase called this morning," she says as she takes my phone to sync it through the speakers. "Their connecting flight got delayed and they didn't make it to Ohio until after midnight."

"That sucks."

"Yeah. And then it took them over an hour to get to Mark's house. Said they are having a horrible snow storm."

When Candace selects The xx to play and sets the phone down, I take her hand in my lap, and ask, "So what do you wanna do while we're away?"

As she leans her head back against the seat, she responds with, "Nothing. I'm so worn out, all I want to do is lay around in my pajamas."

"So I get to keep you hidden away in my bed the whole time?" I say with a smirk, and she smiles back at me.

"No, but I think lying around, watching movies, and eating are all my top priorities."

Bringing her hand up to my lips, I kiss her knuckles as we sit back and listen to 'Angels.'

"I always think of you when I hear this song," she murmurs as she gets comfortable in her seat.

I give her hand a light squeeze as I listen to the love song that is laced with a haunting melody.

Candace and I continue to work together with Dr. Christman, still focusing on the events of that night with Jack, but since running into Charles, we've been discussing more of our childhoods and how they've impacted us as adults. I've learned a lot about what it was like for Candace growing up and how she taught herself to shut down emotionally so she wouldn't be forced into feeling worthless and sad all the time. She learned how to bury it and hide it away, to just move on through life by avoiding. But I do the same thing. Although we've dealt with two very different sets of parents, we both used masks to cope.

Candace still deals with anxiety around crowds. She continues to wake from night terrors, although not as often as she did a few months ago. I have a feeling these things will stick with her, along with the blame she carries. She's still my same Candace, but she's beginning to settle with herself, no longer living inside of her chaotic head all of the time, constantly haunted and shadowed. Her personality is starting to brighten, and I love seeing bits and pieces of the Candace that was so far destroyed when I first met her.

When we finally arrive at my mom's, it's a little after five on Christmas Eve. Trevor helps me unload all the gifts for the kids, and Candace, staying true to her word, is already in a pair of her long red and white polka dot pajama pants and a long-sleeved white shirt.

Walking over to her as she's sitting down with the kids, watching cartoons, wrapped up in a blanket with her glass of

Merlot, I sit down next to her and kiss her.

"You move fast," I tease.

She settles herself into my arms as we lean back against the couch and says, "Your mom insisted I take it easy."

"Oh she did? Did she also insist on getting you drunk?" I joke as I eye her rather large glass of wine.

Her only response is a soft kiss with her hand wrapped around the back of my neck.

"Eww! Gross!" Maddie squeals from a few feet away, embarrassing Candace.

"Don't you kiss your boyfriend?" I tease her with a wink.

"I don't have a boyfriend, Uncle Ryan."

"That's not what your mom says," I say, continuing to egg her on.

She tilts her head at me, clearly in the know that I'm making things up, and says, "Boys are nasty," causing Candace to burst out laughing.

"This boy isn't nasty," Candace tells her quietly as if it's a secret she doesn't want anyone else to hear.

"Don't listen to her, Maddie," Tori pipes in as she sits down on the couch behind Candace and me. "Uncle Ryan has cooties."

"Maddie, do you know what crabs are?" I tease, knowing that the only crabs she's aware of are those in the ocean.

"Ryan!" Tori squeaks as she slaps my shoulder.

Laughing loudly, I turn to Tori and say, "Hey, if you're gonna tell her I have cooties—"

"Ryan, that's disgusting," Candace scolds while smiling at the banter going on.

"Aunt Donna told me that you guys got a cat," she mentions as she sits back, and we turn to face her.

"We didn't *get* a cat; Candace just decided to open our home to a feral," I say and then wait for Candace to get defensive, and it only takes a second.

"She's not a feral. She's super sweet," she tells Tori before looking at me, saying, "Admit it, she's sweet."

Tightening my arms around her, I confess, "Yeah, babe. Ana's sweet."

"Her name's Ana?" Tori asks.

"No, her name's Tatiana," Candace responds.

"So why do you call her Ana?"

Looking at Tori with annoyance, I tell her, "Because no man should have to call any pet 'Tatiana,' especially a random stray."

Tori shakes her head and laughs, "You guys are funny."

"It's a pretty name," Candace says. "But Ryan feels it impedes too much on his masculinity to have to acknowledge her full name."

"Are you guys talking about Tatiana?" my mom calls out from the kitchen. "That is the *cutest* cat."

"When did you see it?" Tori asks.

As Mom starts walking into the living room, she answers, "I visited them before Thanksgiving to see Candace dance since I missed her opening night."

Wrapping another blanket around the two of us, I tuck Candace's head under my chin as the four of us continue to talk.

It isn't long before everyone is finished with dinner and busy giving the kids baths and getting them ready for bed. Candace and I stay downstairs, cleaning up the kitchen and then settling in front of the fireplace with some wine. We enjoy the peace while we wait for my mother. Candace wants to stay up with her to fill the kids' stockings and put the gifts from Santa under the tree. My cousins appreciate her enthusiasm since it means they don't have to stay up and can go to bed.

"It's so dark in here," we hear my mom softly say as she walks into the room.

"It's quiet," I joke. "That's the most important thing."

She laughs and then eyes the bottle of wine, grabbing a glass before joining us. "Ryan, I have all the stocking stuff in the laundry room closet. Would you mind grabbing it for me?"

When I get the bags and return, Candace and Mom have all the stockings pulled from the fireplace and lying on the floor. I drop the bags and watch the two of them working together, filling them up with candy and gifts.

"So how have you been, dear? You're always so busy; I hardly get to talk to you," she says to Candace.

"I know. I'm sorry. Everything is good though. We've been really busy with the Nutcracker and also rehearsing auditions for our next run."

"What's that going to be?"

"'The Tempest.' It'll run in February."

"I'll have to get tickets for that."

"Mom, you don't have to come to all of her performances," I tell her as they continue to fill the stockings.

She sets one down to take a sip of her wine before saying, "I know I don't have to, but I want to." When she looks to Candace, she adds, "It's fun for me to go and to know it's you up there dancing."

Candace's face lights up as my mom says this. "Thanks, Donna. But you don't need to buy tickets. I can get you the same passes I get Ryan. It's not a big deal."

Once everything is filled, they hang the stockings back up above the fireplace when Candace says, "Did Ryan tell you about his newest shoot?"

"No."

"He was commissioned to shoot one of the lead principals in the company to be displayed at the Metro Gallery downtown for a special invitational showing," she brags with a huge smile.

When my mom turns to me, she nearly scolds, "Why didn't you say anything?"

"I just got the gig a few days ago."

"Apparently the director, Peter, is friends with one of my old college dance teachers whose girlfriend works at the Henry Gallery, who Ryan works closely with now. Anyway, a few of his pieces are being displayed and caught Peter's eye, and when he found out the photographer was my boyfriend, he commissioned him for this photo shoot."

"That's wonderful," Mom says. "It amazes me the things you two have going on in your lives."

I laugh at my mom's excitement as Candace continues to chat with her while we start putting the gifts under the tree. When everything is done, we say goodnight and Candace and I head up to my room to crash.

I wake up to the smell of Candace's shower and the commotion from downstairs. I lie there for a moment, trying to fully wake up, when she walks out of the bathroom, dressed and looking amazing for so early in the morning.

Reaching out, I grab on to her arm and pull her on top of me. "Morning."

She giggles and then wraps her arms around my neck, kissing me softly. Pulling back, she stares down at me, whispering, "Merry Christmas," with a hint of a smile.

"I love you," I tell her as I tangle my hands in her hair and bring her back down to my lips.

Remembering this day last year, I was at her house after her parents tossed her out the night before. She was upset and quiet, only wanting to come home with me to hide from everything going on in her life. And now . . . now she's mine, and that day seems like years ago. She's happy and content in my arms, with a whole new family that she fits into flawlessly. I'm happy to have another Christmas with her, and one that isn't buried under so much darkness. Not that the darkness isn't there, but the rim of light is promising.

"I'll wait while you get ready," she says as she shifts off of me.

After a quick shower, I toss on some clothes and we head downstairs into the madness.

"Uncle Ryan's up!" Connor yells out with excitement, making Candace and me laugh, as if Christmas couldn't start until I dragged myself down here.

"Morning, Mom."

"Good morning. You better hurry and grab your coffee because these kids aren't going to last much longer," she says, walking out of the kitchen, stopping to kiss Candace on the cheek before going into the living room.

Candace and I grab our coffees and then head into the other room. I make myself comfortable on the floor as Candace sits on the couch behind me. I lean my head back and she plants a kiss on my forehead followed by a wide smile before Bailey plops down on my lap.

"Wyan," she calls out, finally starting to get the hang of my name as she clings her tiny arms around my neck.

She squeals when I start blowing raspberry kisses on her neck.

"You ready to open presents?" I ask, and when her eyes widen as she nods, I call over to Trevor, "Find me a few for this princess."

After opening several gifts with me, she trades me in for Candace's lap. I sit next to them on the couch as she helps Bailey unwrap the tea set we bought her. They open gift after gift, and when a box wrapped in black paper lands on my lap with Candace's name on it, I interrupt her and Bailey, teasing, "So you can buy me a gift, but I can't get you anything?"

She shoots me a grin and then turns her attention back to Bailey as I peel back the paper to find that she bought me a big tintype kit for my camera.

"I saw you eying that tintype at the Metro Gallery," she says to me.

"This is perfect." I've been wanting to work with something a little bit different and for Candace to know that, picking up on the fact that I spent a little more time observing that piece than the others on display makes it clear how gelled we've become with each other.

"Candace," Mom says as she walks up to us from behind the couch. "Ryan made me tuck this away." She hands Candace the gift I ordered for her and was having my mom hang on to so that Candace wouldn't find out.

She takes the small, wrapped box from my mom and then shakes her head as she mutters, "Ryan, I don't . . ."

"Don't worry. It isn't for you."

She gives me a confused look when I clarify, "It's for Ana."

Her smile is warm, and when Bailey hops off of her lap, she folds her legs underneath herself as she gently unwraps the paper. Pulling out the sleek, brown leather, designer cat collar, her smile grows, showing off her sexy dimple.

"The collar isn't the real gift," I tell her. "Look at the tag, babe."

Laying her palm flat underneath the gold tag, she reads

the name I had engraved on it: *Tatiana Campbell.*

"Campbell?" she questions slowly with a wary eye before asking, "So we're keeping her?"

"We're keeping her."

She wraps her arms tightly around my neck, laughing with excitement. "Thank you."

I laugh at her demeanor, planting a couple kisses below her ear, and when she pulls back to look at the collar again, Tori snatches it and teases, "This is a really nice leather collar."

"I would have tied yarn around its neck, but I saw Candace drooling over this collar when she dragged me into some frou-frou pet store."

Eying Candace, she cocks a brow at her. "Really?"

"Don't make fun of me. I think it's sophisticated," she defends.

"That's what's so funny about this," she jokes as she hands the collar back to her. "I've got to meet this cat if Ryan was willing to *bestow* his last name on her," she jokes with laughter.

"You should see the small four-post bed Candace bought her. It's ridiculous," I tell Tori.

She turns back to Candace, and says, "So Ryan has a tiny four-post kitty bed in his bedroom?"

Candace nods her head with a grin and Tori adds, "God, I love what you're doing to him."

Narrowing my eyes at her, I defend, "She didn't give me a choice. I came home from the bar one day and there it was."

"Regardless, it's still there."

"It's really cute," Candace tells her, and I laugh when I reiterate, "It's a four-post bed!"

"Oh my God, you guys," Tori bursts out laughing, and

we all join in, even Candace, at the absurdity of it all. But in the end, my girl is happy and that's all that matters. She's never had a pet, and she adores having Tatiana.

Once the living room is completely demolished and littered in paper, my mom has everyone get the kids dressed and ready for the day while I do a clean sweep of the place. Candace takes a moment to call Jase and check in with him and Mark.

"I got her and Jase a little something for Christmas," Mom tells me as we take out all the trash.

"Mom—"

"I know, but I saw this cooking school that is down the street from your loft, and after seeing how much Jase likes to cook when he was here in July, I thought they would have fun taking a few lessons together."

We start heading back inside when I turn to her and say, "She's gonna love it. So will Jase. He's been coming over whenever he has free time and has tried teaching her a few things."

"Any luck?" she asks with a smile.

"We wind up going out," I admit with a light chuckle. "Thanks, Mom."

Walking back inside, Candace is standing over by the windows, looking out at the ocean. I step up from behind and slip my arms around her shoulders, resting my chin on top of her head. "Whatcha doing?"

"Just thinking."

"About?"

"Last Christmas."

Lifting my chin, I run my hands down her arms, and when she turns to face me, she says, "Thank you."

"What for?"

She wraps her arms around my waist as I cradle her face.

"For being so patient with me."

"You may be slow to open up and hard to read, but you're not the type of girl you wanna rush anything with. I want every slow second."

When she lifts up onto her toes to kiss me, I pick her up off the floor as we seal our lips together, both realizing how far we've come since last year.

Candace and I decide to get bundled up and take a long walk down the beach alone, taking our time while the mist floats its way down from the dark, grey sky. We don't talk much, just keep close, stealing kisses along the way. When we finally get back to the house, Candace stays with my mom for most of the day in the kitchen, cooking, while I hang out with the kids, keeping them busy and out of trouble.

After dinner, everyone is getting ready for bed when Candace and I decide to do a replay of last year. When everyone finally heads to bed, we pile a bunch of pillows and blankets onto the living room floor in front of the fireplace, and then find an old black and white to watch.

We lie down, and I snuggle her into my arms, but this time, I can kiss her whenever I want, so I do. We make it through 'Swing Time,' and I think this one makes it to the top of Candace's favorites so far, but I figured it would since it's a love story about dancers. She keeps glued to the TV, but when 'I'll Be Seeing You' comes on next, our eyes drift from the screen to each other's. It's after midnight, and we begin to grow tired as we lie here face to face.

Candace slides her hand along my jaw before she presses her lips to mine. Running my hand down her back, I pull her in tight against me. She begins to bury her hands in my hair when I slip past her lips and revel in the sweet taste of her mouth. I fumble my hand in the blanket until I find the remote and shut off the TV, the only light coming from the burning logs in the fireplace.

I'm overwhelmed with her. Having her like this when a year ago I was so nervous around her. Now all I want is what we have. She's given me everything I thought I never wanted. She's given it in her own way, but the most perfect way for me. I used to be so disconnected and cold, but with her . . . she's taught me how to be soft because I can't be any other way with her. I never knew how much I needed that until I had her. It's because of her that I no longer worry about the fears that plagued me throughout my life. She showed me what it meant to provide for someone else. She's always been my priority. I never even had to think about it; she always was. And to see how happy she was today, I know I'm able to give her what she needs. That I can love, and I can do it well. It's because of her that I'm the man I never thought I could be, and she makes it so easy to do.

I'm never gonna stop wanting her—I know that. From the broken girl in the coffee shop on that rainy Halloween night to the vibrant girl who owns that stage at McCaw Theater every time she dances, I want every version of her—forever. I've never known beauty until her. I've never known how good life could be until her.

As I slowly drag my lips away from hers, she opens her eyes as she rests her head next to mine on the pillow. She runs her small hand from my shoulder down to my chest where she keeps it, and I wrap my hand around hers. Her soft skin glows in the flicker of the fire as I stare into her hazel eyes, and I see everything I'll ever want to see. It's all within her. She holds every part of me, and it's in this very moment that I feel it. It floods inside of me. A peace that only she can bring me.

No doubt. No questioning. No hesitation.

"Marry me."

chapter fifty-one
(Candace)

"Marry me."

His softest words are the most powerful and hit hard inside of my heart as it begins to race when shock takes it over.

"What?" I softly whisper because he's caught me so off guard with his question that my mind is spinning.

"Marry me," he repeats with a clarity I can't deny. With a certainty I've always depended on him for. He's the warmth I draw my strength from. My safe place to rest my head when it won't stop torturing me.

Each word falls right through me, and all I can do is give him a nod of my head.

His smile is perfection as he covers me in it, kissing me with his whole heart. The only heart that has been able to unravel me. The heart that showed me *my* heart could still breathe when I felt as if it was suffocating. He walked right inside of me and brought me back to life. He promised me he wouldn't let me fade. I didn't believe him at the time, but he fought for me. I thought I'd lost who I was, but with each day, he gives me a piece of my old self back. A playfulness I thought was gone. A happiness I never thought I'd feel again. A security I thought was forever stolen from me.

When he pulls back, his face is intent, looking straight through me to my core as he says, "Tell me, babe. Give me the words."

Taking his face in my hands, I can't hold in my emotions when the tears slip out. "Let's get married."

He pulls me to his chest as he loops his arm behind my knees, cradling me in his hold as he picks me up. The giggles slip out, the pure reflection of joy as he carries me upstairs to his room, shutting the door behind him. Laying me down in bed, he crawls over me and pulls the sheets over us.

"Tell me you love me," he whispers against my skin as he runs his hand underneath my top and gently squeezes my breast.

"I've only ever loved you," I pant as he slowly grazes my nipple with his thumb.

His lips find my neck, and he begins to kiss and nibble his way down as he grabs the hem of my shirt and slips it off of me. I know what he wants, and I want to give it to him, but knowing the house is full of people, my nerves take over.

"Ryan, wait."

Lifting his head, he looks down at me and reads me well when he says, "Baby, I wanna make love to you."

"But—"

"You're all that exists for me right now," he tells me, and my eyes fall shut with his words.

His warm lips cover mine, and I let go of the worry, handing it over to him because I know he'll always take care of me. Running his kisses down the center of my chest, he moves to my breast and drags his tongue over the lace bra that's still covering me. The sensation is powerful as he gently sucks my nipple into the heat of his mouth. He takes his hand and slides it behind me, unhooking my bra and dropping it to the floor. Ryan stares down at me, then meets my eyes, saying, "I never knew it could be like this."

His words bring a smile to my face when I respond, "Me neither."

We go slow, the same way we always do. He's never rushed with me, always taking his time, but knowing that he wants to be mine—to be my husband—creates an underlying intensity. A piece of the puzzle that we've finally found. A wholeness that we can bring each other. And when we have each other undressed, he quietly slips inside of me and holds himself there. Still. His breathing is heavy, and I can feel the swarm of his emotions take over him. I see it in eyes as he keeps them locked on mine.

I pull him down to me, needing the weight of him to cover me as I press my hands into his back to keep him close. Tonight is different. Bared in a way we've never been with each other. The love I feel for this man is more than my body can handle, and when I release a whimper, he begins to move inside of me.

His head is nestled in the curve of my neck, and I run my hands up his back and into his hair, holding his head in my hands, and when he draws his head back, I see his cheeks are damp with tears. I don't say anything; I know exactly how he feels because his tears reflect the ones that run down the sides of my face.

Rolling to the side, we lie face to face. He takes my leg and drapes it over his hip as he grabs me from behind, guiding me with him. I keep my hands on his face and hold him close, both of us quietly releasing our love and happiness through tears. The room fills with nothing but soft breaths of pleasure as we make love, giving ourselves entirely with the certainty that we are perfect for each other.

Feeling secure, knowing that through it all our love has never stalled. It only grows.

Waking up in the morning, the room is cold, and I snuggle in tighter to Ryan who is just starting to stir. I watch as he slowly begins to open his eyes, and before he can fully wake, he has a cheesy grin on his face when he rolls me on top of him.

"Morning," he says in his sexy rasp before I lower my lips to his, giving him a gentle kiss.

When I shiver in his arms, he rolls me back onto the bed, and wraps his arms around me.

"Mmm, you're still naked," he teases with a grin, and I tuck my head down into his chest. "Why are you so shy with me still?"

"Ryan," I softly nag.

"I'm not complaining. I like that you're still shy and reserved around me."

Peeking up at him, he kisses my forehead, and adds, "But I'm not gonna lie, I love feeling your skin all over me."

"Stop," I say, feeling the blush heat my cheeks as he quietly laughs.

He runs his hands through my hair as he looks at me, saying, "Tell me last night wasn't a dream."

"Which part?"

"The part where you said you'd marry me."

Smiling, I tell him, "I hope it wasn't a dream."

"Do you have any idea how happy you make me?" he asks, not letting me answer when he kisses the smile on my face.

He keeps his lips on me as he starts running his kisses

across my cheek and down my neck. Holding on to him, I close my eyes as he sends tingles down my arms. "I don't wanna wait," I whisper.

"For what," he mumbles against my skin.

"To marry you."

He pulls back to look at me, and agrees, "I don't either."

"Well, I was thinking . . . umm . . ."

"Just say it," he tells me as he brushes my hair back.

"What about Indian Beach?"

"To get married?" he asks.

I nod my head, saying, "I love it there." It's where we went this very day last year when he told me that he wanted to be with me. It's where he taught me how to surf. It's a place the two of us go together every time we come to Cannon Beach. And I know it's his favorite beach too.

"Sounds perfect."

"But . . ." I start hesitantly. "What if we just did it this weekend?"

"In two days?"

"Or three," I say coyly, wondering if he's thinking I'm crazy for suggesting doing it so soon.

"Babe, don't you want a big wedding and have everyone there?" he asks, concerned.

Letting out a soft breath, I tell him, "I never wanted a big wedding. You know me; I don't want all that. I just want us."

He gives me a kiss and then questions, "Are you sure?"

"I'm sure. Just us," I assure him before adding with a smile, "And a pretty dress."

"What about everything else?"

"There is nothing else. I just want you, but no cheesy tux. Promise me no tux."

He laughs at me and asks, "Why's that?"

"Because it isn't you."

"Okay, no cheesy tux," he agrees with a sexy smirk, and the smile on my face can't even reflect the happiness that I feel right now.

After he makes sure he is satisfied from thoroughly kissing me, he says, "We should go downstairs. Everyone is leaving this morning, so we should make an appearance."

"Can we not tell them?" I suggest, and when he tilts his head in question, I add, "I don't want all the fuss. Can we just tell your mom when everyone leaves?"

"Of course, babe," he says and then gets out of bed.

After we take our showers and get dressed, we head downstairs to visit before everyone heads home, except Tori, who is going to stay so that she can go shopping with Donna.

"Hey, Mom. Can Candace and I talk to you for a minute?" Ryan asks as she is finishing up a pot of tea for herself and me.

"Sure," she says with a curious eye as Ryan takes my hand and starts walking back to the study.

"What's going on?" Donna asks as the three of us stand there.

My stomach is filled with butterflies, wondering how she's going to react to this sudden news. I think Ryan and I are still in a bit of shock with the spontaneity of it all, but it's what we both want.

Ryan doesn't waste any time when he comes right out and says, "I asked Candace to marry me last night."

"What?!" she squeals and looks to me, and then down at my hand, and Ryan catches her eyes.

"No ring, Mom," he says.

She shakes her head, questioning, "So . . .?" and I laugh as I assure her, "I said yes."

"Oh my God!" Donna wraps her arms around both of us,

and I can't stop laughing at her reaction. Happy, joyful, and everything else you would wish for from a parent.

"Why didn't you say anything?" she nearly scolds Ryan when she pulls back. "And why didn't you get her a ring?"

"I don't need a ring," I butt in and tell her.

"Because," Ryan interrupts, "I never thought of asking her until last night. It just happened, and before I knew it, I asked and she said yes."

"This is just wonderful news, you two," she beams with an ear to ear smile.

"But we need your help," he says.

"Yes, anything."

"We want to get married here. Either Saturday or Sunday."

"*This* Saturday or Sunday?" she questions.

"Yeah," he says while I nod my head.

"What's this Saturday or Sunday?" Tori asks as she walks in.

Donna doesn't say anything and looks to me, but Ryan goes ahead and tells her as he steps behind me and wraps his arms around my shoulders. "Candace and I are getting married."

"What?!" She gives the same squealed reaction as Donna. "In two days?!"

"Or three," I mumble quietly, starting to feel a little embarrassed with the reactions.

"How are you supposed to plan a wedding in two days?"

"Tori, stop," Ryan tells her, and when she looks at me, she back pedals as I'm sure she can see the embarrassment written all over my face. "I'm sorry, Candace."

"No, it's fine," I tell her and then look over at Donna. "We don't want a big wedding or anything. We were just thinking we could go to Indian Beach in a couple days and simply get married. That's all."

Her warm smile soothes the anxiety that Tori was starting to give me and softly says, "I think that's perfect, dear."

"We just need someone to do the ceremony, so could you call the church you attend and see if one of the pastors is available? We'll work around his schedule," Ryan says to her.

"Of course. I'll call right now, but you two will need to go to the courthouse to get a license today," she tells us.

"What about flowers, or a cake, or—" Tori starts.

"Nothing," Ryan tells her.

"Really?" she asks, looking at me, and I tell her, "Really. I just want a dress. That's all I need." But then it hits me . . . it isn't all I need. Turning in Ryan's arms, I look up at him, and before I can speak, he reads the panic in me, asking, "What's wrong?"

"We have to call Jase. I can't get married without him. I just . . ."

"We'll call him, babe. No worries."

Jase is my family, the closest person I have in my life next to Ryan. I couldn't imagine doing this without him by my side.

"Well, then," Donna says. "I'll get on the phone and start making calls. Why don't the two of you go ahead and drive to the courthouse and call Jase on the way. As soon as I get things figured out on my end, I call and let you know, okay?"

"Thanks, Mom."

Donna walks over to me and takes my hands in hers, saying, "You have no idea how happy you've just made me."

"Really?"

"We'll talk later, dear," she assures and then adds, "I'll

get a list of dress shops together so when you get back, you can decide where to go first."

"I was hoping that you could take me," I say, and when her eyes rim with tears and she nods her head, she tells me, "I'd love nothing more," before hugging me.

After Ryan and I left to head to the courthouse, I called Jase to tell him what was going on. He was shocked, which I expected, but hopped on the computer and was able to switch the flights for him and Mark, and they will be here tomorrow evening.

When Ryan and I got back home, Donna had spoken with one of the pastors at her church, and he agreed to marry us Saturday at five. He wants to meet with the two of us later today, so Donna and I are going to try our best to find me a dress before we have our appointment at the church.

Walking into the first dress shop, I have a pretty good idea of what I'm looking for. So when one of the bridal consultants approaches and asks, I tell her, "Simple. I really like lace."

"Not a problem. You're quite small, so if you are looking to buy off the rack, you're limited," she tells me as she leads us through the mass of wedding gowns.

Donna and I begin to pull dresses. Most are pretty detailed, so I only take a small handful back to the fitting room to try on. I step out and show Donna a couple of the dresses, but it isn't until the third one that I know.

Stepping out of the fitting room and onto the platform in front of the mirrors, Donna stands behind me to tie the satin sash around my waist. Smoothing my hands over the ivory lace, I look at myself in the mirror and just know that this is the dress I want Ryan to see me in. It's sleeveless with a v-neck front and a plunging v-cut dip in the back with a champagne colored satin sash around the waist. It's form-fitting and simple with a tiny sweep-train and solid lace, which I know Ryan has an affinity for.

"I love it," I say as Donna steps to the side.

"It's perfect, dear."

The hem is a tad long, but it'll do. Everything else fits perfectly. I never saw myself getting married. I dreamt about it as a little girl, but never really considered it as I got older.

It's odd to see myself like this. As a bride. It even sounds weird; but I love him. Even when I wasn't with him, I never stopped loving him.

"What do you think?" Donna asks, and when I look at her in the mirror, I nod my head.

Thinking about Ryan seeing me in this dress, thinking about becoming his wife, thinking about this past year—it all overpowers me, and I quickly wipe the tears that begin to drop. Donna steps onto the platform with me and gives me a hug.

"I certainly hope these are happy tears," she quietly says, and when I pull back and see another bride walking in, Donna takes my hand and walks us to my fitting room, closing the heavy curtain.

"Are you okay?" she asks as we sit on the small couch.

"It's a lot," I tell her.

She gives me a questioning look and I assure, "Not like that; I love Ryan. Just . . . this past year has been a huge change. One I never saw coming."

"I can't even imagine."

And out of nowhere, I think about my parents. About my father, and how everything has decayed with them. I was about to leave for New York without ever telling them, and now I'm about to get married. It hurts.

"My parents don't even know," I mumble as more tears fall.

"Sweetheart," she says as she pulls me into her arms. "Well . . . do you think you should call them? I mean, when's the last time you spoke with them?"

Sitting back, I tell her, "Last Christmas. It's been a year. Ryan said he saw my dad several months ago at one of my performances, but he didn't even want to talk to me. He told Ryan to not tell me he was there."

"I'm so sorry."

"It just makes me sad."

"Of course it does," she says. "Love doesn't disappear just because the people do."

"I'm not sure they ever loved me," I choke out around the knot in my throat. "But it feels weird to move on without them."

"What does Ryan say?"

"What can he say?" I tell her with a slight shrug of my shoulders. "He's supportive regardless, but it's hard not to think about them right now. I know them well enough to know that it's done with and has been for a long time."

She takes my hands, and tells me, "I don't claim to have been the perfect mother to Ryan. I let him down in so many ways. I didn't protect him like I should have, and I know that. But I've never once *not* loved him with everything that I am. I don't know your parents, so I can't speak for them, but I feel like I have gotten to know you well this past year. And you have a beautiful soul. I couldn't imagine anyone better for my son than you. To be able to call you my daughter, I can't tell you what that means to me." Her tears fall along with mine, and I soak in her words. "I love you as if you were my own."

Wiping my face, I don't feel like I could possibly speak, but I force the words out because she deserves to hear them when I explain, "It's always been hard for me to talk to people." I stop, trying to take a breath through my shaky voice but then continue with my trembling, strained words. "I don't open up easily, I know that. But you made it easy. You and Ryan both. And when I told you, the night of my solo, that you were the best gift Ryan ever gave me . . . I meant every word. It killed me not to have him for those few months, but it killed not to have you either. I never understood what a mom's love felt like until you."

We spend a few minutes hugging each other before we dry our tears and have a good laugh at our emotional mess.

"Here, let me untie you," she says as we stand up and she loosens the sash. "Should we look for a wrap or something? You're going to be freezing wearing only this."

"This dress is beautiful. I don't want to cover it up," I tell her.

"But it's the middle of winter."

Looking back at her, I say, "Ryan will keep me warm."

When she steps out, I slip off the dress and put my clothes back on. Donna tried talking me into a veil and jewelry, but I politely declined. Unfortunately, there was no declining when she insisted on buying the dress.

The past two days have been a whirlwind. After we met with Pastor Andrews the other evening, Ryan ordered dinner in and watched the new episode of 'Ridiculousness' with me. Donna couldn't believe that I liked that show, and she and Ryan had a heck of a time teasing me, but I know it was all in good fun. It was nice to veg out in front of the TV with the two of them.

I decided to go by myself to pick up Ryan's ring yesterday. As much as he likes to tease me, he loves nice things just as much as I do, so I decided on a timeless, brushed-platinum band. I waited while they engraved it for me, and by the time I got back to the house, Jase and Mark had just arrived. They were exhausted from spending the day traveling, so we all crashed early.

When I stir awake, Ryan is already up. Threading his hands through my hair, he says, "Morning, babe."

"Morning."

Inching his way down in bed, and facing me, he smiles, saying, "I feel like an antsy kid."

"Why's that?"

"Because I get my everything today," he says. "You nervous?"

"No. You?"

He pulls me flush against him, whispering, "No," before kissing me.

When we finally make it downstairs, Donna and Jase are cooking while Mark drinks his coffee and watches. We all sit around and enjoy a long breakfast together before Ryan and I throw on our raincoats to take a walk along the beach.

The skies are dark and a heavy mist fills the air as we head down the beach and find a spot to sit. Settling between his legs, I lean back into his arms. "Talk to me," I request.

"About what?"

"Anything," I say, simply wanting to hear his voice.

He tightens his arms around me, and tells me, "I don't want you to worry about anything. Thinking that marrying me is going to change us."

I smile at his words because somehow he just knew what I needed to hear. "I'm glad you said that."

He shifts me to face him and says, "I love us just the way we are. I want to marry you because I want forever with you. I want it all, and I know you're the only one who can give it to me."

"I don't know what to say," I tell him.

"You don't have to say anything."

Running my hand along his cheek, I give him the only words I can find, "My only wish is that I can give you everything you've given me."

"You already have, babe. You're enough."

I cuddle into his chest as we sit in the cold, in no rush to get back to the house. I need the quiet with him. I always will because I've come to depend on the closeness.

Ryan is spending the afternoon with his mom and Mark, letting me have the next couple of hours alone with Jase before we head to the beach. I sit in Ryan's room while Jase changes in the bathroom. My dress hangs in front of the window, and I sit on the bed, staring at it, thoughts filling my head, wondering how I wound up here when it wasn't that long ago that I was wishing I had died by that dumpster.

And then there was Ryan. The stranger that sat with me while I lay there naked and unconscious on the ground. The stranger who is now about to become my husband.

Ryan is an amazing man. More than I ever thought I deserved. He's always loved me, and no matter what we have dealt with, he's never wavered. He's always held my heart above his. Always giving me a safe place to fall. From the start he saw through my walls, to the darkest part of me, and found my light.

"What are you thinking about?" Jase says as he walks

into the room.

"How I got here."

He sits next to me on the bed and holds my hand. "Remember that morning when Mark and I were talking to you about Ryan? I was being way too protective, worrying that you two might be interested in each other."

Looking at him, I nod my head, recalling that morning. The morning after Ryan returned my leopard scarf I had left at The xx concert.

"And you remember when you told me that you thought you wouldn't ever be able to fall in love, and I told you that one day you'll get everything you deserve?"

"Yeah."

"This is that day for you."

His words make me cry. We've been through so much together. Jase has always been my heart. We've depended on each other for almost five years now. From the moment I met him, I loved him. I couldn't imagine my life without him. Ryan has never questioned our relationship, and neither has Mark. It was always Jase and I—for years—before Mark and Ryan walked in. They blended seamlessly with us, and Jase and I have found a way to open ourselves up to our boyfriends.

"I love you," I tell him.

"I know you do. And I love you."

Feeling extremely overwhelmed by today, Jase sits with me while I let the tears stream down my face. But it's when I see his own tears slip out that I turn to face him as he says, "Tell me that this won't change. You and me."

"Nothing will ever change you and me."

"I know that you're Ryan's, but you are always going to be my girl." He wipes my tears with his thumbs, but they're falling too fast for him to catch.

"You're my heart. You always have been. But now, Ryan holds that heart," I tell him. "My love for you will always be there. I couldn't imagine my life without you."

Jase holds me as we share this moment with each other. He was the first person I ever trusted. The first one I ever shared my heart with. Never once has anything come between us. He's my constant—I've never had to hide from him. But it's because of him that I was able to fall in love with Ryan, and for that, I love him even more. Jase always believed that I would find love, that I would find happiness when I thought my life had been too far destroyed for any hope of that happening. He believed it, and he pushed me when I was scared to open my heart to Ryan.

The tears finally subside, and I freshen up before Jase helps me get dressed. When he's done tying my sash, I turn to face him as he looks me over. He smiles, and when his eyes meet mine, he says, "You look amazing, sweetheart."

"Thank you . . . for everything you've ever been for me."

"It's just the beginning," he says as he takes my hand. "You ready?"

"Just one more thing." I walk over to the dresser and pick up the necklace that Ryan gave me. "Can you clasp this for me?"

I know it doesn't go with the dress, but I wear it every day, and today is no different. So when Jase puts it on me, I know I'm ready.

"Let's go," I say.

Jase helps me into his car and drives to Ecola Park, through the winding streets until we get to Indian Beach. He parks the car, overlooking the beach down below where I see the pastor, Donna, Mark, Tori, and Ryan. I smile when I see him down there, wearing black slacks and a dark charcoal button-up shirt.

"No tux?" Jase says from the driver's seat.

"I told him they were cheesy." Taking his ring that I have been clutching in my hand, I give it to Jase to hold.

Keeping my eyes fixed on the people who mean the world to me standing below, I hear Jase as he reads the inscription, "I see you in colors that don't exist."

I've never been so sure of my life until now, and all I want is to feel his touch, so when I turn to Jase, I say, "Will you take me to him?"

He gets out of the car and walks over to my side, opening my door. I take his hand as he helps me out, and when I smooth down the lace, he says, "Grab the umbrella."

"No umbrella."

"You're gonna ruin this dress, you know?"

"I know."

Taking my hand, I lock my fingers with my best friend's as he starts walking me over to the wooden steps that lead down to the beach. A thick blanket of grey covers the sky as the heavy mist falls from above. The sound of crashing waves fills the air, and when Jase gives my hand a squeeze, he begins walking me down the first flight of stairs. When we hit the landing before taking the last set of steps to the beach, Ryan turns to see me.

(Ryan)

My eyes hit her when I spot her on the stairs. God, she looks incredible, wearing nothing but lace with her hair down. She's clutched to Jase, and I know she's got to be freezing in this rain, but she's never looked more beautiful.

When Jase starts leading her down, she keeps her eyes locked on me, and I can already see the tears running down her cold, pink cheeks. My heart begins to race at the mere sight of her, and I feel like the luckiest man. Everything about her is everything I dream about now.

She walks across the dense sand, rain puddles everywhere, but she doesn't care. She walks right through them, dragging her dress through the water and sand. Before I can touch her, she turns to Jase and gives him a hug and kiss. When he gives her over to me, I run my hands down her soft, damp arms as she smiles through her tears. Pulling her into my arms, I take a moment and hold on to her, needing the closeness. I breathe her in, and when the pastor begins to speak, I keep my arms around her, giving her my warmth. We stand, wrapped up in each other, and no one else exists right now—only her.

We make our vows to each other, and when I take the ring from Tori, Candace keeps her eyes fixed on the vintage ring I found for her. When I saw the aged pearl, I knew it was perfect, and I love what it stands for because she's the purest thing in my life. The pearl is set on a weathered gold band with a stamped filigree pattern. It's simple, delicate, and when I slide it on her tiny finger, it couldn't be more perfect.

We may not have a fairytale meeting, and we may not always have sunshine and roses, but what we do have is a raw love that is honest and true. And when the pastor declares her as my wife, I take my sweet time kissing her cold, rain-covered lips, tasting a life that is so much more promising now that she's in it with me.

Wanting to get my girl warmed up, we say our goodbyes to everyone, and I take her up to my car. But before I open her door, I band my arms around her, and really kiss her.

Moving my lips with hers as I run my hands down the smooth skin of her exposed back. And when I finally drag my lips away, I look down at her and ask, "Now what?"

"Let's go home."

Helping her up into the car, I tuck in the bottom of her lace dress, which is now soaked with rain and dirt. I grab her a blanket from the back seat and wrap it around her before I get in and start driving us back to Seattle. She holds my hand the entire way, and when we finally make it back to the loft, I carry her up the stairs and inside.

When I get her upstairs, we stand in the center of the room as I cradle her cheeks in my hands, saying, "You will never have to doubt your place in this world again because I swear I will spend forever making sure you're right where you belong."

I watch her eyes rim with tears while I run my hands down her neck and underneath the lace on her shoulders as I slowly begin peeling off her wedding dress.

I never knew that a person could be capable of falling as hard as I have for Candace. I spent so many years fearing the fall, but she made it effortless, taking all my fears away. With her, I know I'll never get enough. I'm always gonna want more, and as I make love to my wife, I know I'm gonna spend the rest of my life falling.

epilogue

As I wait for the curtain to draw up, I turn to Jase and watch as he and Mark keep their daughter, Caroline, busy by showing the program to her, reading off the various performance titles. This is her first time at the theater, and I'm surprised with how well-behaved she's being.

Jase and Mark ended up getting married a few years after Candace and I. When they adopted Caroline, simply having Candace and I be her aunt and uncle wasn't enough, so Jase and Mark asked us to be her godparents. She's always been a huge part of our lives, and to see that she is fast approaching her fifth birthday is a test to how fast the years have flown by.

Candace has managed to have a successful career, quickly becoming a soloist at Pacific Northwest Ballet during her second year, and moving to principal her fifth. She's loved every minute of it, and getting to watch my girl dance the lead in so many shows has been amazing.

Shortly after we got married, I took her to New York to attend a performance by the American Ballet Theatre, the company she turned down to stay in Seattle. I wanted to remind her that we could still make New York happen, but she was firm on staying with PNB. I never questioned her decision to stay, but I know a piece of her has always been scared to leave everything behind.

Security has consistently been something she has craved, and Seattle offers her that. Having her friends and family close was also important while she was in therapy and trying to recover from her attack. She continued with therapy for a few years, but through it all, and after twelve years since the attack, she's never gotten over holding herself responsible for that night. It's not something I believe will ever change, so I've simply accepted it and no longer try to convince her that she should feel differently.

A few months after we married, nearly two years since the rape, she finally came off of her sleeping pill. It was a rough transition, but the doctor insisted. She had nightmares for a while, but I feel it was her anxiety that was triggering it. Eventually the nightmares lessened, and then the night terrors lessened. She still has nightmares, but those only happen a few times a year, and they aren't nearly as bad as they used to be.

Aside from a few lingering effects of that night, she's blossomed into a beautiful woman, and I've been lucky enough to watch it firsthand. She's a lot more spunky than I would have imagined from when I first met her. Her laugh is infectious, and she has brightened every aspect of my life.

I wound up selling a percentage of Blur to Max, making him a partner. We remain close friends, but my main business now is my art. When my photos started being picked up by galleries in different states, my commissioned work really took off, but the majority of my income comes from gallery sales.

Candace and I have transitioned through the years with ease. She remains the love of my life, and I spend every day making sure she never forgets it. I'll never be able to thank her enough for giving me this life.

When the lights dim, and the curtain goes up, Caroline is excited as she watches the dancers on stage. I have to wait a few numbers until I get to see my girl. When the music cues, she lights up, sending chills up my neck. She moves across the stage with her beautiful smile, enjoying every second. I can't take my eyes off of her even though there are other dancers on the stage. She captivates me, and I'm stuck on her.

She's the greatest gift in my life. I never thought I could love the way I love her. The music comes to an end all too soon. I could watch her on that stage forever. When she takes her curtsey, she beams at the applause. After the curtain falls, I just can't wait to see her, so I quietly tell Jase, "I'm gonna run backstage."

Making my way out of the theater, I head back to the hall where all the dressing rooms are, and when I spot her, she smiles as she rushes towards me. I hold my arms out for her and catch a glimpse of Candace off to my side as she smiles proudly before my girl bounds into my arms, squealing with joy, "Daddy!"

I See You In Colors

I am pretending you did not exist.
Ink nightly washes black
over my consciousness
and abandons me as morning seaweed
upon a foreign beach.

I am pretending we were simply
the sparkling imagination of some higher being,
our life together set below a singular epic sky
unrepeated
in future histories.

I am pretending I cannot taste you
each day as I do the sea air in my breath
when I am running,
my heart tied upon one foot,
ancient melancholy tied upon the other,
anxiously racing,
madly racing through lifetimes,
to find our brightened souls.

I see you in colors that don't exist.

It is all that I see clearly.
and why I run.

—P. Matsumoto

1 in every 4 women will experience domestic violence in her lifetime. 30% to 60% of perpetrators of intimate partner violence also abuse children in the household. Boys who witness domestic violence are *twice as likely* to abuse their own partners and children when they become adults. Only approximately 1/4 of all physical assaults and 1/5 of all rapes are reported to the police.

Candace and Ryan's story is simply one of example of how so many people live. Although both of them hid what they had suffered through, you don't have to.

National Domestic Violence Hotline
1.800.799.SAFE
Visit www.ncadv.org to find more
information and resources.

National Sexual Assault Hotline
1.800.656.HOPE
Visit www.rainn.org for more information and resources.

acknowledgements

As this series comes to a close, I am taken back to the night I finally swallowed my doubts about writing a book, remembering the moment I turned to my husband and said, "I'm gonna do it." He's the one that, out of the blue, said I should write a book, and it took him time to finally convince me, but eventually he did. No amount of 'thank you's' will ever be enough. I'm not even sure he realizes this gift he's given me.

And so I start with him.

Thank you to my husband, who, through it all, has always seen the light within me. Seen the potential that lies beneath. Seen everything I'm not able to. Always believing and sacrificing to make sure I can act upon every opportunity that comes my way. It's been a crazy year while I have been writing this series, and watching you take control of everything to allow me the time to write these stories has proven to me how lucky I truly am to have you by my side. And just as Candace views Ryan, I also see you in colors that don't exist, because what we have together is a rarity. Don't doubt for one second that I don't see everything you have ever given me. I do.

Gina, what can I say? You have been my partner through it all. Being able to share this journey with you has been amazing. The time you have sacrificed for me is something that I can't thank you enough for. You've been there from the beginning to the end, and I love you for loving Candace and Ryan as much as I do. For believing in their story and believing in me. For all the late night phone calls and texting. Encouraging me when I felt defeated. Guiding me to the end with your constant support. These books would not be what they are if it weren't for you.

And to Lisa, my amazing editor and friend, you constantly push me to make my writing better. You are the queen of cuts, and with each book I resist you less and less. I love that we have been able to share this whole experience together. That you were always a part of it and in the passenger seat with me. It's an amazing thing when you can share the discovery of a dream and passion with a friend. You were by my side when I felt so lost in life a couple years ago, and I love that you were by my side as I dug myself out and found this hidden talent. You're a unfailing support, and I hope to create more and more wonderful stories with you!

Now my family. To my father and step-mother, having the two of you tell me how proud you are of me means more to me than you will ever know. It's something that every child craves from a parent, and something that you have always given me. I'm one lucky girl to have such amazing parents. Cathy, to have you so invested in my writing is so much fun for me. Being able to sit around with you to plot and bounce ideas off of is the best. Thank you for your enthusiasm and unwavering support. Kelley and Traci, my sisters, thank your for taking the time to read my stories and for all of your encouraging words! And to my brothers, Josh and Quentin, thank you for not reading my books because I just don't know how I feel about you reading my intimate scenes. Josh, you have been a great support even if you don't know it. I love that you can be someone I can discuss my writing with and that you offer ways to strengthen my stories. Thank you for showing me around Seattle and Oregon and for being the one who took me to a place I never knew existed—Cannon Beach. You changed the direction of this story from the very moment I set foot onto Indian Beach. It might not be that significant of a moment for you, but it was for me and for my characters.

I want to thank all of my betas for putting in the hours to read and critique my manuscript. You guys do it all, from encouraging me when I get stressed to helping me promote. Your honesty and support has become something I have depended on through writing this series, and I am blessed to have had such an amazing group of women be on board with me.

Last but not least, to Candace, Ryan, Jase, and Mark, I know you aren't real, but it feels like you are to me. It's been an amazing journey getting to know you all. To live inside each of you for the time I was able to affected me in a way I never thought was possible. To learn and grow with each of you has been a true gift. I have spent the past year with the four of you, and it's sad to say goodbye to your stories, but I thank you for giving them to me, because no matter how anyone else feels about these books, for me, you have given me the stories I have always wanted to read but could never find—until now.

THE FADING SERIES
FADING ⁓ FREEING ⁓ FALLING

FADING (book #1)

"Heart-wrenching, jaw-dropping, and absolutely beautiful. If you enjoy not only reading but *feeling* a great story, don't miss this intense tale of love and healing!"

—Aleatha Romig, New York Times and USA Today bestselling author

"E.K. Blair has upped the standards of indie writing forever. This author is an artist. One of the most incredible, breathtaking stories I have ever read."

—Word

FREEING (book #2)

"Another amazingly beautiful, heart-wrenching, yet heart-warming story. Like Fading, Freeing is brilliantly written and once again, it is so easy to get lost in the pages of this story."

—Book Crush Reviews

"A book that's packed with an intensity that is rare to find in today's New Adult Genre. Blair's writing is phenomenal, and the tears her words induced were not like any other's."

—GMB Reviews

e. k. blair

Website:
www.ekblair.com

Facebook:
https://www.facebook.com/EKBlairAuthor

Twitter:
@EK_Blair_Author

www.ingramcontent.com/pod-product-compliance
Lightning Source LLC
Chambersburg PA
CBHW020822030726
47496CB00001B/48